KELLY PARK

Jean Stubbs is a frequent lecturer at writers' seminars and in 1984 she was writer-in-residence for Avon. Her novels and short stories have been translated into eight languages and have been televised and adapted for radio.

She lives in Cornwall with her second husband.

Also by Jean Stubbs in Pan Books:

A Lasting Spring
Like We Used To Be
Summer Secrets

BRIEF CHRONICLES

Kit's Hill
The Ironmaster
The Vivian Inheritance
The Northern Correspondent

JEAN STUBBS

KELLY PARK

PAN BOOKS
IN ASSOCIATION WITH MACMILLAN LONDON

First published 1992 by Macmillan London Limited

This edition published 1994 by Pan Books Limited
a division of Pan Macmillan Publishers Limited
Cavaye Place London SW10 9PG
and Basingstoke
in association with Macmillan London Limited

Associated companies throughout the world

ISBN 0 330 32522 1

1 3 5 7 9 8 6 4 2

A CIP catalogue record for this book is available from
the British Library

Phototypeset by Intype, London
Printed and bound by Firmin-Didot (France),
Group Herissey. No d'impression : 31194.

Acknowledgements

I am enormously grateful to the following people: Pat and Peter Bearman, who transformed Boscundle Manor, Treghan, St Austell, and gave me so much information about running a country-house hotel and restaurant; Mr Ian Atlee and his staff at Helston library, as always, for providing necessary books; Stephen Ivall of the *Helston Packet*, for finding me a corner in his office, where I could research 1978–1979 copies of the newspaper; my agent Jennifer Kavanagh, my American publisher Tom McCormack, my American editor Sandra McCormack, and my English editor Jane Wood, for advice, encouragement, and above all else enthusiasm. And to Felix, who coped valiantly with limping printers and stricken word-processors, and lent something of himself to Tom Faull.

To my mother, most splendid cook,
who would have loved this story.

Bon Appétit!

South of the Thames in the 1970s there used to be a bistro called Bon Appétit, which Egon Ronay once described as having an unremarkable exterior. Indeed, its position within sound and smell of Battersea Power Station, the gas works and the railway seemed unlikely to attract gourmets. Yet the hotel inspector had found his way there at last, drawn by its growing reputation. He sampled the set menu and pronounced each dish to be just as it should, praised the imaginative presentation, the intimate atmosphere, the informal but efficient service, and the French Provincial décor. He mentioned the gamine charms of Flavia Pollard, *chef-patronne*, and the flamboyant personality of her partner Jack Rice. Then he bestowed upon Bon Appétit a chef's hat to indicate the proprietor's personal cooking, an S for friendly service, a cup and saucer for rich strong coffee, and a solitary precious star.

Entreés

CHAPTER ONE

4 February 1978

London was suspended in the aimless hours of early morning, and in that season of the year which demands hibernation. Winter lay on her empty pavements, whistled through barebone trees, blew across the river. We had given a farewell party at Bon Appétit and almost all our guests had gone. They had stood for a few moments on the unpretentious threshold, sniffing an aroma of wine, garlic and bayleaves, exchanging hushed comments and regrets. Then vanished like ghosts at cockcrow, into the man-made world of back streets with their odours of gas, fish and exhaust fumes.

Within the bistro one last gourmand had laid down his head, as upon the softest of pillows, and fallen asleep between his ash-tray and his coffee cup. Our last waiter had bidden us goodnight and yawned his way out. And now Jack Rice and I could survey the débâcle of our last entertainment, and speak composedly of our broken partnership.

I pulled off my white cap and shook out my hair. Jack loosened the bow-tie at his throat and removed his dinner-jacket. Through the bistro archway an immense mirror on the far side of the dining room reflected his handsome, self-loving face and the droop of my shoulders. Reflected crumpled tablecloths, fading flowers, and empty champagne bottles lolling in buckets of melted ice. Reflected chairs pushed back and chairs overturned, and a crushed carnation that once had been a jaunty button-hole.

Jack said, 'That was a damned good evening, Flick. One of the best.'

He demanded, and got, the best of everything. Required hallmarks on silver, pedigrees for cats, women whose value was far above rubies.

He added, staring at me, summing me up, 'Pity it had to be the last. Ridiculous really. Are you sure you know what you're doing?'

I did not intend to justify myself, and certainly not to Jack Rice.

I said, 'You haven't told me what *you* propose to do next. Apart from having an affair with Sylvia Hammond.'

He skirted the hidden dangers in this remark by treating it as the concern of one friend for another.

'Oh, we shall be touring Europe with an eye to business. Sylvia's father made his money in hotels, and she wants to show the old man she can do as well as he can – preferably better! I might well run a place in Switzerland for her. I haven't enough capital to go it on my own.'

Nor, as it happened, had I. The profits from the sale of Bon Appétit would be split down the middle.

I had fought the situation out with myself over the past wretched months. For I could not rid myself of Jack without losing Bon Appétit, and by now I loved that place more than my lover. In the end I won the battle for self-respect, and Sylvia won Jack. They were barren victories, as I knew from experience and she would find out later. She was young and spoiled, you see, and thought that what she most loved would make her most happy. And the losses on all sides were great. Even for Jack, who had been very comfortable indeed with his agreeable job, a complaisant partner and a series of young mistresses. Moreover he was used to calling the tune and letting someone else pay the piper, but in this case the tune was of my making and not to his liking and he had had to pay his share.

He said, almost savagely, 'For God's sake, why couldn't you leave things as they were, Flavia? We had a good working arrangement.'

I said, 'It worked well for you, certainly.'

He gave an angry little laugh.

'And well enough for you to keep your eyes and mouth shut for seven years!' Then he reflected that honey caught more flies than vinegar, and used on me the smiling good humour that made him so popular with dinner guests. 'Come on, Flavie! You can't say there'll be no regrets.'

I said, 'Oh yes, Jack. One very big one. I wish I could have bought you out and kept the bistro.'

And I remembered how we started off, seven years ago, and learned the business from the sink upwards. What a wild chance we had taken! Even our best friends, even Humphrey – looking at our last guest, who was snoring in vast contentment – had told us that the idea would never work, that this was the wrong sort of business in the wrong sort of place, with no custom near enough to make it worthwhile. 'Why, you'd make a better living out of a fish and chip shop!' they said. Didn't they? Didn't they? But we proved to be right. Made them eat my food as well as their words.

As if he read my mind, Jack said, musing, 'Yes, we took a flyer with this place. Didn't we, old girl?'

'Jack, I really would prefer you not to call me old girl,' I said tartly, 'particularly as I'm approaching forty!'

He drew his long black brows together, disliking correction.

'Still, if we had to sell, we sold at the right time,' said Jack, making the best of a hard bargain. 'And young Nick Rackham is paying for the very thing we're taking away with us – the ambience. Even if he finds a chef as good as you and masterminds it as well as I did, he still won't be running Bon Appétit. And he's never done this sort of thing before. New to the business but thinks he knows it all, of course. God's answer to the *Michelin Guide*. Well, that's *his* problem.'

Jack Rice was an excellent businessman. He smelled out unlikely projects, made a success of them, sucked them dry and sold them before they failed. He picked up people with talent and flair, used them, paid them off, and replaced them. He had created this bistro out of me. Out of Sylvia Hammond he would create a hotel. Perhaps in another few years he would meet the daughter of a millionaire and create a chain of hotels. Jack Rice's horizons were, in the material sense, limitless.

'A damned good little business,' he said. 'Pity.'

'I loved Bon Appétit,' I said suddenly. 'I still do. It's meant far more than a good little business to me.'

Uncomprehending, scathing, he said, 'But *of course* you loved it, my dear. We couldn't have made it come alive if you hadn't. But love isn't enough. A bistro has to make a profit or go bust. Even if you serve the best food in the world it can go bust. Sometimes *because* you serve the best food it goes bust. The core of any business is foresight and good management. And if you're thinking of doing something similar in the future you'd be wise to use your head instead of your heart, and to look very long before you leap.'

And he stared coolly through me with his bright, shallow eyes.

He knew that this decision had been an emotional one, that I was devoid of future plans, and covering up the fact that I had nothing to do and nowhere to go. Still, I had freed myself once more from a humiliating situation. We can't have everything.

He resorted to good-natured bullying, trying to discover my plans.

'You should have a jolly good rest before you start work again, Flavia. You haven't had a break since – I don't know when.'

While he had found time to seduce, or be seduced by, Sylvia Hammond as well as others. This he probably remembered because he moved swiftly on without waiting for an answer.

'You haven't had a holiday for ages. Why not go to Venice?'

I said sharply, 'Because I spent my honeymoon there, eighteen years ago, with Guy Pollard. And the city would be full of ghosts.'

Old ghosts of my youth and the marriage which had failed. New ghosts of Jack Rice and Bon Appétit. Yes, I should do well to avoid Venice.

'There are lots of other places,' said Jack idly.

'As a matter of fact I'm thinking of spending a week or two in Cornwall.'

Jack's expression changed from curiosity to derision. He stared at me as if I were a strange specimen on a microscope slide.

'Good Lord!' said Jack. 'What on earth will you do there?'

I nodded towards the sleeping man opposite.

'I've persuaded Humpty to lend me a corner of Kelly Park.'

'That doddering old white elephant! What's happening to it, by the way?'

'Nothing. No one's rented it since the last tenants left, two years ago. And he's always saying how marvellous it is. I thought it might be fun.'

And far, far from London and all its reminders, and all my responsibilities.

'I thought that if it worked out for me I might take Patrick and Jeremy there for a holiday later on. If Guy would agree.'

My two sons had never been of any interest to Jack, who spoke idly, lightly to himself.

'I've often wondered how one *does* live in the country. I suppose people sleep a lot to pass the time.'

I answered sourly.

'Well at the moment I can't think of anything better. Just for once in my life I want to be by myself, and do something for myself, instead of running round after everyone else. Sleeping a lot in the country would suit me nicely.'

His metallic eyes lacked comprehension.

'But why trail off to that benighted hole when you can go abroad, and find the sun and a decent hotel? My dear girl, I can assure you that Kelly Park is a dump. It used to be splendid, I believe, when Humphrey was a boy. Classic feudal estate, run on benevolent lines. I spent some years of the war there as a kid, with my two sisters and an assortment of cousins. Grandmama Jarvis was still alive and ruling the roost, and she took a crowd of us in. But the place was looking threadbare even then, and after the war it went completely to pot.

'He and I went down for her funeral in 'sixty-eight, and it poured the entire weekend. The roof was leaking and we sat there listening to the rain plopping into zinc pails. We had a power failure and the emergency generator wouldn't work. The old biddy who acts as housekeeper doesn't cook, so we lived on pasties and bread and jam from the village shop. Being an absent landlord, Humphrey had lost contact with the local gentry. Once the funeral was over there was nowhere to go, no one to meet, nothing to do, and everyone was in bed by ten o'clock.

'The only person who enjoyed himself in a dreary sort of way was Humphrey, who dressed up in some sort of a Sherlock Holmes outfit with a black band round the sleeve, and passed much of the time in the local pub chatting about the good old days. I spent the entire weekend being cold, wet, hungry and bored stiff, and trying to comprehend the dialect. It certainly wasn't my scene, and I can't imagine how it could be yours.'

His confidence in his own judgement made me doubt mine. In self-defence I joined his mockery.

'Oh, now I can't *resist* Kelly Park. I just know it will be madly amusing! And I've never been that far west. Never seen the house, apart from old photographs. Humpty on the lawn with his teddy bear. Humpty, the budding cricketer, in the paddock. Humpty presiding over the Tenant's Tea. After all, if it's too much of a drag I can always go somewhere else.'

Jack's attention turned from leisure to business.

'He won't get another tenant – not that the last one was any good. No one is going to rent an old pile like that nowadays. And no one will buy it in its present condition. Why on earth doesn't he convert the place into holiday flats? People like to rent a way of life without being committed to it.'

'He has thought about that, apparently, but says it would be too expensive. I think he means too much like hard work. And he can't bear the idea of losing the ancestral home.'

'What can he do with it otherwise? Let it fall down?'

'Oh, you know Humpty. He's waiting for a miracle. The clock turned back. Kelly Park in its glory. And Humpty with his teddy bear on the lawn.'

'If that house had been mine . . . ' said Jack thoughtfully.

But it was not, and he never wasted time in daydreams.

I stared at my reflection in the mirror, and a sad tired waif stared back. Full pale lips, wide grey eyes, broad cheekbones, a pointed chin, a turned-up nose. In my head I heard my mother's plaintive voice. *Darling, you've got such a dear little face and figure. Like a Dutch doll. You could do so much with yourself if you tried!* My hair had been flattened by the cap and I fluffed it listlessly. *A few blonde streaks, darling, would lift that mousy shade so nicely.* My face was nearly as white as my apron. *A hint of rouge, a lively lipstick.* No use. I had put everything I was, and everything I had, into the evening, and there was nothing left. Behind me, Jack raised a glass of champagne to himself and sipped.

He was a man of medium height with the old-fashioned good looks of a 1930s' matinée idol: smooth dark-brown hair, a trim moustache, regular features. We gave the impression of being a disparate couple. And yet we had worked together, planned together, loved together, and I at least had been faithful to him, for seven years. The only thing we didn't do was to live together, but that was because Jack guarded his privacy jealously, and didn't want a home so much as a base from which to travel forth. And I needed some place I could call my own, and in which I could entertain my sons, even if it was only a basement flat in Battersea.

My reflection in the long mirror looked puzzled. The man from Egon Ronay had remarked upon my gamine charms. Was he referring to my short hair, my short stature, my wide smile, or the way I darted about? People liked me, relied on me, tended to lean on me. And when it came to food they bunched their fingers and kissed them. I was expected to turn every meal into a magical occasion. Regular diners would pop their heads round the kitchen door to congratulate me on a particular dish, or ask me to come into the bistro for a glass of wine. When, by popular request, I had emerged at the end of this evening's triumph, a great round of applause, cries of affection, and a bouquet from Humphrey had greeted my appearance. If I was such a success in public, how did I come to be so unsuccessful in private?

Jack's reflection was puzzled, too. It looked my reflection in the face and said, 'You never seemed to mind my flutters before. What went wrong this time, Flavia? I thought we were all right together. I thought you understood.'

I touched the ring in the pocket of my overalls. A platinum silver band. *From me to you, 14.2.71.* A gift on the Valentine's Day of our first year together, but with no names. Always he robbed each gesture of intimacy, and excused the lack with charm. *But you and I know what it really means, don't we, Flick?* The ring had worn better than I had.

'All right is not enough, Jack, and I've grown tired of understanding.'

'You're the only woman I've ever known for so long,' he said. 'The only woman I could ever talk to properly.'

There was no point in allowing him to salt my wounds. I walked away from him, drew back the curtains and looked out at the narrow street. A failed wife, a failed mother, a failed lover, and the only good thing in my life sold up and gone. Failed all the way round. And forty next birthday.

Jack coughed, rattled the change in his pockets, took a turn about the room, talking through and past me.

'You weren't expecting us to marry, were you? I thought we were clear about that from the start. Personal freedom. Remember?'

I sat down, spent and solitary, among the remains of the feast. Selected a pear and began to peel it thinly. I had hoped he would commit himself to me as I had committed myself to him. And yes, secretly, I suppose I had hoped we might marry in the course of time.

A tear dropped on the flesh of the pear.

All I had left was my dignity. I absorbed the tear with one corner of a used napkin, and spoke composedly.

'I remember that we agreed to set each other free and/or to dissolve the partnership without fuss, if ever we had good reason for either or both. Which is exactly what we've done. So what's your problem, Jack?'

'But *I* didn't ask to be set free on either count. And I can't see what upset you so much about Sylvia,' he said, slightly impatient.

'I can't give you any reason you'd comprehend.'

Nevertheless I tried.

'All right, then, I mind being used. I mind being there for you all the time, while you're only there for me when it suits you. I mind doing most of the work while you play the genial host. And I mind everyone *knowing* that I'm being used, and either pitying or despising me. And the reason I drew a line at Sylvia Hammond was because she wouldn't stay in the background like all the others, so that I could pretend she didn't exist. I minded that she hung around here, at Bon Appétit, bringing her friends with her, flirting with you under my nose, invading *my* territory—'

'That wasn't my fault. Wasn't what I wanted. I tried to put a stop to—'

'Well it was the final bloody straw as far as I was concerned.

And seven years of being understanding is too high a price. Even for Bon Appétit.'

I addressed my remarks to the pear. And dabbed it again.

'But to turn your back on all this simply because of Sylvia,' he cried. 'Look, it's not too late.'

Some idea was forming in that shifty self-loving head. Something which might hurt her as well as me, but would benefit Jack.

'No,' I cried. 'I've had enough.'

I pushed the pear away. I hadn't wanted it in any case.

Outside in that unremarkable street which we had made remarkable, someone sounded a motor-car horn gaily, peremptorily.

'I think,' I remarked, controlled and dry, 'that your lady has arrived to take you out to breakfast.'

He walked to the window. She had parked her Mercedes outside the front door. I saw its pale bonnet gleam beneath our street lamp.

'Before you go,' I said, still with the same dry control, 'do our people know they're supposed to clean up before Nick Rackham takes over tomorrow?'

His flamboyance was less evident. The presence of Sylvia Hammond seemed to be an error in bad taste, and Jack's taste in all things was impeccable. I didn't suppose he had asked her to pick him up but she was young, her father was rich, and she was used to having her own way. If she wanted the final curtain to come down early then the curtain came down.

'Oh yes,' said Jack in a lower tone, subdued. 'They'll be in today. There's no more for us to do now.'

He rapped on the window to attract her attention and spread out his hand against the glass. His way of saying, 'I'll be ready in five minutes.'

He fetched my coat and his.

'I'll be a little while yet,' I said flatly, needing time to myself before I left.

'I suppose that's that, then,' said Jack, searching for an exit line. He looked round and found it. 'What are we going to do with old Humphrey?'

Jack's cousin. My father's friend. My swain of twenty years. And our most devoted client.

'I'll look after Humphrey,' I said.

He hesitated, and then caught my cold hands with his warm ones, and shook them in the manner that made him so popular everywhere.

'Oh, well. No point in hanging about like people waiting for a train. So, I suppose it's good luck and goodbye. No hard feelings, eh? You've been a great girl. All the way. The best.'

'Yes,' I replied, withdrawing from his clasp, 'I think I have. Perhaps if I hadn't you might have paid more attention to me.'

He shrugged, gave a rueful grin. The horn tooted again. She would be walking in if he didn't hurry, and neither of us wanted that.

'You could never be anything but wonderful!' he cried, and threw his overcoat across his shoulders, and hurried out to meet his immediate future.

Suddenly I longed to seize the tablecloth and pull, fetching bottles, plates, glasses and cutlery cascading to the floor. But it was not in my nature to destroy what I had created. After a few moments' reflection I bit on the pear. The sweetness in my mouth caused my eyes to fill. One tear followed another. I ate resolutely, wept silently.

A feeble sun rose and illumined the small bistro. This was the only time of day that the buildings allowed him entry, but that had never mattered because Bon Appétit woke in the evening, serving a set menu of authentic French Provincial dishes, with care and attention to detail, from 7.30 p.m. to midnight. Their savours still lingered in the room: memories of meals past.

In my grief I had forgotten our sleeping guest until Humphrey Jarvis's plump manicured hand moved towards mine and patted it gently.

He was surfacing, somewhat crinkled and stained like the tablecloths, smacking dry lips. His bulk bore witness to his appetite. A gentleman of goodly mien: he had pandered to the flesh for so long that he possessed too much of it. Hazel eyes, thinning fair hair, a heavy chin, the remnants of good looks beneath the fat. His voice, whose drawl bore the mark of public school and Oxford education, was pleasing in tone but could turn petulant. He believed himself to be one of life's patrons, a giver of good things, a dashing boulevardier. In fact he was the most self-centred of men, embedded in bachelorhood, anxious for his comforts, distressed by any alteration of his routine, and his generosity was of the convenient kind. He gave of his surplus, not of himself.

He was staring at me sombrely, patting my hand helplessly, and I wiped my eyes with a napkin and shook my head, to show that he had no need to give me sympathy. But when he spoke I was amazed, because out of that mound of over-cherished flesh came words of remorse.

'I blame myself,' said Humphrey Jarvis, 'for introducing you to him. Blood ties and all that. Got him out of many a scrape when he was a lad. Always fond of the rascal. But should never have introduced him to you of all women, and so soon after your divorce. Sorry for it. Very sorry. I do apologise, Flavia dear.'

I said, 'Oh no, oh no, it was the right thing to do. You were helping me out when I was young and green in the catering trade. I was living alone in London, missing my children. If it hadn't been Jack it would probably have been someone else. And the partnership worked well on the whole. For seven years, in fact. Quite a long time, these days. You're not to blame, Humpty. People meet, and that's all there is to it. No blame, Humpty. No blame. I'm not crying for Jack Rice. I'm crying for Bon Appétit – and all the other things I've lost along the way.'

Then I cried harder and he actually wandered off to the kitchen and made fresh coffee for us both.

Watching me sip the bitter black liquid he said gravely, 'I shall not receive him in my home again. I regard his behaviour as unforgivable. I am an old-fashioned person. If that is a fault then I admit it freely. Freely!' He was very proud of it. 'Nevertheless, I can imagine how my grandfather, old Humphrey, would have dealt with a scoundrel like Jack Rice. Taken a horsewhip to him. That's what. You may regard yourself, Flavia, as being under my protection.'

Even in the midst of sobs and sips I laughed a little. His voice, his theatrical cadences, amused me. He took himself so seriously always.

'It was not my good fortune,' Humphrey continued, 'to have the honour of marrying the lady on whom I set my heart' – and here he looked at me meaningfully – 'but in memory of that deep affection, and of your late father's friendship, I honour you above all women. Ah, if only matters had worked out differently . . . well, well.'

He cleared his throat. He was enjoying himself immensely. He meant that he might have married me. He kept this proposal for occasions when I was unlikely to accept it.

A noise between a laugh and a sob escaped me. And yet I needed someone to think I was wonderful. Tired as I was I could not yet stop, could not yet sleep. He must stay with me, keep talking. And there was only one way in which I could persuade him to do that. I stood up.

'Humpty, let's take a taxi to my place and I'll cook breakfast for us.'

An over-sized child, he expanded at the thought.

'Darling girl, I couldn't manage a morsel.'

'I'll grill you some of my home-made sausages.'

'Flavia, Flavia. My doctor has been most strict with me recently.'

I knew how little notice Humphrey took of his doctor.

'Well, I can't help that,' I said briskly. 'My sausages couldn't do you anything but good. Pure meat. Cooked with the minimum of fat. A couple of grilled tomatoes for vitamin C. And only a scrape of best butter on wholemeal toast. How can that hurt you?'

He saw that he need not console me in any way but a practical one, that of eating my food. And as he helped me on with my coat he sang 'Auprés de ma blonde' in a melodious baritone, and murmured to himself, '*Mam'selle*!' though how that applied to me I could not imagine.

CHAPTER TWO

'So, my dear,' said Humphrey, as the taxi sped away, 'a new beginning, a new life. I wonder what lies ahead of you?' And without waiting for an answer added fretfully, 'It's astonishing how all the exciting things happen to other people. Nothing ever happens to me.' He mused on this for a while, and then said conversationally, 'By the way, have you seen Guy recently?'

This reminder of my ex-husband was unwelcome.

'My dear Humphrey, we communicate as little as possible. When we absolutely must, Guy telephones, and I write. I haven't seen him for years.'

'No, I suppose not,' he said vaguely. 'He and I bumped into each other at the regimental reunion the other night. He doesn't change. Greyer than he used to be. He must pay his tailor a pretty penny.'

So Guy was still lean and spruce and self-contained. Humphrey had been fleshy and convivial even in his youth. And nowadays, even though the morning light was gentle with him it revealed a ruined Roman emperor.

The taxi swung me against him, and he patted my knee as I righted myself.

'I thought of your father as we toasted dead and absent comrades, Flavia. I always do, and I'm sure Guy does. The old Major was a fine man. Very kind to the pair of us – green young cubs that we were. I have much for which to thank him.' He turned a moist gaze on me and said sentimentally, 'Not least for introducing us, my dear. From that first meeting, my fate was sealed.'

I said, with a touch of asperity, 'I was six at the time,

Humphrey. I'd torn my frock, climbing a tree in the garden, and I expect my face needed washing. You couldn't have been even vaguely interested!'

'Dear Lily always did let you run wild,' he said, with mild displeasure. 'That was why your father sent you to a boarding school after the war.'

I had been less than gracious, and felt guilty.

'Of course, I adored you and Guy from the first moment,' I said quickly. 'What little girl wouldn't fall in love with two dashing young soldiers in uniform. Even out of uniform I adored you for years and years.'

This was a gross exaggeration, but it pleased him.

'Adored both – but chose the wrong man, my dear,' Humphrey murmured.

I said sadly, 'I always choose the wrong man.'

My father had been a professional army officer. The connection between him and two wartime lieutenants was a tenuous one, and yet it held. I was nineteen when he died. My mother was too empty-headed, and I too young, to cope with the complexities of death. It was Humphrey and Guy who stepped in to help us.

'You were so good to us when my father died, Humpty. A positive cornucopia of theatre tickets, teas at Fortnum and Mason, Christmas hampers, boxes of chocolates and bunches of flowers.'

Guy, being a solicitor, dealt with all our practical problems, and charged my mother nothing for his services.

'You were sweet nineteen, my dear, and wore size three shoes. How could I resist you?'

I was twenty-one and Guy Pollard was forty-two when he proposed to me quite unexpectedly.

'Good fellow, Guy, but a bit of a cold fish,' Humphrey was saying. 'What made you decide on him, my dear?'

I could not say physical attraction, which it was. For that would exclude Humphrey, as indeed it had done.

'I think it was The Elms,' I said, mingling truth with diplomacy.

With the connivance of Lily, Guy took me out for the day, and we had tea at his house in Essex, suitably chaperoned by his domestic help.

'I'd never had a proper home, you see,' I said. 'You know what

Lily's like. She should have been a gipsy, except that her caravan would be full of clutter and she couldn't cook on anything, let alone a camp fire.'

'A thought unkind, Flavia! You preferred to do the cooking when you were at home. Your father told me. He was so proud of you.'

'Sheer self-preservation. I'd discovered, even at boarding school, that there was more to food than a tin of something on scorched toast.'

'Dear slap-dash creature. Always been fond of Lily. About Guy . . . ?'

'Well, there was Guy. A mature man, with an established business and a beautiful house full of cherished furniture in a fine old garden. And there was me. In my salad days, and certainly green in judgement, with nothing apart from a teaching diploma in domestic science from Battersea College. And he did set out to court me. So what alternative had I but to fall breathlessly in love and say yes?'

'I proposed to you, too,' said Humphrey, and sighed.

The following week, over dinner at Rules. He always left everything until it was too late.

He said reproachfully, of the past, 'I was a little hurt, I recall, because Lily was so delighted about the engagement. Still, Guy did ask me to be best man. And then I was godfather to your firstborn, Patrick.'

I was pursuing my own line of thought.

'I remember Lily saying, on my wedding day, "Now you'll be happy ever after, as I was when I met my Mr Right." As it turned out, he was Mr Wrong.'

We were silent for a few moments, looking at the passing scene. Then Humphrey started off again.

'Anne was with Guy, by the way. Not at the regimental dinner, but before and after. She dropped him there and picked him up afterwards. Presumably spent the evening at her club in between. She's not wearing as well as you are, my dear. Very much the Committee Lady in a Hat these days. Still, that would suit Guy better. You were always a bit of a Bohemian, Flavia.'

I leaned forward to tap on the glass and say, 'It's the next turning on the left. The third house past a row of shops. Opposite a street-lamp.'

'Still, it's not all spilt milk. You have your boys.'

'In their school holidays. For brief visits. Yes.'

'Haven't seen them for quite a while,' said Humphrey conversationally. 'I must ask them up to town. Take them to a cinema, and give them a good tea. I don't forget their birthdays, mind. And from time to time I send them a fiver apiece, for tuck. I remember life at public school . . . '

I said, 'The trouble is that I have so little to do with them. Awful, not knowing your own sons.' An old grievance burst out. 'The courts should have granted me custody.'

Humphrey fidgeted. He disliked coming to grips with the bitter side of life.

He protested, 'But, my dear, how could you have looked after them? What could you have done for them? You had to find work for yourself. You had no place of your own, no money—'

'Half of Lily's house is mine.'

'You couldn't have turned Lily out and sold up, now could you, my dear?'

Too much pain. I was silent. She had not wanted us. And because my trouble was inconvenient, she had pretended it didn't exist.

'No, no,' said Humphrey, who also found trouble inconvenient, 'it would have been too much for you, my dear. Besides, you couldn't have supported and educated them and housed them as Guy did.'

The cab stopped. In the chill of early morning I hugged my coat around me while Humphrey paid the driver. Slowly we descended the steps to my basement flat. As I slid my key into the lock Humphrey spoke again, this time in an encouraging tone.

'On the whole,' he said, 'and all things considered, I expect it worked out for the best, in the end.'

Perhaps. But not for me.

CHAPTER THREE

'I have the lease of this flat until the end of the year,' I said, watching my captive eat, 'and then I shall have to find somewhere else to live. Meanwhile a publisher has suggested that I write a cookery book, and I'm pretty keen on the idea.'

Expansive now, affectionate, I used the nickname Jack Rice had given him years ago.

'Humpty, do I have to ask Jack's permission if I want to call it Bon Appétit?' I scribbled the title on a kitchen pad to show him. 'Like that. Bon Appétit! with an exclamation mark. D'you see?'

He acknowledged the intimacy by laying down his knife and fork and touching the back of my hand. Then returned to the business of eating.

'I should certainly get his permission, officially and legally,' said Humphrey with unwonted shrewdness, 'while he is still occupied with La Hammond – a spoiled creature, that one. Running a hotel indeed! I'd be surprised if either of them stayed the course! Where was I? Ah, yes. Later, if things don't work out as he hopes, he may become difficult. These sausages are awfully good, by the way! Now what else can I do for you, Flavia? I must hunt around and find a little place for you near my own. Somewhere larger and sunnier than this. I know you've done what you can with it, my dear, but it is the wrong end of the district, and – being in the basement – just a weeny bit dark, isn't it?'

'Just remember that we pay heavily for light and space in London. I can't afford an elegant pad in a square, like yours.'

'No, no. I understand that. But somewhere near to me. And

then we can eat together often. That would be perfect. I take my responsibilities seriously, you know. I shall see that you are not lonely.'

I realised, with some irony, that I would now be cooking for Humphrey instead of the bistro. Nevertheless I thanked him, for he meant to be kind. And I resolved to deal with that problem later and have a long holiday by myself first.

'Humphrey dear, you must tell me all about Kelly Park, so that I'm not a total stranger when I arrive there. I was thinking of finding out train times and making arrangements this week. I'd like to leave as soon as possible.'

'Good heavens, Flavia. How very sudden you are.' Taken aback. 'I'd thought of your being here for quite a while so that I could look after you.'

'You're very sweet, but I really must get away from London.'

And I felt a lift of spirit, as if that were the answer.

'But they've been having the most appalling weather there recently,' he said. 'Gales and rain. Even a snowstorm, which is a rarity.'

'My dear Humphrey, a little wind and rain won't worry me!'

'But you've no idea what it can be like on the Lizard in bad weather. You're a city girl. It's simply not wise to dash off at the wrong time of year. And those storms! I tell you what, my dear, I'll send you my newspaper when I've finished with it. I may have been absent a while but I keep in touch, you know,' he said proudly. 'I have a copy of the *Helston Packet* posted to me every week.'

'Thank you, and I'd love to read it, but I really want to go anyway.'

'Perhaps I should come with you?' he mused.

And grounded me. I needed to be by myself. Still, I could hardly forbid a man to visit his old home.

'We could go in the Bentley,' he said, brightening up. 'I'll get the garage to service it. It's a pity you don't drive. And I'm somewhat out of practice. But we could do the journey in gentle stages.'

He had once taken Jack and me out to Box Hill for a picnic: an excursion I shall never forget. I can think of few things more horrific than being driven by a man who looks at his passenger while he talks, whose hands frequently lift from the steering wheel to illustrate some salient point, and whose mind is anywhere but on the road. Fortunately the Bentley broke down and we had to return by train. Never again.

'Humpty, I can't hear of it. Driving all the way down to Cornwall simply to make things easier for me.'

He chewed thoughtfully. I pressed on.

'Besides, if it rains a lot, just think of the damp, with your rheumatism! What would your doctor say?' As he hesitated I put my hand on his and said, 'I can't allow you to sacrifice yourself on my account. So the answer is – no, thank you, darling Humpty.'

I kissed his cheek and he subsided gratefully.

'Well, if you put it like that, Flavia, sadly I must agree. But I was more than willing to try, my dear, for your sake.'

'Of course you were. And it's just like you to be so sweet and thoughtful.'

I returned to practical matters.

'Now, Humpty, what's the Kelly Park routine? What should I take with me? How do I order the milk and basic groceries? Jack mentioned a housekeeper. Perhaps you should ring her up to tell her I'm coming?'

'Oh dear,' said Humphrey, overwhelmed by detail, 'this is all most abrupt. And excessively complicated.'

I smiled at him and squeezed his hand encouragingly.

'You see, my dear,' he began, unwillingly, 'Alice Quick isn't a housekeeper as such. We haven't been able to keep up a full establishment since the war. Most of the place was shut down after Grandmama died. And neither of my tenants managed to get it afloat again, in a manner of speaking. No, Alice Quick and her husband are former retainers who oblige me by keeping an eye on things. They live in the lodge rent free. Ben does odd jobs around the place and stokes the boiler in winter. Alice opens windows now and again, pulls the blinds up or down, and so forth. But neither of them will have anything to do with a telephone. If there's any little problem they tell Peggy Crowdy at the shop and she rings me up, and then I get on to Will Soady, the builder, and he usually sorts matters out.' I maintained a smiling, waiting silence. 'I suppose I shall have to write her a letter?'

His bottom lip was pendulous. I was spoiling his breakfast with my plans.

'Humphrey, I can write the letter for you if you'll give me her address.'

He put down his knife and fork and patted his pockets fretfully, saying, 'Now where did I put that address book?'

'Never mind Mrs Quick, then,' I said, slightly impatient. 'I can dash round the shops for myself when I arrive.'

Humphrey pushed away his plate with a touch of temper.

'Elinglaze has only *one* shop,' he said. 'And it's bound to be closed by the time you get there. This isn't Surbiton, my dear, it's a Cornish village! A few hundred souls, a couple of farms, a church, a pub, a bus stop and a telephone kiosk.' He added tartly, 'It's ten miles from the nearest town and two from the nearest decent-sized village. Your lack of transport will be a tremendous drawback – which is why I suggested taking the Bentley.'

He was regretting his long-standing invitation which had been offered, as so many are, without thought of acceptance. But opposition always arouses the best and the worst in me, and now I was determined to go.

'If the village is as small as that, surely a letter addressed to Mrs Quick, The Lodge, Kelly Park, Elinglaze, Cornwall, should find her?'

He said grudgingly, 'Elinglaze, near Helston, Cornwall. Yes, I daresay it would. She'll have the keys, anyway. And she'll order milk and bread if you ask her.' He assumed a distant air. 'By the by, my dear, you really mustn't talk about Kelly Park when you're in Cornwall. That's simply a nickname, an anglicisation. The correct nomenclature is Parc Celli. Spelled like this!'

He wrote it down on my kitchen pad, beneath Bon Appétit!

'Thank you, Humphrey. I'll remember. Tell me more. Have you got basic cooking equipment, household and bed linen there?'

'Yes, yes, of course,' testily. 'It's my old home. Closets full of the stuff. China, sheets, towels. I expect they're still there. And I seem to remember that the kitchen was very large and well equipped, with some sort of a range in it. I used to go down there when I was a lad, and the cook would give me a saffron bun hot from the oven. But it's extremely cold in winter. The radiators simply take the chill out of the air and stop everything from rotting away. The rooms won't be ready or the fires lit.'

'Oh yes, they will. I'll send a couple of pounds to Mrs Quick and ask her to do just that.'

He placed one hand on his waistcoat and asked of himself, 'Indigestion?'

'Not a bit of it. You haven't had your toast and marmalade yet, nor a second cup of coffee. And your table napkin's slipped to the floor. Here, let me sort you out!'

His face brightened as I attended to him. His humour was restored.

'Tell me about Parc Celli,' I said.

'Well now, where shall I begin? When Great-grandfather Jarvis – of Jarvis's Red and White Quince Marmalades, Bristol, established 1855 ...'

I must make quince preserve sometime.

'... made his pile, like many another city merchant he decided to invest some of the proceeds in a Country House and become a Country Gentleman. Parc Celli was built around 1870 when Gentlemen's Houses were proliferating like mushrooms, and he named it after its position – the meadow in the grove. Have I ever shown you this photograph of me on the lawn in 1920?' Taking out his pocket-book.

Yes, Humpty, about four thousand times, but let me take it and look and exclaim with delight once again.

'Well, my dear, that lawn was part of the original meadow. And the trees round the far edge were the grove. My father had this side cleared, so that there was a view to the sea. You observe the house in the background? An architectural pastiche, of course – but charming, charming. Dreamed up by old Humphrey himself and a somewhat eccentric architect, Augustus Parkin of Bristol, who was all the rage at the time but barely rates a footnote now.

'Old Humphrey thought to found a dynasty, you know. Which is why his son and grandson and myself were named after him. I am Humphrey Jarvis the Fourth. The fourth, and the last, I fear. We were not destined to be a prolific family. My grandmother – a beauteous Cornish lady – produced three living children of whom only one son survived. My parents only managed to have me, because my dear mama died young and my father never remarried. Then two world wars and all the death duties . . . '

I was suddenly overwhelmed by exhaustion. As he talked and drank and ate I curled up on the sofa and wedged a cushion beneath each elbow and another behind my head, to keep me in a listening position. Humphrey's words came out of his mouth as balloons and I floated up with them.

'In those days, of course, there were servants a-plenty, and all of them glad to work. And we *belonged* to Elinglaze – at least we did by the time my father was born. It takes a couple of generations to persuade the Cornish to warm to an outsider. But we regarded the villagers as our people and we looked after them. Visits to the sick. Calf's foot jelly and strong broth when they were ailing. Cast-off clothes. Low rents and a benevolent patriarchy in return for service. A feudal system, in short – and a jolly good thing, whatever your Labour people might say. My grandfather was Master of Foxhounds – plenty of good hunting in those days. But it's all gone now. Goonhilly. Animal rights. Socialist scoundrels . . . '

Pictures flickered across my mental screen. My mind swooned after them in a kind of ecstasy.

' . . . never forget trotting forth in the pony cart to Helston with my dear grandmama. A great lady, Flavia, a great lady. Cornish beauty. Arabella Curtys. Daughter of Cornish gentlefolk. Good blood, old family, not much money. Fine black eyes with a touch of fire in them. Short straight nose. Generous mouth. Hair with only a touch of grey, and so long that she could sit on it. The weather wasn't as wet then. I remember life at Elinglaze as one long spring morning. Trit, trot, trit, trot. The smiles, the bows, the doffed hats. Charming, quite quite charming . . . Flavia! Are you asleep?'

'Certainly not!' I said, waking up. 'I was musing along with you and Grandmama in the pony cart. Let me pour you some more coffee. And I'll have some myself.'

To keep me conscious.

I sipped and set the cup down on the side-table, but my eyelids were sliding down again like weighted blinds. I squeezed a yawn into a sigh of satisfaction.

'Do go on, Humpty.'

He had not yet begun to regret the richness of my sausages, and was becoming expansive over his third cup of coffee.

'Alas, Flavia! The house in its glory is no more. Like a woman who has once been beautiful, the structure is there, the air, the style – but faded, my dear. Faded. Much of the surrounding land was sold, and someone built little houses on it. Not very nice little houses, either. But the grove remains, and the view to St Mawes across Falmouth Bay, so the immediate privacy of the house and stables is assured . . . which reminds me. Flavia!' I jerked upright. 'Flavia, did I ever tell you the most amazing story about a sailor called Tom Faull?'

'I don't think so. Tell me again.'

I drank black coffee and willed my eyelids open.

'Actually, I didn't mention it, come to think. Because in broad daylight the whole thing seemed rather far-fetched . . . '

He paused so long that I felt bound to ask, 'Do tell!'

He gave a little laugh, part deprecating, part confused, as if he were about to impart an amorous secret.

'Sounds absurd, even now. He came out of the blue, quite unsolicited, spent the evening with me, and then vanished. But he did give me the impression of being perfectly sincere.'

I sat up. I had always suspected Humphrey of being more interested in men than women, but if he were then he either repressed his desires or concealed his lovers awfully well.

'Come on, Humpty! Tell me about your sailor!'

'Actually, he comes from my part of the world. He was one of our people. His father worked on the estate. There's a rumour that Tom was born on the wrong side of our family blanket – my widowed papa having his wicked way with the parlour maid! I've never been quite sure how true that was, although his mother, Tegan, married quite suddenly and Tom was born six months later. Fine-looking girl as I remember. Soft-voiced, ladylike, took a pride in her appearance. And dark, dark. Spanish blood there somewhere, as so often happens among the Cornish. Tom inherited her good looks, and he was her darling, and a great favourite up at the house. But his father – Kevin Faull, that is – never had any time for him' – he retrieved the dropped stitch of his narrative – 'Yes. I best remember Tom as a high-spirited lad of sixteen in the village cricket team. Highly promising fast bowler. Black as a gipsy. Wonderful action. Tall, slim, handsome fellow, too. Bright and quick and interested in everything. Intelligent beyond his station in life. A bit of a scapegrace. A little wild. There was no future in Elinglaze for such as Tom Faull. He went to sea to make his fortune, like many a lad before him. And like most of them he has come back a great deal older and no richer than when he left, except in experience. He must be in his middle forties by now, and he's tired of roving and wants safe harbour. Flavia! The moment he saw me he swept off his hat and gave a little bow—'

'His sailor's hat?'

'No, no, no!' Testily. 'He was on shore leave. A sort of green baseball hat it was. But anyway, he swept it off. Called me Mr Jarvis, sir. Spoke to me as one of my father's tenants would have spoken to him. Respectful, trusting, man to man. By God, Flavia, it took me right back to the good old days!'

'And what did this courtly sailor want?' I asked, now wide awake.

'A favour – which would actually be a favour to me as well. He needs a place to call his own, but he only has his savings, you see. A few hundred pounds, he told me. And that won't buy anything. He's been cycling round Cornwall on each of his last leaves, looking for some ruin he could rebuild. Bit of an innocent, really. All the ruins are being bought by city businessmen and tarted up as holiday cottages. Anyway, at the end of this leave, having drawn a blank as usual, Tom Faull decided to visit Elinglaze. He's been something of a prodigal son, I fear!'

At this point Humphrey laughed indulgently, winked slyly.

'Unfortunately, his homecoming brought forth no fatted calf! He hadn't kept in touch with the family since his mother died . . . the lady with whom Papa was rumoured to be' – here he wriggled his fingers and lifted his eyebrows – 'anyway, he didn't know what had happened to anything or anyone. Expected to find the place as he left it, ten years ago. But the Faulls had either died or departed and all was changed.'

Humphrey now moved into the present tense, reliving the sailor's return.

'He thinks that the old squire might help him – meaning my father, you know. So off he goes to the house. All locked up. It starts to rain. He takes shelter in the deserted stables at Parc Celli. Eats his sandwiches, looks round, sees what could be done, and makes enquiries in the village of Mrs Quick, who tells him that the young squire – meaning me! – lives in London. Now this is the astonishing part, Flavia! He coaxes my address out of her, and cycles up from Cornwall, which takes him five days. Finds my flat, discovers I'm spending the evening at the Garrick Club, and tracks me down there!'

'And how did the Garrick Club react to a sailor in a green baseball hat, on a bicycle, demanding to see the young squire?'

Humphrey gave me a reproachful look.

'Everyone acted very correctly. They pretended not to notice. And when I found out that he hadn't eaten I took him to a more suitable place for a meal.'

'More suitable to his station in life, the bicycle and the baseball hat?'

'Flavia, dear, I wish you'd take this seriously. It's a perfectly serious matter! Anyway, he came straight to the point. He wanted my permission to restore the stables and make them into a home for himself. He'll keep the outside exactly as it is – as it used to be. But inside it will be a private dwelling. He's prepared to do the whole of the restoration and rebuilding himself, whenever he's on leave. Of course, that will take two or three years.'

'And who's going to pay for this?'

'He is paying for it himself, but I feel it would be only right to offset some of the expense. After all it's my property and will remain so. And when it's finished he'll retire from the sea and live there, keeping himself by doing odd jobs. He's a chief engineer, by the way, and can turn his hand to anything.'

There was a tinge of pride in Humphrey's voice, as though Tom Faull belonged to him. Personally, I smelled the faintest odour of fraud.

'And what happened after the meal?'

'We shook hands and parted – he was going back to his ship. A couple of days later I had a postcard from him at Southampton, thanking me and saying he'd be in touch. But I haven't heard a word since.'

'How long ago is *since*?'

'Three months,' Humphrey admitted, watching my face. And as it evidently bore out his own fears he said uncertainly, 'Seems odd, doesn't it? The long silence.' He became querulous. 'I believed in him at the time. But now I've had a while to think it over I'm not at all sure.'

A possible explanation of this fairy tale occurred to me.

After a pause I said, 'Did he ask you for a loan?'

Humphrey turned a darker shade of crimson.

'Not a bit of it. No, no. Not asked. Certainly not.'

I recognised evasion.

'Did you lend him money without being asked, then?'

'Not exactly lent.' I looked disbelieving, and he added hastily, 'I offered him fifty pounds to replace the money he'd spent on tools and slates. He'd patched up the worst part of the stable roof which was open to the sky. I felt quite touched when he told me that. I thought it sounded – so genuine.'

'And presumably he accepted the offer? I thought so. Humphrey, how do you know he patched the roof? Did you write to Mrs Quick and ask her?'

'Not exactly. No. It didn't seem necessary. I, well, I took his word. A man's word is his bond. He was one of our people.' He drew his squirearchy about him and said haughtily, 'It's something which is very difficult to explain to an outsider. Tom Faull and I *understood* each other.'

I was unimpressed, except perhaps for the audacity and possible mendacity of Tom Faull.

'So he leaned on your sense of family and past history, spun you a likely story, touched you for a free meal and fifty quid and cycled off? I think, myself, that you've seen the last of him.'

I was sorry I'd said it when I saw Humphrey's face. Chap-fallen, I thought – oh, what a pun!

He turned from red to white, clasped his waistcoat, and said faintly, 'Flavia dearest. My tablets – breast pocket – glass of water—'

'I'd better call a cab for you,' I said, conscience-stricken, as I ministered to him. 'There, there, Humpty. Sit still while the tablets work. I shouldn't have cooked you a big breakfast after that rich food last night, and well I know it! I'm never to be trusted with a man who likes to eat, and that's a fact.'

Humphrey's eyes were moist and frightened. He sought my fingers and kissed them. He smelled of gentlemen's toilet water. Floris No. 89.

'So sweet to me always. Someday, Flavia . . . '

I was anxious in case he proposed and regretted it, but I need not have worried. Even in an extremity he would never do anything so rash.

'Someday,' he said, with sombre pleasure, 'I know I'm going to keel over after an especially splendid dinner. Keel over for good, I mean. And, dear girl, I hope it's after one of your dinners!'

'I should always remember that,' I said wryly. 'Now let me call a cab. Go home and rest quietly, and I'll ring later today to see how you are.'

As I helped him into the taxi, Humphrey spoke again in a wheedling tone, willing me to give him the answer he wanted.

'Flavia dear, I suppose you can't imagine a faithful tenant wanting to restore the squire's ruined stable at his own expense, can you?'

I was not to be wheedled.

'No,' I replied firmly. 'It sounds most unlikely.'

'Yes, it does, doesn't it?' said Humphrey, wistful. 'And yet he mended the roof before he knew I would give him permission to live there, and he cycled all that way from Cornwall to London simply to see me.'

'He only said he did,' I reminded him gently.

'But he did have the bicycle. He chained it to a lamp-post and one of the neighbours complained.'

'The bicycle is not evidence of good faith. He could have cycled from Brixton and you wouldn't be any the wiser.'

'No,' said Humphrey heavily. 'I suppose not. And I took him at his word. Well, well.'

I kissed his cheek tenderly, closed the door, and asked the taxi-driver to wait a moment. Surreptitiously, I slipped a pound note in the man's hand, and spoke too softly for Humphrey to hear me.

'Would you be kind enough to see him safely into his flat? He had rather a bad turn when he was with me, half an hour ago.'

'Yes, lady, I'll do that!' Then glancing back at Humphrey, leaning forward and speaking for my ears alone, he said, 'You want to watch it with a man his age. My sister's husband went that way.'

'Indeed?' I said coldly. And then, 'Oh, what is it now, Humphrey?'

For he was rolling down the window, seeking yet more comfort from me.

'But Tom Faull did write a postcard from Southampton, thanking me.'

'Yes,' I said firmly. 'So he did. And I'm sure he's the nicest sort of rogue to know, but a rogue nevertheless – so don't you forget it!'

And watched him being driven disconsolately away.

CHAPTER FOUR

This place is at the end of the world.

It was dark by the time I got here and I arrived in the midst of pouring rain, so my first impressions were blurred and faintly hostile. The taxi-driver was new to the job, took a wrong turn, and lost us down miles of narrow winding roads. Some of them were only wide enough to take one vehicle at a time, and we met several others coming the other way. The iron gates of Parc Celli were chained and padlocked and he had to rattle them and shout for the lodge-keeper. Further time was expended while Ben Quick let us in, made extensive enquiries as to my identity, and explained that his wife was waiting for me up at the house. In a fine black temper, by this time, the taxi-driver charged me eleven pounds, dumped my suitcases on the gravel and roared off, leaving me exhausted.

Jack's summing up of Kelly Park seemed justified. The incredible slowness of Mrs Quick, her inability to find what I wanted, and a power failure which robbed me of light when I most needed it, all contrived to give me the feeling of being unwelcome.

The radiators were huge, old-fashioned, and tepid. A coal fire had been lit in my bedroom, and a large range which needed black-leading made the kitchen inhabitable, but outside these patches of warmth great wells of coldness waited to engulf me. The bathroom, high, spacious, and glacial with white tiles, was a North Pole. Accustomed to small rooms and efficient central heating, I suffered. There was no such thing as an electric blanket, and the only rubber hot-water bottle I could find had perished. The night silence, dark and deep and velvet, made me feel as if I were wearing ear plugs. The very lack of noise disturbed me. I missed the sounds of late-night traffic. Finally the electricity was restored with brutal suddenness at 5.30 a.m. and switched me wide awake, to sit up in bed, heart hammering, crying, 'Oh! Oh! Oh!' as Kelly Park became an illuminated, if dilapidated, palace.

At that point I gave up the idea of sleep, pulled on my scarlet wool housecoat and thick fur slippers, and went downstairs to the kitchen. And there I huddled by the rusting range for an hour, drinking hot tea, waiting disconsolately for dawn to break, and wondering whether to leave at once, and if so where to go.

I do believe in the value of eating a good breakfast. When I was with Guy and the boys I used to get up early to prepare something special for that first important meal of the day. I love food: choosing, buying, planning, preparing, presenting, and eating. I never had any trouble in feeding my children. They ate everything I gave them in the spirit with which it was given: eagerly, joyfully, adventurously. Whereas Guy's second wife, Anne, complained about their fads and fancies and poor appetites.

Best not pursue that trend of thought.

Mrs Quick had left a cardboard box of groceries, a small white sliced loaf, six eggs, bacon and tomatoes and a bottle of silver-top milk. I grilled some bacon and a tomato, poached an egg, toasted the bread and resolved to bake my own if I decided to stay here. The food warmed me. A watery February sun rose. My spirits lifted. I took a mug of hot sweet coffee with me, to sustain my heart and stomach while I made a grand tour of Humphrey's childhood kingdom.

Warmth and light revealed an error of judgement on my part. I had misunderstood Parc Celli, misread the signals. There was no ill will here, simply the forlorn spirit of a house once busy and hospitable and now without purpose or employment. And its presence was so manifest that I found myself talking aloud, as if to a companion in misfortune, while I walked through chilled rooms and draughty corridors. And later, wrapped and Burberryed against the wintery weather, I walked round the gardens in order to see the house from without as well as within.

Parc Celli had been built by a man of social ambition, and

designed to look as if it had been in the family for generations: an Elizabethan E in shape, subtle-stoned, grey and secluded, with mullioned windows, scrolled gables and fanciful chimneys. The desire of a Bristol jam manufacturer to acquire instant history had dictated a great hall to the left of the passage which rose through two storeys and had a vast open fireplace, a long refectory table fashioned out of a single oak trunk, a troop of carved oak chairs, and dark oil paintings in elaborate gold frames. I recognised Humphrey's heavy chin and portly bearing in the three male ancestors, and Grandmama was unmistakable at any age. But I could not help feeling that the other portraits, some of royal personages, had been bought as an upmarket job lot to fill the wall-space and lend an ancestral air. They all looked dirty and disconsolate. And though my knowledge of architecture is minimal I could see that the owner and the architect had mixed their styles with considerable abandon.

On one side of the hall a Georgian drawing room led into a linen-fold panelled library, where again I felt that many of the tooled leather books didn't belong to anybody and had never been read, but bought by the yard for appearance's sake. To the other side was a Victorian dining room, and beyond this an Edwardian lady's boudoir. Both these rooms overlooked formal gardens which must have been lovely in their day but were now a sorry tangle of their former selves.

On the north side, the kitchen quarters, connected to the dining area by a service lift and hatch, were pure Victorian: light, high and spacious, with flagged floors and a multitude of little sculleries and pantries, requiring a large staff to clean and run them, but at the moment furred with dust and run only by mice.

On the first floor, one bathroom had been considered adequate for the occupants of six grand bedrooms and two dressing rooms, all in various states of neglect. On the second floor front a humbler bathroom had been provided for the nursery quarters. And along the back wings were the servants' bedrooms, greater in number, small and close and spartan, certainly too cold in winter and probably too hot in summer. Pinewood fittings, peg rugs and plain wallpapers had been thought good enough, and instead of a bathroom they were supplied with plain cream basins, ewers and chamberpots.

I returned to the ground floor and sat with the cloaked ghosts of furniture in the drawing room, and thought, and thought, and thought.

The property which eventually became our bistro had been in a similar state of neglect when Jack Rice and I took it on. In those early days, though wisely leaving rewiring, plumbing and fitting to the experts, we had been poor enough and keen enough to do the decorating ourselves, and the whole place had been finished in a matter of weeks at a reasonable cost. But this house must be twenty times the size of Bon Appétit and involving work far beyond amateur ability. Scaffolding would be needed to reach the ceilings. Discoloured stone must be cleaned, carpets mended, floorboards repolished and intricate cornice-work regilded. I was looking at months of painstaking effort and considerable expense. And yet.

And yet, it was perfectly possible.

Imagine that you are a stranger, from town or city, coming to spend a few days at Parc Celli. Seeking to get away from it all, you arrive at the end of the world: remote, but highly civilised.

Someone (not Mrs Quick) hurries down the front steps to greet you, takes your bags, guides you to your room, chatting pleasantly. Here is luxury. A four-poster bed. A cavernous wardrobe for clothes. A half-bottle of champagne in an ice-bucket on the side-table. *With the compliments of the house.* And through the long windows lies a view which sweeps across the newly mown lawn to the glittering bay beyond. *Accessible to the coast.*

Tea will be served in the drawing room whenever you're ready.

Downstairs, you mistake the turning and find yourself in a Victorian dining room, already laid for the evening meal. Twelve to twenty covers for special parties. *The atmosphere is gracious and hospitable.* You come out again and walk through the great hall – could use the long table plus smaller ones, or use the long table as a buffet and have small tables – say thirty covers. *Non-*

residents welcome. You are advised to book well in advance. And into the drawing room.

Fellow house guests are there before you. It is that hour on a spring/summer/autumn/winter afternoon when one pauses and reflects, sipping china tea from china cups, looking out on to the headland. Sunlight, chintz, little tables covered by lace-edged cloths, cucumber sandwiches, home-made cakes and scones. *An atmosphere at once serene and intimate.* The conversation is friendly. Have you been here before? You haven't? Oh, what treats are in store! This is our third visit. We recommend it to all our friends. Nothing is too much trouble. And of course *the food is noted throughout the county . . .*

I, who was perilously adrift, without people to feed or man or child to cherish, began to perceive stability and purpose and a personal future in Parc Celli.

My first home belonged to my husband and I was merely its housekeeper. Bon Appétit was shared with but betrayed by Jack Rice. My present flat was mere accommodation. But this house could be my future home and living, created by myself.

We communed in that ghostly drawing room, Parc Celli and I. Dignified in her decay, hinting at the splendours that had passed, perhaps she could sense in me, as I sensed in her, the means of restoration and redress. Woman to woman, we said silently to each other, 'Save me, and I will save you.'

'But no checked tablecloths, blackboard menu and *table d'hôte* for you, Madame!' I said aloud to her. 'This time we're aiming for the silver and damask and *à la carte*!'

Mrs Quick's provisions being of the most basic kind, I managed through Sunday, and then on Monday morning set out for the village with a large basket and an even larger umbrella, which I found in the butler's pantry. There at the post-office-cum-stores I introduced myself, quite unnecessarily as it happened, because Mrs Quick had reported all she knew of me and they recognised the basket and umbrella and told me to whom they had belonged.

Everyone asked after Humphrey respectfully, and two or three elderly customers who had known his father and grandmother recalled tales of the old days. Mrs Crowdy, the reigning post-mistress-cum-shopkeeper, was in no particular hurry to serve anyone, and joined the conversation. In a London shop this would have caused considerable friction, but time seemed to be of little importance here. After a decent interval for socialising, I then presented my list to Mrs Crowdy, who crossed out many of the items, saying she didn't get no call for they, and I would have to take the bus into Helston.

'But the butcher's van calls here Tuesdays and Fridays,' she said helpfully, 'and the fish van on Wednesdays. I'll ask them to come up to the House, if you like.'

And she laid reverent emphasis on the word as if it had a capital H.

I said I should like that very much indeed.

'And Parc Celli farm, the Home Farm as we used to call it, sell fresh eggs and clotted cream and home-made butter and poultry. He's just down the lane from you, to the right.'

I thanked her.

'And you'll find the bus-stop just two hundred yards up the hill. He runs the school children into Helston at half-past eight in the morning and the shoppers at two o'clock in the afternoon. And there's a school bus back at four o'clock and a workers' bus at half-past five.'

I wrote the times down in my diary.

'But if you want a morning paper,' said Mrs Crowdy, 'you'll have to order it, and walk down here for it, because there aren't no delivery.'

'Thank you,' I replied, 'I'll just have the *Observer* newspaper on a Sunday while I'm here.' She wrote this down, rather coldly I thought, and I remembered something. 'Oh, and a copy of the *Helston Packet*.'

This went down better.

'That's a weekly paper. You don't want no daily newspaper, then?' she asked, pencil poised.

I hesitated, and another customer said, 'The lady don't want to walk all the way down here from the House every day!' And, turning to me, 'If you look in the shed, or else the stables, you should find the gardener's old bike. You can ride a bike, can you?'

'Oh yes,' I said confidently, who had not ridden a bicycle since my school days. But once learned never forgotten. I hoped.

'He'll need a drop of oil, and his tyres pumping up, but he should go.'

Someone else said, 'That'd be Martin Skeggs's bike.'

'Ah, but he don't use it since he had the arthritis.'

'No more he don't.'

'You use 'un, Mrs Pollard!' said my adviser. 'And then you can c'llet the *Western Morning News*. That be a good paper.'

I thanked him, and asked Mrs Crowdy if she stocked Cornish picture postcards. She found a packet of sepia reproductions in the bottom of a drawer, and I was delighted to see Elinglaze in the nineteen twenties, and a romantic study of Parc Celli in her prime. The cards were passed round when I had bought them, and everyone could recall some story or relative pertaining to that era. Then it began to rain and they insisted that I shelter in the shop. So by the time I got home again I had an hour in which to eat a sandwich lunch, and walk briskly down the drive and up the hill to catch the two o'clock bus. But Helston stocked everything I needed, and I returned at dusk, laden with good things, and as the evening settled in, so did I.

On Tuesday morning, busy cleaning and oiling the gardener's old bicycle, I met the postman, Jeff Kennack, who rode up on *his* old bicycle, saying prophetically, 'I think this letter be from Mr Jarvis, Mrs Pollard.'

And so it was. I thanked him and slipped it into my apron pocket.

'And you got some here that's been redirected from upcountry,' said Jeff Kennack, doing a Sherlock Holmes on the post. 'One mail order catalogue about catering, and two that look like bills, but there again they could be receipts. Is that your kettle whistling?'

The kettle had no whistle and was not even on the range, but I felt I should ask if he would like a cup of tea, and he accepted, and said he hoped Mr Jarvis was well. So we both sat down at the kitchen table, and I opened my letter in order to assure him that Humphrey was flourishing. By the time he mounted his bicycle again I had heard the early morning news from Elinglaze, and given him the information he wanted.

He also told me that he delivered post throughout the parish, and always had time for a word with everyone, and everyone had a word for him. As I wobbled experimentally up and down the drive, I thought it must take him all day.

On Wednesday, I heard a milk float jingle up to the back door, and caught the milkman before he could jingle away. I told him my name, which he knew already, and asked his.

'Henry Blewett, my dear,' he said.

'Well, Mr Blewett, I wondered if I could have a pint of gold-top milk?'

He was a large rosy Cornishman with a large rosy smile and, as I was to discover, a mind of his own.

He said, 'Here you are, my dear,' very nicely and gave me a pint of silver top.

'No, Mr Blewett,' I said, 'I want *gold* top. Jersey milk! Because the creamy bit is so good in coffee!'

'Oh, gold top!' he said, as if enlightened.

'Yes, please.'

'Oh, you don't want tha-at,' he said, elongating the 'a' very contemptuously. 'I don't carry tha-at!'

And as I stood there, clutching the unwanted bottle, with my mouth open, he gave a huge smile and said, 'Don't you bother none, my dear. I'll look after you. All right?' And walked off.

So silver top it is.

Far from behaving as the Cornish Riviera should, the weather continued to be atrocious. On the following Sunday morning I woke to a cold white silent landscape, and discovered that Kelly Park and I were isolated. I was not in the least apprehensive, in fact a childlike excitement and delight possessed me. But I did realise that I must connect myself to the outside world. So I pulled on my wellington boots, donned two coats and a woolly hat, found a spade in the shed, and began to dig my way towards the main gate.

At eleven o'clock, as I rounded the bend in the drive, I saw three stout Cornishmen digging their way chivalrously towards me. We hailed each other with shouts and a flourishing of spades, and then set to again with a will.

Old Ben Quick made the introductions when we met a few yards later.

'Now this here's my son-in-law, Brian Angwin,' he said of a large, red-faced, middle-aged man. 'And this here is Arthur Crowdy, and his wife she run the village shop. And he come up on the tractor and brought Brian with him, to help me out.'

'Seeing as Parc Celli be cut off in this sort o' weather,' said Arthur.

'And you a stranger from upcountry,' said Brian.

'And Mrs Crowdy says to tell you there's been no papers delivered.'

I thanked them all warmly, and we shook hands.

'And there's that old boiler to stoke,' said Ben, breathing heavily, 'which you don't know nothing about. And he do have to be stoked regular.'

There was a long pause.

'Well, us'll be going now we've helped out,' said Brian, and stood smiling at nothing in particular.

'Yes, now us have helped out we'll be going back,' said Arthur, and did not move.

'Oh no,' I cried, waking up to my responsibilities. 'You've been so kind, and worked so hard, and it's so cold. Won't you come up to the house and have some tea and a slice of cake?'

'We don't want to bother you none,' said Brian, leading the way.

I had intended to take a complete holiday from cooking, but love and habit and the desire to try out an old-fashioned kitchen range, had proved too strong for me. A handsome Genoa cake, which I should never have eaten by myself, was decimated and deeply appreciated by my rescuers.

Conversation remained somewhat stilted, though we all smiled a lot and nodded at each other like a set of mandarins, and I said several times how grateful I was for their efforts. But apparently the name of 'Squire' Jarvis was held in tremendous regard, and as I was the Squire's guest they felt duty bound to help me out.

So I thanked them again, and Ben Quick showed me how to stoke the boiler, in case there came a day when he couldn't get through at all. It seemed to be a dirty and exhausting process, but I decided I could manage it in a crisis. Then they all had another slice of cake and a third mug of tea, and left me and Parc Celli to ourselves again.

I find old household inventories and account books mouldering in drawers, rescue them, and check present contents against past reckonings. I plumb the depths of the cellars and mount to the attics. I examine the furniture, noting its state of shabbiness or need of cleaning and repair. I count every article of glass, china and cutlery, and discover a hoard of silver and brass. And I set up a large black notebook, purchased in Helston, in which I write down every detail. On the leaden winter nights I wrap myself in an eiderdown and sit in the kitchen with my feet on the fender, poring over my notes, drawing up plans and writing out my work schedule for the coming day. I send sepia postcards, with ecstatic messages, to Humphrey and my two sons. I also write a letter to Humphrey, to tell him that I should be home again at the end of the following week, and will give him dinner at the flat. But I do not mention my proposal, nor say that I mean to return here as soon as I can. I tell no one of that.

Sometimes I think I must have gone gloriously mad. Here I am, living alone in a decaying house, on the southernmost peninsula of the wildest county in England, at the stormiest time of the year, with the wind coming up, the trees coming down, the drive flooded, and yet another power cut. It sounds like the beginning of a Hammer horror film. But instead of combing my long gold hair and hoping to meet a duke in disguise, or shivering at the prospect of a nightly haunting by some departed Jarvis, I am preparing to put Parc Celli to rights and turn it into a country-house hotel.

Yet, busy as I am, I still have time for reflection. Every evening at seven o'clock I think of Bon Appétit opening up: menu written out on the blackboard, tables laid, candles lit, the air savoury with coffee and garlic. Sometimes I lie awake and wonder where

Jack Rice is and how he is, and whether the lure of Sylvia Hammond comes from her youth or her total difference from me, and if he thinks of me sometimes.

For, however glad I am to be rid of the worry and misery he caused, I still regret the joys I have lost. And I think how good it would be if he were working here with me on this project, and how we would laugh together about a hundred pleasing Cornish absurdities. A seven-year partnership is not dismissed so lightly. He had been life and adventure and hope and youth and fun to me, after that long cold marriage. He had brought out the Flavia that Guy Pollard never wanted. And I had loved him.

CHAPTER FIVE

First I fed Humphrey royally on favourite and forbidden dishes. Then I settled him in the only comfortable armchair, with coffee, chocolates and brandy. I cut the end of his cigar and lit it for him. Finally I sat opposite, with my hands locked round my knees, and began to speak of Parc Celli, of my feelings for her, and my belief that she should not be left to decay.

Gradually, Humphrey's expression changed from bliss to suspicion. He guessed that something was afoot, but in an effort to ward off the moment he tapped the ash from his cigar, and pretended to be amused.

'So those ecstatic postcards were not mere good manners? Why that's absolutely splendid. Such a sophisticated Londoner as yourself might not – I wasn't *quite* sure whether you'd find it entirely – of course, I know exactly what you mean. A feeling of presence, as if the Parc Celli were a person. Well, so she is. A grand old Victorian lady in an Elizabethan manor, dressed up in eighteenth-century costume!'

'A very dilapidated costume, Humphrey. And an old lady on the verge of extinction.'

'Ah, yes, but a great lady nevertheless. "I am Duchess of Malfi still!" Remember, my dear?'

I took a deep breath and said, 'Humphrey, I know exactly what I should do about Parc Celli in your position.'

He laid his cigar aside and murmured to himself, 'Oh, dear!'

He crossed his legs with some difficulty, but nonchalantly nevertheless. One foot and one hand betrayed his nervousness. The fingers tapped. The shoe tossed pettishly.

He said with a hint of sternness, staring me down, 'Do you really, Flavia? You astonish me, my dear. You've only been there for a couple of weeks, and already you've solved a problem which brought my father to his grave and continues to haunt my modest self. Well, you *are* a clever girl!'

I said outright, 'There's no need to be sarcastic, Humphrey. I've gone to a lot of trouble over this, and I'm perfectly serious.'

He was at once contrite.

'My dear girl, I'm not being sarcastic. I'm kneeling at your swift little feet in humble admiration!' Then he sighed and said, 'So by all means tell me what you think I should do.'

His expression of displeasure conveyed that you never could trust a woman to mind her own business. And as I outlined the plan, and brought out my notebook full of figures and calculations to prove it, he became annoyed.

'A country-house hotel?' he cried. 'Good God, Flavia, my grandmother would turn in her grave!'

'Humphrey, it would be a very upmarket hotel. Like a private country house in which the guests are treated as friends. You wouldn't be encouraging charabancs and trippers. You could accommodate ten resident guests the first year, and up to twenty in the second year. By the third year you should be able to open a licensed restaurant for the public. Just run through these figures, and you'll see what I mean.'

He put on his half-moon spectacles and turned the pages distractedly, muttering, 'The hoi polloi tramping through! My grandfather would have set about them with a horsewhip! What a very aggressive black notebook. It gives me a headache just to look at it, let alone read it!'

'There's no need to tackle everything at once. Just the bare essentials.'

'Well, that's a blessing! What do you suggest I do first, dearest?'

'The principal rooms on the ground and first floors, and both bathrooms, should be decorated by the beginning of August. If I have a criticism of Parc Celli it is the shortage of bathing facilities. So it would be a good idea to convert the two dressing rooms into shower rooms.'

He read aloud, with derision, 'Improve kitchen facilities. Tidy the garden. That should keep someone busy! A trial run of autumn and winter weekend breaks while converting the second-floor rooms ready for a major opening in the spring of 'seventy-nine. I see!'

He laid down the book and said, 'I can feel my indigestion coming on!'

Inexorable now, I replied, 'It should be advertised in the national papers and I've made a rough sketch for an illustrated brochure which tells the story of Parc Celli, the meadow in the grove.'

'Well, well, well. You *have* been doing your homework!' Bitterly.

Humphrey changed course. He dabbed his face with an immaculate white handkerchief, smiled, and spoke unctuously, benevolently as if to an idiot.

'Flavia! Dearest girl! Will you listen to a few practical words from a sober old man of the world? How much will this cost?'

'Approximately ten thousand pounds,' and as he wagged his head in jocular disbelief I said, 'I found your builder and asked him to give me an estimate.'

'You found my . . . ?'

'Yes. Will Soady. My bedroom ceiling was leaking, and when I told Mrs Quick she gave me his address. I thought I'd mention this to him while he was there.'

I handed the estimate to Humphrey, at which he stared incredulously.

'I didn't commit you. I simply told him that you were wondering what it would cost to renovate.'

'Renovation is one thing, but running a business is another. Do I take it that you are prepared to be involved in this delightful daydream?' he asked coldly.

'If you would put up the ten thousand I'd be prepared to organise and run the whole thing. Board wages until the hotel was paying its way, and then when we'd cancelled the debt to you – fifty per cent of the profits.'

'Dear girl, I must just – one moment, Flavia – pouring myself a spot more brandy – this is so *sudden*! Flavia, I really must have time—'

'I realise that, Humphrey, of course. But time is valuable, and the sooner we start the better. If you look at the inventory,' – handing it over – 'you'll see that there's a lot to do. We shall need to choose wallpapers and fabrics and buy some modern kitchen equipment.'

Humphrey struck the paper pettishly, 'Surely there are sufficient copper warming pans and suchlike – well, of course I understand that one or two things may have to be updated, but what is this about a freezer and a refrigerator? Have you not noticed that we already have larders and cool rooms for such culinary fantasies as – no, I am *not* behind the times! It's simply that we managed without a freezer and a refrigerator then and I do not see why – and I do feel, Flavia, that there is nothing worse than discussing business matters after a heavy meal. It leads to bad judgements or indigestion or both. I am not prevaricating. I am thinking. Thinking, dearest, not dealing in wild speculations! Yes, wild speculations!'

I leaned forward, looked at him intently, and asked, 'Have you heard from Tom Faull recently?'

'Tom Faull?' Humphrey cried, flushing up. 'What in heaven's name made you think of him? What has he to do with this?'

'He had the same sort of idea, as I remember, and you were terribly thrilled about it, and gave him full permission and fifty pounds.'

'I have not heard from him, and he did not have the same sort of idea. He is prepared – was prepared – well, anyway he said he was prepared to rebuild the stables himself and pay for the materials. Ha! Yes, indeed. Tom Faull's modest plan would not have cost ten thousand pounds, board wages, profit percentages, wallpaper, new kitchen equipment, and an enormous lot of worry and responsibility on my part!'

'Humphrey,' I said, very quietly, 'I am offering you my professional services for a pittance and taking on all the hard work. You simply have to put up the money and let me get on with it.'

'Well, yes, of course I realise that. And I'm touched, dearest, positively touched to think of you investing yourself and your considerable expertise – My dear girl, no one knows your qualifications better than I. One has only to say Bon Appétit!'

'One could also say that I was loyal, truthful, dependable – and not in Southampton.'

'Now that was just a thought unkind, Flavia, and unlike your usual . . . Flavia, I am not comparing Tom Faull's humble dream of home with an ambitious business project.'

'A business project which would also enable you to restore Parc Celli.'

'But such an undertaking—'

'Otherwise Parc Celli will just fall down.'

'That sounds something of an overstatement.'

'But true.'

'Well then, a little dramatic perhaps, but I suppose it is true. I'm not denying the fact.'

I felt that silence would persuade him more subtly than words.

Finally he said hesitantly, 'I suppose I could scrape up ten thousand – at a pinch – I'm not a rich man, you know—'

Then he cleared his throat and spoke authoritatively.

'But I shall have to ask my accountant – who is very severe about capital expenditure – and he will insist on looking into this scheme very carefully,' – tapping the notebook – 'and then, of course, I must come down to Parc Celli and speak to Will Soady. No one will do anything unless I say so.'

I believed that the reference to his accountant was more of a safeguard than a fact. I had known him use his solicitor in the same way. 'Personally, I'd be delighted, but my solicitor is very dodgy about this sort of thing!' And far too often he prefaced an evening out with the remark, 'I must warn you that my doctor has put me on an extremely strict diet,' before eating and drinking himself to the point of insensibility.

Now I, too, lied in a business-like fashion.

'Well, I have an interview on Monday, Humphrey, and there are one or two other irons in the fire, so I want to know where I am. I shall need to hear what he and you decide, as soon as possible. And meanwhile, you had better take all this information with you.'

His face and tone changed.

'Of course, I shall tell him that I am for the scheme. Absolutely for it!'

'Nevertheless,' I replied demurely, 'you're proposing to invest a great deal of money in this, and I'm proposing to invest myself and my professional reputation. So we must both be certain that we're doing the right thing.'

He leaned forward and patted my knee.

'Leave it to me, my dear,' he said portentously. 'Just you leave it to me!'

I observed Humphrey's metamorphosis from man-about-town to country squire with amused interest. He arrived on Paddington Station, exactly a week after our conversation, clad in well-cut tweeds, sporting a tweed hat, and holding a walking stick. A letter had warned, a telegram had alerted, Mrs Quick as to the time of our arrival. We travelled first-class and lunched at leisure on the train, but were back in our compartment in time to see Brunel's bridge spanning the Tamar and bringing us into Cornwall.

'Home!' said Humphrey, with the utmost sincerity, and wiped his eyes.

The journey to Elinglaze was quite unlike my own. At Camborne station a taxi was waiting, and the driver knew his way. The gates of Parc Celli were open, with Ben Quick holding a storm lamp aloft to greet us, and Alice waiting up at the house with far more fires lit, rooms warmed and dustcovers removed, than when I was there. She must have gone to Helston for supplies, because as well as my order of groceries and greengroceries there was an unopened bottle of Johnnie Walker on the drinks' tray in the drawing room. And in the meat larder I found neighbourly offerings of poultry and game, for which I made immediate plans.

Though I would have been content with a Welsh rarebit for supper, Humphrey was not to be deprived of his comforts, so we dined out that evening, and came back in another taxi, full of high hopes. The wine we had consumed, plus a nightcap of Johnnie Walker, veiled our eyes to Parc Celli's inadequacies. But waking next morning was a different matter. The house seemed to be peeling, crumbling, sifting to pieces round us: an elderly actress, discovered without costume or make-up, her lines forgotten.

'For heaven's sake pull yourself together!' I charged her, under my breath.

And took Humphrey's breakfast to him in bed lest he change his mind.

But he was cheerful under the childhood spell, though careful not to put himself out on any account.

'What time is Will coming up?' he asked, buttering every corner of toast.

'Ten o'clock, Humpty. With all four sons.'

'Ah! Good of him. On a Saturday,' said Humphrey graciously, accepting the gesture as of right. 'And then I must take a walk to the village and look up a few people, and have a drink in the pub.'

'And this evening,' I said, 'I shall cook for us. What about a partridge apiece?'

'Excellent. I'll find us a couple of bottles of wine. There's still some in the cellar worth drinking.'

'Breakfast in bed for you again tomorrow,' I said. 'And then a classic Sunday lunch with all the trimmings?'

Humphrey looked thoughtfully round his bedroom. A sheet of cardboard wedged in the top pane of one window blew out with a sudden gust of wind. A sheet of wallpaper, its corner tugged away, turned enquiringly towards us and then rolled gracefully to the floor. Rain spattered furiously over the top of a chest of drawers. Humphrey averted his eyes.

Oh for God's sake, I urged the house silently, make an effort!

'That would be splendid. And then, dear girl,' he said grandly, 'I think I shall take an afternoon train home.'

'I thought,' I said apprehensively, 'that you were going to see your Helston bank manager on Monday. To open an account for Parc Celli.'

'Oh, I don't think that will be necessary. I'll write to him instead. You can pop into Helston with the letter and introduce yourself. After all, you are the person with whom he will be dealing. And I'm sure you have plenty to do here, without troubling yourself about me.'

'As you think best, Humpty,' I said, secretly relieved.

'And when the house is more habitable I can come down for a little holiday.'

Normally, as Humphrey informed me, we should have held this conference in his father's office. But we were short of coal and staff. So at ten o'clock on a mad March Saturday morning he and I sat at the kitchen table in conference with Will Soady and all four sons. Etiquette being strictly observed, Humphrey introduced me to them officially as his friend and business partner. He commended me to their care, and asked them to regard any orders from me as if they came from himself.

'Which, naturally, they will do,' he added, 'since Mrs Pollard will consult with me before she gives them.'

They all swore allegiance.

Then, with my notebook before him, he outlined our plans, and announced that Parc Celli must open on the first of September. And, metaphorically speaking, declared the meeting open for discussion.

'Now that's not going to be so easy, Mr Jarvis and Mrs Pollard,' said Will Soady, taking a thoughtful sup of tea, 'seeing as how Easter comes early this year – the end of this month, in fact – and Easter to October is the time for us to do outside work. What I mean to say is, we've got other jobs to go to that was promised. And though there's a handsome lot of decorating to do inside Parc Celli you'd be advised to make sure of that roof first. They storms didn't do him no good. Leaking all over. And the flashing's gone on one chimney.'

He was a small, gnarled, brown Cornishman in his sixties, with a face not so much lined as cracked by age and weather, and two grey cracks of eyes through which he viewed us acutely. His four grown sons waited for their father to pronounce judgement before airing their own opinions.

'We did ought to make all right and tight outside afore next winter, Mr Jarvis,' said Ken. 'Downspouts and guttering and that.'

'And take a look at all they roofs and chimneys, Mr Jarvis,' said Albert.

'Running repairs,' said Humphrey, dismissing them. 'Patch it up, Will.'

'Patch on patch don't do no good, Mr Jarvis. What you need is a new roof.'

'Can't be done at the moment,' said Humphrey firmly. 'Later, perhaps. Do whatever is absolutely necessary, but Mrs Pollard and I want you to concentrate on the inside decorating. We'll talk about a new roof when we've made some money.'

I sensed from Humphrey's tone and the expressions on their faces that this conversation was a repeat of past building conferences, all of which, judging from appearances, had come to nothing.

Will Soady rolled a cigarette between stained finger and thumb, thinking.

'Now an old house like this 'un,' he said, 'is as full of surprises as a bran tub. You don't know what's inside him, see? Start one job and you find three more.'

'And when we've done him inside and out, right through,' said Henry, with gloomy satisfaction, 'he'll need doing again. My word on that!'

'When he's finished,' Terry echoed, 'he'll need doing all over again.'

And the five men nodded at each other wisely.

'My dad's cousin,' said Will Soady, 'was estate carpenter here when Ben Quick's father was mason. And the two of them spent their livelong days – forty year or more! – keeping up the property. That was all they did. Keep up the property. Forty year or more.'

He lit his cigarette, which fizzed wildly before settling down.

'But they'm dead and gone long since,' he ended.

A brief respectful silence ensued.

After this decent interval Humphrey said, 'Have you anything to say, Flavia?'

I addressed Will directly.

'I do understand what you're telling us, Mr Soady. This is an enormous job, which will probably take longer than any of us have estimated.'

A chorus of assent from Will Soady and sons.

Ken said, 'A damn sight longer if you ask me!' And in response to a stern glance from his father, 'Begging your pardon, Mrs Pollard and Mr Jarvis.'

'But we *must* open in September. There's only so much money to spend and we must keep afloat financially until next Easter, when the real holiday season begins.'

They looked up at the high ceiling and down at the long scrubbed table, and were silent.

'Then we'd best start work on Monday, lads!' said Will Soady, closing the discussion. 'Thank you for the tea, Mrs Pollard.'

Obediently, the sons emptied their mugs, fitted their caps back on their heads, and followed him. At the kitchen door Will turned back for a final word. His tone was solemn and held a hint of reproach.

'All I'm saying is we'll do our best, Mr Jarvis and Mrs Pollard. Cain't do more than that, now can us?'

'No, no, no, of course not,' said Humphrey easily, waving one hand in acknowledgement, in dismissal.

I had to add, 'But if you could keep the first of September in mind.'

They nodded and filed out stolidly. At the door Will paused again to throw fresh light on the conversation.

'Now with it being Easter soon and us having work elsewhere, Mr Jarvis and Mrs Pollard – jobs that's been promised – we mayn't all be here all the time. But there'll always be some of us, and others as'll help out, and I'll keep an eye on all of them. But I cain't promise what we won't find. All right?'

I realised that he would go at his own pace and in his own way.

'All right!' I agreed.

And wondered whether praying to a neglected God would rank as moral cowardice.

Mrs Quick, who had been unhurriedly black-leading the kitchen range so that she could listen, said, 'There aren't no better builders than Will Soady and his sons, Mr Jarvis and Mrs Pollard. And they do always do their best.'

Lest we had missed the point.

'Well,' said Humphrey, stretching and yawning, 'that seems to have sorted everything out. Alice, did you light a fire in the library? I rather fancy spending my morning there. And, Flavia, might I have a cup of coffee?'

CHAPTER SIX

PARC CELLI, ELINGLAZE, nr HELSTON, CORNWALL

Sunday, 12 March 1978

My dear Pat and Jem,

How are you both? Sorry that my recent letters have been so scrappy, and my plans up in the air, but everything has now been settled and Parc Celli will be my home and business for, I hope, many years to come.

This brief note is to announce a change of plan for the Easter weekend. Instead of pigging it in my flat and doing London museums, I want you both to come down here and have a real holiday. I shall be in the midst of chaos, of course, but I know you won't mind that. I promise to feed you royally, even if the surroundings are a bit rough, and as you've never been down to Cornwall there are lots of places for you to explore. I am writing to Daddy by this same post, to explain my new situation, and perhaps you'll have a word with him, too?

Must dash. I have just completed my first week here as general dogsbody and must write a letter to Uncle Humphrey to keep him up to date. Looking forward *so* much to seeing you both at Parc Celli. Only just over two weeks to go!

I enclose a little something to enliven this blustery month of the year.

Lots of love,
Mum

I read the letter through, passed it as fit for young man consumption, and slipped two clean five-pound notes between its pages. I should have liked to say, 'Write soon!' but was afraid of sounding importunate. All mothers should be careful not to clutch and bind. Ex-mothers should be doubly careful.

I sighed, licked the flap of the envelope, stuck it down, stamped it, and stood it up on the kitchen mantleshelf for Mr Kennack to collect the following day.

15 March 1978

'Humphrey Jarvis speaking. Flavia, dearest, you sound a little breathless. Is this a convenient time to ring?'

'Yes, of course, Humphrey. I was sitting with my feet on the kitchen fender, doing the accounts, and I've had to sprint down the hall. I do think it would be a good idea to have a telephone in the kitchen.'

'Yes, I suppose so. The servants didn't need a telephone, you see – but there's no reason why you shouldn't have an extension in there sometime. No sense in spoiling a ship for a—'

'Actually, Humpty, I've already ordered one.'

'Oh. Good. Well . . . '

He cleared his throat and spoke briskly.

'Flavia, I really rang to thank you for your letter – or should I say *business report*? Ha! Dearest girl, all these mundane details about boiler pipes and drains and so forth are really not in my province, but no doubt very kind of you to keep me informed. I'd far rather have photographs showing progress when the work gets underway, and then I can visualise the house for myself.'

His voice became genial, but guarded.

'Flavia dear, I have no wish to interfere with your plans but there is one tiny point I should like to make. I was somewhat dismayed by the remark in your letter about wanting to *sack* Mrs Quick.'

'But I understood that I was to have a free hand in choosing my staff.'

He was paternal.

'Even as an *absent* squire, my dear, I must observe the unwritten laws of squiredom. Let me explain the position. Now if Alice

Quick were a foreigner – that is, a person born outside Elinglaze – or if she had stolen the silver spoons or dropped a Dresden figurine, there could well be grounds for dismissal. Being slow, obstinate and disorganised does not count. And in any case she is employed for a pittance. Five pounds a week!'

'Five pounds wasted, Humphrey. Take my word for it.'

He said sharply, 'Surely that is for me to judge, Flavia? I do not grudge Alice Quick her modicum of salary.'

'Then wouldn't it be a good idea if she treated the modicum as a retirement pension, and kept out of my way?'

He was reproachful.

'But that would hurt her feelings, Flavia! Now this may well sound sentimental to a hard-headed London businesswoman like yourself but I feel something for Alice Quick to which you are a stranger. She has worked for my family in one capacity or another since she was fourteen. I remember Alice as a bonny young lass, raking out the ashes in the grate and laying my nursery fire in the mornings. And she takes her position very seriously. There is no question of getting rid of her in any way whatsoever. By all means employ an extra house or scullery maid if you need to, but you must allow Alice to make her contribution or she'll feel unwanted.'

I felt encumbered, and no doubt sounded it.

'Humphrey, I am not running a charity, and I have no use for the lady, worthy though she may be.'

He spoke as to a froward child.

'Cornwall is not London, my dear. You must come to terms with Alice Quick or risk being at odds with the entire population of Elinglaze, *and* losing the services of her husband! Flavia, I hesitate to say this, and I don't mean to sound rude or unkind, but you must realise that you are a *foreigner*. Not only a foreigner but an *English* foreigner from upcountry. Whereas Alice Quick has lived in Elinglaze all her life, and she and Ben have served Parc Celli in one capacity or another since they were youngsters. And I can assure you that the villagers could be extremely, if not totally, obstructive, if you dismissed her. No one would work for you, help you, or possibly even speak to you. Believe me, my dear girl, I do know what I am talking about. Banded together they could even defeat a local council! "Here's twenty thousand Cornishmen will know the reason why!" and all that.'

'But, Humphrey, she seems not to have a specific timetable. And I like to know which days, and which times, she's likely to turn up.'

'I'm afraid I can't help you there, my dear. Alice is a law unto herself.'

'I can't say I'm terribly thrilled about this, Humphrey. What *does* she do?'

He was growing slightly impatient.

'Well, keeps things going, and so on. Look here, my dear, why don't you find her something to do which keeps her happy and out of your way?'

'Like what, Humphrey?'

'Well, she was a housemaid, in various degrees of importance, all her working life. Can't she do whatever they did?'

I realised I was beaten.

'All right, Humphrey. I'll put her in charge of polishing the furniture,' I said thoughtfully. 'There's an awful lot of it. And I'll buy her a pile of large new cleaning cloths and a jar of beeswax cream from the WI market in Helston.'

'An excellent idea.'

'And I won't specify what should be done when, nor how long it should take, nor what her hours or days should be. So she can go round and round and round the house for ever.'

And good luck to her, I thought.

Humphrey was delighted.

'Very sensible! Splendid! Problem solved! So pleased you take my point.'

'Until we open, that is. And then I must review the situation.'

But he was not to be drawn.

'I'm sure you will deal with it in your usual tactful style. So glad all goes well, my dear. My regards to everyone. Take care of yourself, and don't work too hard.'

Mindful of village sensibilities, I employed Alice Quick's youngest married daughter as my personal assistant, but this was a better bargain than I expected, and Vera Angwin took on both the job and the caretaker with a sense of diplomacy worthy of the Foreign Office.

'Mother, she be slow but she be sure!' Vera remarked. 'And once she know what she have to do, she do make a proper job of it.'

I took that to be her way of saying that she understood my difficulties, but would not be disloyal to her mother. She was a small dark rosy woman with trusting blue eyes, who deserved more of life than life had given her. Her husband was a farm labourer, and as they had three teenage youngsters to feed and clothe she was glad of the wages. Three days a week, at one pound fifty pence an hour, is not to be mocked.

'Would Mondays, Wednesdays and Fridays from nine o'clock until five suit you, Mrs Angwin?' I asked.

'Oh yes, Mrs Pollard. And you can call on me any time, and I'll come. And my daughter Marianne, she leaves school this summer, and she'll help out for a pound an hour. And my son Sean left school last year and he's looking for a job.'

'I'll keep that in mind, Mrs Angwin.'

I could not say we were close, though she did say she would prefer me to call her Vera. There was a certain reserve on both our parts, but we respected each other.

Side by side we worked, taking down curtains and bed hangings and examining their state: parcelling some up for the dry-cleaners; carrying others, all holes and moth and dust, down the garden to be burned.

'Some old house, Mrs Pollard!' Vera would say, as witchlike, with scarves tied over our heads and mouths, we charged at yet another floating curtain of cobwebs with our brooms.

I will say this for Mrs Quick, nothing deterred her. She had her own system which must have been a relic of her housemaid days, and she did not depart from it under any circumstance or for anyone. Rooms were inspected and dusted in rotation, furniture was polished whether in use, in storage, or shrouded in cotton covers. Slowly but thoroughly, she worked her way through Parc Celli, deciding to turn out the great hall on the day Will Soady and sons began to decorate it. Due to technical difficulties, the long oak table had not been moved, so she polished it and replaced the dustsheets. When part of the plaster cornice fell down she took off the dustsheets and polished it again.

PARC CELLI, ELINGLAZE, nr HELSTON, CORNWALL

21 March 1978

Dear Guy,

I take it very much amiss that you should suddenly decide to take the boys to Germany for the whole of the Easter holiday, and completely over-ride my own plans. We had arranged that I should have them with me in London, and I see no reason why my departure to Cornwall should have made any difference. I offered to pay their fares and they were both willing to make the journey there and back, even for a few days. What I had hoped was that you would allow them to stay a little longer. But I never expected you to cancel the whole thing. And yet why not? Experience reminds me that this is not the first time you have disappointed me.

It is now more than ten years since we were divorced. You have remarried, you have custody of our two sons, and you see far more of them than I do. And I have long suspected that you undermine any affection they might have for me. Isn't it time that I was treated with some consideration?

You have behaved badly over this, as over so many other things. If you can't play fair with me then I shall deal with the situation through my solicitor. And what will that do for either of us, apart from giving us a lot of unnecessary hassle, and upsetting the boys as well?

I wiped my eyes so that not a drop should fall on to the page and delight him.

I signed it with a flourish. *Flavia.*

CHAPTER SEVEN

April

Towards five o'clock, one late, wet, squally afternoon a cyclist knocked on the back door and stood there, smiling through the rain, as if he were an expected visitor, well known and well beloved. He was a big man, dark as a gipsy, bearded as an Elizabethan, sunburned a rich mahogany, and dressed in a glistening yellow cape and hat and leggings. And he was hung about with possessions like a travelling caravan. The rucksack on his back, the panniers on his bicycle, bulged with personal belongings.

At first glance I took him to be an out of season wayfarer in search of food and lodging, and said, 'I'm sorry, we don't do bed and breakfast here. But you'll find people in the village, half a mile away, who do!' and smiled and nodded and began to close the door.

But behind me, Vera Angwin cried, 'Mrs Pollard – that be Tom Faull!'

So I opened the door wide again and stared at the stranger in mute astonishment.

In spite of the pouring rain he doffed his hat, revealing a good head of thickly curled hair which had once been as black as his eyes, but was now brushed with grey. And held out a large brown hand saying genially, courteously, 'I reckon you'll be Miss Flavia! Mr Jarvis told me about you.'

He wore a youthful and jaunty air, but time had worn him. At first sight and sound I would not have taken him for a Cornishman. He was far bigger than average, for one thing, and his accent was difficult to define. A lifetime of seafaring had layered the original with English-speaking tongues and their idioms. There were colonial stratas not far beneath. But now the Cornish bed-rock showed through, rich and dark and deep, as he unbuttoned his cape and came into the kitchen, holding out his arms to Vera Angwin in welcome. He was dressed in a medley of old clothes which might have been bought in a jumble sale, over which he wore a green anorak.

'Well, my girl, didn't I tell you I'd be back?' he cried. 'And back I am. This time for good.'

He lifted her clean off the ground in his embrace and gave her a smacking kiss, which she received with obvious pleasure, though scolding him throughout. Then he turned to me, who had latched the door and was leaning against it dumbfounded. His face was bright with hope and achievement.

'Taken me five days to cycle here from London,' he said conversationally. 'I slept in barns, and kept myself as dry as I could. But it's grand to be under a roof again. Mr Jarvis said you'd put me up here while I settled in.'

When I did not reply immediately, his face and tone changed. This was a man who had to cut his coat according to other people's cloth.

Embarrassed, confounded, he said, 'Is that not right, then? Mr Jarvis did say he'd telephone.'

No it was not right, and the toad had not telephoned, and I knew why. Humphrey, no doubt swollen with triumph at Tom's return and pettish at the distance I was keeping between us, had chosen to surprise and burden me simultaneously.

I said as quickly as I could, 'Yes, of course, and you're very welcome, Mr Faull. But there are only two warm rooms in the house at the moment, and this is one of them.'

'Oh, Tom'll sleep in the kitchen!' Vera Angwin cried. 'He don't mind.'

And reassured, he echoed her, 'Oh, I can doss down anywhere, Miss Flavia. Don't you worry about me.'

I was piqued that Vera had issued the invitation, and was now putting the kettle on and asking him to sit down as though this were her house instead of mine. Her tone was warmer, her air younger. She glanced round at Tom Faull again and again, as if to satisfy herself that he was really here. I guessed that long ago, when Vera was young and slim and single, Tom had meant much to her. That he was glad to see her no one could doubt, but his affection did not match her delight. He acted like a favourite brother.

In the fever of his arrival she had overlooked me and my position in Parc Celli. He had not. Dropping his Cornish accent, he turned to me, speaking with an agreeable deference which held no trace of servility. Humphrey, it was clear, had stressed my importance. Tom bowed to that without question, as he bowed to Humphrey's status, but remained his own man.

'I shan't be troubling you more than a night or two, Miss Flavia, just while I tie a tarpaulin over the stable roof and sort myself out. I've got all I need, bar a few groceries, on my bike out there. And I can get them tomorrow from Peggy Crowdy.'

'It's no trouble at all,' I said, donning my role as lady of the house. 'Would you like to put your cycle in the shed? There's a lock on the door, and I'm sure Vera can find the key for you.'

'No need for that,' said Tom. 'No one locks a door in Elinglaze – or used not, when I was a lad.'

Vera Angwin was smiling at him as if she could eat him up.

'You'll come home and have your tea with us tonight, Tom?' she asked, and the question was a demand.

Personally I should have preferred that arrangement, yet I had to say for Humphrey's sake, 'Of course, this must be your decision, Mr Faull, but you're very welcome to have supper here.'

Then Vera turned round quite fiercely and faced me for the first time as an equal instead of an employee, and I saw that she was jealous. And Tom saw it too, but did not betray his knowledge by so much as a flicker.

He said to her smoothly, 'Nothing I'd like better, you know that. But Mr Jarvis told me to ring the moment I got here, and I've a heap of things to do before dark. But I can come tomorrow if that's all right by you and Brian.'

Then the kettle boiled. I beat Vera to it by a whisker. Yet though we all sat down at the kitchen table together companiably with our mugs of tea their conversation excluded me.

'You got your learning books with you, have you?' she asked.

Tom said self-consciously, 'Oh yes. I'm coming on pretty well.'

'You must read us some of they long poems tomorrow night,' said Vera. 'And some of they short ones, too.'

'Go on with you,' said Tom, reddening. 'You don't want poems, my girl!'

'I didn't know what they was about,' said Vera honestly, 'but I did like the sound of them. And so did Brian.'

Tom threw back his head and laughed long and loud and deep. His teeth were still good, and had been splendid. He laughed from his belly, like a big black curly giant in a children's storybook, and the sound made me smile in response even though I felt annoyed. His eyes glimmered. He courted Vera directly, his tone teasing, caressing.

'Brian fell asleep last time I read to you, my love.'

'He never!' cried Vera, flushing in her husband's defence. 'He just closed his eyes a bit while he listened.'

Tom laughed again and said slyly, 'Does he always snore when he listens?'

Then he became mindful of my isolation and turned to me and said in apology, 'You'll excuse us, Miss Flavia, but we've known each other a long time.' And made a great show of searching the pockets of his anorak, saying, 'I should've given you this in the first place!'

Stiffened by a piece of cardboard and protected by a plastic bag was a letter from Humphrey.

'Oh, thank you,' I said, glad of a pretext to occupy myself while they talked. 'Will you excuse me?' I asked, opening the packet.

But I needn't have bothered. They were off again, segregating me.

Even the hand-writing looked jubilant, shouting from every line the words *I told you so, and I was right!* And as I read the letter I could hear which particular phrases Humphrey wanted to stress, as well as their underlying message.

London, 16 April 1978

Dearest Flavia,

I know you will be as delighted as I am to meet my remarkable friend Tom Faull, *whose story I daresay you recollect.*

He has decided to retire from the sea, and will be living and working in the stables at Parc Celli from now on. You will find him to be *an independent and hardy fellow who will be no trouble to you.* Nevertheless, the stables are barely habitable, and *it would oblige me if you offered him the hospitality of Parc Celli* on rainy days. He will not expect a bedroom, simply a dry corner somewhere in the servants' quarters. A storeroom or pantry, or something that is not in use at the moment.

I believe he is carrying camping equipment as well as most of his worldly goods. I have never in my life seen any bicycle so heavily loaded. We tried a practice run round the square this afternoon, to make sure he could ride it, and I had to hold the machine up while he mounted, and give him a helpful push. He managed remarkably well but the effort quite winded me. Anyway he pedals off into his new life tomorrow. *I do hope he arrives safely.*

As I gather you do not wish to be disturbed in these early stages of house restoration *I did not telephone you*, but thought it best to allow Tom to announce himself. He is a friendly, intelligent and articulate man and *he will be ringing me once a week to report his progress.* Please allow him to use the house telephone, and *if, dear girl, you feel like having a word with me* about your own progress *nothing would please me more.*

I should be grateful if you could keep an eye on Tom. He has a Primus stove and will provide his own food and do his own cooking, but it will be simple fare at best. *Perhaps you would supplement his lowly diet*, from time to time, with some of those exquisite delicacies and wonderful savoury dishes for which you are so justly famous? Tom is quite a gourmet in his humble fashion, having knocked about the world and mingled with all classes of person. You will find him a good fellow and a highly amusing raconteur. We were yarning together until three in the morning.

Dearest Flavia, I bow before your talents and your industry. I kiss your fair hand, and am ever.

Y[r] devoted Humphrey

I folded the letter and returned it to its envelope. Marching orders, I thought, wryly. Damn the pair of them.

The conversation had become intimate in my mental absence.

'Then you sort him out, my love,' Tom was saying sternly. 'If he don't put his pay down on the table then don't you put yours. Tell him he's off luxuries until you see the colour of his money!'

'Oh, Tom!' said Vera, reproachful, wistful, admiring. 'I cain't do tha-at!'

She looked up at the kitchen clock. Time to go home, it ticked and tocked. Your day's work's done. Her expression was forlorn.

Tom put his hand on hers and said, 'Tomorrow night, my girl, you can make me a pasty a yard long with the gravy running out of both ends, and a bowlful of trifle! Right now I'll take it kindly if you'll let me escort you home.'

She lit up at that, flashed a smile which even included me, and whisked away to fetch her plastic raincoat and headscarf.

Tom Faull took my measure, and I took his, in silence.

I had not trusted what I had heard of him, and now I saw him I trusted him less, for he was both shrewd and intelligent, possessed of considerable charm, and knew how to use all his assets.

Vera came back, still lit up, and watched him put on his yellow oilskins. They went out into the late afternoon arm in arm like a courting couple.

It was six o'clock when Tom returned. Left alone together we were a little awkward at first. To fill in the silence I asked him when he last ate a hot meal. He said he had bought a bacon sandwich and a mug of tea from a mobile refreshment van at eight o'clock that morning, and eaten a bar of chocolate on the way.

'I wanted to get here, you see,' he said, 'but don't you bother yourself. Eggs and bacon'll do me, Miss Flavia.'

The prospect of feeding a hungry man always softens me. Whereas I had been regretting the loss of a Welsh rarebit with fresh fruit to follow, my tone was now cordial as I translated this into a hearty meal, and asked if he could eat macaroni cheese and apple pie.

A sudden blaze in Tom's black eyes signalled assent before he did.

I said, 'As it will be about an hour, and you've been travelling, perhaps you'd like a bath while I cook the meal? Mr Jarvis tells me that we must make you as comfortable as possible, and since the stables' – which I could see that moment through the kitchen window, steaming with wet and in a state of dire dilapidation – 'aren't exactly waterproof, I've been thinking that you could keep your possessions in the little room at the back, off the hall. It will be one of the last places to be decorated and we could warm it for you with an oil stove or an electric fire. And it's near a door to the courtyard, with a cloakroom next to it, so you can come to and fro and be quite private there.'

I meant that he needn't trouble me with his comings and goings, and I wanted him to respect my privacy as well as his own. He was not stupid. He answered the meaning rather than the statement, looking steadily at me.

'I know what you're thinking, so I'll say it for you, and I'll tell you what I said to Mr Jarvis. I can live in my tent in the stables if need be. By the end of the summer the roof should be on and I shall have two stalls fitted out as a bedroom and living room, and there I shall camp warm and snug through the winter. I have all my cooking equipment and, though I'm not a cordon bleu like you, I can cook. I've lived rough before and shall live rough again, I don't doubt. I'm not here to take advantage of Mr Jarvis, nor of you neither. If the nights are too cold or too wet I got friends in the village who'll take me in. There!'

I did not want to upset either him or the villagers through him or Humphrey's feelings as his squire, though inwardly I cursed everybody all round for being feudal, clannish and touchy.

I said, 'But you won't be in anyone's way in that room, Mr Faull. And Mr Jarvis did suggest the idea. So do accept the offer.'

'Well, then,' said Tom, capitulating with relief, 'I do accept, and I thank you. To tell you the truth, I'd be glad of it. There's my books and typewriter and record player need proper housing, even if I don't.'

'Then that's settled. I'll show you the room I mean.'

'Oh, I know which one you're talking about,' said Tom. 'It used to be the steward's room in the old days. I went there with my dad once.'

He assumed a stance which I was to connect with his story-telling: hands on hips, head thrown back, eyes half closed, looking into the distance, the beginnings of a smile on his mouth, remembering.

'My dad was the carpenter on the estate. He left me in the

passage and told me stay outside and not move till he came out. Well, I was only a little chap, and a curious little chap at that, so I crept round the corner and walked down the passage towards the hall. And the lady's office was there – that was Mr Jarvis's grandmother. And I turned the knob and took a peep in. The lady was sitting at her desk writing letters, and it was a grand room and she was a grand lady. Her hair was the colour of iron, and she had fine dark eyes that flashed at me and she held her head very high. I stared as if I was in a shop full of sweets. Never seen nothing like that before, you see. The lady wasn't vexed, but she flashed her eyes at me and said, "And who might you be?" And while I was telling her – because I was never shy, you understand – my dad came after me, and doffed his hat to her and said he was sorry. Then he took me outside by the collar of my shirt, and smacked my head till it rang.'

'I can imagine!' I said coolly.

I would have done the same.

My response did not dampen him. He laughed aloud in recollection.

'I was always like that,' said Tom. 'Boy and man, I wouldn't be gainsaid.'

His black eyes gleamed with more than memory. He had enjoyed flouting authority, treading on forbidden ground. Unabashed, he would have charmed the lady into giving him sweets or a sixpence if his father had not cut short their interview. I saw the mischievous lad, the rebellious youth, and the mature man who still harboured both delinquents. I had not forgotten how he conned fifty pounds out of poor old Humphrey, and then disappeared without trace for months. I should have liked to know why he had decided to retire from the sea, not the tale he presumably told Humphrey but the truth.

He was quick to see that I had not been beguiled by his childhood memory, and returned to practical matters.

'I'll take my bike round to the passage door then, shall I?' he asked, affable, respectful. 'And since you offered, I'd be glad of a bath, Miss Flavia.' Then, as if to emphasise that he knew his place, he said, 'You'll need to tell me where the bathroom is. Never been that far into the big house before.'

* * *

Once settled, he left a distinct feeling of space behind him, and I breathed again. He and Humphrey had much for which to answer. Between them they had wrecked my present paradise.

I looked forward to the evenings on my own, when Kelly Park and I kept each other company. During the day our alliance was quiescent, but when the workers had gone we opened to each other. I walked her rooms, approving, imagining, planning, even – I admit – talking to her. And she listened, make no mistake about it. Nor was I ever afraid, as Vera felt I ought to be, of living here alone. Creaks and sighs and faint echoes did not disturb me. They were the sounds of the house, pondering to itself, mulling things over. We were renewing each other, but now our privacy had been violated and I must reckon with a lodger/neighbour, with telephone calls to Humphrey, with cups of tea and little chats, with Vera hanging about Tom Faull instead of getting on with her work, and never a moment when the wretched man wasn't within sight and sound.

I tackled the apple pie first. There is something restorative about making pastry. Ideally, you should be light of heart as well as hands to do it justice, but the act of rubbing fat finely into sifted flour soothed me. After all, I reflected, Tom Faull was not my responsibility but Humphrey's. I knew that my role in the house was crucial. If the man became impossible I could say, 'Humphrey! I have money of my own, qualifications and the reputation of Bon Appétit behind me. I can find a job anywhere and go if need be. So it's Tom Faull or me! Make up your mind which!'

I improved on this dialogue while the pastry rested in the new refrigerator and I peeled the apples. By the time I rolled the top crust over the pie I had won every argument with my invisible foes and was feeling charitable. I even admitted that the light in Vera's face and Tom Faull's bear hug had stirred up anger and desire. There was no man to put his arms round me any more.

'Off luxuries indeed!' I remarked sardonically.

And then, 'Oh, damn the fellow!'

I had forgotten to put out clean towels.

As I approached the bathroom I could hear him splashing and singing with equal enthusiasm, and the song was one which made him stop and chuckle now and again. I waited for a decent break between verses, while he presumably soaped himself, and knocked on the door.

'I've just remembered the towels,' I called. 'I'll leave them outside.'

An abashed, at least I hope it was abashed, silence followed.

Then he called back cheerfully, 'No need, Miss Flavia. I've got my own towel. Thanks all the same.'

I left them there nevertheless, and ran down to make the cheese sauce. Out of habit I laid the table with a red-checked cloth, and stuck two red candles in two old wine bottles, and fetched a jar of daffodils from the windowsill to give a festive air. Finally I chose a robust Rioja from my personal rack along the wall. Opened it. Tasted it. Good, but not too good: suitable for both meal and man. Then I threw off my apron, darted back upstairs and changed my pants and sweater for a light wool dress. Dashed down again, drank a preliminary glass of wine, and felt much, much better.

'Oh my word!' said Tom Faull half an hour later, rubbing his hands, sniffing the mingled aromas of hot apples and bubbling cheese. 'Oh – my – word!'

He had dressed himself in honour of the occasion in a white embroidered shirt and black suit and, although he needed a haircut, was looking surprisingly distinguished. His clothes were of good quality and cut but neither new nor fashionable. This had probably been his best outfit for a number of years and he still carried it off splendidly. Growing heavier and wilier with age, he was still a very handsome man and in his heyday must have been a god-like youth. I could see why Humphrey was half in love with him and Vera still sighed. He held himself well, if a little self-consciously, hoping for some comment.

'Goodness, how smart you are!' I cried lightly.

And then I saw that he was wearing brown plaid carpet slippers.

He followed my glance down to his feet and said, 'I hope you don't mind, but I've been living rough for five days.'

'Not in the least!' I said, but could not resist adding, 'The restaurant isn't officially open yet!'

I know I have a sharp tongue. Fortunately the wine warmed

my tone, took the sourness out of that remark, and made it sound amusing. He responded with goodwill.

'Ah, that'll be some grand day for us all. And let me say this, Miss Flavia, although I've got my hands full – and more than full – rebuilding those stables, if you want me to do anything for you then just say the word.'

I did not commit myself, but answered, 'Thank you, Mr Faull!' as nicely as I could, and poured wine for us both.

I had forgotten, in the last few weeks of snacking, how very good a hot supper could be. We ate the macaroni cheese between us and finished the wine, and Tom had three helpings of apple pie and cream.

He asked me to call him Tom, since everybody else did, but refused to call me Flavia.

'It wouldn't seem right,' he said stiffly.

Apart from that we got on pretty well. I talked about Bon Appétit, speaking of Jack as impersonally as if he had simply been a business partner. I told him my plans for Kelly Park and he brought out his plans for the stables, which looked surprisingly workmanlike and quite agreeable. I still considered him to be a plausible trickster, but at least he was professional enough to take trouble over details. He declined coffee but accepted a pot of strong brown tea, and insisted on washing up while I cleared away. Then I found a two-bar electric fire and a pillow in the housekeeper's room, and he unpacked his bicycle and set up house in the steward's office.

He called me in to inspect his quarters before he retired for the night, and I understood then what ship-shape really meant. He had found a place for everything and used every available inch of space. His sleeping bag was rolled out under the window, with a pair of violet cotton pyjamas neatly folded on the pillow. His transistor radio was on the mantelpiece, his cassette player on top of the filing cabinet, his typewriter and a pile of textbooks and notebooks on the table. He rubbed his hands and chuckled as he had done when he saw the supper table.

And God saw everything that He had made, I thought uncharitably, and behold it was very good.

His Cornish forebears spoke through him.

'Proper job, eh?' Tom Faull enquired.

Amused by his complacency I answered, 'Proper job indeed!'

He was at peace with himself and the world.

'It's good to be home,' he said sincerely, 'and I thank you for everything.'

Then I felt kindly towards him and answered, 'You're very welcome.'

'I'll be up early tomorrow,' said Tom, 'but I shan't disturb you.'

'I shall be up early, too. At least, I call seven o'clock early. But I've left the table laid. Help yourself to whatever you want. There's eggs and bacon in the fridge. Vera doesn't come tomorrow but I start work directly after breakfast.'

Lest he think that I was there to drink tea and gossip all day, I added, 'There's a lot to do, and we have a time limit in which to do it, you see.'

He nodded gravely, but there was a gleam in his eyes which might have been amusement and could have been malice.

I could think of nothing else to say apart from, 'Good night, Tom.'

'Good night, Miss Flavia.'

He knocked at five minutes to seven the following morning, to say he was leaving a cup of tea outside for me. He had gone when I opened the door, and in his stead sat a little silver tray bearing a flowered china cup and two plain biscuits. He had even found a paper doily to set beneath the cup.

I was amused and irritated simultaneously: a state of mind which Tom Faull would continue to generate in me. He had taken time and trouble to find the tea things and my room, but for what reason?

I heard Humphrey's reproving murmur of, 'Honest gratitude, my dear. His little way of saying thank you!'

Placation with intent to future fraud would have been my verdict.

But I drank the tea and ate the biscuits, and felt pampered just the same.

Downstairs I found that the kitchen range had been riddled and stoked up, and the coal scuttle filled. He had breakfasted on toast and jam, washed up his dishes, and left the kettle simmering on the hob for me.

In my head Humphrey murmured, 'The perfect house guest!'

Personally, I was disquieted by the thought of how many houses Tom Faull must have frequented to bring his manners and perception to this pitch, and how many hostesses he had beguiled in the process and to what purpose. But my conscience smote me two or three hours later, when I saw him pulling a vast blue and white striped tarpaulin into the courtyard on a hand-cart. Where he had found, borrowed, purchased or stolen either the tarpaulin or the hand-cart I would not know, but the haul home had been long and hard. He had shed the previous evening's distinction and was back in his working clothes again, but they did not demean him. His big body wore them gracefully, like a good sort of joke. He stood for a while getting his breath and wiping his face, before setting the green baseball hat firmly back on his head and addressing himself to his task.

I was brewing tea and would have called him in, but Vera was there before me. Vera who should have been enjoying her day off and minding her own business. Vera, who made some remark about 'seeing to them curtains' straightaway forsook me and carried out his mug and hers together with a tin of chocolate biscuits, calling over her shoulder, 'I left yours on the hob, Mrs Pollard.' And was greeted by a cheerful shout and compliment from Tom.

'You're looking bonny this morning, my girl. Come in out of the cold.'

Such a sense of loss assailed me, as he put his arm round her shoulders and drew her inside, that for a moment I hated the pair of them. The next moment I was myself again. But nevertheless, seeing that he hadn't had time to put the tarpaulin to use, I hoped devoutly that the skies would open and rain right down on them through the holes in the stable roof.

CHAPTER EIGHT

Music while you work was Vera's motto. She brought her transistor radio with her and tuned into Radio One or Two as soon as the day's chores had been decided. Over in the stables another transistor sounded faintly. But this one was tuned to Radio Three, playing Schubert. My unwanted neighbour was classical in his tastes. He sang with the music when deeply moved, in an agreeable bass voice, and had been known to conduct a few bars at his peril: ladder swaying, roof creaking ominously. So far he had returned to the factual world in time to avert an accident. I didn't actually wish him harm. But . . .

As I whisked out to the dustbins Tom called down from the roof, 'You got a minute, Miss Flavia?'

Damn and blast. I should have checked that he was out of the way.

'Well, yes. But only a minute!' I called back, and slammed the lid.

He began to descend from the ladder and I tried to look amiable. His pace was easy, his smile friendly, his spirit light. On this fine April morning his speech was in the Cornish mode, and leisurely. I had never felt more of a Londoner in my life. Faster, faster, for God's sake!

'Been thinking,' said Tom, looming over me benevolently. 'You need a car for your shopping. Just a small car, I mean. Nothing grand. Couple of hundred pounds or so. When Parc Celli opens you'll be relying on Helston for some supplies.' He grinned at the thought of local limitations. 'Elinglaze doesn't stock fancy food and wine. Peggy Crowdy's shop isn't Harrods, you know.'

'I know that only too well. Nor does Mrs Crowdy want it to be Harrods. She refused Parc Celli's future custom. Too much trouble, apparently.'

He pursued his own thoughts.

'And you can hardly go shopping on the bus when the house is open, now can you? Take you all morning to get there and back. You couldn't carry all that food, either.'

'I'm well aware of that problem, too.' Keeping him at a distance. 'And I've been thinking it over.' So far without success. 'I'm sure I can get the grocery orders delivered.'

He did not ask for my conclusions but went on to his own.

'Find you a nice little car,' said Tom. 'No need to fret yourself with garage bills. I can keep him going for you.'

'I'm sure you can. But there's another problem. I can't drive.'

This checked him for a moment.

Then he said, 'I can teach you to drive in no time.'

'I really don't think that would be a good idea. And I have a notion that it might take quite a while – even if we remained on speaking terms.'

'I can drive you, then. Just give me the word. Take you anywhere you want to go.'

I wondered what this was all about, and my tone sharpened with anxiety.

'But you have your own work to do, and your own life to lead. Suppose you need to mend your roof and I need to shop in Helston at the same time?'

His face was earnest and curiously trustful. For some reason he seemed bent on my having a car. And of course I did need regular transport of some sort.

'We'd sort it out.'

He adopted his storytelling stance: hands on hips, head thrown back, eyes on some distant horizon. I foresaw him talking for several minutes, and fretted about the bread I was baking.

'Now let's take it,' said Tom thoughtfully, 'that I'm on the roof. Right? And you want to go shopping in Helston—'

'Yes. As it happens I do have to keep an eye on the oven.'

'Then I'll come inside while you do what you have to do.'

I hurried ahead of him, and made a great business of checking the loaves, which were not yet ready for turning. He leaned against the doorpost and waited until I had closed the oven door and risen, pink with heat, to listen to him.

'Now then,' said Tom, 'let's take it—'

'You're on the roof and I want to go to Helston. Yes?'

I pulled a saucepan off the stove to hint that I was extremely busy and should be left alone. He took not the slightest notice.

'I say to you, "Is it an emergency?" And you say, "Yes. I have to buy a jar of preserved ginger!" – or some such thing—'

'Oh, really! I would hardly drag you out to buy a—'

'I say, "If it's an emergency, then I'm your man!" And down the ladder I come. We get the car out – nice little car! – and off we go.'

I was not as impressed as he evidently expected me to be.

'And suppose your work on the roof was an emergency?' I could not resist adding, 'And it certainly looks like that! What about my jar of preserved ginger then?'

He was triumphant.

'That's why I want to teach you to drive, Miss Flavia. See what I mean?'

I dug my nails into the oven cloth and said I would think matters over, and could he please excuse me at the moment?

He departed quite cheerfully, and a few minutes later I heard him alternately whistling and swearing as he carried slates up to the roof.

Vera had become reconciled to me as soon as she realised that Tom Faull was no favourite, and was now disposed to reconcile me to him. How their renewed friendship was developing I did not know. One evening a week he went round there for his pasty and trifle, and when her husband had been more disappointing than usual she took her morning tea to the stables, seeking advice and comfort.

Now, amused and philosophical, she said, 'Tom Faull don't change none, Mrs Pollard. Always did have a head full of wild notions.'

I refused to be won over.

'Well, I'd rather he didn't impose them on me!'

She thought about this for a while and then spoke up in his favour, and with some reproach.

'But he do like to help. And he can turn his hand to anything and make a proper job of it, too. And what he says is right. Stands to reason you need a car for the shopping, Mrs Pollard. And if you cain't drive then either you got to learn or someone got to drive you.'

I did not like having my problems spelled out for me.

'I can manage the shopping quite well once a week by bus while I'm by myself, and I had given the matter considerable thought. In fact I intend to discuss it with Mr Jarvis when I next telephone him. Meanwhile we shall need to employ a general handyman – I mean, apart from your father, who is so helpful with the boiler – someone who would tidy the garden and do odd jobs, and if I had a car he could act as chauffeur.'

'Mart'n Skeggs cain't drive.'

I had heard the name, but could not remember in what connection.

'Who's Martin Skeggs?'

'That was his old bike in the shed.'

'Oh! *That* Martin Skeggs!'

'He be the gardener.'

In dramatic fashion I threw out one arm in the direction of our wilderness.

'Then where in God's name is he? And what has he been doing?'

'Oh, he don't bother none while the weather's bad. He's eighty-four and his arthritis don't get no better,' said Vera, 'but he'll be round to cut the grass any day now. I been wondering whether he couldn't do with some help. My Sean could do the digging and that. He be good with gardening. Doing odd jobs since he left school but he needs work regular. Wants to learn. Mart'n Skeggs would learn him.' She added, lest I had missed the point, 'But Mart'n cain't drive.'

I had the distinct feeling I was being manipulated by everyone from Humphrey downwards. Dear God, I thought, what have I taken on? Jack, where are you?

'And Tom'll see that Eddy Johns don't ask too much for that car.'

'What car? Who is Eddy Johns?'

Vera's face closed up, which meant I would find out only as much as was good for me.

She repeated, 'You cain't manage without a car down here, Mrs Pollard. And Tom's the man to do right by you. See if he aren't.'

The following Monday I wrote out a cheque for one hundred and eighty pounds, and became the owner of a very old two-seater Austin Seven.

'He's in good nick,' said Tom proud as a father with a new baby. 'Only one careful owner. Been in a barn for twenty years. I got Eddy Johns to put new tyres on him.'

The car looked to me as if it ought to be in a museum.

'Does it go?' I asked incredulously.

In answer to my disbelief, Tom took me for an hour's run round the Lizard peninsula. We had to stop at a garage for a refill of oil, and we rattled and banged a bit, but apart from that it seemed to be all right.

'Now don't you worry if he seems a bit smoky,' said Tom, as we drew up to the front steps of Parc Celli. 'He could probably do with a rebore, but we'll get away with a new valve-guide and rings.'

'Oh. Good,' I said, mystified.

'You can put all your shopping in that boot!' said Tom proudly, slapping the car's rump affectionately. 'And when it's fine weather you can have the hood down.'

He illustrated this with some difficulty, and with even greater difficulty forced it back again.

'Needs a drop of oil on the hinges,' he said, momentarily disconcerted.

How I wished Jack Rice had been here, to kick the new tyres, lift the modest black bonnet and inspect its contents, and give a sharp, sure verdict which would probably be, 'Don't buy this old heap on any account!' But Jack had long since roared off in his new love's Mercedes to Switzerland, where he was probably inspecting hotel kitchens at 5.30 a.m. and being lucky enough to catch sight of an early morning rat which would bring the price down beautifully. So I was stuck with Eddy Johns's Austin Seven.

At least it was mine. Yes. It was mine. My very first car.

Out of the blue I said suddenly, proprietorially, 'In any case, it isn't a he. It's a she. And as she's got a boot like a bustle I shall call her Victoria.'

Later that afternoon Tom ran out of materials and asked if he could borrow the car. He also suggested that I should in future telephone my weekly orders to various shops in Helston, and he could pick them up for me. As it happened I was running out of a few items so I took his advice, which did not make up for seeing him career off in Victoria. He was away an incredibly long time and I worried in case the car had broken down. But Vera explained matters to me, as we spent the afternoon disposing of the attic curtains and chasing away a world of spiders.

'Tom do make friends easy, and folk like him, you see, and they talk to him, and one thing leads to another. So everything take longer. But it do come out all right in the end. I known him go out in the morning for one thing and come back at night with twenty.'

He returned just as she was about to leave, and I was transfixed by the sight of a large hip bath roped on top of my car and covered by another tarpaulin.

'Picked him up at an auction!' he called, rapping the side of the bath. 'Shan't need to bother you none now, Miss Flavia.'

'Did he also buy three Primus stoves and a cauldron to heat the water?' I asked the universe drily. 'Or will that be done in my kitchen?'

For there was only one cold tap in the stables.

'He be only trying to help out,' said Vera reprovingly, and put the kettle on, although this would make her late home.

Tom wiped his hands on the seat of his pants and began to unload a quantity of unwieldy parcels.

'Told you this boot'd hold plenty!' he said, striding across the courtyard, well pleased with himself. 'And I got you one or two things you didn't ask for but will be glad of.'

'I see what you mean,' I said to Vera, raising my eyebrows.

Then he astonished me by producing a fish kettle which must have been in service at the beginning of the century.

'Needs re-soldering,' he said, 'but I can do that. Got it cheap.'

I took the mug from Vera's loving hands and gave it to him myself.

'Sit down, Tom,' I said, impressed for once. 'I've got about four thousand pieces of Victorian equipment in this kitchen. How did you know we were short of a fish kettle?'

He took a swig of tea and grinned at me.

'Because the other's down at the Home Farm. Been used as a feed trough for the chickens.'

I let this pass and examined the kettle closely. Soldered and cleaned, it would be a valuable acquisition.

Vera, inspecting it after me, said, 'That'd shine up handsome.'

'How much was it, Tom?' I asked.

'I swopped some scrap for it.' He saw that he had impressed me, and was quietly elated. 'Got you some other things as well. They're in the bath.'

Tom's bargains belonged to the category Jack and I used to describe as 'poor but promising'. A rocking chair, scuffed and de-wormed, which several hours of loving care would bring up beautifully. An engaging blue and white flowered basin and ewer, cracked but decorative. And a china soup tureen without a lid which would make an elegant cachepot.

'Also swopped for scrap?' I asked ironically.

'Didn't cost me a penny,' said Tom evasively.

'But I should give you something for them,' I offered, out of fairness.

He shook his head and said, 'You do more than enough for me.'

He had me at a disadvantage, not for the first time in our acquaintance, and I felt I would rather not owe anything to Tom Faull. There was no knowing when the debt might be called in, or in what way. Still, I could hardly snub him, as he had probably reckoned. So I thanked him instead.

'Fixed myself up for cricket, too,' said Tom, opening a vast brown paper parcel.

The white shirt and trousers, the sleeveless and long-sleeved pullovers, socks and broad-brimmed white hat, all sporting their modest price tickets, had been purchased from an Oxfam Shop.

'Had some chat with Jim Jewell last night,' said Tom, addressing himself to Vera, 'and he wants me to play cricket for Elinglaze again.'

'I know that,' said Vera, shining with pride. 'Brian and him had a pint at the pub soon after. Jim says you was the fastest fast bowler they ever had. Put you in the First Eleven, have he?'

She was asking a question to which she already knew the answer. I recognised the over-casual manner. Tom's expression was inscrutable, his tone jaunty.

'Yes, my bird. For the time being. But at forty-three, and out of practice, I might not be able to keep up with the First.'

I could tell that neither of them believed this.

'They're moving our Sean up to the First this year,' said Vera, also proud of her son. 'He be a fast bowler, too. And Brian can still swing a bat – though he do have some belly on him these days! Well, I'll be there when you play at home, Tom. When do you start?'

'End of this month. I'll be going to nets practice on Thursdays.'

'You'll come to our house on Thursday nights then, after practice, and have a cup of tea with us and a saffron bun?'

He did not commit himself, but thanked her, patted her bottom, and returned to the day's haul.

'One more thing,' he said to me, with immense satisfaction.

From the seat of the car he brought a dead pheasant wrapped in newspaper. I received it with caution. The body was still warm.

'I suppose this dropped off a passing lorry?' I said, trying not to laugh.

I knew very well where it came from. An estate not too far from us reared pheasants.

'Found him by the side of the road,' said Tom blandly, stroking his beard and smiling into it. 'Must've been hit by a car.'

A sound of suppressed amusement and admiration from Vera.

'And where did the tarpaulin come from?' I asked, staring at that torn and filthy covering. 'Also hit by a car?'

'Found him floating on a pond,' said Tom. 'So I fished him

ashore. Good old tarpaulin, he is. Only a couple of rents in him. Soon patch him up.'

This time I laughed aloud at his impudence and his ingenuity.

'Well, wherever anything came from,' I said cordially, 'I'm obliged to you, Tom – particularly for the fish kettle and the pheasant. Let me invite you to supper tonight, by way of thanks.'

Vera's face changed.

'Tom be having his tea with us tonight,' she said firmly. 'Brian said to me this morning, afore I left, "Now you be sure and fetch Tom home tonight. I aren't seen him for days!"'

I was tempted to question this spurious invitation, but stopped myself. For it would look as if we were quarrelling over possession of Tom Faull. So I accepted gracefully.

'Then I'll invite you when the pheasant's hung, Tom, and we'll share it.'

He had watched and listened to our exchange with some interest, arms folded, leaning against Victoria's bonnet.

He said to Vera, 'I'm obliged to Brian, but I ought to get this tarpaulin scrubbed before dark.'

'You bring him along and I'll scrub him for you at home, Tom,' she replied.

There was no gainsaying her. Her little face was flushed, her mouth set firm. Tom turned to me.

'It'll be heavy and awkward to carry, Miss Flavia. Would you mind if I took the car?' he asked deferentially.

My goodwill began to fade.

Yes, I certainly would, I thought. The damned car's been out all day, and although it's my car you seem to be using it all the time, and . . .

'No, I don't mind,' I said coolly.

Polite, but unenthusiastic. So that he understood there were limits.

He nodded, and said to Vera, 'I'll be ready in half an hour, my girl. You go and get that fish kettle cleaned up and then I can solder it tomorrow.'

And she did. Without a murmur.

Left alone, I hung the pheasant in solitary state in the appropriate larder and defrosted a chicken leg for my supper, puzzling over

Tom Faull. That he was generous and helpful in his own way, I admitted. And amusing, and attractive, though not my type. But I had reservations. I felt that he had conned me over the car, despite myself. I could not see how, but then I did not see why I was still lumbered with Alice Quick, and how I seemed to be employing most of her relatives. I resolved it would go no further. The next time I should be ready for them all.

Kelly Park seemed very empty that evening, and I tried to think of a treat for myself. So I began my weekly letter to the boys.

> My dear Pat and Jem,
>
> How are you both? Work here is going well, though rather more slowly than I could wish. It seems a very long time since we last saw each other, and I'm so tied here at the moment that I can't come up to London to meet you. You said that you are thinking of taking a hiking and walking holiday by yourselves sometime this summer? I wish you could hike as far as Cornwall and come to stay here with me, or use this house as a base while you explore.
>
> You would love Kelly Park. She (they all call things 'he' here, and I've picked the habit up, except that some of them are 'she' to me!) is a lovely old house and we are bringing her back to her former grandeur. By August, most of the principal rooms should be ready. Of course it will be another year before we can say we have truly finished work on the house, but you should be able to get a flavour of my future life – and it will be a wonderful place to come for holidays.
>
> There are lots of things to interest you here. The sea is only a short distance away. We have the Aeropark near Helston, and you could visit Culdrose and the Earth Satellite Station, and there are wonderful coastal walks – not that I've had time to try any of them yet. And I promise to make chocolate layer cake and Queen of Puddings!
>
> Do let me know if you can come, and when. Any time would be convenient.
>
> Lots of love,
> Mum

I read the letter through, and enclosed two clean five-pound notes. The money seemed inadequate.

CHAPTER NINE

The pale blue envelope meant trouble. It was a letter from my mother. No one could mistake that impetuous hand, the baggy loops and frilly capitals, the high-flying dots, scooping dashes, violent exclamation marks and dramatic underlinings, the words charging from side to side as if time were running out. Well, I suppose it is. My mother does not admit to being seventy.

Lily, an arch romantic, used to be a musical comedy actress back in the 1930s, and not a very good one. My father, Major Harry Clough, saved her from facing reality by marrying her when her juvenile charms were fading. In another year or two she would have been unemployed and unemployable. Instead she was able to retire from the stage gracefully, with a good excuse for doing so, and to play the role of an adored wife. Her talk is of love, love, love, and many of her phrases are lifted from sentimental songs. She was a dazzlingly pretty girl and is still a pretty woman, though her type of beauty and the way she presents herself is essentially passé. Like a film star of the thirties she is always immaculately made-up, with golden wavy hair which nowadays I suspect to be a wig, and has a proclivity for fox furs, floating clothes and high-heeled shoes.

My father, the most considerate of men, died first, and left her sufficient money with which to continue making a fool of herself. And since his death Lily has once more enjoyed the company of gentleman admirers. Outwardly she is well preserved. Inwardly she is still the same silly girl who won Harry Clough and a lifetime's devotion and protection. She overcomes hard facts by gliding over or past them, so she still regards herself as being in her prime, and I am still 'Flivvy'. She has never acknowledged herself as a grandmother, referring to Patrick and Jeremy as 'your boys', insisting that they call her Lily, and seldom making enquiries about them. When they were young she would look at them vaguely as if they belonged to a stranger, saying, 'Such sweet things!'

To my knowledge she has never conducted a sensible conversation on any subject, and her letters are not sensible either.

20 May 1978

Darlingest Flivvy,

Humphrey took me out to lunch today to cheer me up, and told me that everything was going wonderfully well at Parc Celli, and I need no longer fret about you – which I confess I have been doing, darling, while hiding an aching heart. I know you will be horrified to hear that Godfrey [one of her regular gentleman friends] has behaved extremely badly – not to say treacherously!! You may remember that he went on one of those coach tours last autumn (which I always thought rather common and how right I was!) and apparently met some widow whom he has been meeting in a clandestine fashion ever since!! And now, if you please, they have decided to get married!!! And to honeymoon in the Seychelles!!!! It's all so terribly sly and underhand! He had the impudence to say that when they got back we must all meet, and that he hoped the three of us would be good friends! Can you believe it? I was very Cool, as you may imagine, and said I would be spending the summer Away and had Other Plans.

I did confide in Humphrey, and he was so sweet and very understanding. Such a good friend, and only waiting for a word of encouragement from you, darling, to take you away from all this – and be a loving and devoted husband to you, as Daddy was to me. Every woman needs to be loved and protected. But I know what an independent little thing you are, so, 'nuff said!

Actually, Flivvy, as you're so much in my thoughts, and we have always been such a comfort to each other when we're lonesome, I wondered whether you could find a tiny corner for me and my doggie in Parc Celli? Poor little Beau, he always knows when his Mummy is blue, even though I keep on smiling! I know you're busy, darling, and we shan't bother you a bit. All I need is a little something on a tray in my room now and again – and to breathe fresh air – to rest my weary spirit in the purple dusk – and to heal myself in that wonderful West Country peace and quiet. Life can be a bitter cup . . .

My mother is the only person I know who actually leaves sentences unfinished and substitutes a row of dots to indicate that there is much, much more she could say. She does it in conversation, too. You can hear them puttering on in the silence.

In contrast to the poetic body of the letter her PS was strictly practical.

> I shall travel mid-week to avoid the rush and take advantage of the cheaper fare. Find me a good train with a restaurant car, darling, and give me a tinkle to let me know when and where you'll meet me and Beau.

'Oh my God!' I said aloud. 'That's all I needed to make life difficult.'

My mother and I were strangers, though she would never have admitted it. Indeed, our supposed devotion to each other was a necessary fact of Lily's existence: largely fictional, like the rest of her life.

Sadly I asked the empty house, 'Oh, Jack, where are you?'

For one of the wonderful things about Jack Rice was his outright refusal to be inconvenienced by Lily.

'Terribly sorry,' he would say to her over the telephone. 'You know we'd love to see you, but quite imposs I'm afraid. Working like blazes at the moment.'

Of course it meant that I had to give my mother lunch in London when Bon Appétit was closed, or pop down to Surrey to see her for a couple of hours, but his attitude liberated me.

I am too much of a female coward to deny my mother access. I need a selfish male to say my nays for me. Unarmed against her demands, I miss Jack now. I miss him anyway.

She stepped off the train looking impeccable, and close behind her, bidding a fond farewell, hovered a white-headed gentleman of military appearance whom she had evidently captivated during the long journey. They had probably lunched together and exchanged stories – Lily's largely fictional – and written down names, addresses and telephone numbers. A young hitchhiker, realising that the gallant swain was too shaky to leap on and off trains, kindly assisted him with the heavier bags, and finally handed the lady and her Sealyham terrier down to the platform. Safely balanced once more on her high heels, Lily uttered a cry of joy at seeing me waiting for her.

'Darling,' she cried, 'how *sweet* of you to come!' as if my presence were a big surprise.

At my request Tom had driven me here and left me, for I could not imagine my mother either approving of Victoria, or caring to be squeezed three abreast in front while her excess luggage was tied down on the roof.

She embraced me lightly while Beau sat down and panted as if he had run all the way from Paddington.

Turning for the last time to her conquest she called, '*A bientôt*, Raymond!' blew him a delicate kiss and watched him wave himself out of sight, saying, 'Darling, we shall need a porter!'

There was no porter available and the young hitchhiker felt forced to offer further help, which she accepted. She thanked him effusively.

On her way out of the station she was also fulsome with the ticket collector and charmed the taxi driver on sight: a wise move on her part, considering all that baggage. He ended up less charmed, with her cabin-trunk looming over him in the front seat.

'Flivvy,' she said, putting a white-gloved hand over my ungloved one as we sped towards Kelly Park, 'you must tell me all about yourself. You've been so much on my mind.'

And that was the last time I was mentioned, for she immediately added, 'Darling, if you could guess what I'd been through . . . ' and began a long-running saga on the perfidious Godfrey.

Lily was able to take up more time and space than anyone else I know. We never had a home in the real sense. During the war we followed my father about and rented furnished accommodation. When the war was over he bought a house in Polesden Lacey and spoke of us as being settled for good, but Cherry Trees always felt like lodgings.

A professional army officer of what is known as 'good family', he should have married a woman of his own kind who could run an orderly household. But Lily treated every room as her personal boudoir, heated up snacks in the kitchen, and was a stranger to time and purpose. In select Surrey her deficiencies became manifest. I remember my father installing a cleaning lady and a mother's help, in an attempt to make a home for me. Finally he sent me to boarding school to be brought up properly, and there I did pretty well.

At Kelly Park she spread and shed herself all over the house, and in fine weather all over the garden too. Gloves here, parasol there, her rings in the bathroom and her personal laundry on the floor of her bedroom. Assembling her for the day occupied most of my morning, and reminded me of early motherhood when I could only work while my children slept. Fortunately she was a late riser, so I had time to set my kitchen, house and garden staff to work before I bicycled to Elinglaze to collect my *Western Morning News* and her *Daily Mail* from the village shop. I no longer rode Martin Skeggs's boneshaker but another of Tom Faull's bargains: old-fashioned, but in good condition and only six pounds.

'Take care of your mother,' my father had said.

And because I had loved him dearly, and he had astonishingly loved her, I always did my best.

So I took up the little breakfast tray, with an elaborately laid breakfast, let out Beau who was either bursting or had inconveniently burst already, and had a little chat about what she should do and wear.

That first morning she said she felt strong enough to walk to the village and buy a few little things she had forgotten to pack. I hoped they were nothing more elaborate than toothpaste and cottonwool because Mrs Crowdy's choice of goods was limited. The great decision made, I worked madly until her entrance at the door of the kitchen an hour or so later, dressed as for a Buckingham Palace garden party. Lily did not like kitchens, and she could never understand why I spent most of my life in one. It was twelve noon. And I had just dished up a snack for Vera and myself.

'Darling,' she said, 'I don't think I'm quite up to a walk after all,' – ignoring our congealing scrambled eggs – 'I think I'll sit in the garden instead. Would you mind awfully . . . ?'

I left Vera eating and found a patch of lawn which Martin Skeggs had reclaimed from the jungle. He helped me to carry out the garden chairs and table, and paid his respects to the lady while I collected together a portable radio so that she would not be, as she said, 'lonesome', her reading-glasses and novel so that she would not be bored, and finally a little tray of coffee and cake which I hoped she might regard as lunch. But as I prepared to leave her for another hour or two she called me back, saying that she thought she could manage a little something at two o'clock, and would then skip dinner and go to bed early with another little tray. Mentally I rearranged the menu, which meant that I should be snacking all day.

Lily always enjoyed a little nap after lunch, so I worked in her absence. At four o'clock I carried up a little afternoon tea tray and we had another little chat, this time about the treacherous Godfrey, who was all of seventy-three, and his lady of seventy-two. I marvelled that Lily could be so enraged by this venerable liaison, which I found rather touching. But she was.

'Life and Love are bitter-sweet!' said Lily, sipping Lapsang Souchong.

Faded forget-me-nots, her eyes still searched for a blue horizon.

Reviving, she said, 'Flivvy, I feel so rested after my little nap that I think I can manage dinner downstairs after all. What culinary treat have you planned for us this evening, darling? Such talent, such industry, such a clever Flivvy! I must change, to do justice to the cuisine. What should I wear, do you think?'

She and Tom Faull did not get on. How could they? He was a realist with a dream. Lily was a dreamer who had been sheltered from reality.

Humphrey evidently gave her a misleading description of his protégé. This, coupled to my mother's incorrigible romanticism, led her to expect Ramon Novarro dressed as a scholar gypsy: too young to be a gentleman friend, but old enough to admire and revere her. She cultivated that kind of satellite, too.

So Lily paid Tom a courtesy visit the day after she arrived, for which she dressed carefully and inappropriately in lilac voile and a picture hat. And Beau was brushed until even he protested, and she decorated his forehead with a baby-blue ribbon to show he was a boy.

From the kitchen window I watched my mother pick her way across the cobbled courtyard, with the little dog pattering after her. It was noon, the hour when all good Cornishmen have their mid-day meal. Tom was sitting on top of the stable roof, eating a thick home-made sandwich, drinking strong brown tea from a Thermos flask, listening to Mozart and reading Rabelais. He wore his green baseball hat, a faded red plaid shirt, a pair of very old and shapeless blue cotton trousers, and dirty plimsolls. His hair and beard needed trimming, and he was wearing National Health spectacles mended with adhesive plaster. Even Lily could not imagine him in a romantic role, but she put both hands to her mouth and called hopefully, coyly, above the joyful strains from the transistor radio, 'Ahoy there, Mr Faull!' while the Sealyham sat down and panted, and blinked upwards through its fringe.

Tom nodded amiably, swallowed a mouthful of bread, turned down Mozart and closed Rabelais, sized her up in an instant, and replied with an irony which would escape her, 'And the top o' the morning to you, my lady!'

'I am Mrs Clough. Mrs Pollard's mama!' cried Lily.

She paused for him to cry out in astonishment, 'This is not possible!'

As he didn't oblige her she continued roguishly, 'Mr Jarvis is an old friend of mine, and I've heard all about *you*.'

'Oh, I hope not,' he said genially, and took a swig of tea and stared hard at the Sealyham's baby-blue ribbon. 'There are some things I'd rather a lady like yourself didn't know.'

She smiled uncertainly, and decided to appeal to his manly chivalry.

'I've come here for a holiday,' she ventured. 'Well, to convalesce, really. Such a healing place . . . '

'Oh, yes?' said Tom easily. 'Been ill, have you?'

Lily laid one manicured hand over the place where her heart

should be, and said insinuatingly, '*Les affaires de coeur*!'

Tom's face was as bland as a baby's, but I could imagine the satanic gleam in his black eyes.

He said gravely, 'Ah, you want to be careful with that sort of thing. It can set the neighbours talking.'

Lily considered this statement for a few moments while her smile faded. Then she tossed her gilded head, tossed her lilac stole over one plump shoulder, and turned her back on him, saying peremptorily to the Sealyham, 'Come along, Beau. Time for walkies!'

But first she tottered straight back to the kitchen, and standing in the doorway said loud enough for him to hear, 'That Person is quite Impossible! What on earth does Humphrey see in him?'

Up on his roof Tom laughed and threw the crust of his sandwich to a waiting rook, emptied the dregs of his tea into the nettles, and went back to work. He was singing 'Lili Marlene'.

I envied him his temerity. I admired his honesty. Lily would never expect anything of him ever again.

Yet my mother attracted admirers, and before the end of the week two of my staff were in thrall.

Vera Angwin, who in another walk of life would have made an excellent actress's dresser, was always willing to take up Lily's little trays and wash her lacy underwear. In return for these services, my mother told her inflated, if not misleading and sometimes downright untruthful, stories of the splendid past, and offered her chocolates from a lordly box.

'Oh, Mrs Pollard,' said Vera one morning, turning out the broom cupboard, 'I'd sooner listen to Mrs Clough than read a book. Real life romance, I call it. To think she knew the Duke of Windsor – and might have been a duchess if she'd been so minded. Some life she had before she married the General.'

Major, I said mentally, but did not correct Lily's fancy. My father had been promoted several times since his death. One does not give up a Prince of Wales lightly.

And then there was Martin Skeggs the gardener, who doffed his mangled hat whenever she sailed into view, kept her room supplied with fresh flowers, and cut a rose each morning to lay on her breakfast tray.

How did she do it?

I would hazard one guess. She never let anyone come near enough to find her out. She held herself at mystery distance. The wretched Godfrey, like a number of other gentleman friends, hung round her for years. What he needed was a satisfactory wife to replace the one he had lost. Instead he was kept in a condition of perpetual courtship by a coquette. I am glad he escaped Lily's clutches. I hoped that he and his lady would enjoy many twilight years together.

'Darling,' my mother was saying, back from her walkies, 'all this peace and quiet is so good for the soul, and the weather is so warm, that I feel strong enough to have afternoon tea in the garden. Do you mind awfully?'

The only thing which cheered me up and on was the thought that she might soon get tired of us. An old stage friend of hers lived in Somerset, and her letters, full of the joys of country living, sometimes tempted Lily to dash off for an idyllic month in the country; from which she always returned early, saying how artificial life was in London before throwing herself gleefully back into the social whirlpool. So I told myself to be patient, looked after her with the best will I could muster, and was to be bitterly disappointed.

One Friday afternoon in mid-June Tom Faull had gone to Camborne station to collect a box of London goodies from Humphrey; and, I suppose, whatever else took his fancy on the way. I had made strawberry jam and tried out a new recipe for scones; and Lily and I were sampling them and drinking tea in the drawing room.

'Tell me,' said Lily, spreading new strawberry jam on her scone, shaking clotted cream from a spoon. 'Does that funny little car belong to Mr Faull, or is it yours?'

'It's mine, but he has the use of it now and again in return for teaching me how to drive and taking me shopping.'

'I see,' said Lily distantly. 'And I notice that he has recently begun to call you Flavia. Surely a smart and civil Mrs Pollard every time he speaks would be more appropriate to your respective positions?'

'That,' I said, as lightly as I could, 'is the result of the driving lessons.'

'Look out, Flavia! You bloody fool! You're nearly in the middle of the road!'

He grabbed the steering wheel to correct our course. His hands clamped over mine. One arm accidentally brushed my breast. A car coming from the opposite direction just managed to avoid us, and the driver shouted something uncomplimentary as he drove past.

Greatly disturbed by all these events I cried angrily, 'Take your hands off that wheel! I'm going to stop the car.'

Embarrassed in his turn, Tom relinquished his grip. I drew into the nearest crossing place, trembling with reaction, and sat with my head in my hands for a few moments.

'And don't you dare call me a bloody fool again!' I said, when I could speak.

As pale as I felt, he shook his head, as if to shake off the situation, and answered in a subdued tone. 'All right, I'm sorry, but you took that bend too wide. If I hadn't grabbed the wheel and he hadn't swerved we'd have met in the middle.'

I knew he was right.

'Scared the hell out of me,' Tom mumbled. 'That's why I yelled like that.'

I said with an effort, 'Well, I'm sorry too.'

'Didn't mean to be familiar either, Miss Flavia,' Tom added stiffly.

'Oh, let's not start the feudal address all over again!' I said, half amused and half annoyed.

The incident had been cathartic. I pulled myself together and managed a touch of humour.

'If you call me Flavia I shall feel I can yell back at you.'

After a while Tom grinned, and said, 'Right. Flavia.'

We glanced at each other, smiled, and glanced away again.

Considerately, Tom said, 'That's your first brush with the terrors of the road. Must have given you a shock. Shall I take over, and drive us home?'

'It's very kind of you,' I said, recovering breath and equanimity, 'but I'm fine now, and I do want to go on with the lesson. I'd like to learn to drive before I kill the pair of us!'

I drew a deep breath, concentrated, and drove off without clashing a single gear.

'Driving lessons have a most curious effect on the people involved,' I told Lily, joking, because I still remembered the incident with some confusion. 'We found it difficult to shout and swear at each other and remain on formal terms.'

She made Beau beg for a bite of scone.

'I'm sorry to hear that. Shouting and swearing doesn't sound like my Flivvy. And I shouldn't encourage that man, if I were you, darling, or he'll be coming in here for his meals, next!'

She was wrong about that. Since her arrival last month he had refused all invitations to supper, and to tell the truth I felt relieved because the thought of coping with them both together was just too much.

'I believe he and I understand each other's limitations, Mother.'

When I was annoyed with Lily I called her mother, which she disliked.

She huffed and puffed in her lime-green chiffon.

'Oh, you know me, darling, I never interfere – though he seems something of a village Romeo. But I'm sure you've had sufficient experience of the wrong sort of man to avoid making a gaffe.'

I was instantly insulted that she should have thought of such a thing. The remark was waspish and deliberate, and only the sight of Victoria whizzing up the drive, with a Fortnum and Mason box tied on her roof, luggage sticking out of her open boot, and four faces staring from her windows like a child's drawing, prevented a very sharp retort.

Lily paused, scone held aloft. We looked at one another, long and hard.

'Darling?' Lily asked incredulously. 'Did you invite . . . ?'

'No. No one. I know nothing about them.'

Since Vera had gone home to feed her flock we hastened across the hall to open the front door in welcome: Beau scurrying round our feet.

Walking towards us was a tall and elegant young woman who looked like a model, hand in hand with two curly red-haired cherubs. And behind them loped Tom, alight with chivalry and adventure, carrying two enormous suitcases. The strangers halted at the threshold, and he made introductions.

'Flavia, this is Mrs Clarissa Gibbon. Mr Jarvis's cousin. And her nippers. Can't remember their names . . . '

The children chorused, 'Bella and Bee!'

Towering gracefully above me, the model held out her hand and said faintly, 'Flavia – may I call you Flavia? *Do* call me Clarissa – Flavia, forgive the intrusion, but Humphrey spoke so *warmly* of you. And I promise we'll be *no* trouble.'

'Do come in!' I cried hospitably, though my stomach turned to a large cold stone of apprehension. 'We're just having afternoon tea. This is my mama, by the way. Mrs Clough . . . '

A cross-fire of explanations accompanied Tom and the luggage into the hall.

Lily touched Clarissa's fingers in a token handshake, fluttered a chiffon handkerchief at the two children, and murmured, 'Sweet things!' doubtfully.

'*Dear* Mrs Clough. Are you *really* Flavia's mother? I can't *believe* it! So *young*! Humphrey told me what a *delightful* lady you were. *Lovely* to meet you. *Please* call me Clarissa . . . '

'Yap, yap, yap.'

'*Excuse* my asking, Mrs Clough, but does the little dog bite?'

'No, but he doesn't like his ribbon being pulled by these sweet things.'

'Yap, yap, yap, yap.'

'Bella! Bee! Leave the little dog alone, darlings.'

'No.'

'Shan't.'

'Spotted them at Camborne Station,' said Tom, well pleased with himself. 'Asking the ticket collector the way to Parc Celli. So I took them aboard. I'll get the rest of the stuff.'

He padded back to unpack the car and I marvelled at his ingenuity. How he had managed to stow four people and three suitcases into Victoria I couldn't imagine.

'Flavia, Mrs Clough, I hope you don't *mind* children. They're really no trouble at all. At least, Bella isn't, and Bee's learning. Real names Arabella and Beatrice. Bella and Bee say how do you do nicely.'

Bella takes my hand and says confidentially, 'I'm five. She's only four.'

Bee says, chin up, mouth set, fists clenched, 'No.'

I love children, particularly because I was deprived of mine, but I received them with decidedly mixed feelings. They bore no resemblance to their mother: small, sturdy, red-cheeked, full of mischief, staring up at me with black boot-button eyes. She had dressed them identically in green gingham smocks. Bella held a teddy-bear, and Bee clutched a cloth dolly.

'What a lovely surprise!' Lily was saying insincerely. 'But why . . . how . . . ?'

'Here's your tucker from Fortnum's, Flavia,' said Tom. 'I'll take it through to the kitchen?' And walked off with the box on his head.

Bella and Bee turned round to watch him go.

'I *do* like Tom!' said Bella.

He was back in an instant, saying, 'I set it down in the dry goods larder. Reckoned it was dry goods stuff. And now I'll be off.'

'No, Tom. Stay and have tea with us,' I said, ignoring Lily's distant air.

'Oh, yes,' Clarissa cried. '*Don't* leave us, Tom. You've been such a help. Flavia, we'd have *died* without him!'

Bella and Bee deserted us without a qualm and clung to his cotton trouser legs, begging him to stay. Lily looked across at me with the grandeur of stage resignation.

'I suppose we should ask Mr Faull to stay,' she said coldly.

Once settled in my chair, Clarissa shrugged off her daughters in the same easy way she shrugged off her cream cloth coat. Apart from saying plaintively, 'You *are* going to be good, aren't you?' she then abdicated her responsibilities and left them to whoever was interested.

Tom enjoyed himself thoroughly, piling his scones with jam and cream and showing the children how to throw a piece in the air and catch it in the mouth; which they did with a singular lack of success. I checked my tongue and temper with difficulty, for the carpet had just been cleaned, and now I should have to clean it again. But he ate his tea with such relish, and praised it with such eloquence, that I wondered if he got enough to eat. In the kitchen, thanking him again, for he had been kind, I offered the rest of the chicken terrine from last night's supper, and he accepted it gratefully.

Bella and Bee, who had followed us out, now refused to part from him.

'Shall I show them the stables?' he asked. 'I expect you three ladies will want to talk? You needn't fear. I'll take good care of them.'

I realised that he guessed or had probably been told, why Clarissa came and for how long. And as she seemed glad to leave her daughters to anyone who might be interested in them I agreed to this. So he hoisted the children up in his arms, squealing and giggling, and bore them away.

Clarissa had contained herself until my return. As I appeared she flung her arms in the air with a superb gesture, tossed back her raven's wing of hair, and cried, 'I've left home. I don't love my husband any more! I don't care if I have to starve or beg in the streets. I shall *never* go back!'

Lily, recognising a fellow Thespian, took her cue and said, 'Oh, my dear! How we poor loving creatures suffer at the hands of men!'

They gazed deeply at each other, playing the scene for all it was worth. They were enjoying themselves enormously.

'Are you staying here long, Mrs Clough?' Clarissa asked, wooing her.

'I *was* thinking about going home next week,' said Lily, 'but, of course, if *you're* staying.'

Clarissa put out a long white hand, which my mother clasped in both hers.

'Oh, that would be *lovely*!' cried Clarissa.

'We'll have lots of little talks together,' my mother said. 'Do call me Lily.'

I shall ring Humphrey this evening, and tear strips off him, slowly.

* * *

'But Flavia – dearest girl – if you will allow me to explain . . . '

His voice wafts like a timid zephyr across the wires, as well it might.

' . . . Clarissa is a sweet girl, and one of my god-daughters. Her mother was a Bristol Jarvis. I believe I told you that quite a few of them were evacuated to Parc Celli during the war. I'm sure I showed you the photograph of us all on the lawn together—'

'Humphrey!' I said, warning him to stick to the point.

'Yes, of course I did. Well, my dear, the poor girl rang me, at her wits' end, not knowing where else to turn. Her husband is Dick Gibbon, you know, the explorer. *Former* explorer, I should have said. He was past his best when she met him, though still very much of a live-wire!' He laughed in reminiscence. 'If you wanted to make a party go you invited Dick!'

'Humphrey, however lively he was, she has now left him and is here with the children, and I want to know why.'

'Why indeed?' he said nervously. 'We do well to ask ourselves that question. They were all right for the first few years. Bashing about the world together, living it up, but nowadays he's something of a burnt-out case. He's a great deal older than Clarissa, you see, and she's a girl who likes to have a rattling good time. Living in the depths of Devon with the children, while he writes his memoirs, is not her forte . . . '

'Why can't she go to her parents?'

'Papa is an invalid, and Mama looks after him. They can't possibly have children in the house. Besides, they didn't want Clarissa to marry Dick Gibbon in the first place. More or less prophesied what would happen in a May and December partnership. So it's a question of pride with her. She won't slink home and admit that they were right.'

His tone changes to one of dignified displeasure.

'I must say, Flavia, that I'm a little surprised to find you so unsympathetic about her plight. After all, you've been in the same position – well, probably not exactly the same, but you know what I mean. Besides, Clarissa is family. All she needs is a month or two to sort herself out.'

That point made, he became affable once more.

'Placed as I was – until your wondrous intervention – a bachelor in a small flat, I could have done nothing for her. But now Parc Celli is restored I can offer her shelter, dearest. Don't you see?'

Beneath his courteous pleading lay the adamantine hospitality of a Cornish squire. And this is his house, not mine.

'Parc Celli,' I said, controlling my anger and fear with difficulty, 'is being restored as a country-house hotel, Humphrey.'

'But they are guests, my dearest girl. *Our* guests.'

'But our guests must pay as well as stay, if we're to run this place as a business— Yes, I understand that you look on Clarissa as a special case. But I'm working eighteen hours a day to get this place open in September, and I can't have the responsibility of feeding and caring for three extra people—'

'My dear, I shall send a little cheque to you in the next post. And by the by, has my little present arrived from Fortnum's?'

'Humphrey, a little cheque in the next post is always welcome, and I do thank you for the lovely treats from Fortnum's, but that is not the point. I need time and space even more than money. Have you any idea of the amount of work involved in this project?'

'My dear. Regard this as a little favour to me.'

'It is *not* a little favour, it is a very great imposition. I don't want to quarrel. God knows, I'm trying to avoid trouble! All I ask is to be left here in peace, so that I can put Parc Celli on her feet as a viable concern . . . '

'A lovely, lovely girl. Always delighted to join in . . . '

'Yes, very handsome, but you're being wildly optimistic if you believe she'll help me. I put the children to bed myself, this evening, and she's left a basket full of washing for Vera to do . . . '

'And such sweet little girls. Flavia, did you know that Bella was named after my grandmama?'

'I'm sure that's very gratifying.'

'And Bee. Such a little tease . . . '

'Humphrey? Humphrey! Will you please *listen* to me for just one moment? This sort of thing was not in our original agreement. I'm being asked to undertake far more than I should and it isn't fair. It isn't fair and it isn't *right*, Humphrey! And you must jolly well *do* something about it!'

Bang. Let him think about that!

CHAPTER TEN

July

There are dark, deep and devious gods in this county, who play tricks on English invaders and adventurers. They lure us with Cornish mists and beguile us with Cornish dreams, they make straight the way to the trap. And then amuse themselves at our expense.

I needed fine weather in order to lose my guests and was given rainy days. Lily and Clarissa either swamped us with small demands or impeded us by looking after themselves. The children were in everyone's way, clamouring for attention, pressing their faces against the streaming windowpanes, running and shouting through the house. Then an unseasonable high wind riffled yards of slates and uncovered the horror of the rafters beneath.

A finer day has dawned and we are standing on the roof, Will Soady and I, gravely exploring, talking of major repairs. We disagree on only one point. He refers to Kelly Park as he, whereas to me she is she. But we make allowances for each other.

'I daresay they storms, back in February, did the real damage. So he only needed one good blow to riffle him. Lucky we hadn't decorated they attics. We'd have had to do them twice over! He's been let go too long, you see, Mrs Pollard. Haven't been touched since the old squire died – like the rest of Parc Celli. By the way, did you ask Mr Jarvis about they boiler pipes? Well, Ben Quick had another word with me and Tom and I looked at them and they'm none too smart. Now Mr Jarvis don't want them to go and flood the place, do he? And the boiler is an old 'un, too. Could be an explosion. I should ask him again, if I was you.

''Es, that's how it be with these old houses. Set one thing right and find two wrong. Take this roof, now. This be a sou'-westerly roof. Takes the worst of the wind and rain. We can do a cheap job and patch him where he's gone, but come another wind and he'll scat him up again. Tis my belief that he's rotten all the way along . . . '

Dwarfed by chimneys, awed by the size and extent of Kelly Park's various slate hats, I listen to Will Soady talking familiarly of this strange terrain.

'So this 'un'll be your worst, but I shouldn't be surprised if they'm all dodgy. If I was to look too close I'd be talking about a fortune in repairs. But I aren't meeting trouble afore trouble comes. We can do them one at a time. And while we're about it, Mrs Pollard, we'd best have this old boy down!'

He gives the chimney nearest to him a friendly slap. The giant shudders.

'One good squall,' says Will appraising his adversary, 'and he'd go through three floors and no mistake. I'd best look at the other chimneys, too. And you tell Mr Jarvis from me, ma'am, that he'd be better to spend five thousand now than twenty thousand later.'

Five thousand pounds? I feel as if the full weight of that brick giant had fallen and lain on my chest. I have a place to put every penny of Humphrey's money without the present crisis. The question is, can he afford to go on?

Will Soadby muses aloud.

'May as well make a good job of it and be done. Else you're forever trimming and patching. That's why Tom aren't as far forrard as he hoped. He been patching, you see. That's what I said to'n. "You been patching, Tom, and it's one patch atop of the other. Take the whole lot down, boy, and see what he be about." And sure enough, when he stripped that roof down he found what we've found here. Needs new rafters right the way along, and all the slates rehung. And all the window frames are rotten, and the doors, too. That's why his tarpaulins are back on.'

Distracted from my present predicament by a future one, I ask, 'Does that mean Tom won't be living in the stables this winter?'

'No chance,' says Will Soady cheerfully, and confides in me.

'There wasn't hardly no chance o' that, anyhow. Tom aren't no builder. Leastways,' and here he corrects himself, out of fairness or loyalty, 'he'll turn his hand to anything and make a proper job of it, and there aren't no harder worker nor better worker than Tom Faull, but building aren't his given trade, if you follow me.'

'I follow you,' I say flatly. 'He's one of those people who have a bright idea without realising how much work and trouble and expense is really involved. And now he's too far in to get out.'

I am thinking of myself and of those for whom I have made myself responsible: of Humphrey, whom I persuaded into the project, of Kelly Park who cannot now be abandoned, of the little troop of employees who rely upon their wages here, and others hoping for employment when we open.

Will takes my remark to be directed at Tom. Not best pleased by this summary, he strokes his cheeks thoughtfully with one hard worn hand.

'I wouldn't go so far as to say that,' he answers slowly, 'but he do have his work cut out to get a roof on and windows in and doors rehung before autumn. And with the weather like it have been lately . . . '

Too much rain, too little time, a shortage of cash. And no going back.

Look forward, then, Flavia. Always forward. To September, when the autumn visitors begin to pay. To 1980 when the public restaurant opens.

'And what about this work then, Mr Soady – with the weather like it is?'

'We'll need to buy tarpaulins for when he's stripped off,' says Will briskly, and adds to himself, 'Have to ask Tom where he got his from.'

'He found one of them floating on a pond,' I say.

Will Soady gives me a sceptical look. There is a silence between us.

Eventually I say, 'Well, I must tell Mr Jarvis. You did warn us that we should look at the outside first.'

He nods sagaciously.

'Thank you for not saying, "I told you so!"'

'Didn't have to do tha-at, Mrs Pollard. I knew I was right.'

Another silence. Then I close the conversation.

'There seems to be no choice, Mr Soady. The roof will have to be repaired.'

I stay there when he has gone and nurse my trouble, try to assuage the fear that I am trapped in yet another situation which spells f-a-i-l-u-r-e. I shall have to coax more money out of Humphrey, which means inviting him down for a weekend as soon as possible, and cosseting him before I mention the roof. The only difficulty is that once he comes down he is likely to stay indefinitely, and revel in the assembled company.

I droop at the thought. For I have neither the emotional nor the physical energy to cope with a group of non-paying residents and Kelly Park too.

And yet, as the evening light tinges the chimneys and I look down on the Jarvises' demesne and out to the bay, the reason is made manifest. I am queen of all I survey. Without me Kelly Park is derelict. I am wanted, needed, relied upon. Oh, I realise that this is an ancient female snare, baited with love and concealing metal teeth. But realisation makes no difference. To desert her now would be to desert myself.

I have had to be cunning in order to survive. I make sure that my unwanted guests disturb me as little as possible. In the evenings, the kitchen becomes my private domain.

Lily and Clarissa are drawing-room ladies. They keep each other company for hours, chatting about those feminine fantasies which they call personal experience. Occasionally they talk at cross purposes, or unwittingly interrupt each other, since neither of them is a good or attentive listener. Hamsters in twin cages, they trundle their wheels endlessly, side by side. Parallel lines, they resemble each other but never meet.

I spend the merest fraction of time with them, courtesy time, and then retreat to a place and an occupation which makes sense of the present and holds promise of a future. For Lily and Clarissa, circling round and round themselves, nothing changes. Their future is their present which was their past. Lily's tales I know by heart. From Clarissa's list of grievances I have formed an opinion of her husband which she would be chagrined to hear.

I like Dick Gibbon. He rings every weekend and speaks to me and to Bella and Bee while Clarissa is found. He is a frank and simple man and his greatest sins are probably of omission. Patently he adores and spoils his wife, but has failed to keep her entertained, admired, and in public view. I believe she married him, as I married Guy Pollard, because she was young and green and looking for a mature man to provide her with all the answers.

In my case I was seeking the home Lily was incapable of making. In Clarissa's case she fell in love with Dick Gibbon's way of life, no doubt picturing herself the object of all male eyes at his distinguished lectures, or being photographed for some international magazine in a safari hat and veil: *Clarissa, the beautiful wife of explorer Dick Gibbon, admires a pride of lions.* Now he is burnt out, home from the hill, asking nothing more than a quiet country life with his loved ones about him. She is trapped in his retirement, and he grows old and dull.

Bella and Bee love him dearly and cannot understand why he doesn't join us. He tells them little lies which they are bright enough to interpret and spirited enough to resent. Their behaviour after one of his telephone calls is diabolical, and can only be curbed by the threat of no bedtime story: a treat instituted and carried out by me.

I could sympathise if Clarissa were a different kind of woman, but she is a clinger and a taker. Also she causes emotional problems as well as that major one of lodging herself and her children. So I listen to Dick Gibbon's plaints, and soothe him with innocuous advice, and hand him over to his dark lady who wears a frown between her brows and only wants him to supply her with money and leave her alone.

'Flivvy,' Lily calls plaintively, as I bolt out of the side door to speak to Martin Skeggs, 'do stay and talk to me for a moment. There's a little something I feel I should mention.'

She is sitting on the back lawn today beneath her flowered sunshade, about to take afternoon refreshment.

I had been hoping to pass unhailed, and my expression probably says so, for she then adds, 'Such a busy person. Always dashing about and no time to talk. Sit down and let me look after *you* for a change.'

This idea gratifies her, particularly as there is little to do. Her ringed fingers teeter among the china cups. I see she is old and lonely and needs to unburden herself. I hesitate, sigh, and sit. Behind us the ever-willing Vera is wending her way back to the kitchen, carrying an empty tray. Spread before us is a sumptuous tea fit to feed an army.

'Where are the rest of the troops?' I ask satirically.

This is the question my mother was hoping to hear and she launches into its answer with gusto.

'Well may you ask!' She offers me one of my own saffron buns and says, 'Do try one. So delicious!' before beginning her saga.

'Darling, I think perhaps you should give that Mr Faull a word of warning. Mind you, I thought it most unwise when you asked him to stay to tea that day. He's taken advantage. As I could have warned you he would. I know men, my dear! And I know how weak and trusting a girl like Clarissa can be.'

She dabs her mouth and feeds Beau a piece of buttered bun.

'Naturally, a person like Mr Faull thinks he's on to a good thing. And he's preying on her in a very cunning way through the children. The three of them have been over at the stables this afternoon, Vera tells me. And they were there this morning, too.'

'Doing what?' I ask peremptorily. 'Tom's having building problems, just as I am. I should have thought he was too busy to entertain idle visitors.'

'Oh, they're helping him. Vera tells me that Clarissa brought some things over from the house to make him more comfortable. And Bella and Bee fetch and carry for him in their little way!'

I was infuriated to think he was now paying court to Clarissa as well as Vera. Was there no end to the man's vanity?

'How *dare* she take things from the house!' I cry. 'What has she taken?'

I bang my cup down on the saucer, and immediately regret it because they are both old and frail and pretty.

'Darling, it's no use being angry with *me*!' Lily protests, hand on bosom, blue eyes wide. 'Vera didn't say. You'll have to ask *her*. But apparently Clarry and this Mr Faull are very thick. I noticed myself, on Saturday evening when he came in to telephone Humphrey, that she went out to meet him in the hall. And when I passed that way, some time later, they were still talking together. You aren't aware of these things, darling,' she says with reproach, 'slaving away in that kitchen.'

And she pays tribute to my slavery by cutting a slice of sandwich cake for herself and the dog.

'You say things from the house. Do you mean furniture?'

'I have hinted,' says Lily, disregarding me, brushing crumbs from her frilled bosom, 'but Clarry is very innocent. She doesn't understand – as I didn't, my dear, until after your father died! – she simply doesn't know how men can behave with an unprotected woman.'

'I'm going straight over there to inspect the stables, and if I find so much as a single cushion . . . '

'And then there's poor Vera. Simply broken-hearted, my dear. I'm not suggesting that there's anything wrong between herself and that wretched Faull creature, because of course she's married, but she still thinks the world of him. He's let her down before, you know. They were engaged when they were young. Well, not exactly engaged, but there was an understanding, and then he simply walked off into the blue, and she didn't see him for eighteen months . . . '

'I've had enough, and more than enough. I shall go back to London and let Humphrey sort his own mess out . . . '

She is eating and talking while I sip hot tea and seethe twice over.

' . . . a few weeks after he'd disappeared she married Brian Angwin. On the rebound, she told me. But I did wonder. Then the Faull man came back again and picked up where he left off, expecting everyone to be pleased to see him, just as he did this time. And he gets away with it, that's what annoys me . . . '

'I should never have got caught up with this in the first place . . . '

'Vera is a trusting simple soul,' says Lily, and adds, 'like me. He may well have led her up the garden path again. I can't help thinking that things went further than they should have done the first time. She married Brian Angwin so quickly, and I've been doing my arithmetic . . . '

Arithmetic is Lily's sole intellectual achievement. By some miracle she can count her change correctly, know how much to tip, and calculate the date of conception from the time of birth or vice-versa.

' . . . and I shouldn't be a bit surprised if that son of hers isn't Tom Faull's child. The dates would be about right. Mind you, from what Humphrey tells me about his own family, that sort of thing does seem to go on! And Sean Angwin is as dark as a gipsy, just like the Faull person. Unusually dark.'

My rage is diverted from Clarissa to Lily. And as I have wondered the same thing myself, I become doubly wrathful.

'Unusually dark? Sean's Cornish. Of course he's dark. Vera's dark. Mrs Quick was dark. They're a dark family. Dark, indeed! Why, my father was dark, come to that – and he's got nothing to do with Sean Angwin!'

'Oh, well,' sighs Lily, momentarily quelled, 'I only wondered.'

So had I. So do I now.

Lily recovers her equilibrium. Her displeasure with me is expressed with tremendous hauteur. She sweeps the crumbs from her lap.

'I can tell you have something on your mind, darling,' she says, 'and as I can't seem to enjoy my tea today I'll take myself off and have a stroll with Beausy-Boy – who loves his mummy.'

Lily has eaten heartily and with great enjoyment. It is my cup which contains gall and wormwood.

She stands up, unfurls her parasol, and makes absurd tutting sounds, tongue on palate, as if she were about to eat something especially delicious.

'Is a boy coming with his mummy, then?'

Beau naturally scrambles into a begging position, cocks his head on one side, and looks round for more cake. As it is not forthcoming he falls down again dejected.

'Walkies?' Lily enquires tenderly.

He perks up immediately and trots ahead of her. The turquoise bow on his forehead bobs with anticipated pleasure.

* * *

I march off to the stables, where Tom Faull is alone on the roof, swearing and hammering simultaneously. His transistor radio is playing Schumann, but faintly. It needs new batteries. As I wish to avoid a confrontation I slip into his quarters unnoticed, clutching the paper bag of cakes which is my excuse if he asks what I am doing here.

Inside, the apology for furniture consists of a series of greengrocer's wooden boxes covered in oil-cloth and cretonne. Whether or not the material has been supplied by Clarissa I don't know, and judging by its quality I don't care either. Everything is very tidy, but I attribute that virtue to Tom who likes things shipshape. Clarissa leaves a trail of debris wherever she goes.

He has converted six of the stalls into bedroom, sitting room, study, dining room, washroom and kitchen. The place is bare and shabby but as clean as he can make it, swept as you might say but ungarnished. And though he has turned out and burned all the straw the air is musty and damp.

Heating is supplied by an extremely old oil stove with a fretted top. Such a stove I remember from my childhood, slanting a pattern of distorted lace across the ceiling of my room. Sanitation is a chemical closet. Washing facilities are the hip bath, and what does look like a servant's cream earthenware jug and basin from the attic, but I am not about to quarrel over those. A clothes line, stretched across the end wall, holds a dripping change of underwear and a dank plaid shirt. His chairs are oddly assorted, and I recognise none of them.

I can create his daily life from this, his humble habitation. A partly darned sock stretches over a wooden mushroom. A Spanish grammar book lies open, with a notebook and biro beside it. A typewriter holds a half-written letter. I would not trespass on his private correspondence but cannot help reading the opening lines:

> Dear Squib, Please note my new and permanent address! Here I am at last, 'in my expected country' as the poet says.

A frayed tea-towel dries over a yellow plastic washing-up bowl. What food he has, and there is little enough of it, is covered and weighted to defeat the rats. He has the minimum necessities, all of them poor and plain. Comforts are non-existent. The only feminine touch is a bunch of wildflowers in a jam jar on the crumbling sill.

I place the cakes in a dish, cover them with a saucepan lid and weight them down with a spanner. On the paper bag I write a note, half-false, half-true:

> Didn't want to disturb you. Thought you would like to try these.
> Flavia.

I wish I had brought more food with me: a loaf of freshly baked bread, half a pound of Cornish butter, a pot of home-made strawberry jam. I should do more for him, subtly, so as not to hurt his pride and further rouse his independence. Should say, for instance, 'Oh, Tom! I'm trying out a new recipe for game pie. Would you mind being a guinea-pig?' Or 'Oh, Tom! Could you possibly find a home for these few things? I find I've cooked far more than they've eaten.' Something like that.

I return to the house without troubling him, without being seen. His circumstances have scoured me free of anger. Now I feel guilty, though my suspicions were quite justified in the circumstances. It is not my fault that I have a foolish mother who does not check her facts. So I tell myself. And yet still feel ashamed and sorry.

That evening I sit in Tom Faull's reconditioned rocking chair, notebook on lap, and think, and rock. The kitchen clock is ticking my thirty-ninth year away. The fat sweet smell of roast Cornish spring lamb, the sharp sweet tang of mint sauce, lingers. On the scrubbed table my account book waits to terrify me. Next to it in a folder marked boldly Bon Appétit! are a sheaf of favourite recipes scribbled on odd sheets of paper, which is as far as my future cookery book has gone. On the mantelpiece is a letter to my former husband, seemingly insouciant, in reality asking permission for my sons to visit me next month.

I concentrate on composing the advertisement with which Kelly Park is to burst upon a waiting world.

> Looking for an autumn break? Why not try a genuine Victorian country-house weekend in a secluded part of the beautiful Lizard

peninsula? Parc Celli offers you the delights of fine food, four-poster beds . . .

. . . only one bathroom on the same floor, and a Spartan fixture up the next flight of stairs!

I should have insisted on another bathroom being built before we opened. Two dressing rooms converted to shower rooms, and a handbasin in each bedroom are hardly the last word in washing facilities. But as Jack Rice used to say, if something's not up to scratch either ignore it or make a feature of it.

I add 'old-fashioned service and captivating features', and read the advertisement through again. Suppose I brought the slipper-baths down from the attic and had them repainted?

I cross out 'captivating features' and write over the top 'a slipper-bath in every bedroom'.

A slipper-bath in every bedroom? Sounds like a quotation from Hoffnung – 'a French widow in every room'!

Oh, blast it all. We shan't be able to open on the first of September anyway.

Humphrey may adore me, or imagine he does, but he is far closer to Tom Faull. The two of them are very thick, even if they do remain squire and tenant, and there is a male camaraderie between them which excludes me. And then, they are both Cornish. I am not jealous, of course. This is a hangover from the Jack affair. I should like to come first in someone's affections.

Reluctantly, as Tom's telephone evening comes round, I have to ask him not to mention the Kelly Park roof when he reports the week's progress to Humphrey. As a reason, I say that I am inviting Humphrey down in order to discuss the matter, and don't want him to worry unduly beforehand.

Tom's voice drops to its deepest and most confidential tone.

'Don't you fret! You can rely on me,' he says.

His tone perturbs rather than soothes me, and I wait apprehensively for his return from the telephone.

'Mr Jarvis would like to speak to you, Flavia,' says Tom, apparently well pleased with his own conversation.

'Hello, my dearest girl!' Humphrey begins breezily. 'Just been having a reassuring word with poor old Tom about his roof problems. Nothing desperate, one feels. Simply a minor setback.'

The stable roof is a minor tragedy at the moment. Come to that, the south-western side of Kelly Park roof could be called a major one.

'Anyway,' Humphrey continues, 'I'm glad to hear that all goes according to plan with you. Tom says it looks as if the house could be open on time.'

Damn the fellow for overdoing it!

'Of course, we do hope so,' I say, with misgiving. 'But at the moment we're slightly behind schedule.'

'Then what is all this I have been told about teas on the lawn and picnics in the park?'

I am being diverted from my plan of campaign, which is to beg the favour of his company while concealing the real reason for asking him. I manage a merry laugh.

'Not for me, Humphrey. For Lily and Clarissa and Bella and Bee!' Then the truth surfaces sourly, abruptly. 'Personally speaking I'm working against the clock and I wish they'd all go home!'

'Oh ho, ho. You don't mean that, Flavia. A little bird tells me that you've invited your boys down at the end of next month, and are hopeful that they will be coming. Quite a house party!'

I turn to give Tom a piece of my mind and glimpse him disappearing down the passage. I am sure he has done this on purpose.

'So it's not all work and no play, despite your protestations. You *do* find time to entertain,' says Humphrey.

His tone is arch but conceals a reproach.

I start to say that I have no choice in the matter, decide that this would be bad tactics, and am rephrasing it into an invitation when he takes the words away from me.

'How very nice it would be if I could join you all for a few days!'

I draw a resolute breath and do the best I can.

'But so you shall!' I cry.

I am quite proud of myself and the voice that now rings out loud and true.

'Why not make it a long weekend? Next weekend if you like!

We'll have a lovely quiet time together, and a good *tête-à-tête* about Parc Celli, and you can see everything that's been done. And then we can talk about one or two things which perhaps ought to be done.'

The short silence that follows is breathless with gratification.

'Dearest girl!' says Humphrey, deeply moved, 'I was beginning to think that you didn't want to see me.'

CHAPTER ELEVEN

The house was in an uproar, preparing for the advent of its owner. All my helpers, those I needed and those I did not, were assembled for the fray.

Final shopping had been accomplished in a series of trips, and I spoke sharply to Tom Faull on two counts. Firstly, because he said Victoria was too small to fetch and carry like this, and he knew of a good little van I could buy. Secondly, because I was driving and he cried, 'For Christ's sake, overtake that dozy pillock! You want to be here all morning?'

To which I answered loud and clear, 'Don't you shout and swear at me! I'll overtake when I feel it's safe! And as for a new van, you should have thought of that before I bought this car – which was your idea, remember! I haven't money to throw about on whims and fancies!'

Nastily, I wondered why he needed a van, but could hardly put so direct a question.

Tom did not speak for a while. He had been out of sorts in flesh and spirit recently. The transistor radio was silent. He no longer came in for a joke and a chat with Will Soady and sons or found an excuse to visit Vera in the kitchen. I wondered if he were ill, for his dark skin was the colour of tallow and he had lost his confident sailor's gait.

Now he said slowly, 'Well, if I'm in the wrong then I'm sorry. But you've got a clear road ahead, and that old fool's doing no more than twenty miles an hour.' He swallowed, and added, 'And if I was wrong about the car I'm sorry too, but I didn't realise how much food you'd need to carry. And Eddy Johns has a good little van he wants to sell.'

I indicated to the traffic behind us that I was moving out, and slammed my foot down on the accelerator. Coughing, jolting and smoking bravely, Victoria shot past the car in front, ground into third gear and nearly made fourth.

'Just a shade smoother on the changes,' Tom growled softly.

Wait until I had passed my test!

Yet I could not manage without him, and I still felt guilty about the poverty of his quarters. So I insisted on treating us to coffee when the last box had been loaded, and persuaded him to have a Danish pastry.

We sat without speaking, which made me uneasy. Usually it was difficult to stop Tom from swamping any conversation with ideas, opinions, information and sea yarns, but today he remained taciturn. I did not flatter myself that my rebuke had checked him. Driving lessons were usually stormy, ending in an apology on both sides. So a morose Tom Faull was a phenomenon.

I made a special effort to be cordial.

'I expect you'll be glad to see Mr Jarvis tomorrow,' I said.

He wet his forefinger to pick up the last few crumbs, and stared down at his empty plate, subdued.

He said heavily, 'That stable roof should have been finished by the time he came home. It looks worse now than when I started. And that sticks in my throat. Looks as if I've done nothing, and am nothing.'

I said, 'But Mr Jarvis knows how hard you've worked. Will Soady said no one worked harder or better than you.'

'That was good of Will,' said Tom, uncomforted.

'Have another pastry. Or a sausage roll. Or something.'

He shook his head and thanked me. I tried to cheer him by pointing out that he was not alone in his sorrows.

'Well, I've got roof trouble too, as you know. That means a huge bill and a delay before we open. But none of us can do more than our best.'

He did not reply to that, but looked up and said, 'Anyhow, I might as well make myself useful. If you want me to help in the house while Mr Jarvis is here you've only to say the word.'

'Thank you, Tom. I will.'

His inner light dimmed further.

'And then, when he's gone, I'll be looking round for a job.'

'But surely you've got plenty of work to do on the stables?'

He hesitated before he answered, and his tone was clipped.

'I've got as far as I can with the stables. For the moment, that is. I've run out of materials.' Then in a lower tone, 'And I've run out of money.'

I said soberly, truthfully, 'I'm very sorry to hear that.'

'So I need to earn more,' he continued, 'before I can go on.'

And meanwhile how was he to live?

He said quickly, 'I'm not asking favours of you or Mr Jarvis. So you've no cause to worry about that.'

'But of course I shall worry. I'm wondering how I can help.'

Smiling grimly, he said, 'You mean, feeding me in a way I shan't notice?'

I should have tackled this directly and said, 'Don't be stuffy, Tom. I want to help you any way I can!' But his look and tone flurried me.

I said defensively, 'I shouldn't like you to go hungry . . . '

His austere stare made me depersonalise this statement.

' . . . I shouldn't like *anybody* to go hungry.'

'That's my business,' said Tom Faull sternly.

There was no need to add, 'Not yours.' The words were implicit in his tone. Grave and forbidding, he held my gaze as if he could see right through me.

'But we all belong to Parc Celli,' I said, floundering now, 'and you're more than welcome to eat up at the house – or to take the food away if you prefer. Whichever you like.'

'But I shouldn't like it,' said Tom Faull stubbornly. 'That would be sponging off Mr Jarvis. And hard up as I've been, sometimes, I've never yet had cause to beg from a soup kitchen.'

Evidently he had finished trying to please me, and just as I was making an effort to please him.

He got up and said politely, coldly, 'Shall we be going, then?'

I drove extremely badly on the way back, but he made no comment even when one driver rolled down his window and swore at me. When I apologised he said it didn't bother him, but he thought it would be a good idea if I had a few lessons from a professional for my own sake, because driving instructors knew all the tips about passing the test.

I was astonished to realise that I had expected Tom to be there whenever I needed him. Consequently I was badly rattled even before I walked into the kitchen to find Vera and Clarissa quarrelling and crying, and Lily making matters worse by trying to make them better. Between them squatted a broad old-fashioned washbasket brimming with dirty clothes. On top of the basket, watching and listening raptly, sat Bella and Bee. And clutched to Bee's flat little chest was a petrified Beau, ribbon askew, dressed in a doll's bonnet.

The women greeted me with a triple chorus of explanation and complaint, while Tom carried boxes of groceries and greengroceries through to the pantries and steadfastly ignored all of us.

Vera stated her case, chin trembling, 'I aren't doing no more laundry for Mrs Gibbon, Mrs Pollard. I aren't paid to do laundry. I don't mind helping Mrs Lily none. That's different. Mrs Lily been here some while, been some kind to me. But Mrs Gibbon, she be ikey-tikey.'

Whatever that meant it was not complimentary.

Clarissa protested, sweeping back her raven's wing of hair, 'Flavia darling, I simply asked, ever so nicely, if Vera could rinse through a few little things for my babies.'

She had no regard for the children except as arrows in her quiver, but she was adept at using them. Poor Dick Gibbon must often have been impaled on these infant shafts.

Lily fluttered, 'It was the timing that was wrong, Flivvy, just the timing. Clarry didn't mean any harm. And Vera is probably overtired. I know we're all far too fond of each other to disagree.'

The cross-currents of emotion at Kelly Park ran fast and deep. Vera, who was devoted to Lily and Tom, looked on Clarissa as an importunate rival. Clarissa, who used Tom for flirtation and Lily as an audience, had made the mistake of disregarding Vera. Lily detested Tom, but needed Vera as a personal maid and Clarissa as a fellow gossip. Tom, I was certain, made fools of them all. And the children, delectable but undisciplined, played us off one against the other.

Vera wiping her eyes on the skirt of her overall, cried, 'Fact is, I got too much to do already, Mrs Pollard, with the master coming. And in this house there's some as works and some as don't. I aren't meaning you, Mrs Pollard – aren't nobody works harder than you. But I won't flog myself to noth'n over someone as does noth'n.'

I was in full agreement on this, and my conscience smote me, for I knew that I had allowed them to take advantage of Vera's willingness to serve.

Clarissa, one of those rare women who look charming when they cry, dried her dew-drops on a square of white cambric embroidered with her initials, and murmured to it, 'Darling Flavia, you know I wouldn't dream of upsetting your servant, but if Vera won't do the laundry, who will?'

The use of the word 'servant' infuriated me. I should have liked to slap her. But physical violence was not my forte, nor was I tall enough, so I kept my distance and controlled my anger for the moment.

'Vera is not a servant, she is my assistant!' I said. 'And she is not obliged to do anything for you at all.'

And had the satisfaction of staring Clarissa out.

Frightened, Lily babbled, 'It would be so much easier, Flivvy, if Parc Celli wasn't so far away from the shops. Is there a launderette in Helston? Oh, but then there's the question of transport . . . '

In the washbasket war was being declared.

Bella said to Bee, 'It's my turn to hold our baby!'

'No!'

'It's my turn, give him to me!'

'Shan't!'

Bella snatched. Bee tugged. The Sealyham's ribbon and bonnet were the first casualties. The children grabbed the weapons to hand, and Beau squealed for mercy as they flailed him and each other with damp and sandy towels. Before we could intervene the basket had heeled over and taken them all with it.

I rescued the hysterical animal and gave him to Lily, plucked the children from the debris and stood them abruptly upright.

Their sandals went thump thump on the slate floor. They received the first blast of my temper.

'You naughty girls! How dare you behave like that! Pick up those clothes and put them back, at once!' I said.

They rubbed their eyes with their fists to stimulate tears.

'And don't you dare cry, because I won't have it!'

Their fists dropped. They looked round for support and found no one prepared to confront me. In red-cheeked silence they obeyed.

'My boy's lost his ribbon,' Lily said tremulously, appealing to me. 'They've taken his ribbon. His favourite ribbon.'

I put one hand on my mother's arm and steered her towards the kitchen door, saying gently, 'Lily, why don't you and Beau sit in the drawing room? I'll find his ribbon and bring it to you in a few minutes.'

Then I turned on the real troublemaker and delivered my ultimatum.

'You must make your own laundry arrangements in the future, Clarissa. I should ask Mrs Crowdy if there's anyone in the village who takes in washing. Or look in the *Yellow Pages* and find a laundry who will collect and deliver. When Parc Celli opens we shall be sending the house washing to Penryn. I can give you the address, if you like. But you'll have to deal with this yourself.'

The lady was bewildered. She turned from one to the other of us, long white hands outstretched. I thought of the lilies of the field who sowed not. I intended this one to reap.

'But darling Flavia, Vera dear, my babies haven't any clean socks.'

Bella and Bee clutched her skirt and stared from Vera to me, round-eyed. I could tell that they were revising their former good opinion of us. I no longer cared what anyone thought of me.

'Then I suggest that you use the laundry room here. Vera and I won't be needing it today. And I must stress that we're both too busy, from now on, to help you out. You must look after yourself – and your children. And please keep out of the kitchen altogether.'

Behind me I heard Vera murmur, 'That'll be tell'n her!'

She and I at least had arrived at an understanding.

'But I don't know how to do washing. I've never had to do it.'

'Oh, it's very simple,' I said, smiling like the proverbial tiger. 'Pick up this basket and follow me. I'll show you how to do it in five minutes.'

Later, when I was drinking tea with Vera, I said uneasily, 'Whatever happened to Tom? I never saw him go.'

'Oh,' she said, subdued and sorry, 'he come through when you was in the laundry with Mrs Gibbon. But he wouldn't stop. Some changed he is, these days. Don't have his supper with you nor me, Mrs Flavia.'

I was at once amused and delighted by my new title. She had elevated me to Lily's rank. A favourite. But I felt the sting of Tom's rejection sharply.

Vera said, head bent, 'Did you know that Tom was my sweetheart, once?'

Diplomatically, I answered, 'I know that he's very fond of you.'

Vera consulted the tea leaves in her cup, sighed, and refilled it. 'Brian's a good man, and a good 'usband, as 'usbands go. But I did like having Tom back again.'

'I can understand that,' I said slowly. 'He's both thoughtful and kind.'

She looked up at me with those trusting blue eyes.

'I still think the world of Tom, but he don't feel the same about me.'

I was moved to be sorry, and in another way to be glad.

'There aren't nothing wrong between us,' she said. 'I don't want you to think that.'

So I had misjudged him once again.

She looked down at her hands, which had worked so hard for so long.

'But he do make me feel somebody special, see, Mrs Flavia.'

I reflected that that was part of his charm, and was sorry for her, and wanted her to be happy.

'But you are somebody special,' I said reassuringly. 'You're my right hand. I couldn't manage without you. We've been working side by side for nearly half a year. I count on you as I count on myself.'

That pleased her. She smiled a little, but was too sad to smile much.

'But Brian have been teasy about Tom. And there's talk in the village of Tom and me. Folks do like to talk. And Mother says I'm living in a fool's paradise. Tom wasn't no good to me then, she says, and he aren't no good to me now. I've made my bed with Brian Angwin, Mother says, and I must lie on it. And I daresay she be right.'

Vera was mourning and needed to be comforted. And she had trusted me.

I put my hand on hers, and said, 'Use your talents, Vera. That's what I did, and what I do. Use your talents. It's the best cure for sorrow. By the time you've trained for a year here as my assistant you'll be able to find a job anywhere. You'll be working full time when we open, and I'm putting up your wages too. That'll be something to reckon with.'

A shimmer overlaid the trusty blue. She nodded. Smiled. Wiped away the shimmer.

I squeezed her hand, got up, and said briskly, 'And now I must see what the Lady of Shalott has done to our laundry room!'

But I also had my mind on Humphrey's possible reaction to the scene with Clarissa, should she report it to him or to the zealots of Elinglaze.

Turning back, I said, 'I just hope she isn't going to make trouble with Mr Jarvis or in the village, Vera. She is one of his cousins, you know.'

But Vera despatched this notion with disdain.

'Far enough back!' she said contemptuously. 'And on the grandfather's side. Along with they Rices and that lot. No, don't you bother yourself none about her, Mrs Flavia! She aren't one of us. She be one of they Bristol foreigners.'

Relevés

CHAPTER TWELVE

In Humphrey's childhood Parc Celli had employed a coachman, a groom and a stable-boy for the horses and carriage, and a chauffeur for the car. Two gardeners and a boy, a gamekeeper, an under-keeper, a water bailiff, a mason and a carpenter worked on the estate. Indoors a butler and a housekeeper headed the staff. Chamber and housemaids kept Kelly Park spotless. A cook directed the kitchen, two under-cooks and a scullery maid. A valet and a lady's maid served the master and mistress. A nanny nurtured the son and heir. And always at the master's homecoming a little platoon of servants would be assembled to greet him.

But on this radiant afternoon in late July, more than half a century later, only Vera, Alice and Ben Quick, Tom Faull and Martin Skeggs line up outside the front door, punctually at five minutes to four, to await the squire's arrival. The great gates are open, and Sean Angwin has been posted as a look-out. Meanwhile the rest of us sit on the lawn, prepared to serve tea the moment Humphrey appears.

Tonight we shall be an intimate four for dinner. Vera is coming back to help me with last minute preparations and to give Bella and Bee their high tea in the kitchen. She is also bringing her daughter Marianne to wait, so that I can join my guests. The dinner is arranged from starter to Stilton and port, with leeway for Humphrey's appetite. On the cork notice-board in the kitchen I have pinned my hand-written menus for his visit. Sauces and sorbets, prawns and Dover soles are in the freezer. In the refrigerator lies a tray of fillet steaks. One of Tom's friends knows a gamekeeper who has been culling deer. So we have an unexpected haunch of venison, as well as the usual selection of game, about which I no longer ask qeustions. And all this so that Humphrey's holiday will be as congenial, and my part in it as uncomplicated as possible; so that we may enjoy ourselves and come to that very necessary understanding before Kelly Park can be opened to the public.

But I shall be astonished if he arrives at all, let alone at four o'clock as he promised, for he is driving himself in the Bentley. In my concern for Humphrey's safety I have consulted Tom Faull, and we have decided that if the squire has neither arrived nor telephoned by six o'clock tonight, Tom will head Victoria towards Plymouth to see what has befallen him.

Not for the first time events conspire to make a fool of me.

Sean Angwin now sprints up the drive shouting, 'Mr Jarvis be a-coming!'

The short line of servants straightens up. The tea-table company rises to its feet. Clarissa plucks out her handkerchief, ready for an emotional reunion. Lily's diaphanous stole floats behind her as she teeters on high heels across the lawn. Beau frisks after it. Bella and Bee, forgiving and forgiven, demurely clasp hands and follow the welcoming committee. And just as the stable-yard clock chimes four Humphrey's Bentley sweeps round the bend in the drive, and draws to a standstill in exact alignment with the steps.

Tom Faull has been patronising the Oxfam shop in honour of the occasion, and is looking unusually smart in an open-necked shirt, grey flannels and a navy-blue blazer. His hair and beard have been trimmed in Humphrey's honour, and I must admit that he looks every inch the gentleman. I think of the pretty parlour-maid and the lonely widower, and wonder once again, as he steps forward and opens the passenger door with an inclination of the head in homage.

The passenger door?

I should have known that Humphrey is incapable of arriving on time, of driving so smoothly and judging the correct place to stop. Humphrey has been driven. We must cater for an unexpected guest. Companion or servant? Dining room or kitchen? Five for dinner, anyway. No problem. The menu can be stretched.

'Well, well, well,' I hear Humphrey cry. 'Ha, ha, ha!'

He is upon me. His bulk blocks my line of sight. I feel his body shaking with mirth, smell Floris aftershave, and receive a damp kiss on each cheek before I can see the chauffeur. The guilt in Humphrey's voice, his too jovial laughter, should have told me the identity of this stranger before he did.

'Flavia dearest, you'll never guess who came with me.'

Who indeed? Walking jauntily towards me, hair slicked back, smile in place, dapper as ever, is the last person I ever expected to see at Kelly Park.

What do I feel? God knows! Total confusion of mind and emotions. A prickle of apprehension and desire. And a profound wish that we had met without an audience. I see that Humphrey is looking coy: hoping no doubt that he has done the right thing by accident.

'Hello there, Flick! How's life?' says Jack Rice.

Years of learning how not to mind in public come to my rescue.

I place a cold hand in his warm one, and reply airily, 'Never better!'

For I must not seem disturbed.

I am grateful to Clarissa, whose vanity draws her forward with her babies clinging prettily to her skirts, crying, 'Dear Cousin Jack! We've never met but mamma's told me all about you. She was evacuated to Parc Celli with you during the war. You remember? Valerie Jarvis?'

'Could I ever forget?' cries Jack, who has clearly forgotten, and kisses her extended hand gallantly. 'Haven't seen Val since she married Jim Starky. How are they both these days?'

While these cousins at some uncertain remove swarm into the branches of the family tree, Bella and Bee hop up and down smiling, hoping for sweets or cash from this unforeseen relative, and Humphrey inspects his household troops. A few cordial words with each of them draws a curtsey from Alice Quick, despite arthritic knee joints. Ben Quick and Martin Skeggs duck their heads and touch their bald brows. Vera and Sean, being younger and more democratic, simply nod and smile and answer politely.

In this reunion of the squire and his people I am naturally excluded. Also, personally speaking, I am in total disarray. Of course it is unforgivable of Humphrey to invite Jack to Kelly Park when he knows how I feel about the man, but it is even more disquieting that Jack should agree to come, or worse still should have invited himself, for he does nothing without a purpose. And what might that purpose be?

I am momentarily diverted by Humphrey saying roguishly, 'Now Jack! Now Tom! Do you remember each other after all these years?'

Yes, they have remembered, and do not relish the memory. Tom's black eyes grow denser. Jack passes a hand over his well-groomed head and smiles into the distance, as if Tom were a cloud in the blue sky. Then he recovers.

'Hello there, Tom! Take these bags up for me, will you, like a good fellow?'

Tom does not answer him. Turning his back on the order he speaks to Humphrey politely.

'Now, sir, let me take your bags up for you.'

Oh, how Humphrey enjoys this interchange. Another family joke about which I know nothing.

In lordly fashion Jack has acknowledged the staff's greetings. Now he signals to Sean Angwin to pick up his luggage. I am disquieted to see that he treats them as servants, whereas Humphrey treats them as friends who render him a service.

Now the squire wipes his eyes, places one arm across Jack's shoulders and the other across mine, and says fatuously, 'Good to be together again!' And as we mount the steps, 'Home sweet home, eh?'

'It's looking a damned sight sweeter than it did when I was here last,' Jack answers irreverently, and Humphrey neighs with delight.

They have made up their differences and come to some mutual agreement. About me? Certainly without me!

Tom and Sean Angwin follow us, carrying the bags. As always I look for a likeness between them, and would ponder on it, except that I have more important concerns than Tom Faull's illegitimate progeny. I note that my guests' luggage seems excessive for a long weekend. More like a long month.

In the hall Humphrey's arms fall from our shoulders and he

stands alone, pale eyes watering. The sun comes through the mullioned windows and lays down a carpet of rainbows. He bows his head, and for fully a minute we are silent with him: Jack amused, me forbearing, the others understanding.

On returning to the present the squire says briskly, 'Wash first. Tea after. Flavia, where are we going to put old Jack?'

We have at the moment only four of the bedrooms complete. Humphrey occupies the Green Room, with shower. Clarissa and the children spread over the adjoining White and Blue Rooms opposite, also with shower. Lily has turned the Lilac Room into her personal boudoir: no shower but adjacent to the bathroom. The other two are shrouded and swept bare.

'What about the Hall Room, next door to yours?' I say. 'We can make it habitable, if not smart.'

Vera will unroll the carpet, take off the covers, dust round and make up the bed while we're at tea. But who will play waitress then?

I address my unexpected visitor laconically, but avoid his eyes.

'I'm afraid the room's somewhat Spartan, Jack. The curtains and bed hangings are at the cleaner's. It's due to be decorated next Wednesday.'

Hint, hint. I expect you both to be gone by then.

'Oh, I don't mind. I can kip anywhere,' says Jack, refusing to be undermined.

'And whereabouts are you, my dear girl?' Humphrey asks tenderly.

'I'm in the housekeeper's room on the next floor.'

'But is that adequate? Is that right?' he enquires, shocked.

'Of course it's right,' I answer, far too pointedly. 'Good rooms are for guests. House staff must make do.' I amend this ungracious statement. 'I'm very comfortable there, truly, Humpty. You can come and inspect it if you don't believe me.'

His bottom lip is pendulous. A puzzled frown peaks his brows.

'I thought you would have taken Grandmama's room. I expected us all to be together, my dear. I've promised Jack a good old-fashioned house party. I don't want you hiding away in the kitchen.'

I manage to frame the truth in a fairly vivacious fashion, hoping he will grasp its deeper meaning.

'But the meals won't cook themselves, Humphrey. Someone has to look after everyone else, and that someone is obviously me!'

And I grow cold, and colder yet, as I realise that this new partnership springs from different motives and has different objectives. I am in business, and in earnest. But he has been given the means to return to his childhood and is playing the same old sweet song over again.

My former partner takes in every nuance, and smiles and smiles, cat-like beneath his narrow moustache.

The Green Room faces south, and in the late light of a summer afternoon is both mellow and reflective. Humphrey runs a soft white hand over the carved bedposts, strokes the embroidered coverlet, and sits down smiling. His face is guileless, rapturous.

'Everything is as it was,' he says, with infinite satisfaction. And turning to us, his entourage, courteous but brooking no denial, 'I'd like to have a private word with Tom first. You're dining with us tonight, of course, Tom?'

Tom and I glance at each other, for neither of us had expected this.

I say, 'Of course he is, Humphrey!'

And in my mind I slice the duck more thinly.

'Good, good. Then if you'll all be so kind as to leave us for a while, I shall join you for tea directly.'

I should have been warned by his use of the word *directly*: the Cornish equivalent of *mañana*. The clock is close on half-past five when he pads across the lawn, rubbing his hands, wearing a cream tussore suit, an old-fashioned straw boater and two-tone shoes.

Vera has had to return to the bosom of her family to feed them, which means that Jack's room must wait until later, but Tom places himself at my disposal. The meeting with Humphrey has healed and restored him. He is wearing the look of the well-beloved once more. I wish I were, and know I am not and have no reason to do so.

'Now, Flavia,' he says, rubbing his hands, 'I can tell that you're short-staffed. So just tell me what I can do to help.'

'You can buttle for me, if you would, please, Tom!'

So he tramps to and from the kitchen, keeps me supplied with hot water, and hands round cups and plates and cucumber sandwiches with great good humour. Apparently at his ease, he jokes with Humphrey, avoids Jack as far as is possible, ignores Lily's efforts to crush him, and keeps the children under pleasant but firm control. I preside over Grandmama's Georgian silver tea-pot, cut the cardamom cake and exchange small talk, while pondering new problems and rearranging my timetable.

I am not surprised by the evident intimacy and good fellowship between Humphrey and Tom Faull. Plainly, the others are, but they accept their host's eccentricity in this as in all matters. And though Tom addresses Humphrey as sir, it is not a servile sir but an easy and affectionate sir: the sir of a favourite on excellent terms with his prince.

'How's the Elinglaze cricket club doing these days, Tom?'

'Not too badly, sir. Win some, lose some.'

'And how are you doing personally, Tom?'

'Three for seventeen last Saturday. Plus a dropped catch. We play Trebeddo away tomorrow.'

'We must all come and watch you, Tom! Everyone!' addressing his attentive audience. 'We shall drive over to Trebeddo tomorrow afternoon to back the local team. Flavia, my dear,' turning to me in afterthought, 'we shall have to set out at one o'clock, so could we lunch early and dine late tomorrow?'

'Yes, of course.' I suspect that we shall also dine somewhat late this evening.

'And could we take a picnic tea with us? There are some wonderful old hampers somewhere. Mrs Quick could find them.'

'I know where they are, Humphrey. Yes, a picnic would be a lovely idea.'

And if they all go out I can catch up on my altered schedule in peace.

'But you're coming with us, aren't you? Oh, do, Flavia! I shall hate it if you have no free time.'

Free time indeed. He must be joking.

'Dearest girl?' Humphrey persists, and clasps my hand so plaintively that I say, withdrawing it, that I will see what I can do. But my smile is insincere and they all perceive that I have no intention of going with them. I shall get up early tomorrow and prepare everything, and then sit out in the garden by my blissful self.

'Good heavens!' Humphrey cries, consulting his fob watch. 'Time we changed for dinner! Flavia, shall we eat in the hall tonight?'

The table has been laid in the dining room. Never mind. Transfer the contents and lay two extra places. But the distance between kitchen and hall is far greater than that between kitchen and dining room, and it will be difficult to keep the food hot. I wonder if Tom could mend that ancient portable hot-cupboard?

Humphrey is still reorganising my schedule.

'And we'll let the children dine with us for once, shall we? Did you pack their best bibs and tuckers, Clarissa? Oh, good! They can sit up straight, and look pretty, and eat their boiled eggs and toast soldiers while we gorge on richer provender!' In explanation of this gesture, for Humphrey is not particularly fond of young children, he adds, 'Grandmama used to allow me down to dinner when I had been especially good, and Bella and Bee really are most awfully sweet.'

So we must lay four extra places, put high cushions on two of the chairs, and serve different food for Bella and Bee at the same time as our own. It was easier to cook a set menu for forty at Bon Appétit!

Humphrey recollects his general factotum, whose smile by this time is fixed by sheer willpower.

'But it is not I alone who must decide! What do you say, Flavia? It is Flavia who has to look after us all!'

So he did get the message but is merely paying it lip service.

I say coolly, 'I think that can be managed.'

For this is Humphrey's house and Humphrey's holiday, and I must not feel beset. I must look on it as good practice for the future. Have I not learned that the customer is always right, even when he or she is not? And don't I know that emergencies are a part of life, and taking them in one's stride is the mark of a professional? Still, I am irked.

'Oh, and let's have a grand old log fire in the hall,' says Humphrey, inspired. 'Unless there is a heatwave the English summer is considerably enhanced by a fire in the evening.'

Ask Tom if he will chop logs and light the fire while they dress.

'Oh, that will be the finishing touch!' I say ironically.

I mean it my way, but Humphrey takes it his way and kisses my hand.

Tom and I collect the tea things while the others wander off. I have observed the tension between himself and Jack with some interest.

I say, as we stack the trays, 'I didn't realise that you and Jack Rice knew each other so well.'

To which he replies briefly, 'It was a long time ago and I never expected to see him again.' And returns the ball to my court. 'He was your partner at the bistro, wasn't he?'

I can find no answer to this, apart from a feeble, 'Yes, he was.'

Tom looks at me keenly for a moment or two, hands on hips, and then says, 'Seven years, wasn't it? I remember your telling me, the first evening I arrived here. That's a long time. I'm surprised you didn't ask him down before. Both being in the same sort of business.'

'We haven't been in touch recently. He's been abroad.'

'I see,' says Tom. And then, 'I'll carry these trays in, Flavia. They're too heavy for you.'

And marches off. Subject closed.

Vera returns, bringing with her a sixteen-year-old maiden with a long rope of butter-coloured hair, whom she introduces as, 'My Marianne. I named her after Marianne Faithfull and she do be a bit alike, don't she?'

I agree.

'And I was named after Vera Lynn, but I never looked nothin' like her.'

I agree again and we move on to more relevant matters.

Being short-staffed we have to entrust Marianne to lay the hall table by herself, after an initial lesson in the placing of glasses and cutlery. Tom automatically begins to wash up, humming Schubert's 'Death and the Maiden' under his breath. I am concerned about Grandmama's Royal Doulton teacups but he seems competent enough and besides I have no choice. I must assemble the food in time for dinner, which will now be served at eight-fifteen. Vera, in this first trial run, shows initiative as well as common sense, which is one comfort.

The three of us talk aloud as we work, expecting no answer. Our diverse remarks are not addressed to each other but spring from personal preoccupations.

'Thank God I resisted the temptation to roast a poussin apiece, or do Humphrey's favourite tournedos. I shall get fourteen good slices out of that ballotine of duck, which leaves two slices over for second helpings. Wish I hadn't done individual starters, we need two more. Well, I can go without . . . '

'I don't mind washing up. Not me. But what we need is an industrial dishwasher. I know the manager of a hotel who has a dishwasher for sale. Buy it for a quarter the price of a new one. Good old machine he is, too . . . '

'And now she be leaving they dirty clothes all over the laundry floor and hanging her tights in the best bathroom . . . '

Jack Rice sticks a smooth head round the kitchen door and says, 'Someone on the telephone for you, Flick!' He sniffs ostentatiously, like a Bisto kid and cries, 'What delicious aromas!' Then adds maddeningly, 'Why on earth haven't you got a phone in the kitchen?'

My answer is brief and acid.

'Because the telephone company has promised to put one in *directly*!'

'Ah! The year 2000! So soon?' says Jack, refusing to share my troubles.

Just like old times is written all over his smooth face. I walk past him without answering.

Leave me alone and mind your own business is written all over mine.

His responses are so familiar. For months I have missed Jack, and his quick tongue and his sly-sour wit. And now that he is here, and the first confusion of meeting is over, I find that I have recovered from him as from a long and unpleasant illness. Free, I shout within myself. Free! But there is no time to savour that knowledge for the moment.

The receiver lies on the hall table like a black trap and I lift it warily and say, 'Hello. Flavia Pollard speaking.'

A young man's voice says politely, nervously, 'This is Pat, Mum . . . your son, Patrick.'

The hall is illumined. In an instant I am breathless with joy.

'Pat? Oh, Pat! How lovely! I wasn't expecting you to ring.'

For they were supposed to be in Scotland with Guy and Anne until the middle of August.

'I've got Jeremy with me. He's mouthing hello.'

'And hello to both of you. How lovely! How are you both?' A familiar terror assailed me. 'Is anything wrong? Can't you come down here at the end of the month?'

'Well, in a way, no.'

I knew it. Guy had switched dates again.

'Scotland's been cancelled, Mum. Anne caught some sort of virus and we had to come home early. Hasn't Dad rung to tell you?'

'No. I haven't heard from him,' and lest that sounds hostile I add, 'yet.'

A whispered discussion between the two of them. Pat's voice returns, sounding uncertain.

'Mum, I hope it's all right. You did say we could come any time . . . '

Oh, surely they don't want to come next week? I'll never get rid of Humphrey and Jack if the boys turn up.

' . . . and Dad and Anne are fussing over her virus thing. So we thought – well – why not now? So we left a note for Dad, asking him to ring you, and set out at the crack of dawn this morning, with our rucksacks and tent. We thought it'd take much longer to get down here. We planned to camp on the way. But we hitched a couple of lifts and got as far as Devon.'

Next week was too optimistic. They will be here tomorrow.

Stoically, I ask, 'Pat, whereabouts in Devon are you now?'

He answers apprehensively, 'Actually, we thumbed another lift from there, too. We're in a telephone box in Helston.'

Helston? They are here. This moment. Two more for dinner, and another bedroom to be prepared. Well, no help for it. Remember not to sound as overtaxed as you feel.

'Darling, how wonderful! Tell me exactly where the telephone box is, and then wait outside. I'll find someone to pick you up, but it will take about half an hour for them to reach you.'

'Mum, don't bother. We can have a cup of tea somewhere and catch a bus.'

'At this time in the evening you can't do either,' I said drily, 'because they don't exist. But if you'll stay near the phone box someone will come as soon as possible. I can't come myself because I'm cooking the dinner.'

'Mum, I do hope it's all right . . . '

'Oh, it's wonderful!' I say with all the conviction I can muster. 'Absolutely wonderful. You don't know how thrilled I am.'

And I am. I am. But I wanted them to myself. I saw this, the first real holiday I had been able to offer them, as being momentous to the three of us. My role in their lives had been such a minor one. Now I could provide them with a home that was worth visiting, spend time with them, so that we could get to know one another. Whereas now they will become part of the hurly-burly while I run round looking after everyone else.

Inside me someone is crying silently.

Tom will drive into Helston for me. I will not ask a favour of Jack Rice. And dinner must be delayed yet again, and the menu recreated. Forget the present starter. No time to make more. So heat up a batch of frozen consommé, add sherry and tomato purée. Consommé madrilène. Defrost a dozen home-made dinner rolls to fill up the corners. Thank God that I prepared two cold desserts, in deference to Humphrey's sweet tooth. Enough to go round. But we'll need more potatoes. Make them look special. Served creamed as well as sautéd. And what about that over-worked ballotine of duck? No time to fry up a separate meal for the boys in the kitchen. Nor can Vera cook for them and serve up our food and the children's eggs as well. Besides, the boys must eat with us. And we need the top of the range for soup, vegetables and the *bain-marie*. So?

So slice the duck thinner, and no seconds for Humphrey. Can't be helped if it seems a bit sparse. Add an extra vegetable. Something easy that looks exotic. Break a house rule about fresh vegebles, and use the emergency frozen peas and frozen baby carrots, ecorated with sprigs of mint. Serve with a flourish. *Petits Pois flamande*. Who's to know the difference?

I summon up enough fortitude to look into the drawing room where they are all laughing, drinking and chatting together, and speak gaily to our host.

'Humphrey, dinner will be delayed until about a quarter to nine. We have two extra guests arriving. My harum-scarum sons hitchhiked down to surprise me!'

Glass in hand, he turns on me his face of shining hospitality.

'My dear girl, how lovely for you – and for all of us!' And to the assembled company, 'My charming godson and his brother will join us. Now this is what I call a house party. Just like the old days . . . '

I could break down and cry but haven't the time.

In the kitchen Tom Faull is attacking the hot-cupboard with a blow-lamp.

'Pipe was leaking,' he shouts, over the roaring flame. 'Don't you fret. I'm just going to solder it.'

'Tom, you've forgotten to light the fire in the hall!' I shout back over the roar. 'And I need you to do something else as well – at the same time if possible but preferably sooner.'

'I'll light the fire, Mrs Flavia,' says Vera, placating me, 'and then I can keep an eye on Marianne with they cut-glass glasses. She be quick but sometimes she be careless and we don't want none broken.'

'Thank you, Vera. And Vera, will you peel another pan of potatoes and put them on to boil. And Tom! Tom! I'm speaking to you!'

He lets out the blow-lamp and mutters to himself that he bets the bugger won't bloody well light again. I tone my voice down and ask him meekly if he would mind picking up the boys in Helston. He gives me a long look, in which I read amusement, understanding and something I cannot define.

'Which do you want me to do first?' he asks pleasantly.

'Please pick up the boys, and forget the soldering for the moment. They're waiting outside a telephone box next door to Bowden's.'

'Right you are!'

He sets down the blow-lamp, scrambles to his feet, and go[es] out. A couple of minutes later I hear Victoria refusing to start up. Five minutes after that I hear another vehicle leave the yard, and [I] am standing in puzzlement when Vera comes back for candle-ends because the logs won't light.

'Oh, that'll be Eddy Johns's van that you was interested in,' she says, in answer to my question. 'Tom did tell him to leave it with us this week, so's you could try it out.'

I am now overwrought and Tom takes far too long to bring the boys back. So joy is mingled with apprehension when the van shoots into the yard and discharges two tall slim youths. My sons are reserved and slightly wary. Tom has evidently tried to make friends with them, and not entirely succeeded. Still, he makes the best of it. His grin is genial, his black eyes lustrous, his air piratical. They remain polite but sceptical.

He rubs his hands, saying, 'Here they are then. Safe and sound. Now all you have to do is say the word – and I'll do it.'

Patrick and Jeremy rid themselves of their rucksacks, and hover shyly by the door. I too hang back, uncertain whether one kisses young men of fifteen and seventeen. How they have grown and changed in the past six months, and how beautiful they are, with their flushed young faces and clear grey eyes. And what will they make of me, so insignificant and harassed in the cauldron of my kitchen?

We stand and smile awkwardly. Make our way towards each other. Hug, kiss, laugh a little, in the attempt to disguise the fact that we are strangers. They are too ready with their explanations and apologies.

'Thought you'd be by yourself . . . '

'No idea there was a house party . . . '

'That don't matter none!' says Vera roundly. 'Family be welcome any time.'

And she comes forward to be introduced, wiping her hands on her apron before she shakes theirs.

Marianne eyes Patrick openly and brings the rope of butter-coloured hair over one slim shoulder. I notice that both sons are very pleased to meet Marianne, and much more at their ease with her than with me. The Angwins have lightened the atmosphere considerably.

Patrick says, embarrassed, 'We're a trifle smashed, I'm afraid, Mum. Mr Faull took us to the Blue Anchor for a glass of spingo.'

'Oh, Tom, you didn't!' I cry. 'They're both under age!'

'Only a half apiece,' says Tom sheepishly, 'as a Cornish welcome.'

He was not too happy about being addressed as Mr Faull, and I guessed he had been skilfully snubbed. Well, he is not the only one. I have been snubbed more times than I care to recollect.

'We've been hearing about your new van, Mum,' says Jeremy, who is younger and more malleable than Patrick. 'Mr Faull's been telling us how useful it will be, and how much food it will hold.'

Tom joined in, saying, 'And I've told them I'll do Victoria up for them, so that they can knock about in it while they're here.'

'Awfully kind,' said Pat.

'I didn't know you could drive,' I said.

I know nothing about my sons.

'Oh yes. I've just got my driving licence.'

Tom says quickly, 'Now, Flavia, you tell me where you're putting these young men of yours and I can take them upstairs and show them where everything is. Be one less thing for you to fret yourself about.' He turns to the boys and adds, 'We must do all we can for your mum, because she's got her hands full tonight.'

'Yes, of course,' says Patrick. 'We certainly don't want to be in the way. Do we, Jem?'

Vera is wearing what my father would call 'an old-fashioned look'. She does not understand this sort of relationship. But nor do I, Vera. Nor do I.

I speak matter of factly, as if all was well.

'We'll put them in the room next to Mr Rice, Tom. And will you find them some towels from the airing cupboard, please?'

Then I say to the boys, 'We'll sort your room out later. Meanwhile have a quick wash and change, and be down again as soon as you can. I'll join you just before dinner.'

'Is it a shirt and tie do?' Patrick asks the kitchen at large.

'Yes, it certainly is,' I say tersely. 'And, Tom, on your way out would you please suggest to Mr Jarvis that he serves a final round of drinks? And we'd better forget about mending that hot-cupboard. We haven't time to sort it out tonight. Perhaps you could do it tomorrow? Oh, and would you mind chopping up some more logs, and keep the fire going in the hall? And later on we shall need some help with the bedroom furniture and carpets.'

'Aye, aye, captain!' says Tom, and stands to attention and salutes smartly, which everyone but Patrick and Jeremy finds vastly amusing.

I dash upstairs and change. Cover my finery with a clean white apron. Slice the duck and return it to the warming oven. Taste the soup for seasoning, test the rolls for crispness. My orders are brief and to the point.

'Marianne, tell them that dinner is served. Vera, I'll come into the kitchen between each course. Just have everything ready for me to inspect. Now will you pass me the tomato garnish? And line this wicker basket with a dinner napkin, pile the dinner rolls up and cover them over. That's right. Are the soup plates really hot? Good. Bring me the butter curls from the fridge.'

I turn to my stalwart helper, who has accomplished all his tasks and is ready for more.

'Tom, could you be a dear and push the trolley into the hall for us? And please, please, push it very carefully. Nothing, but nothing, must be slopped.'

A few fine strips of scarlet on the tureen of clear red-gold soup. A pyramid of crusty rolls. Butter curls on a fresh lettuce leaf.

I survey the result.

For the first time in hours I smile with sheer relief.

We shall dine in style, after all.

CHAPTER THIRTEEN

The day was beautiful, bright, blue and breezy. I had been up since six o'clock and so had Tom. Everyone else slept on. Since my prepared menu was too meagre for our extended house party I was creating a huge *boeuf bourguignon* and a mound of rice for the evening, while collecting things together for a picnic tea. And as Vera and Marianne were not coming in to help before six o'clock, Tom had volunteered to act as scullion in return for his breakfast. Despite the subject of Eddy Johns's van, about which he must be tackled later, I felt kindly towards him. For under the present circumstances he was not only useful but indispensable.

'So you've changed your mind about the cricket match? Coming with us after all?' he said, peeling onions and wiping his sleeve across his eyes.

'I couldn't resist seeing the Elinglaze fast bowler triumph, you see!' I replied flippantly.

'Don't you give me that!' said Tom, and chuckled. 'You'd never have come if those two lads of yours hadn't turned up.'

This was true.

'It's a good thing we've got three lots of transport between us,' Tom offered, light and airy but waiting to be bitten.

I said nothing.

Relieved, he continued, 'I'll spend the morning on Victoria, so that your lads can drive him.'

I said, in apology, 'They don't mean to be formal with you, Tom. They're just feeling strange at the moment.'

'That's all right,' said Tom. 'They can help me with the car. There's nothing better than getting oiled up and having a bit of a swear together, to make friends. And, talking of transport for this afternoon, I don't see how all of you are going to fit in the Bentley.'

My knife paused over the chuck steak. Nor did I.

'I tell you the best way we can manage it,' said Tom. 'I've got to be there early. So supposing I take the squire with me in the van? Then Mr Rice can drive you and the other two ladies, and Bella and Bee can sit on your knees.'

'That's a very good idea,' I said, impressed.

'The team'll be proud to meet Mr Jarvis,' Tom went on. 'The family have always stood high in Elinglaze. His grandfather gave us our ground, you know, and took an interest in us. And Mr Jarvis used to come and watch us play when I was a youngster. He knows a lot about cricket. Turned over a good arm in his time. Have you ever seen a cricket match, Flavia?'

'Humphrey took me and Jack to Lord's once or twice. It seemed to be a leisurely sort of game. Rather elegant and terribly English. I dozed off in the sun between wickets, but the shouts woke me up. And when anyone was caught out they all leaped in the air like ballet dancers.'

'Well, this won't be like Lord's,' said Tom, 'but it should be a decent match. Trebeddo's a good team. I haven't played them before. I'll draw you a diagram, if you like, and write down the main points so that you get a flavour of the game. Oh, and you might need to wrap up. Weather looks as if it might be sunny this afternoon, but it could rain, and with this breeze it'll get cold in the evening.'

I resolved to pack a couple of woollies, a pair of sunglasses, a mackintosh, and my notebook, so that I could rework my menus between wickets.

'Do you good to have an afternoon off,' said Tom.

We worked peaceably together in the sunny kitchen, in the quiet house.

Trebeddo cricket ground must have been constructed on a Saxon burial site, for the field sloped away from the pitch in a most astonishing manner. Consequently players on the near side of the spectator seemed unnaturally tall, while those on the far side had been apparently amputated at the knees, the thighs or the waist. From one end of the pitch the bowler appeared head first, toiling up an incline. I checked my diagram. The man who took the position of deep long on was a mere bust against a background of scrub and straggling trees. And the scoreboard could only be read in its entirety from the pavilion.

We were quite a party.

Patrick and Jeremy and Jack, supervised by Humphrey, struggled chivalrously with folding chairs, cushions, cardigans, car rugs, raincoats and picnic baskets until Lily and Clarissa and I were settled. Then sank down beside us. Tom's influence was made manifest in my sons. They sat on the grass at my feet, now much more at their ease, and talked about Victoria. Inspection of her engine had proved to be a delightfully dirty and rewarding job, and I noticed that they were on first name terms with Tom.

The sun shone brightly but could not warm us because of a persistent breeze, which blew down our necks and round our ankles, carrying with it an odour of pigsties from a farm next to the cricket ground. The men constructed a windbreak of car rugs and we kept our handkerchiefs at the ready.

Since we were Elinglaze's only supporters we stayed together, fortified by the Bentley, Victoria and the van, and surrounded by a battalion of Trebeddo cars. Lily and Clarissa were lamentably overdressed for the occasion, as if they were about to open a fête, and the little girls seemed to have been attired in frilled organdie since Humphrey arrived. Behind us a scatter of mothers and grandmothers exchanged conversation, some of it palpably about ourselves, and kept an eye on their children who were playing on a patch of grass behind the pavilion.

'It seems to be quite a family occasion,' said Clarissa, with a pleasure which was soon explained. For she answered Bella's and Bee's query by saying joyfully, 'Yes, darlings, run along and find some new little friends!'

I watched the two little girls running gleefully, hand in hand, into a crowd of strangers. I supposed, and hoped, that they could look after themselves through childhood because their mother certainly would not. Humphrey selected a cigar from his case. He must have been the only person there who really wanted to come.

'I should have thought,' said Jack, lounging at his ease, 'that a man who regularly buys a season ticket for Lord's would hardly be interested in watching the antics of a set of country bumpkins.'

'Then you would be quite wrong, my dear fellow!' said Humphrey severely. 'I have an enormous admiration for village cricket.' He became philosophical. 'I know of nothing more delightful than a good old-fashioned game of cricket between country parishes – where each team plays, to quote Mary Russell Mitford, "for honour and a supper, glory and half-a-crown a man".'

'Oh, I didn't know they were paid and given supper!' I said, interested.

Humphrey glanced reprovingly at me and cut the end off his cigar with some deliberation.

'Not nowadays, my dear. I am speaking of the nineteenth century.'

'So it's different now?'

'Not in any way that matters, my dear. *Spiritually* it is the same!'

'It looks spiritual,' I said frivolously. 'All those white clothes . . . '

'I'm afraid you're talking nonsense, Flavia. So there is no further point– Oh, my God! I had not noticed. The wretches are an umpire short and that rogue, Tom Faull, will assure them I am available!'

And he stood up in his apprehension and glared around as if to find a means of escape.

'But if you admire village cricket so much . . . ' I said unsympathetically.

'Hide me!' cried Humphrey, blundering among us like an overladen bee.

But Tom was already striding jauntily in our direction with a muscular Cornishman by his side.

'I shall never forgive him!' Humphrey whispered, turning to meet his fate.

'Mr Jarvis, sir, our captain would like a word with you.'

Humphrey's face was suffused.

'Ah ha, ha! Tom, my boy. And Jim Jewell, of course! Met you earlier, didn't I? Yes, yes. Your grandfather was one of our gamekeepers in my father's day. Ha, ha, ha! What? Tom has told you that I'm an expert? Aha, ha! Nothing of the sort – though I've turned a useful arm over in my day, you know. Taken a few wickets. Ah ha, ha! Yes, well, I'm perfectly capable of umpiring but I doubt you have a white coat in my size. I'm a shade stouter than I used to be! Aha, aha.'

'Most Cornishmen are your size, sir,' said Tom pleasantly.

'Oh, yes. No trouble about tha-at, Mr Jarvis,' said Jim Jewell, ignoring his reluctance. 'And we're very much obliged to you for stepping in.'

'But will these dear ladies be all right on their own?' Humphrey asked tenderly, as though we were being abandoned in a red-light district at night.

I said briskly, 'Don't be ridiculous, Humpty. Run along and enjoy yourself.'

'Darling Humphrey. *Do* go and save the day!' pleaded Clarissa.

'Go on, old chap. Show 'em what you're made of!' cried Jack, laughing uncharitably.

Clutching her hat as the breeze whipped it sideways, Lily murmured, 'Humphrey dear, you'll look so splendid all in white. Like Dr Kildare or one of Ouida's guardsmen – now was it Ouida?'

Beau, sitting up in her lap, barked his approval. And Humphrey was led disconsolately away.

The Elinglaze First Eleven was mostly composed of veteran players. On to this venerable scion the committee regularly grafted a new shoot or two which had been nurtured in the Second Eleven. But as there was a reluctance on the part of the elders to retire, and the youngsters were seldom trusted with great responsibility, the team tended to have an uneven quality, which was perhaps hardly surprising. And because their record was disappointing, and they stood low in the league, their supporters had fallen away. Playing at home they could reckon on a few loyal relatives. Playing away they were usually left to their own devices, so our party was doubly welcome.

The opening ceremony was leisurely and impressive. First of all the two umpires came out, full of self-importance, and put the bails on the stumps. The coin was tossed, and Jim Jewell cried, 'Tails!' quite rightly, and chose to bat, rightly or wrongly. The fielding team came out, casual and smiling, throwing the ball to one another. Then Henry Blewett the milkman and Jeffrey Kennack the postman, as our opening batsmen, marched solemnly down the steps and out on to the field, and we clapped as hard as we could.

Further ritual, while Henry consulted Humphrey, made a scratch mark with his shoe spikes, tapped the ground to form a hole where his bat would rest, then put his left shoulder forward, tucked the bat close to his legs, and looked sternly at the field.

The bowler paced gracefully back from the wicket, made his bowling mark, and waved the fielders into position with lordly gestures. The wicket keeper squatted behind the stumps. Humphrey held out his arm as if to turn left, then turned round and spoke the noble word.

'Play!'

The opening bowler for the Trebeddo team had been greeted by a ringing round of applause from their supporters. His name, Lily discovered by enquiring of our neighbours, was Chris Fowler, familiarly known as Speedy Fowler: a player of growing reputation on this wild and windy peninsula, and a man of great pace and ability with a venomous delivery.

Seemingly unmindful of his fame, Mr Fowler removed his pullover in a leisurely fashion, and handed it to the other umpire. He was a long lean pensive fellow, who sauntered away from the stumps as if he had better things on his mind, while polishing the ball on his groin with a diffident air. At seventeen steps from the pitch, transformed from thinker to doer, he wheeled round, leaned forward, paused for a moment to concentrate his powers, and began to lope down the field, faster and faster. As he reached a crucial place and time he leaped into the air, crossing his feet so rapidly that they seemed to twinkle, and let fly.

The boys took it upon themselves to instruct me.

'That's called bowling off the wrong foot, Mum,' Jeremy said.

'Personally I'd rather take my chance against a bullet!' I replied.

I was being honest, but felt gratified when they both laughed.

Our two opening batsmen stood up to him nobly: swiping at everything, very occasionally hitting something, and running earnestly whenever they had the chance. But after a while the bowler grew tired of indulging them, smacked down Henry Blewett's middle stump, caught Jeffrey Kennack out in the next over, and retired, pulling on his sweater in a business-like manner.

'So you enjoyed your morning with Tom?' I said, as we clapped each of the defeated batsmen back to the pavilion, and heralded Jim Jewell and young Terry Soady on to the field with equal vigour.

'Yes, we haven't done anything like that before . . .'

They wouldn't, of course. Guy doesn't soil his hands.

'He was yarning away about being in the merchant navy . . . '

They both laughed, and exchanged covert looks. Their masculine world had been enlarged. Pat, who usually acted as spokesman for the two of them, now gave his verdict.

'Tom's a good sort,' said Pat.

In Speedy Fowler's place came the Trebeddo slow bowler, George Lockitt: a plump ginger-haired man with a pale skin who merely stepped up to the popping crease, lifted freckled arms into a tasteful arch, wrung his hands together as if in prayer, and cast a guileless ball which rolled hopefully down the pitch. This seemed such an unlikely way of getting anyone out that I wondered why they allowed him to do it. So apparently did Terry Soady, who clocked up eight scornful runs before one slyboots trickled past him into the stumps, and the bails rose in slow motion.

'Mum, excuse me,' said Pat urgently, 'but you mustn't clap when one of our team is out.'

'Oh, I thought everybody was clapping.'

'Only the Trebeddo lot, Mum.'

He and Jeremy exchanged smiles at my expense, but they were warm amused smiles. I didn't mind them at all.

'Tom's been telling us what the house was like before you took it on, Mum,' said Jeremy.

'Some job!' said Pat. And then, astonishingly, 'You're a regular David, Mum, tackling a Goliath like that.'

Jeremy murmured to himself, 'And the food's always good.'

Jim Jewell and Arthur Crowdy, being old hands at the game,

resisted the temptations of slow balls and formed a steady partnership. For half an hour they held their dogged own and garnered the occasional run. Again Trebeddo sent in Speedy Fowler to despatch them, at which all runs ceased, but still they could not be moved. Fifteen minutes later, realising that they would neither be beguiled nor browbeaten, Trebeddo called upon Mr Quarterman: a gentleman of advancing years and goodly girth who had once played for the county. Respectful handclaps greeted his appearance while Arthur Crowdy shifted his stance, tamped down the turf with his bat, and waited.

'Why bother to bring in a professional like old Quarterman?' Jack asked the company at large. 'I told Humphrey this match would be a shambles.'

'Oh, I don't know,' said Pat coldly, back turned on the speaker, 'they're doing pretty well at the moment.'

Jack leaned forward and tapped me on the shoulder.

'By the by, Flick. We must have a word together when you've got a spare moment. I've come down here to see you.'

Patrick and Jeremy stared ahead of them, frowning.

I made a non-committal sound, and resolved to avoid him.

Meanwhile the breeze had dropped and the sun was not only warming us but heating the pigsties. We cast off our extra clothing, and Lily brought out a small bottle of eau de cologne and sprinkled it on our handkerchiefs, which we held over our mouths and noses.

Mr Quarterman took his measure of the batsmen, the pitch, and the sunlight, and rambled off, polishing his missile. He came serenely up the slope at a medium pace, and his first ball was graceful but unremarkable. Arthur took a single run off it. The second ball gave Jim Jewell a run, and we innocents clapped in anticipation of more. Then Mr Quarterman sent down a minx of a third ball so inviting that I muttered, 'Swipe it!' under my breath. And Arthur did. The minx rose in an equally inviting manner from his bat, soared across the field, caught sight of an uplifted face and a pair of waiting hands against the bushes, fell gladly into them to the accompaniment of gleeful shouts . . .

'Oh, he's *got* him!' Patrick shouted in anguish.

. . . and slipped capriciously through them.

'No, he *hasn't*!' cried Jeremy in relief.

The young fielder disappeared into the scrub in shame, while his team-mates shuffled their feet and stared at the turf. Mr Quarterman stood still for a few moments, head on one side, communing with his soul, then shrugged his shoulders and returned impassively to the fray.

'He's found his line and length,' said Jack. 'It's only a question of time now.'

The fifth ball seemed to be headed in one direction and then unexpectedly curved in another. Arthur stepped forward and swished at it forlornly.

'Howzat?' shouted Mr Quarterman in a great voice.

Humphrey admitted that it was leg-before-wicket. And Arthur strode back valiantly to the pavilion amid a spatter of handclaps from us, exchanging a curt nod with Sean Angwin, who was out for a duck and followed him back again almost immediately.

In a couple more overs Mr Quarterman dispatched Jim Jewell, saw Will Soady and Brian Angwin installed, and left them to the alternate mercies of George Lockitt and Speedy Fowler.

I studied the scoreboard. Six wickets for thirty-six runs.

'How are we doing?' I asked my sons.

'Ruddy awful,' said Patrick.

'But no worse than I expected,' Jack observed.

Anxious to learn I asked, 'Are they playing well or are we playing badly?'

Jeremy said, 'Our team is doing its best, but they're outclassed.'

Jack said, 'Shouldn't be too long now!' And yawned.

My notebook remained unopened on my knee. I watched absorbedly, clapped every run, and once stood up and called, 'Oh, well played, Mr Soady!' when Will hit a boundary. I admired Humphrey, full of portent in his white coat and hat, making imperious gestures like a policeman in a traffic jam. But towards half-past four we arrived at our last man, and his name was Tom Faull. By this time the enchantment of the game was upon me and I had become a champion of the Elinglaze First Eleven.

'I suppose they keep the best batsman to the last?' I said to Jeremy, feeling sure that Tom could be no other. For was he not one of our very own?

But Patrick said apologetically, no, not really. And Jeremy said, anyway, Tom being the sort of chap he was you never could tell.

But Jack said, 'The last man might poetically be described as the dregs in the team's cup!' And yawned again and glanced at his wristwatch.

Out came Tom in borrowed cricket pads, swinging his borrowed bat with stupendous style. His bearded good looks, his stalwart figure, harked back to W.G. Grace. The spurt of handclaps from our party sounded thin against the anticipatory silence, but I sat up full of hope. All Tom's sins I forgave him in that awesome walk from pavilion to wicket. Lines from Kipling rang in my head and brought tears to my eyes. 'You're the last man in, the captain said.' Ah, yes. That was it.

I would not allow Jack to diminish him.

'Well I think,' I said confidently, 'that he's going to surprise us all.'

Then we were very quiet as the head of Speedy Fowler emerged, to be followed swiftly by the rest of him. He was muscular, young and fleet, and the sight of Tom's doughty stance did not deter him. At the height of his speed he leaped clear into the air, his feet twinkled, and the ball came down the pitch like a rocket and exploded on the off-stump.

Trebeddo cheered their hero to the sky. In our group there was a short and sorry silence.

Then Jack said, with a sunless smile, 'And that, my friends, is that. All out for fifty-one. And time for tea.'

Humphrey did not join us so we ate without him, faintly subdued by events, but Jack, exercising his right as cousin to a Cornish gentleman and a cricket enthusiast strolled into the pavilion to speak to him. He came back to report that our team had been fed like kings.

'Oh, I'm glad of that!' I said, for we had picnicked splendidly.

'You shouldn't be,' said Jack, smiling thinly beneath the stripe of his moustache. 'Your team's fielding directly afterwards. I set it down to a dire conspiracy on part of the Trebeddo ladies. Humphrey's made an absolute hog of himself and he's already half asleep. The others aren't much better.'

This judgement was borne out a few minutes later when our team emerged for the second half of the match.

Jeremy, gauging their lethargic progress on to the field, said stoically, 'I think we've had it, Mum!'

Then Tom came into his own. Most of the First Eleven had gorged themselves partly out of habit and partly to soothe their misery. Apparently he had been one of the very few to restrain himself amid the welter of assorted sandwiches, home-made sausage rolls and savoury quiches, of airy scones capped with WI strawberry jam and clotted cream, three different iced sandwich cakes, chocolate biscuits and buttered saffron buns, and unlimited tea and lemonade. Had they backed him up, he said later, he could have taken three wickets in his first couple of overs. Unfortunately they didn't run very fast or observe very closely, and showed a distressing tendency to miss catches or else to let them drop.

I observed Humphrey standing, hands clasped behind his back, watching his protegé's prowess with gloomy pride. And listening to the comments of our male experts I realised that this was the sunset-hour of a genuine talent. According to Patrick and Jeremy and even – grudgingly – Jack, Tom gauged his line and length well. He judged his opponents accurately. He employed strategy. He bowled gently and lulled them into a false sense of security. He bowled aggressively and astonished them out of it. He did not allow them to rest. And they, in turn, ceasing to be complacent, raised their game to meet his and fought back. When he came off after his ten overs, with two wickets for twelve runs, he received a general ovation.

Henry Blewett took his place, and showed an ability for slow-bowling. Will Soady was our humbler answer to Mr Quarterman: deliberate, well balanced, experienced. And looking to the future were Sean Angwin and Terry Soady, allowed an over or two to try their arms. But with brilliant sixes, cunning fours and impudent singles Trebeddo knocked off the remaining runs, and the match was over.

While Jack and the boys packed the Bentley I retrieved a soiled and boisterous Bella and Bee and we all waited for the return of our heroes.

Plodding towards us, Humphrey held out his arms for comfort, was affectionately entwined, and said, 'Well, well. Not such a bad showing, eh?' And, indicating Tom and becoming lyrical, 'You should have seen him twenty-odd years ago. I said then that he should play for the county, you know. But many a flower is born to blush unseen.'

So we made much of them both, while Jack Rice smiled to himself, cat-like under his moustache, and smoothed his glossy head.

'They gave us a tremendously good tea!' said Humphrey to me, and looked at Tom meaningfully.

'Better than we have at home,' said Tom, taking his cue. 'It's all shop cake and paste sandwiches at Elinglaze.'

Humphrey cleared his throat and adopted his best manner.

'I'm sure you'll agree, Flavia, that the honour of our village team should not be tarnished. I know that if I mentioned your name the tea ladies would be delighted to accept you as their caterer.'

Patrick said for my ears alone, 'That's called a bouncer, Mum!'

I saw Jack grinning at my annoyance, but could not hold back my retort. I had had enough, and more than enough.

'And how do you suppose I can run Parc Celli on Saturdays at the height of the tourist season while I'm serving cricket teas?' I cried. 'The answer is no, Humphrey!'

Jeremy muttered to his brother, 'But it didn't catch her out!'

My temper was not improved when we arrived home to find that Tom had also been blessed with uninvited visitors. Three old shipmates were sitting at the kitchen table, yarning and flirting with Vera, while she brewed tea and cut up a cake I had been saving for tomorrow. Since the hospitality of Parc Celli must not be imperilled, and Tom could neither feed nor house them, we made up three of the servants' beds on the top floor, and Humphrey invited them to dine with us.

I had planned that weekend with such loving care, and this was one of the moments when I ought to have been able to survey my dining table with pride and affection. Tonight we should have consumed Parma ham and melon, braised pheasant in cream sauce with exquisite trimmings such as celery bundles and fried apple rings, followed by orange soufflé.

As it was I looked down a long abundant board, at which we were about to sample a menu notable for ingenuity and variety rather than beauty and symmetry. Unaware of what he had missed, Humphrey sat benevolently at the head of the hall table, and beamed upon me as hostess at the foot. My two sons sat on either side of me, and unequally divided between us – in more ways than one – Lily graced Humphrey's right and Clarissa his left; Tom was keeping the peace between Bella and Bee; and Jack Rice had been thrown among sailors. Thirteen in all. I am not a superstitious person but it did occur to me that the number was propitious to the occasion.

As one dish jostled or succeeded another, and I wondered what to feed everyone on Sunday, they kept on eating and saying how wonderful I was.

'Such a clever girl! She taught herself to cook when she was only eleven or twelve, you know. I can't cook at all. I live on snacks when I'm at home.'

'*Darling* Flavia. I don't know how you *do* it. I can't even boil a *kettle*!'

And, for once, accolades from my two sons.

'Mum, this is just out of this world. Honestly.'

'Honestly, Mum. Absolutely super food.'

A triple variation on the theme of, 'Thanks very much, lady. Bloody good grub. You should see what we eat on board ship! Tom, do you remember that cook on the Aden run?' from the sailors.

Jack lifted his glass and said, 'Here's looking at you, Flick. And probably only I know just what an ingenious girl you are!'

At this remark Tom, who had been enjoying himself, gave Jack a hostile stare, and said, 'Only the workers in the kitchen know that!'

Bella and Bee, no longer restricted to a suitable diet, were roving indiscriminately among the dishes, praising me with their mouths full. Later on, they would probably be sick. Well, I thought, if Clarissa isn't prepared to rein them in she must clean them up.

Tom, eating hugely and appreciatively, was telling anyone who listened that he had prepared the vegetables, that he accounted this task an honour, and had only to be asked to repeat the whole performance.

But Humphrey's comment capped them all.

He cried, raising his glass, 'I drink to the chef! Who has produced, as by a conjuring trick, a choice of starters, two main courses, all those vegetables Tom prepared, and three different types of dessert! How you spoil us, my dear! But of course,' speaking confidentially to the others, 'this is nothing to Flavia. She is used to cooking for a restaurant. Our little house party is a mere bagatelle compared with that sort of catering.'

He meant it as a compliment, but I could have stood up there and then, and bowled a complete over of caramelised oranges at him.

CHAPTER FOURTEEN

August

'A word at last, Flick,' says Jack Rice, sitting down beside me. 'I've hardly seen you since we arrived.'

I am shelling peas on the doorstep leading to the back garden, believing I have found a time, place and occupation which will protect me from the remainder of my guests. I have lost five of them.

Tom, who has been a Trojan throughout, told his sailors to roll away the following Monday, which they did in good humour and good heart. He was also influential in persuading Patrick and Jeremy to stay on longer than expected, and we all watched the Lizard Omnibus Service Cavalcade on the 17th. But Humphrey and Jack continue to delay their departure. And Lily and Clarissa and the children seem to have become permanent fixtures.

September is approaching, and I should be advertising Parc Celli, but Humphrey has so far avoided discussion of money, and the roof must be repaired and the remaining bedrooms on the first floor decorated before I can even think about opening.

'Here, let me help!' says Jack, in his friendly fashion, cracks open a crisp green pod and begins shelling and eating in equal quantities.

I say nothing. Nothing at all. Let him make all the running. I have never felt more confused and afraid. But my silence does not worry him.

'I told you you were being too hasty, Flick,' he begins amicably. 'Sylvia and I had hardly reached Switzerland before we realised that we were on different wave-lengths. All that talk about buying a hotel was just a new idea on her part. She amuses herself with new ideas. As soon as I asked her to put Daddy's money where her mouth was – she shut it.'

He gives me a chance to reply, but I can't, and won't. So he carries on.

'I should think you're up against a similar problem with old Humphrey,' he says, keeping his tone light and artless. 'He likes the idea of restoring the old home, so long as he's not required to put himself out. But you're the one who's going to, well, shell the peas, shall we say?'

I stop shelling peas and look him in the eyes. No matter where this conversation leads he must acknowledge my achievement. At Parc Celli I stand in my own right. If he is looking for a renewed partnership it must be between equals.

'Jack, this was my idea, and I chose to go through with this scheme by myself. So far I've had my own way, and that's how I like it. I prefer Humphrey to remain a sleeping partner.'

He puts his finger accurately, painfully, on the flaw in my argument.

'Yes, so long as he keeps away, pays the piper, and lets you get on with running the business. But if he insists on throwing house parties throughout the best season of the year, and inviting non-paying guests, you'll be in deep deep trouble, my girl. Personally speaking, I'd sooner deal with the devil than a good-natured fool.'

I dare not argue this point.

'And to have entered into a friendly rather than a legal agreement,' he says in disbelief, 'is damn silly. I know you haven't invested your capital but you've invested your source of income, which is yourself. This house is still Humphrey's property, and he can do what he likes with it. He can change his mind about running it as a business, turn you out as soon as it's finished, and come and live here if he wants to. At the very least you should have made him pay you a decent salary and all expenses, instead of board wages. Board wages! Dear God, Flick, you were born forty years ago, not yesterday. What happened to your common sense?'

Having to defend myself at last, I split pods and rattle peas furiously into the colander.

'I am not yet forty and my common sense is intact. It told me how much I could persuade Humphrey to do, and warned me that if I pinned him down too hard and too soon I should frighten him off. And I wanted to make a go of Parc Celli. She – it – the idea – can work. Will work. And if for any reason it doesn't then I still have my earning power and my capital.'

He shakes his head from side to side, smiling, incredulous.

'My dear Flick, you're simply repeating the same old mistakes in a new way. You've run away from a situation instead of standing up to it, as you did with Guy Pollard. And how did you come out of that mess? With precisely nothing! Then, instead of thinking how best to look after your own interests, you've fallen in love again – in this case with a house! Surely, by this time, you must know that love doesn't provide any answers – only a fresh set of problems!'

Wait a minute, I am crying wildly inside myself. I fell in love with you, once upon a time, and Bon Appétit came out of that. So all right, I'm in love with Kelly Park, but think of her as she was and look at her now. And what do problems matter when you've got a centre to your life?

But I know how he can laugh this argument out of court, and I say nothing.

'You make all that fuss about silly little Sylvia Hammond,' Jack is saying, turning my torment into the best of jokes. 'Cast me for the part of the villain. Force us to sell up a damned good business – and then chuck yourself away! And all in five minutes, for God's sake! Old Humps told me that you hadn't been here more than a week when you bounced him into parting with ten thousand quid . . . '

'Humphrey told you that?' I cry, betrayed, enraged.

'Well, not in those words, of course. But that's what it amounts to.'

He was impatient of Humphrey.

'Oh, he'll mew if the weather changes. I'm not bothered about him. This is a jolly good thing as far as he's concerned. I'm trying to show you where you've gone wrong again.'

'Thanks a lot!'

He ignores all the signals that tell him to shut up and go away, or else change the subject.

'And that's another of your faults, Flick. You decide on a plan that suits you and charge off without looking more than one move ahead. I could have told you that Humps and his Dump meant Trouble with a capital T. You can no more rely on the one than the other.'

'Jack, why and how do you happen to be down here?' I ask abruptly.

'As I told you, Sylvia and I split up. So I came back to London and rang old Humps, and he gave me a paternal earful about treating you badly. And I said it was all my fault and I'd like to make amends.' Here he glances at me to see my reaction, but I am not in a mood for reconciliation. 'So he asked me round to dinner, and talked about you and this Parc Celli scheme all evening. I was greatly intrigued . . . '

At this point one of our regular sparrows alights on the grass a few yards away, watching and pecking and hopping casually nearer, on the look-out for friendly offerings.

' . . . so when he said he was coming down here I offered to drive him. He's bloody dangerous by himself, as you know, but the real reason was curiosity . . . and hope, of course . . . but I wanted to judge the situation for myself.'

Jack picks up a bit of gravel and flicks it at the bird, who flies away.

And that, as far as I am concerned, is that. I shell the last pod, lips tight.

'Since then I've been looking round here,' he continues, ignoring my lack of response, 'and I've come to the conclusion that you and he could be on a winner, providing you update your plans.'

I rise and walk away from him without answering, to shake the pods out of my apron and into Martin Skegg's compost bin. Jack saunters after me, hands in pockets, undaunted.

'At the moment you're on a hiding to nothing, Flick. Even if you manage to keep Humphrey in line, and everything comes up roses, you'll do no more than keep afloat. There's a ceiling to the profit you can make in a country-house hotel. After that you need to invest more capital on extensions or improvements before you can increase your income. And this isn't a bistro. You'll be living on the premises, and on call, for twenty-four hours a day, and taking on a neverending spiral of bank loans in return for slave labour.'

I stalk back in silence to pick up my colander and saucepan. He follows me: easy, jaunty, still talking.

'Whereas, if you and I got together again and invested the proceeds of Bon Appétit into this old pile, and went into a watertight legal and financial partnership with Humphrey, we could make enough money to live on without working ourselves to death.'

Then he slips his arm around my waist and holds me as I used to like being held. But no longer. I push him away with the help of the colander.

'When did *you* ever work yourself to death?' I cry, stung. 'And why suddenly do you want to do business with a man you distrust and despise?'

I have thrown him off course for a moment, but the Jack Rices of this world soon find their way back.

'Distrust and despise? Oh, that's coming it a bit strong, Flick,' said Jack laughing. 'I'm very fond of old Humps. Blood's thicker than water, and all that. But I'm a realist, and I'm telling you this – you'll never make it by yourself, Flick. You've used your heart instead of your head, again. I'm not against that. Your heart brought this old dump back to life. That's your touch of genius. But genius alone won't work. Put your heart and my head and our joint capital together, and you're looking at an all-round winner.'

I also have a touch of genius for falling in love with men who can, and do, extinguish my confidence. At this moment I feel that I have failed once more, and the weight of every stone in Parc Celli sits on my stomach.

Now he presses his argument home.

'It isn't the idea of a country-house hotel which draws you, is it, Flick?' he says, and his voice understands me, caresses me. 'The country-house hotel is simply a means to an end. You're quite prepared to slog your guts out as a landlady for a few years, providing you can run your forty or fifty-cover restaurant at the end of it. And then what? Hand the bed and breakfast side over to a competent assistant – such as Vera Angwin! – and concentrate on the cuisine?'

Probe, probe, probe. Tread, tread, tread.

'But I can prophesy that you'll find it very difficult to work in tandem with someone who will become just as necessary and important to Parc Celli as yourself, and has been there longer, and is by way of being an old family retainer. Our Humphrey will still be trying to live here when he feels like it, and playing you two off against each other. And don't forget that you're the foreigner here. He'll never run short of friends and locals to back him up, and there'll always be our cuckoo in the nest,' nodding his glossy head towards the stables, 'swearing loyal allegiance to the squire while using him for his own purposes. An interesting rogue,' said Jack thoughtfully, 'who could many a tale unfold, I'm sure, without ever telling the real story. It might be worth your while making a few enquiries about his recent past.'

So Jack Rice, too, believes that Tom Faull is a charlatan. Well, it takes one to know one. And I could lie down and die. To die would be most merciful.

'You know, of course,' said Jack, who guessed I did not, 'that Humphrey had a long and intimate chat with our favourite mariner, and has written out a cheque to cover the cost of the materials he's bought? Five hundred smackers, so I understand. Just like that. So that the gallant sailor can potter on with whatever nefarious scheme he has in mind.'

Throughout the past fortnight Humphrey has sedulously avoided any discussion of the money he owes me, and I am speechless.

'Yes, Flick,' Jack says, reading my expression, patting my shoulder, 'you need a champion. Someone who can spot the cracks and weaknesses. Someone who's on your side. Someone who can cut the sentiment and deal with the facts, and is just a shade more ruthless than the opposition.'

I stand immobilised: my face turned away from him. He will have his say, and I must listen so that I know with what and with whom I am dealing.

'So forget the lovey-dovey bit, and let's get down to business. You could still make your home here, Flick. Create a comfortable flat for yourself. Fetch your few sticks and ornaments down from London and settle in. We'll keep one of the top floor rooms for our own convenience – like having a box at the theatre. You can invite your boys down, for instance. Or old Lily, if you feel like playing the martyr. We shall have to let Humphrey have a room too, and a good one, but only on condition that he sticks to it, and understands that anyone he invites here must either pay full whack or be paid for – no concessions. I can pop down from time to time to see how things are going, and sort out any problems. Otherwise Parc Celli would be yours.'

I am sick and angry with him and myself, but more so with myself, for had I not known him?

Still I cannot help asking, 'In what way mine?'

'Personally I'd turn this place into holiday flats. Something for everyone at a price they can afford. Little bedsitters. Grand apartments. All self-catering. Remember what I said about people feeling they can buy a lifestyle without committing themselves to it? It's true. The English have always been sentimental about living in the country. Actually it's a myth. The real thing would appall them. But think of paying only a few hundred a year – and letting someone else have the headaches! – for the privilege of outdoing your friends and enemies! To be able to say, "Just off for a couple of weeks to my place in the country!" does wonders for your image. And when they enquire where "my place" is, the address completes everyone's downfall except your own. "My place? Oh, Kelly Park!" '

Now I stare at him in amazement. For that is what I call her, though mindful not to say so in Cornish ears.

'Kelly Park?' I cry. 'Why not Parc Celli?'

He is courting me now, sure of a return to favour. He wears his clever smile and smoothes his clever head, and his bright, brown shallow eyes see no further than the present opportunity.

'No, of course not. What would Parc Celli mean to an outsider? You could be talking about a tarted-up cottage or a converted barn. And the clients we need all live in cities, where the big money is. So it would be Kelly Park. The name has style and presence. It implies the gentry. And that's what people want to be for a while. Cornish gentry.'

'And what about my restaurant?' I say, from between my teeth.

'We're all going to make a lot of money out of this project,' says Jack, being generous after his fashion, 'but you're going to make more, because you'll be the resident manager and we'll pay you a salary. Not fantastic but more than fair, and you'll live rent free, you can save up, and with this sort of collateral behind you – and our backing – you can borrow money to start a restaurant. How you run both jobs is up to you, but it's perfectly possible. I shan't mind if you delegate as long as Kelly Park doesn't suffer.'

So he will be free to come and go, while I am stuck here as a caretaker, a sort of upmarket Alice Quick, trying to get a restaurant off the ground somewhere else. I notice that he doesn't mention the slave labour and spiralling bank loans that these two projects will involve. But then, Jack only argues his own case. And though his criticisms of my present enterprise are justified, and may even prove right, at least I am working for myself on my chosen project. Whereas Jack is proposing that I work for him, in a way I should detest. In fact he is proposing to use me again, and that makes up my mind for me at once.

'It may be a brilliant idea,' I say coolly, 'but it's not what I envisaged, nor is it what I want. So – no thanks, Jack!'

For the second time in our lives I have astonished him, and I glory in the brief pause that ensues.

Then he shrugs and smiles, says, 'It's early days yet. Think things over, Flick. Let me know if you change your mind.'

And strolls away.

The prospect of August Bank Holiday, with its traffic jams and tourists, speeds the time of departure, and as I help Humphrey to pack he gives me the opportunity for which I have been waiting.

'My dear girl, I can hardly bear to leave, and the only thing which supports me is the thought of returning soon. October is a lovely month, here – and your birthday month, too. Suppose I come down for a week or two – just by myself, this time! – to make sure you're not working too hard? I can take you out to dinner, spoil you a little. You deserve to be spoiled, my dear . . . '

What I deserve is a fair deal, some clear understanding of my situation, and no interruptions. I keep my tone light and easy.

'Humpty, darling, you know I shall be busy throughout the autumn, filling Parc Celli with paying guests and making as much money as possible. How about a Christmas house party instead?'

'But surely there is more to life than working and making money?' he cries impatiently. 'I must confess to becoming a little tired of your constant preoccupation with the mundane, Flavia!'

So it is to be a battle after all.

I answer carefully, 'We agreed to run Parc Celli as a country-house hotel. This sort of undertaking involves both work and money, and I really do need to talk to you seriously about both.'

'Oh, how I detest the term country-house hotel!' he says haughtily. 'Parc Celli is and always has been a gentleman's residence!'

His tone has an edge which is being turned on me. I address him by his full name so that he will know I am in earnest.

'Humphrey, Parc Celli *was* a gentleman's residence until that gentleman stopped living here twenty-something years ago. When I arrived in February this place was a financial liability in a state of decay!'

A gentleman never fights. He simply slides away.

Humphrey says fretfully, 'One would like – in one's house – in one's dear old home – to be able to spend the occasional week or so in convivial company, and without the necessity of booking in advance as if one were a day-tripper. Surely that seems little enough to ask?'

Fretfully, he hands me his Jaeger dressing-gown.

Folding the burnished silk, I say, 'Let's take our present house party, and the time of year, as an example. If you chose to fill Parc Celli with personal guests for two or three weeks in high season, we should – in business terms – lose some thousands of pounds by having them here, and it would cost us a few hundred to keep them.'

This is a delicate hint, for Humphrey has not yet paid what he owes me. Does he assume that food is a free perk of the catering fraternity?

He snaps his suitcase locks with emphasis, pads over to his bureau, disgruntled, and examines the silver-framed photographs as if he had never seen them before.

Over his shoulder he says loftily, 'I find the discussion of money matters so distasteful. And to allow them to come between us, my dear. Between us!'

Unable to communicate with him I cry, 'But who am I to talk to about money if not to you? We are business partners.'

No reply. He hums 'La Petite Bérgère' under his breath and murmurs to himself, '*Mam'selle*!'

'And, Humphrey, though you and your guests have been on holiday here I have not.'

He says waspishly, 'My dear, since we are being so very business-like and talking of my guests, I feel I should remind you that Lily – whom I adore, and am always delighted to meet – has been in residence here since May. And your own boys have recently graced us with their very pleasing presences.'

I find an answer to that, too.

'Yes, but to be fair to Lily she does pay for her keep. And I've paid for the boys. And while we are on the subject of residents,' I add, finding an opportunity to raise this issue also, 'Clarissa has been here with her children almost as long as Lily, and has never offered me a penny nor lifted a finger to help nor even suggested that she should!'

'But I sent you a little cheque to cover that.' Quickly. Indignantly.

'Yes, you did. You sent me *a* little cheque. For fifty pounds, Humphrey. Fifty pounds does not keep an adult and two small children for ten weeks.'

'Then allow me . . . ' he begins grandly, bringing out his cheque book as if he were conferring a favour instead of meeting an obligation.

I am infuriated. How dare he drive me into a corner and then make out that somehow I am at fault?

I say resolutely, 'It costs me at least twenty pounds a week for their food. And while we're talking of costs, you've paid for domestic wages and building materials and builders' wages, but so far you haven't given me a penny towards this holiday and you've never paid my board wages. All these months I've been living on my capital and working for nothing.'

Fractiously, he throws down his cheque book, crying, 'You seem to think I'm a millionaire. I tell you, this restoration business has pretty well cleaned me out. The proposed cost of the roof alone is far beyond my means. I've had some very nasty letters from my bank manager, and my accountant has insisted that I see him when I get back. I can't pay for everything now. I simply can't. Suppose we leave it for a week or two, dearest? And when I've sorted out my finances I'll give you a bonus for waiting.'

I hesitate. I feel ill-used, but I know my man. Better a part-payment in hand than a bonus in the bush.

'All right, Humphrey, we'll forget my wages until you're on an even keel, but I'll take Clarissa's keep and the holiday food. I've costed everything out,' bringing a detailed account from my apron pocket, 'and you'll see that I've paid for my guests and I haven't charged for the sailors . . . '

I wait for him to say something about that and the catering, but Tom's guests and my labour apparently come free of charge, so he does not. This tactless omission on his part enables me to tackle the next problem easily and with some asperity.

'And, Humphrey, I want Clarissa to leave as soon as possible. I can't see us opening before October as it is. It would be pleasanter for everyone if you explained the situation and asked her nicely. If you don't then I must.'

His mouth drops open in a childish 'oh' of disbelief. My voice thickens as frustrations mount.

'Because quite frankly I've had it up to here, Humphrey!' indicating my throat, 'and I want to know right now if you're prepared to run Parc Celli as a business, or whether you would rather forget the idea altogether.'

I use Jack's argument.

'The house is in reasonable working order, and you may prefer to use it as a country residence. I shan't be here, of course, because I can't afford to act as your unpaid Cornish cook–housekeeper. You'll have to find someone else to do that. And the way I feel at the moment I don't care if you do. In fact, I have a good mind to wind things up and leave at the end of next week to find myself a proper job in London.'

Robbed of energy, I sit down on the edge of the bed and try to breathe deeply and evenly. But the peaceful tenor of Humphrey's way has been threatened, and he responds with alacrity.

'Oh, I say, Flavia!' Hurt and reproachful. 'You wouldn't do that, would you? I mean – I've always relied on you, dear girl. Everyone relies on you. What should we all do without you?'

'I don't know. But it's time I was unreliable and stopped everyone from taking me for granted. And why do I say that I'll stay until the end of the week, to sort things out? Why don't I leave you to sort out your own mess, pack tonight, and take a train to London tomorrow? Yes, I'll do that instead!'

He says quickly, 'Dearest girl, not so fast! Of course I shall render unto Caesar the things which are Caesar's. Aha, ha. And I insist upon paying you every penny I owe you, Flavia. There is no question about that. No, my dear,' holding up his hand, 'I insist upon the board wages as well as – what did you reckon for this last week or two?' He consults the list with chagrin. 'So much? Goodness me, how very expensive food must be! Very well. And poor Clarissa's keep? And how much did we agree I should pay you?'

I am glad Jack Rice is not there to scoff when I say ten pounds a week. I never did eat much, anyway, and I hadn't intended to make a profit out of a friendly concern.

Humphrey takes out his calculator, stabs it importantly with his forefinger, being very particular as to the pence, gapes at the result, writes out the amount and presents his cheque with a flourish.

The quarrel has shaken us both. I tuck the slip of paper into my apron pocket without looking at it and stare at the pattern in the carpet. He hums a little tune and taps his fingers on the bureau. Making up our minds together we both turn and speak at once. Then gasp and laugh and hug each other.

'Ah! Flavia!' says Humphrey, moist-eyed. 'If only things had turned out differently – what a happy man you would have made me.'

I resolve to start afresh, and in good heart and spirits.

'I'll tell you what I have made you, Humpty. A delicious picnic for the journey home. Packed in one of the old picnic baskets.'

We are back to normal.

It is not until he has departed that I realise how normal. The cheque is made out for the food he and Jack have eaten, ten weeks' keep for Clarissa – which brings us up to date but no further – and ten weeks' board for me who has worked six months. He has, as Jack would say, pulled a fast one. Well, for the moment that will have to do. I can hardly resume negotiations now.

Jack Rice is still smiling as we come out to see the travellers on their way.

'Thanks a million, Flick,' he says, shaking my reluctant hand. 'I have a feeling we'll be seeing each other again quite soon. Here or in London.'

I am free of him. I feel as crisp as my tone. I can mean my reply.

'I doubt that, Jack. I shall be too busy for light entertainment.'

He smiles, and shrugs at Humphrey as if to say, 'Women! Funny creatures! But we still love 'em!' And gives a final salute before he drives away.

CHAPTER FIFTEEN

September

On the following Friday morning I sat at Arabella Jarvis's escritoire and read Humphrey's letter for the third time.

Dearest Flavia,

First of all, my dear, a thousand thanks for that wonderful holiday we spent together at Parc Celli – would that it had lasted longer, but needs must when the devil drives!

Which devil does he mean?

I have decided to write rather than telephone because this is a somewhat difficult and delicate matter which needs to be considered carefully. Briefly, dear girl, I have – as I feared! – been spending far too much money in recent months. My accountant tells me that I must retrench, and I may even have to sell a few precious things to keep my London bank manager happy about the overdraft.

So anything he happens to owe me must wait a little longer!

However, I have been most business-like about this, as you would wish me to be. I showed my accountant photographs of the work done so far, and explained the situation. He seems to think that the property is now in a fit state to interest a buyer with the same goal in mind, and has advised me to sell. Two aspects of this notion trouble me. I am loath to lose the home of my childhood, and I do not wish to jeopardise the future of Tom Faull and *his* home.

There is a third aspect which seems to have escaped you. What about my future and my home?

However, my solicitor tells me that I may possibly be able to exclude the stables from the sale, or to make Tom's residence there a condition of the sale. After all he is not exactly on view, except through the kitchen windows . . .

And only the workers use the kitchen, and they don't count!

. . . and he did make himself very useful and agreeable during my delightful visit with you.

But not half as useful and agreeable as I was!

Yet another possibility has been mooted in our discussions of late, which is to attract another investor, or investors. In point of fact, our mutual friend Jack Rice has shown a marked interest, and is willing to come into a legal partnership with me, bringing his share from the sale of Bon Appétit. You would, naturally, continue to be the presiding hostess of Parc Celli, at a salary to be agreed by us all.

But taking my orders from the pair of you, because those who have the money wield the power!

The only snag here is that Jack's ideas are not quite in line with ours, and this would mean certain compromises on your side and mine . . .

Especially on mine!

. . . but Parc Celli would remain my property and be restored, which is surely the main concern. According to Jack – whom I have always regarded as an astute businessman – the three of us could also enjoy the amenities of the house, as well as making a good living out of it. Although I am bound to say that I think his scheme sounds somewhat commercial.

It's entirely commercial! Jack isn't interested in Parc Celli except as a source of profit.

Dear girl, I realise that this news will be a sad blow to you after all your wonderful efforts, and I am truly sorry. There is no immediate hurry to reply, but when you have had time to think things over perhaps you would let me know how you feel about this? You may have suggestions of your own which are more in sympathy with the spirit of Parc Celli. For I know that you and I are as one in our desire to preserve the house as a beloved home.

Ah! Now the screw begins to turn. Tighter. And tighter.

Anyway, we have these choices. No Parc Celli. A stranger's Parc Celli. Jack's Parc Celli. Or – dare I hope! – *our* Parc Celli? Meanwhile, until more money flows into my depleted coffers, I am informed that present work on the house must stop, and all expenditure be curtailed. I have written letters to that effect to my Helston bank manager and Will Soady.

So you can move speedily when you have to!

Yours, as always, my dear Flavia,
Humphrey

The phrases 'his share from the sale of Bon Appétit' and 'Or – dare I hope! – *our* Parc Celli?' stood out from the text, salient, foreboding. I knew what was being asked of me. Humphrey was holding Kelly Park to my head and saying in effect, 'Your money *and* your life!'

I knew who was manipulating Humphrey, but the reason puzzled me. Was Jack Rice trying to force me out so that he could take over? Was he hoping that I would invest all my capital and eventually lose everything? Or was he giving me an ultimatum, via Humphrey, believing I could be coerced into partnership with him again?

I pushed the letter away and sat back, hands in trouser pockets. My present way of life and its future promise were under threat. This comfortable little room, from which Humphrey's grandmother once controlled her household, had become my office and personal sanctum. Upstairs I had made the housekeeper's bedroom my own: its simplicity matching my single and single-minded existence. The kitchen was my working world. The first and second floor rooms, their prices graded to suit different pockets, would be occupied by a passing throng of satisfied guests. And some fine day, when I had repaid Humphrey and was making a profit, the great hall would become my restaurant.

In Kelly Park's metamorphosis lay mine also. We were recreating each other. I felt that I could neither give up the venture nor compromise on it, and under no circumstances would I have anything to do with Jack Rice. Yet to invest my capital would be to incur a crushing responsibility.

Humphrey was not a good bet as a business partner. He was

a child who lived in a dream of childhood. Save him now and I should carry him on my back to the end of his days or mine. He would never face facts. He would always ask more of me than anyone should be expected to give. His image of himself as Parc Celli's squire demanded unlimited money and service. His selfishness, amusing at a distance, was disastrous at close quarters. His very weakness became a terrible strength. Unless I fought and mastered him I should be at the mercy of his whims, his squirearchy and his family feelings. I could be lost.

A knock on the door announced an unwanted presence. Quickly I tucked Humphrey's letter under my blotter. Whoever it was would be curious, and though they could not read it from that distance they might recognise his handwriting.

I sat down, pulled a sheet of accounts towards me and called, 'Come in!'

Tom stuck his head round the door jamb saying mildly, 'Eddy Johns is here about the van, Flavia . . . '

'Oh, Lord,' I said, in despair. 'I'd forgotten about the van, and we've been careering round the countryside in it for the last three weeks.'

Tom waited patiently while I thought aloud.

'And having driven Victoria for a fortnight, the boys must feel that I bought her for them. I don't see, quite honestly, Tom, that I have a choice.'

'You can say no if you want to,' he said. 'Eddy Johns is an old mate of mine. He doesn't mind me trying the van out.'

The decision was delicate, not to say untimely. If I stayed here I should certainly need a van. But if I went back to London it would be a further encumbrance. I asked for information, and played for time.

'Is it licensed?'

'Got six months to go.'

'When is it due for an MOT?'

His face fell slightly, but pulled itself up again.

'Sometime in the autumn, I think.'

I guessed he meant this month, if not this minute, and was amused in spite of myself.

'In your opinion, would it pass its MOT?' I asked drily.

He hesitated, and said, 'It would if I did a bit of work on it.'

'I see. And how much does Eddy Johns want for it?'

'He says five-fifty, which is a fair price. I daresay I could beat him down to five hundred and it's worth every penny of that. I'll do that for you.'

I had been backed into another corner. I prevaricated.

'Well, I'm very busy at the moment, Tom, and I'd rather not buy a van today. Could he give me twenty-four hours to think it over?'

'Eddy Johns says if you don't want it then he'll take it away. But if you do want it then perhaps you could write the cheque out now because he's waiting in the kitchen.

I breathed in deeply. I breathed out again.

I said desperately, 'This is costing me a lot of money, Tom. You see, if I'm keeping Victoria as well – and I'm not proposing to get rid of her – I shall be paying for two lots of licences, road taxes and MOTS!'

'Ye-e-es,' he said soothingly, 'but you can put it all down to expenses. Being a hotel, in a manner of speaking, you need plenty of transport. And it'll be grand for those two lads of yours to have their own car in the holidays.'

He rubbed the door jamb thoughtfully with his forefinger and gave a confidential smile. All would yet be well, that smile seemed to say.

'Besides,' he said, 'a car is a big draw for two lads of their age. They'll be down here every holiday like a couple of shots. See if I'm right!'

I knew he was right. That made matters worse. I wavered, and he looked straight at me, very quick and black and bright, and changed the subject.

'Have you set your official opening day yet, Flavia?'

'No, I'm afraid I haven't.' I searched for a good excuse. 'I'm waiting for Will Soady to finish decorating the bedrooms.'

'I reckon that'll be some while,' said Tom, watching me closely, 'seeing that Will Soady had a letter from Mr Jarvis this morning. Jeff Kennack was having a cup of tea with the family while Will read it, so when he delivered Vera's parcel from her sister in Plymouth he told her the news. And he told her there was a letter from Mr Jarvis for you too. It's all over Elinglaze that work's stopped on the house. They're saying that Mr Jarvis has gone bankrupt, and you're only staying here long enough to close Parc Celli, and then you'll be off back upcountry.'

I flared out, 'For God's sake, why does everybody know my business and make up my mind for me before I've had time to think?'

Tom grinned as he replied, 'Folk do say that you only have to kick one person in Elinglaze to make them all limp!' More seriously, 'Anyhow, that's why Eddy Johns is here. He wants his van or his money. And Vera's in a tizzy because she's afraid of losing her job.'

I sat for a few moments, beaten, while Tom waited for my answer.

Reluctantly, I said, 'I did have a letter from Mr Jarvis this morning. And round about now,' as my little mantelpiece clock struck half past nine, 'the bank manager in Helston should be reading his instructions to freeze the Parc Celli account.' I could not resist adding sarcastically, 'But I don't expect the local grapevine to pick up *that* piece of information before it goes shopping this afternoon!'

He came inside and closed the door silently behind him, full of concern.

'Sit down, Tom,' I said wearily, 'and I'll tell you all.'

'I won't sit, if you don't mind, Flavia. I've got my work clothes on and they're none too clean.'

'Oh, for heaven's sake! Let me spread this newspaper on that chair and then you can sit down! That's better. Humphrey isn't bankrupt, he's simply short of spare cash. And Parc Celli won't be closed, it will be run as a business concern. But whether by me or by somebody else I don't yet know.'

He said, 'You're not going back upcountry, surely?'

I answered emphatically, 'I haven't yet made up my mind to go back there, but God knows, at the moment I wish I'd never left!'

He was grave and attentive, waiting for me to explain, and I was frank with him.

'At the moment I don't know what I'm going to do, Tom. So could you tell everyone – including my mother and Clarissa, whenever they happen to feel like getting up! – that I've got a lot to think about and I need to be by myself? I'll let you know my decision as soon as possible. In the meantime, I'd like a quiet hour or two by myself.'

He said, 'Surely!' in a quiet sober way. 'Should I fetch you a cup of coffee?'

'Thank you. That would be nice.'

He paused on his way to the door, saying over his shoulder, 'Did you have any breakfast?'

'No,' I said. 'I read the letter first, you see. And I didn't feel like eating anything afterwards.'

'I'll be back,' said Tom.

And back he was, within twenty minutes, bearing a tray full of hot buttered toast, a soft-boiled egg, my home-made jam, and a pot of coffee: all laid out with the best china on a tray cloth edged with crochet-work.

'Tempting the invalid?' I could not help enquiring, for I have a sour tongue in times of stress.

'You can call it what you like,' said Tom, standing no nonsense from me. 'Just get it down you!'

And departed with as little ceremony as he had spoken.

CHAPTER SIXTEEN

Tom returned for the tray as soon as he judged me to be well nourished and feeling up to a little conversation. He had changed his work clothes for the open-necked shirt, grey flannels and navy-blue blazer with which he greeted Humphrey's arrival.

'I suppose,' said Tom cautiously, closing the door behind him, 'you wouldn't like to talk to me about it? Bounce a few ideas off me?'

'I should have thought,' I answered wryly, 'that you and Elinglaze knew all the answers.'

He smoothed his beard at that and regarded me sombrely. Then he drew up a chair and sat down.

'Whatever you say won't go beyond these four walls,' he said solemnly. 'My word on that.'

'Not even to Humphrey?' I asked.

He shook his head and said, 'Not to him, nor to anyone else.'

We took the measure of each other, as we had done that first evening. I decided I had nothing to lose by honesty, and perhaps something to gain by being blunt.

'If you're worried about losing the stables you needn't be,' I said. 'Mr Jarvis is making sure that you and they are protected whatever else happens. That's what you really want to know, isn't it?'

He sat forward, clasping his hands between his knees, and addressed me just as forthrightly.

'Flavia, I've got nowhere else to go, so I'm bound to be worried about the stables. But there's more than me concerned in this. There's many a one from Elinglaze that'll feel the pinch if their jobs go, and the village itself will suffer, losing the trade and custom of a big house. Besides that, Will Soady's been left with two thousand pounds' worth of slates and roof timber on his hands.'

I was dumbfounded.

'But Mr Jarvis hasn't yet asked him officially to repair the roof . . . '

'No, but you have,' said Tom. 'Will told me at the time that you said the roof had to be done, and you had no choice – which, to be fair, you hadn't.'

'But I also said I must tell Mr Jarvis. I meant, ask his permission first.'

Tom shrugged and said, 'You've been giving the orders all along. Will took your word for it.'

'And he's actually got the materials?'

'In his yard this minute. Delivered yesterday.'

'But can't he use them up on somebody else?'

'He could,' said Tom, 'when the next roof job turns up. Meantime he'll be two thousand pounds out of pocket.'

I reflected, somewhat bitterly, that had the materials been promised *directly* we should still be waiting.

Finally I said, 'Then I owe Will two thousand pounds, whatever happens. And I've got a load of timber and slates on my hands. That's all I needed!'

I stood up and walked about the room, restless with apprehension, pressing my fingers together to stop them from shaking.

Tom said tentatively, 'You short of money, too?'

'Oh no, I have money,' I answered despairingly, no longer caring how much he knew about my private affairs. 'I possess enough capital to pay for all the remaining bills and float Parc Celli until she gets on her feet. It's sitting in my London bank in a special deposit account, earning interest. And what Humphrey wants now is a legal partnership, into which I invest my savings as well as myself. But that money is all I have in the world, and it represents a number of things that I *don't* possess, such as a home of my own, a steady job, and a sense of security. I'm afraid of risking it. Because if I lose it then I have nothing at all – except the boys – and Victoria, of course.'

This sounded so funny, and I was so disturbed, that I came out with a laugh which turned to a sob. Then I sat down suddenly and poured tears.

'That's right, Flavia,' said Tom comfortingly. 'You have a good cry. Make you feel better. Don't mind me, my bird.'

He put one large warm arm round my shoulders and offered me the handkerchief from his top blazer pocket, which was folded into a triangle. It was probably the only clean white ironed handkerchief in his wardrobe.

Furious with myself, I sobbed and wiped my eyes and blew my nose and sobbed again.

When I could speak, I said thickly, hoarsely, 'I was a fool to – get involved with – this project – in the first place. The best thing I can – possibly do – is to cut my losses – and get out while I can.'

I had told him no details but he went straight to the point.

'I suppose Mr Rice is at the back of all this?'

And instead of softening, explaining or evading the question, I cried angrily, 'Yes, he is – the villain! – and he's manipulating Humphrey!'

'I thought so,' said Tom. 'There's money in it, you see. And you've given him the idea and done the groundwork. That's what makes a man like Jack Rice tick. Money. And power over people.'

I dried my face and swallowed a hiccup. Tom's handkerchief was a mess.

Inconsequently, I said, 'I'll wash and iron this for you.'

'Never mind that, Flavia. You just sit here a minute,' said Tom, making up his mind about something, 'and I'll be back.'

I sat. I had nothing else to do and no better idea of my own. I felt very tired. I should have liked to put my head down on my arms and sleep.

He returned bearing a butler's silver tray on which stood a bottle of whisky, a syphon of soda water, two glasses, and a small Pyrex basin filled with ice-cubes. He poured two generous measures into Grandmama Jarvis's best crystal tumblers. His manner was firm and friendly.

I noted these attentions and anomalies with gratitude and a flicker of humour.

'Drink up!' said Tom Faull, clinking glasses. 'And between the two of us we'll sort it out. And while I'm about it,' he added, feeling in the back pocket of his flannels, and bringing out a roll of banknotes, 'you can borrow this to hold Will Soady while you make up your mind. It's the best part of five hundred pounds,' he explained, 'that Mr Jarvis gave me to cover the cost of new materials for the stable. Leastways, he wrote me a cheque, but I cashed it and stowed the money away.'

Even in my present state it did occur to me that he had been wise to cash it, and possibly wise enough to have guessed that.

Although my jangled self cried inwardly, my better self was able to say, 'No, I can't take that, Tom. He meant it to be yours, not mine.'

'Neither mine nor yours,' said Tom factually. 'It belongs to Parc Celli, by rights. So what's the odds if it's spent on the house roof or the stable roof? You're welcome to it.'

I said earnestly, 'I'm truly grateful, Tom, but I can realise my own capital within a week or ten days. So put it back in your pocket.'

Which he did, stuffing it away indifferently, as if it had been no more than waste-paper. Then he settled himself back in his chair, crossed his legs, took an appreciative swallow of whisky, and began to talk.

'Now, let me put the position to you as I see it. You've done a proper job on Parc Celli, and he looks like his old self. Nobody's going to make a fortune out of him, but you and Mr Jarvis don't mind that so long as he pays his way and yours. And I'll be happy living in the stables, and lending a hand when needed. I'm not an ambitious man. Never was . . . ' here his voice became profound ' . . . but I know one when I see one.'

Storytelling while sitting down took the form of addressing the tumbler: holding it up against the light and squinting through it from time to time, staring into its depths, and taking an occasional thoughtful swallow.

'Mr Rice – Flash Jack, as he was called in the servants' hall – was evacuated to Parc Celli during the war. The old lady took in a bunch of the Jarvis and Rice cousins from Bristol, and as my mother worked up at the house I used to play with them. Flash

Jack was the sharpest of them and a plausible little monkey. He was the sort that looks for trouble and can always find somebody to take the blame or get him out of it. He hasn't changed. And I was the mischievous sort that used to be accused of anything that went wrong. He got me into scrapes and let me take the stick for them many a time. We never liked each other. He was older than me, too. Two or three years. And bigger – then. And he fancied himself as a boxer. Used to put his gloves on – I had none – and dance round me. He'd give me a black eye and a bloody nose while I stood there. Then when I got home my dad would wallop me for fighting with the gentry.'

Humour got the better of rancour.

'Not easy!' said Tom, and grinned. 'But I could wait,' and his eyes glinted.

'They weren't here all through the war. They went back to Bristol when the blitzes were over. And then came down again when the V1s and V2s started. I'd put on some height and weight by the time he came back, and I'd learned how to fight. This time *I* picked the quarrel and took Flash Jack behind the garden shed and beat the living daylights out of him. He left me alone after that. Mind you, my dad knocked hell out of me after!

'Drink up, Flavia. You've got a bit more colour in your face. That's good.

'Now if a man like that was to interest himself in Parc Celli he'd want a lot more than you and the squire do. He'd want quick returns and big profits, and he wouldn't care how he made them. Given Parc Celli, he'd be thinking along the lines of a motel or a block of flats. He might go so far as to pull the house down altogether and build on him, or sell the land off in building lots, because that's how the big money's made. Am I right?'

I nodded, and sipped, and listened and watched a Tom Faull I had not seen before. In a crisis he dispensed with charm entirely, and became a formidable adversary.

'So that's where Parc Celli stands,' said Tom, refilling our glasses, 'and now I'll tell you where I stand. You say that I've got nothing to worry about, that Mr Jarvis will protect me and the stables. I believe that's what he means to do, but it isn't what's likely to happen. If Flash Jack Rice is going to run this place then he'll get rid of me and use the stables for his own purposes – either knock them down to make room for a car park, or convert them into garages. And whatever the squire feels or says it won't make a ha'porth of difference because Flash Jack is a man who likes his own way and generally gets it. So that'll be me out of here and done for.'

He shrugged, held up the glass, squinted through it, drank.

'Last but foremost we come to you, Flavia. You can pull out and go back to London. That means giving up the sort of future and the quality of life that you promised yourself in Parc Celli, and lowering your sights as to the kind of business you can afford to run. On the other hand, you've still got your money and you'll be back on home ground, and there's no reason why a talented lady like you shouldn't find a new partner and a new bistro, or set up on your own and make a success of that. So *you'll* be all right. But if you do decide to go back upcountry then Parc Celli as we know him—'

'Her!' I cried, hot with whisky. 'If you're talking about what *I* feel then Parc Celli is a *her*. And *I* call her Kelly Park.'

The room was in a melting mood.

'Well then,' said Tom, mollifying me, 'whatever the name and gender, if you leave Kelly Park to Flash Jack Rice *she's* finished!'

His tone now sharpened, became as urgent as the terrors which whispered all about me.

'But!' And here he put up a finger which looked as unsteady as I felt. 'But, you say to me, if I decide to stick with this house and sink my capital into her, and she fails for whatever reason – what then? And the answer comes the same as mine. There'll be nowhere else to go and no one else to turn to. And that's the sort of fear that keeps you awake at night! Am I right?'

I nodded, mesmerised. His tone and expression mellowed.

'Now you've had a lot of hinderment the past few weeks,' said Tom, 'on account of people being here that shouldn't be, and not understanding that you've got more to do than run round after them. And I'm to blame as much as anybody – though I never invited Squib Bristowe and the lads, and I got rid of them soon as I could. But you've been fretting, and maybe laying out your own money as well – though the squire would always see you right in the end – and you've naturally got to thinking that you ought to walk out and let them all go hang anyway. Now am I right?'

I nodded again, and nursed my whisky, and sipped it whenever I could synchronise the glass with my mouth. Yet, fuddled as I was, I knew that he was pleading the case for Kelly Park and himself and Vera and the little troop of workers as well as me.

His voice had risen as he laid the facts before me. Now it dropped to an emotional low, and I thought what an excellent barrister he might have been.

'Well, you'd be wrong,' said Tom softly, 'because your word is law in this house and what you say goes! You've made Parc Celli your home, and made yourself the heart of it – a home and a place such as your two boys haven't seen before. I've got a fair picture of the life you led in London. Taking them out because there was nothing else to do in a small flat. All treats and no substance. But what happened here? Why, they couldn't get enough of it. They didn't want to go back to their dad, did they? For the first time you got a fair crack of the whip, didn't you? And the way I see it, you've done wonders for yourself *and* them by coming here.'

He lifted his hand as if to quell any interruption on my part, but there was none. He had healed an old raw place in me, and even if that was by intent, and with an ulterior motive, I could forgive him.

'What I'm saying is,' Tom continued, 'that it's right you should stand up for yourself – even against the squire if need be. He's a gentleman born and bred. He can't help being what he is and doing what he does. But he'd be the first to knuckle under if you were to make a stand. So my advice to you is this – if you're going to run a tight ship the first thing to do is to clear the decks. And once you've cleared them they'll stay cleared!'

There was an impressive pause, as if he said, 'And here I rest my case!'

Then he added gently, 'So think it over carefully, Flavia.'

And kindly removed my empty glass, which was hanging from the tips of my fingers.

* * *

Vera woke me, quietly setting down a tray of tea, and was about to withdraw when I put out my hand to stop her. The alarm clock by my bed had ticked its way round to four in the afternoon. My mouth was too dry to talk and the light hurt my eyes. I swallowed, and motioned towards a chair.

'Here, sit you up!' cried Vera with vigorous good nature. 'You don't know where you'm to!'

She helped me into a sitting position, punched a couple of pillows into submission, and pushed them behind my back. She poured out a cup of tea and put it into my hands. She sat down, smoothed her apron over her knees, and waited, head bent, for the oracle to speak.

I drank it up and focused. I remembered as far as ten o'clock that morning and no further. I needed information.

'You want some more tea?' she asked.

'Yes, please – Vera, why didn't you bring a cup for yourself?'

Her face brightened.

She said, 'I did, too!'

And fetched it from outside my bedroom door.

I decided not to prevaricate, apologise or explain. The entire household probably knew that I was sleeping off the effects of too much whisky too early in the day.

'Vera, what's been happening while I was asleep?'

She pulled her chair nearer to the bed and launched into her tale.

'Well, Tom come in and said you had a lot on your mind and wasn't feeling too good, and that you'd gone to lay down, and we was to manage without you.'

Oh, God, I had bared my soul to him. The thought embarrassed me as much as if I had bared my body. Then even more shockingly it occurred to me that I had been in no condition to stand, let alone walk up two flights of stairs. I remembered the glass being taken gently from my fingers, and a feeling as if they and I were eddying down a bottomless pit. And I prayed to any deity who might be listening, of whatever creed, that no one had seen Tom support me or – even worse! – carry me up.

Vera, at least, seemed unaware.

'There,' she said. 'Your colour's coming back. The tea's done you good. Anyways, Tom told Eddy Johns to come back tomorrow. The little maids was running wild in the kitchen and Tom took them off to the stables with him. So I take Mrs Lily's breakfast up, but I knock on Mrs Gibbon's door and tell her that if she want any breakfast she have to get it herself seeing as you'm not well and we'm busy . . . '

Here Vera drank long and deeply, and her eyes shone in remembrance.

'. . . then I give Mart'n Skeggs and Sean and Mother their croust in the kitchen. They ate the rest of those Welsh cakes from yesterday. And Mother dusted all the bedrooms except yours this morning, and cleaned the bathrooms, and they look some smart. Mother might be slow but she's sure. Then I looked at your menu for today and made sure everything was made ready for you to cook this evening. Then Tom and the little dears and me all had our dinners in the kitchen – I used up the cold lamb from yesterday, and some of your apple mint jelly, and baked jacket potatoes with it, and made pancakes for pudding . . . '

I had listened to him, probably lolling drunk and garrulous. Disgraced myself! And what had I said which should have remained unsaid?

'. . . then when Mrs Lily and Mrs Gibbon come downstairs Tom had some talk with them. Polite, he was, but he told them straight you was suffering from too much work and worry and they should look after theirselves today. So they ask him to drive them into Truro, and they'm having lunch there, and doing some shopping, and he's to pick them up at five o'clock . . . '

Had I said too much? And about what?

'. . . and Marianne come in after dinner to help me, and she's been cleaning silver in the butler's pantry all afternoon – you can see your face in it! You said a pound an hour for her? All right? She's saving up to buy herself a pair of gold shoes for dancing. Mart'n and Sean have been 'arvesting, and they brought a basket of runner beans and a basket of tomatoes besides the other vegetables, and a bunch of chrysants for you. I've left the chrysants in a bucket of water. And Mart'n says to tell you that he'll have all the greenhouses going next year and there'll be melons and cucumbers and whatever else you want . . . '

She stopped for a second, and looked at me quickly. I focused my attention and said, 'Do go on, Vera. It sounds wonderful.'

So she rattled on.

'And Tom's been banging away with they slates on the stable roof all afternoon. Nearly finished, he is. Then I looked in the cake tins, like you do, and saw we was low, and I made a chocolate orange cake out of your recipe book, and it's come out lovely. And I give the little maids some pastry to play with. And they was as good as gold. They'm waiting for you to see their pies before they go into the oven. Some pies they be,' said Vera, grinning, 'more like putty than pastry, and more jam on their aprons than in the pies! You wouldn't want to eat none, but, dear o' them!'

She stopped speaking, and put her cup on the tray and folded her hands in her lap and smiled.

'They do grow up so quick!' she said. 'One minute you'm wishing they wasn't underfoot. The next minute they'm saving up for a pair of gold shoes.'

Mine hadn't been underfoot long enough.

'So we done good,' Vera ended, 'and I thought as you'd like a cup of tea and come to yourself quiet-like.'

I thanked her, and said they had all done very well indeed.

'And we're hoping,' said Vera bravely, 'as you'll not go back upcountry, Mrs Flavia, but stay with us and see us right. And we'll see *you* right – my word on that! And Marianne, she say she want to work here full time because she left school this summer, and there warn't no job she liked as much as this one. She do think the world of you, and she want to be a proper cook like you, and train for it. But I tell her she have to do the washing up and vegetables for us while she's learning! And since she waited on, when the master was here, she been telling Julie all about it– that's my youngest that I named after Julie Christie! – and now our Julie want to come with her, and learn how to wait on, and help out when we're extra busy. She can come in the evenings, and in school holidays, and she says is it a pound an hour for her, too – but I shouldn't give her as much as Marianne, with her being younger . . .'

Here Vera ran out of breath, and waved the teapot about as if to exhort us both to drink and be merry.

I had already decided to stay, for I could not leave Parc Celli to any fate but the one I envisaged. I had intended to sleep on my decision. In a way, so I had done. But to hear from Vera that I was needed and wanted for my own sake was irresistible. Instead of delivering a neat speech to the assembled household on the following morning, I blurted out the truth to her at once.

'You can tell everyone that I'm not going back upcountry, Vera. I'm putting my money where my mouth is, and staying here. And we're going to make such a success of Parc Celli that people will come from all over England to stay with us. Yes, Vera, they're going to hear about us!'

My mind was made up, my spirits were high, my words valiant, but I must confess that my heart quailed at the thought of seeing Tom again.

CHAPTER SEVENTEEN

This was one of the strangest days in my life. Vera went home, leaving me with Bella and Bee. I mixed and drank two fizzing Alka-Seltzers, praised the small grey pies and put them in the oven to harden further, set the children's aprons to soak and washed their hands and faces, and read them three *Mr Men* books. Then I waited on tenterhooks for the next instalment of my home-made drama.

At half-past five Lily and Clarissa were delivered to the door of Parc Celli as if by magic carpet. Tom was nowhere to be seen. I was grateful for that. His influence lingered on, and he had evidently been extending it to the two subdued ladies who hovered before me, carrying smart plastic carrier bags.

Lily unleashed Beau, saying, 'Stay, boy!' to which he responded by immediately rushing off to find Bella and Bee. Either his intelligence was low or his memory short, for he had never learned that they meant trouble. In a few more minutes he would be dressed up as a doll and squealing for mercy.

'You're looking better, Flivvy,' said Lily timidly, patting my right cheek. 'Such a pretty colour!'

Clarissa said, kissing my left cheek, 'Darling Flavia, Lily and I have been out shopping to buy a you prezzie for being so sweet and kind to us always.'

My stomach clenched. I had brought myself up to the pitch of having a firm talk with the pair of them, but could hardly do that while accepting chocolates, bath essence, initialled hankies, or whatever they had conjured up from Truro. But, I reflected, if not now then later; if not this way then that way. Unclench, stomach!

Prezzies or no prezzies, the ladies are for burning. I shall have no scenes of any sort, since both Lily and Clarissa would dominate the stage and prevent me from saying my lines. Nor shall I be frank, giving them time to twist my facts and deny my accusations. No, I shall do a Tom Faull on them and win by low cunning and smiling bonhomie.

I waited until Clarissa and my mother were bathing the children before I rang Dick Gibbon that evening. He knew better by this time, poor man, than to think that Clarissa would want to speak to him, and was grateful to hear news of her at second hand. We enquired as to each other's state of health, and spoke of the weather, and then I said my piece.

'Dick, I hope you'll forgive me for interfering, and this is strictly between the two of us, but I think that Clarissa is missing you and doesn't know how to say so.'

'Really?' said Dick, incredulous as well he might be. 'She gave me the impression of being most reluctant to come home.'

'I can't help feeling that it's simply a matter of pride with her.'

'She is proud,' he cried. 'She's always been a beautiful, spirited creature.'

Sounds like a horse, I thought.

'Yes, indeed. And the children are longing to see you . . . '

'Sweet pets! Missed them fearfully . . . '

'Dick, might I make a suggestion? I'm sure Clarissa would respond to a positive approach. Why don't you turn up here and take them all back home?'

'I'm – not – sure – that . . . '

'Faint heart never won fair – or dark – lady. I'll bet you didn't hang about like this when you were courting!'

'No, by God!' he said, becoming animated. 'But I was younger then.'

'Clarissa needs a spot of dashing courtship. Save her pride, sweep her off her feet, give her a slap on the bottom or whatever, and tell her you're not having any nonsense. I'll bet she doesn't give you a ha'porth of trouble.'

'No,' he said, on a deeper note. Thinking. 'No, I'll bet she wouldn't!'

'And don't tell her you're coming to fetch her. Just do it.'

'Surprise tactics, eh?' He made up his mind. 'You're on, Flavia!'

'Good for you, Dick! It doesn't matter what day or hour you arrive. There'll be a welcome in the hills, as they say. Looking forward to meeting you, however briefly.'

'Oh, we'll be back!' he cried. 'We'll come as a family next time.'

'When we're officially open,' I said, pleasant but firm, 'I'll send you the brochure. We shall be making a reduction in prices for families.'

Lest there be any future misunderstanding.

Rejuvenated by guile, I whisked into the kitchen, and for once wondered how to make life easy for myself. So I prepared three cold salmon salads and opened a tin of baked beans for the children. I reckoned I could sort everyone out by half-past seven and have the rest of the evening to myself.

It was twenty-five minutes past seven when Tom knocked at the back door and walked in. We stood looking at each other in apprehensive silence for a few moments, and should have been lost for an opening sentence but for the aroma of his newspaper parcel. Then we both spoke at once.

'I'm just taking Lily's supper tray up to her—

'Fish and chips. Thought we might have a bite of supper together—'

We stopped and began again.

'Clarissa's already collected hers—'

'I've got a surprise for you in the van outside—'

'Sorry, what did you—?'

'Sorry, what were you—?'

Another silence. Then Tom put one finger on his lips, set down his parcel on the kitchen draining board, and said firmly, 'I'll carry that tray up for you, Flavia. You're too good to be running about after idle folks.'

I laughed rather tremulously, saying, 'I'm not really good. I wanted to keep them out of the way, you see. It's actually a form of selfishness.'

'Rubbish,' said Tom, smiling. 'How about putting the kettle on? I'll be back.'

He returned a few minutes later followed by Beau, pattering on paws of silk and in search of adventure. Looking soulfully at me, the dog sidled towards the sink, and sat beneath Tom's parcel, nose uplifted, tail waving in anticipation. At that moment the kettle boiled, and Tom and I moved towards it simultaneously. He was more in command of himself than I was.

'I'll make the tea for us, Flavia. Do you want cups or mugs?'

'Oh, mugs will do.'

'Are you very hungry?'

'No, actually, I'm not. I'd rather sit and drink tea for a while.'

'So would I.' He nodded towards the fish and chips. 'We can warm them up anytime.'

At that moment I saw that Beau had jumped on to a chair near the sink, reared up on his hindlegs, and was nosing into the parcel.

'Beau! Beau! Be off with you!' I ordered.

The Sealyham dodged my slap, trotted rapidly across the kitchen floor, trailing a cod in batter, and disappeared into the hall.

'Oh well, never mind,' said Tom philosophically, watching him go. 'We aren't all that hungry.'

The awkwardness between us had been warmed away. I sat in the rocking-chair he had provided, and he sat opposite. Companionably, we sipped and watched the coals fall in the grate. Then while I was wondering how to frame my thanks and apologies, he put his mug on the hob, folded his hands across his stomach, and began his personal saga with the line, 'I've always lived on the fringes of other people's lives . . . '

'An interesting rogue,' Jack had remarked, 'who could many a tale unfold, I'm sure, without ever telling the real story.'

But it sounded a real story to me, and one much like my own: the desire to improve his lot; the opportunities which turned out to be traps; the giving of hard labour and being cheated of its rewards; the search for what one hoped would be home.

His voice rumbled, lifted, grew sonorous, was gentle and harsh in turn. His accent accommodated itself to the occasion: straightforward English when he talked to me directly, semi-colonial as he roved the high seas, broad Cornish as he dived into his past.

'I never wanted to settle down with any woman. I didn't like what marriage did to a woman. I'd seen it with my mother. I thought the world of her, and she of me, and he – my father – was jealous. That's partly why I went to sea. Oh, I wanted to get away from Elinglaze. But I thought that if I went he'd treat her better . . . '

I set my own mug down, and folded my hands in my lap, and rocked and sometimes listened to him, and sometimes talked of myself.

'Our honeymoon in Venice and the first year at The Elms were intensely happy. It was some time before I realised that Guy Pollard and his house were finished products. He didn't want anything to change, including me. But of course I did. I grew up, and he could never come to terms with that . . . '

'But I also wanted to see life. Travel the world, and keep on travelling. See everything. Do everything. I lived it up along with the rest of them. Drank them under the table. Had any girl I wanted. I was a heller . . . '

'Guy was possessive. I was his property, and when the boys came along they were his property too. But he was too set in his ways by then to enjoy the noise and mess that children bring. So I kept them out of his way, and Pat and Jem and I lived in our own world. Lots of fun – and food, of course. When they went to primary school I wanted to take a part-time job as a domestic-science teacher. That was our first major row. Guy couldn't allow me any independence . . . '

'Then it palled on me. I made friends with a man who said I'd got a brain and why didn't I use it? I'd fooled about in Elinglaze. It was as much as I could do to read and write. So I started from scratch, and went on . . . '

'I stuck it for as long as I did because I thought he loved me. Loved me in the wrong way, but loved me. Much later I realised that he married because he thought it was time for him to settle down. And though I'm sure he wanted me, and thought I'd make a good wife, he really chose me because I was young and innocent and could be recreated in his image . . . '

'And then even the learning wasn't enough. The still point of the turning world – that's what I wanted. To be somebody, somewhere, with people who knew and liked me. That's why I came home, and tried to make a home . . . '

'I left him and took the boys with me. I planned to live with Lily, and take a job, so I could keep them. I started by cooking for other people's dinner parties. But she didn't really want us. And then Guy came down one evening when I was out working, and took them back with him. He started divorce proceedings. He must have had Anne – his second wife – in the background even then. He married her as soon as the divorce became absolute . . . '

Sometime in between I made bacon sandwiches and coffee, and we despatched them with relish. Outside the late summer sky darkened, the noises of day were silenced, and the owl hooted.

We talked out old wrongs and disappointments. We talked in new achievements and fresh hopes. As soon as we emerged into the present Tom remembered his surprise, unloaded it from the van, and staggered in with an immense dishwasher on a trolley. It had seen better days, but was on offer at the bargain price of one hundred pounds.

'Now you tell me where you want it, and I'll fix it up and get it going this minute!' said Tom, radiating goodwill.

The chimes of the clock sounded midnight, and halted us. Being hungry again by then, we decided to leave the dishwasher until morning and warm up the supper he had brought in. But Tom's newspaper parcel had long since vanished from the kitchen draining board. We followed its trail into the darkest corner of the hall, and found it, still aromatic but hollow. And by its savoury shell lay Beau: fast asleep in a ring of cold chips.

As we parted at one in the morning Tom said, 'It's good to be friends at last, isn't it?'

Something more than friendship was between us, but not yet ready to come forth. He put his hands on either side of my arms, but did not give me the bear hug he gave Vera. He kissed my cheek, and I smiled at him. And we told each other to sleep well.

* * *

On a mild, bright September afternoon, soon after my reconciliation to Tom, Martin Skeggs came to the kitchen dressed in his best black suit. In one gnarled hand he held a bouquet of late-flowering roses fit for a prima donna to receive on the first night. In the other he carried a top hat whose nap was worn in places like the skin of an old mole.

'Heavens! How smart you are!' I said, astonished.

Vera glanced up from her sink, sly and knowing, then went on washing and sorting the little blue-black Kea plums from Truro.

'I hear tell that your lady mother be going home tomorrow, Mrs Pollard,' said Martin, holding the top hat to his chest like a presentation plate.

I gave him the explanation I had given Lily, mindful of her self-regard and remembering that, however inexplicably, she had her devotees.

'Yes, I'm afraid we shall have to part with her for the moment. But the London season is beginning, and of course she has so many friends and social obligations in London. But she'll visit us again.'

'If I could have a word with her, Mrs Pollard, I'd be obliged.'

'Vera, would you mind?' I said, checking the thermometer, stirring the jam. 'This is almost ready.'

Unhurriedly, she dried her hands and smoothed her apron. As she walked past Martin Skeggs she gave him a long look, and he looked away.

'Do sit down, Mr Skeggs,' I said. 'I hope you'll excuse me if I carry on with this, but it's almost at jamming stage.'

The rose in his buttonhole, and the crimson three-cornered handkerchief in his breast pocket, were for show. From his trouser pocket he drew a clean old white rag and dabbed his forehead. Then he polished the seat of the kitchen chair before he sat down, though there was no need for that.

'Warm for the time o' year, Mrs Pollard!' he observed.

And then fell into a profound silence, from which my sociable conversation could only draw, 'Right 'nuff!' or 'Pretty good, thanking you.'

I was relieved when Vera bounced in saying grandly but quite seriously, in the manner of drawing-room comedy, 'Mrs Clough will receive you in the library, Mr Skeggs. Please to come this way.'

'Dear God, what next?' I asked the plum jam, and drew it off the hot plate.

Vera bounced back. Herself once more.

'Here, let me get those jars out of the bottom oven,' she cried.

And over the clashing tray, blue eyes gleaming she asked, 'Do you know what he've come for?'

'I haven't the slightest idea.'

She set her burden down with a jingle of satisfaction.

'He've come to propose to Mrs Lily.'

'Never!'

Vera nodded, full of news and importance.

I said, 'I'll fill them. You seal them. All right?'

'Now how do you know?' I asked, ladling.

'Oh, everybody knows tha-at!' she replied scornfully. 'And he never wear that suit unless he be going to church, or courting like.'

A spurt of laughter escaped me, which I pretended was a cough.

'She could do worse,' said Vera judiciously. 'He've got plenty of money and his own cottage, and he be a good few years older'n she!'

And she paused in her task to nudge me, as if to say that Lily would not have to wait long before being a rich and landed widow.

We looked at each other across the last jar.

'I'd best go back in case he lose his way,' said Vera insincerely.

'I'd better come with you – just in case,' I said vaguely.

Bonded by common curiosity we reached the library door together and were in time to hear Lily cry in enraged dignity, 'Get up off your knees, Mr Skeggs. At once! At once!'

There was a scuffling noise, at which Vera snorted in delight and said, 'Poor soul. It's his arthritis. He cain't get up!'

Cautiously we opened the door and peered round it.

In the centre of the Wilton carpet stood Lily, pointing a finger of wrath at her unfortunate suitor. Martin Skeggs was endeavouring to haul himself up by means of an armchair without treading on Beau, who was sniffing his boots in ecstasy. Between them all lay the bouquet of late roses, a single glorious note in the scene.

We ran forward and lifted Martin, one either side, and he thanked us and stood for a while getting his breath back. Beau sat at his feet, head on one side, and watched him wistfully.

Vera whispered to me, 'I'll see to Mart'n!' and picked up his top hat from the library table. 'Come along wi' me, Mart'n,' she cried, in the loud voice with which one speaks to foreigners or the feeble-minded. 'I'll see you right.'

'Beau!' Lily cried in a terrible voice. 'Stay where you are!'

Which he did for once, though very sorry to lose the boots.

Then Lily turned her back on me and swept over to the window, where she remained looking out and waiting for her next cue. I am not a theatrical person, but I did my best to supply it.

'What on earth was all that about?'

Evidently the line was adequate because Lily put her handkerchief to her lips and said tragically, 'Do not ask me! I never encouraged him to hope.'

'But he worships you!' I replied automatically.

'I cannot help it. Our worlds are too far apart,' cried Lily, thoroughly enjoying herself. 'This alters everything.'

'Everything?' I asked, wondering what she was talking about.

'My peaceful haven . . . ' she began, in a tremulous voice.

What haven is that? I wondered, for I could distinctly hear Bella and Bee overhead, apparently throwing wardrobes at each other, though surely this was not possible.

Ignoring the pandemonium Lily said, 'My peaceful haven is no more!'

We heard them throw another wardrobe and then scream in unison, fling open a door, and thunder down the stairs, still screaming.

'Excuse me a minute!' I said, leaving Lily to cope with her own script, and ran out to intercept them.

But even as I shouted, 'Now what's all this commotion about?' I knew.

For a long rambling man, with a lion's grey mane of hair and a full moustache and beard, was holding out his arms, into which the children hurtled, crying, 'Daddy! Daddy! Daddy!'

So I walked forward, smiling, hand outstretched, and said with the utmost sincerity, 'Welcome to Parc Celli, Dick!'

'Oh, what a day!' Lily cried, smoothing the bedclothes and motioning Beau to jump up beside her. 'What choices. Heartache for me. Heart's ease for dear Clarissa. The tides of life and love run strong, Flivvy!'

I unfolded the legs of the supper tray and set it across her knees, saying, 'Just so. The bell's on the bedside table. If you want anything – ring!'

Lily laid a hand on my arm.

'I shall never forget the radiance in Clarry's face when her husband came to claim her!'

'Nor shall I,' I said with relish. 'Let's hope it lasts.'

'I shall miss her, of course. A sensitive girl. A sympathetic companion.'

'You can write to each other.'

Further fictions, on forget-me-not blue paper.

Lily's hand clutched and squeezed my arm.

'Be kind to Mr Skeggs, Flivvy. Tell him it was not to be.'

'I shouldn't worry. I expect a Cornish pasty will put him right in no time.'

I had fluffed my lines. Lily glided over them.

'To think I've been here all summer! London will seem strange at first.'

'One lungful of dirty air at Paddington,' I said irreverently, 'and you'll be back in the social swim.'

She ignored me, saying, 'How I shall miss you, darling – and this dear house.'

'No doubt you'll be here again sometime, Lily.'

'But my conscience is clear. I feel that I have seen you through the worst.'

'You do?' I asked, astounded.

'Oh yes! You're such an independent little thing, but I knew you needed moral support. And now my task is done I can return.'

To thank her would have choked me. I said, 'Oh, well. Eat up and – *bon appétit*!'

Lily surveyed her tray with immense satisfaction, and said,

'Darling, just one little favour. Could you possibly pack for me in the morning?'

'I'm packing for you tonight. As soon as I've eaten.'

'So kind to me always. Darling, one more tiny favour.'

'Breakfast in bed, to save your strength? An early lunch on a tray in your room? A little basket of goodies for the journey?'

I was giving her options.

'Thank you, darling.'

'Which?' I asked.

Lily said smiling graciously, opening the faded cornflowers of her eyes, 'All three, if it's not too much trouble, Flivvy.'

Tom, sworn to keep his mouth shut except for words of farewell, drove us to Camborne in a taxi which he had borrowed for the day, presumably in return for scrap. He cleaned and polished it first and then changed into his naval uniform for the occasion. The uniform smelled of mothballs, but he looked incredibly handsome and Lily was impressed. She leaned forward and tapped him girlishly on the shoulder.

'I didn't know you were an officer, Mr Faull.'

Tom, reading my expression in the driving mirror, fought his darker self and won.

'Yes, ma'am. A four-ringer!' he said good-naturedly, indicating the gold stripes on his cuffs.

Lily sank back in her seat and said to me in a stage whisper, 'What a difference life at Parc Celli has made to Captain Faull!'

Amused, but on his best behaviour, Tom saw Lily, her suitcases and her dog safely installed, bowed over her extended fingers, and then stepped back as we made our farewells: feet slightly apart, hands clasped behind his back as if he were indeed a captain, surveying his ship from the bridge.

'Safe journey!' I was saying, at the carriage window. 'Ring me as soon as you arrive home.'

Lily's chiffon handkerchief made motions at her lips and eyes. She held Beau up to be kissed.

'I've packed a nice bone for him,' I said. 'There, there. Good boy!'

I do hate being licked.

Lurch. Oh, thank God. Lurch.

'Allow me, madam,' said an elderly gentleman appearing behind her, 'to escort you safely to your seat.'

He raised his hat to me, and steadied himself and Lily as the train moved purposefully forward.

'Thank you so much. So very kind!' I called to him. And, 'Goodbye, Lily! Goodbye! Goodbye!'

'Goodbye, darling Flivvy!'

I saw the gilded wig turn to conquer. I imagined Lily's opening gambit.

'I've been staying with my daughter all summer. Well, my only child, really. One of life's sad stories. She needed someone to look after her, someone to see her through, and of course she's always relied on me.'

As the carriage windows rolled by me I caught sight of a funereal figure reflected many times, faster and faster and faster. And turned to see Martin Skeggs standing humble but resolute at the back of the platform, dressed in his best black suit, holding the top hat to his chest with both gnarled hands as if it were a presentation plate.

Entremêts

CHAPTER EIGHTEEN

Towards the end of September I travelled up to London to buy the bed linen, china and cutlery, discuss business with Humphrey, and close the flat. Apart from that first brief return, when my head was full of Parc Celli, I had not been back for nearly seven months. My time in Cornwall, looked upon first as a retreat from battle and then as an answer to my problems, had simply removed me to another sphere of war and posed different problems. Now, the thought of eating food cooked by someone else, being entertained by other people, and freed from my responsibilities for a week, put me in a holiday mood.

From the moment that I drew in a lungful of used air at Paddington station an old self possessed me. Her pulse and pace quickened, her shoulders dodged through or challenged the press of people. She beat a businessman to a taxi, settled back in her seat, exchanged views with the driver on the state of traffic, and watched the passing show. Once more she belonged to the city.

The basement flat called up old memories and unfulfilled hopes. A geranium on the kitchen windowsill, forgotten, had dried to dust. With difficulty I pushed up the bottom window, wedged it with a substantial copy of *Mrs Beeton's Household Cookery* which lay to hand for that purpose, and let in scents of spice and tar and soot and coffee. I lit the gas ring, and its narrow blue blade of flame, its hiss and tang, reminded me of other homecomings at different times and seasons. The tea in the Oriental tin caddy had lost its fragrance. I opened a fresh packet. Sat, stirred, sniffed, sipped and called up my younger past. The city's nostalgia returned to me. Suspended for a while between two worlds, I decided to let life unfold instead of pushing or persuading it.

Later I went walkabout, renewing old acquaintances, savouring the pleasure of finding anything and everything I wanted in a handful of shops nearby which were in no hurry to close. I rummaged in the bargain bins at the wine store on the corner. Bought a bunch of miniature roses and an *Evening Standard*. Sat at a table on the pavement and ordered a *cappuccino*. Spread out the entertainments page and marked everything I wanted to see or hear. On the way back I dropped in at the hairdressing salon which I had patronised on great occasions, and as a special favour they tucked me in for a cut, a blow-dry and a gossip.

Victoria in the rain. Sitting in Overton's restaurant on Monday evening I look down on a flock of wet black bobbing umbrellas, and bring Humphrey up to date with our Cornish news.

'Of course, you do realise, don't you, Humpty, that with all these delays we can't possibly open before the end of the year? Will Soady won't commit himself to a particular length of time on the roof and chimney. He says it depends what he finds and we're better to spend a shilling now than a pound later. That's metaphorically speaking, of course. It will probably cost an arm and a leg – so far *my* arm and *my* leg – and he's absolutely firm about replacing the present heating system, which is antiquated. And Tom's finished the stable roof and he's putting in new windows and doors. But after that he says he's prepared to start on the indoor decorating, and he has quite a few good ideas about the second floor.'

At this Humphrey lifts his head from the menu, smiles beatifically, and says, 'What a tower of strength Tom is! What an asset!'

'Yes, Humphrey, he really is a tremendous help.'

He looks at me closely.

'So you're friends now? You were uncertain about him at one time, I remember.'

'Oh yes, we're excellent friends now.'

'I'm glad,' says Humphrey, observing me benevolently over his half-moon spectacles. 'Very glad of that. And how is the dear fellow?'

I recount a tale to please him.

'He borrowed a taxi to take me to Camborne station, and dressed up in naval uniform – oh, and saluted smartly as the train pulled out!'

'Oh, ha, ha! Oh, ho! Oh, Tom. What a wag the man is.' He signals to a waiter and says we will begin with a dozen oysters apiece and a bottle of Chablis.

'As well as the champagne?' I ask. 'Can we drink it all?'

'I'm sure you'll find it's disappeared by the end of the evening!' says Humphrey archly.

Then becomes serious and confidential.

'Flavia, far be it from me to interfere with your household . . . '

On the contrary, I have known him turn my household upside down and inside out.

' . . . but surely you're not going to allow poor Tom to sleep in the stables through the autumn and winter, are you? I daresay they'll be waterproof, but I cannot see that they would be habitable, my dear.'

I am glad to be given the opportunity to explain our new arrangements.

'No, that occurred to me, too. So he'll be living in the house. I've given him the butler's room on the second floor and he's moving into it while I'm away and making himself comfortable, and he'll be keeping the steward's room downstairs as a study. He's partway through an Open University course, so it will be useful for him to have a decent radio and television at hand . . . '

'Ah, yes. The Open University. English literature, I believe? I know he studied for his O levels and A levels at sea. What an amazing person he is, don't you think, Flavia?'

'Yes. Yes, he is.'

'I do so admire people who educate themselves . . . Ah! Oysters!'

We are silent for several minutes, swallowing appreciatively. Then Humphrey finishes his glass of Chablis and replenishes it, tops up mine.

'So you're here for the week, dear girl. Doing what, precisely?'

'Oh, packing up my things and closing the flat. I know the lease doesn't run out for another three months but I can't keep bobbing up and down to London. Might as well get rid of it for good and all. Then there's the shopping for Parc Celli. Bed and table linen, china, glass and cutlery. We can't use your family antiques. They wouldn't take the wear and tear. And I'd like to see a couple of shows and look up one or two old acquaintances.'

'You'll be seeing Jack?'

I am shocked at the thought, and unceremonious with the suggestion.

'No, I certainly won't. So please don't tell him I'm here, Humphrey. I don't want any nasty surprises!'

'No, no, no,' he replies pacifying me, glancing at me slyly. 'I just wondered. And shall you be visiting Lily?'

'No. She only left me ten days ago. We've seen quite enough of each other for the time being.'

'Well, well, well. Quite a busy schedule, dear girl. But don't leave without seeing me again, will you? We must have another dinner together. Perhaps take in a show, a concert, an exhibition? Something like that.'

Doubt assails me, as I watch him tackle a Dover sole with relish. My own appetite deserts me. I lay down my knife and fork.

'But of course I shall be seeing you again, Humphrey. Aren't we visiting your solicitor this week to draw up our contract of partnership and sign it?'

He lifts his head, surprised, and says blandly, 'Oh, there's no particular urgency about that, is there?'

'Well, yes there is. I've committed myself and my services, and as we've spent your money I'm paying for everything at the moment. I must know where I stand.'

'But, my dear, what's the hurry?' Humphrey asks, taking his time over the Dover sole. 'I have given you my word. Tom, I might remind you, was quite content with a gentlemen's agreement. Tom trusted me.'

He dabs his mouth with his napkin and looks at me reproachfully.

'It's not a question of trust, Humphrey. It's a matter of business. There are points we should discuss.'

He flings the napkin down, saying peevishly, 'You know how I dislike talking business over a meal.'

All my new-found confidence in our partnership has vanished. I doubt him once more.

'Very well, Humphrey. We'll waive the discussion until we meet your solicitor. When is the appointment, by the way?'

As I feared, his tone changes from petulance to placation.

'Dearest girl,' he says, 'I have not exactly, that is to say not yet, not quite, *made* an appointment with the solicitor. Aha, aha.'

My doubt becomes a certainty. I was a fool to expect anything of him apart from charm, day-dreams and shilly-shallying.

I sip my wine and think and grow cold, and he watches me uncertainly.

'But of course I shall get in touch with him immediately – if you want me to!' he says.

When I answer him my voice is as chilled as the Chablis.

'The decision is up to you entirely, Humphrey. I leave it in your hands.'

This frightens him very much, and he asks when he will see me again. I say that depends on him, and when he has made an appointment with the solicitor he can ring me.

He has disquieted me once too often and I am already planning a way out of this impossible situation. I am on home ground in London. I can look after myself and am beginning to think I might prefer life that way.

So I pick up my knife and fork and try the Dover sole, which is delectable, and speak of other things.

That night the traffic keeps me company. In the distance the city hums and shines and promises to turn its pavements to gold. And Kelly Park is fast becoming a dream I once had, and Tom Faull and our growing fellowship are fading away with her.

In the morning I ring up old friends, book theatre tickets, and fill the week with engagements and appointments. My calendar floweth over.

Always return to places you have loved. The antidote lies in them.

Nick Rackham, looking elegant and distrait in a plum-red velvet jacket, striped shirt and matching bow-tie, is apprehensive when I walk into his bistro on the Tuesday evening.

Bon Appétit has a new name. She has changed sex and is called Nick's Place. Basically, apart from the cuisine, she remains the same: spindly chairs, check-clothed tables, a blackboard upon which the menu is scrawled in white chalk, and a provincial French décor.

I try their soup of the day: yesterday's left-over vegetables and stock cubes, or I'm a Dutchman. Their dish of the day: *coq au vin* made with cheap red wine and cooked too hard and too long. I suspect the chef's boasted fresh vegetables of being frozen. I try small helpings of two desserts: a gritty sorbet called autumn blackberry to make it sound more enticing, and a lemon meringue pie which must have been made from a packet. The wine list and the cheeseboard are still good. The coffee would no longer rate attention.

Nick, who has been watching nervously from a distance, now joins me, and hopes I have enjoyed the meal. I evade this poser by saying how lovely it is to be back in London. At which he gives up all pretence, orders two cognacs, sits down with me, and asks if there is any hope of my return. He is prepared to pay me a salary which I recognise as generous to the point of desperation. He will give me free rein in the kitchen, my own choice of menus, even a change of staff if I want it, and I can start as soon as I like.

Jerking a thumb over one shoulder in the direction of the kitchen he says, 'The bastard drinks!'

To which I reply, 'That wouldn't matter if he could cook.'

Nick Rackham laughs. He is a long and lanky young man, with melancholy dark eyes and a certain cadaverous charm, and he treats me with deference. We could get on well together. He begs me to consider. I say I will think it over and give him my decision at the end of the week.

Jack's voice tolls in my head, 'New to the business but thinks he knows it all, of course. God's answer to the *Michelin Guide*. Well, that's *his* problem.'

Apparently it was.

I am enjoying the sort of London visit known only to outsiders, greedily cramming everything into the space of a few days, instead of thinking I really must see that play, listen to that concert, see that exhibition – and doing nothing about it. But time is running out and Humphrey still has not telephoned. In the meantime I have been packing. I inspect my few possessions and discard some. There is no furniture worth keeping. I strike a high-spirited bargain with a second-hand dealer and ask him to remove it all when I have gone. My books and records, and what Humphrey would refer to as my bibelots, will fit into four tea-chests, and I arrange to store these for the time being. I take the contents of my wardrobe to the dry-cleaner's just down the street and return with them, pristine and plastic-bagged, twenty-four hours later. I am in the middle of nowhere, and finding it restful. I am in no place, and have escaped.

This Thursday evening I kneel on the floor before my old school trunk, packing clothes. Outside, I can hear the subdued roar of that enticing tiger called London. Unknown legs walk purposefully past my basement window. When I first came here, ten years ago, I had nothing but my ability to cook. I lived on hope, black coffee, and leftovers. Now I have a handsome sum of money in the bank, a reputation which has not been forgotten, and the offer of my old job at Bon Appétit without the responsibility of partnership. Housing in London is always scarce and expensive, but it should be possible to find another and a nicer flat. Why change an entire way of life and travel an unfamiliar road? Why take on so much and go so far away?

'Do you know why we live in a metropolis, Flick?' Jack Rice had said once. 'Because we're gipsies, and the city is nobody's resting place. We move on. We're genuine vagabonds. We change our addresses, our friends, our favourite haunts – and those we meet there. And our home is the road.'

He and I had walked, stumbled, fallen, picked ourselves up again, and run down that road for seven years.

I had assumed we were travelling together, and so made a home of him. Scraps of his philosophy, which had become my philosophy, continued to return and disturb me.

'Never give in to life. Play it – like a fish on a line!'

A lamp lights suddenly on the wall of a house opposite, and it seems to me that I am on the verge of a tremendous discovery, and must not imperil it.

On Friday a letter is delivered by special messenger and I open it with a sigh. The Prince of Procrastination has written at length on sheets of thick creamy parchment paper.

29 September 1978

Dearest Flavia,

What a coward I am! I find myself unable, after all, to lift up a telephone receiver and talk, or speak to you face to face, so I must write to you instead.

I realised that you were in a state of indecision when you dined with me on Monday, and consequently I felt that it would be foolish to pursue the question of partnership at that particular moment.

Oh, you liar! Hindsight has given you an excuse for doing nothing.

The reason I am writing to you is not to prevaricate about this suggested partnership . . .

Though prevarication is your middle name.

. . . but to shed a new light upon the word itself. It seems to me that I have been very remiss in expecting you to carry the full responsibility of Parc Celli upon your small but valiant shoulders. Flavia dear, I have often said you were the one lady with whom I could have shared my life. Now it occurs to me that if you are prepared to make such a commitment to me and my house I should make an even greater commitment to you.

I am asking you to become my partner in both senses. Dearest, would you be my wife?

At this I drop the letter and sit, appalled. I shall refuse him, of course, but that is not the problem. What does trouble me is the knowledge that Humphrey never proposes without knowing he will be rejected. He has done it twice before: on the eve of my engagement to Guy, and on the eve of my love affair with Jack Rice. So why should he believe it is safe to ask me a third time?

I turn to the next page.

As one grows older the question of continuity, in the human sense, grows ever more important. When I am gone there will be no one to inherit my estate. I am speaking not of money – such a vulgar necessity! – but of beloved possessions: my precious bibelots, my mother's furniture in this London flat, and above all of Parc Celli. Once certain legacies have been honoured – to my godchildren, close friends, old servants and so forth – my relatives will sell up and divide the rest of the spoils between them. Parc Celli and I will be no more than a memory.

Oh my God, he's perfectly serious!

I am not so foolish as to persuade myself that you could love me in the full sense of the word, nor would I expect that. Indeed, my dear Flavia, I am too old a dog to play the lover. What I am offering you is a marriage of dear friends who have known each other for many years, who share a common interest and look to a promising future.

I realise that Parc Celli cannot revert to its former status as a private house, nor would you be happy unless you practised your craft, but perhaps we could compromise on the present situation by making Grandmama's bedroom, her small parlour and the dining room our own? I should not be living there all the time, possibly just the spring and summer months. We could spend Christmas week together here in London, and I hope you would come up for short holidays with me from time to time.

And for your next offer, O Life – a country house, a flat in a London square, and a husband who absents himself for six months of the year.

You would of course inherit the bulk of my estate, and Parc Celli. I first opened my eyes on that consummate little kingdom sixty-odd years ago. I should like to close them there, knowing it will continue through you and your sons and – God willing! – their sons.

I am aware that I have asked too much of you many a time and oft, dear girl, but I will try hard not to be an encumbrance. An elderly and fairly useless husband is not what you deserve, Flavia. I would be the first to acknowledge that. Yet I do not come to you empty-handed. I honour and admire you. I am deeply fond of you. And in Parc Celli I rest my case.

Your always loving – whatever the answer – Humphrey

'Humpty? It's me, Flavia. Humpty, I don't know what to say.

At least, I do know what to say but not how to say it. Humpty, that is the most beautiful letter I have ever received in the whole of my life and I shall keep it. And I love you very much – but the answer is still "no".

'Sorry, sorry, sorry, but it wouldn't work. I'm not going to marry anyone ever again anyway, Humpty. I don't want to know another man that well. I'd like to keep an illusion or two. Yes, I do sound croaky. My throat is sore. What I needed was a good cry, and your letter did it. I've been howling for an hour, and I feel a lot better.

'Humpty, I don't want to sound unpleasant or ungrateful in any way, but all I'm prepared to do is to invest my capital, and run Parc Celli for a fair salary and half the profits. You were afraid I would want that? Darling Humpty, I'm sad it must be so. But I am serious, and I've had another offer. This time from Nick Rackham. He wants me back, giving me carte blanche and extremely good money at Bon Appétit – known as Nick's Place these days, by the by. You haven't been there since? Well, don't bother. The chef can't cook. I've promised to ring Nick at home on Sunday. So you have until then to think things over. And this time, my dearest Humpty, it must be yea or nay.

'Yes, I'd love to see you. Well, I shall be out today, but I'm free on Saturday evening. Yes, we could meet then for dinner. That would be lovely! Can we try one of those nouvelle cuisine places? No, I'm not following suit. I have my own ideas for Parc Celli. And I very much doubt whether your average Cornishman would thank you for a sliver of white fish in a pool of red sauce, decorated with seven mange-touts. They prefer large helpings of recognisable provender. Still, I'm always fascinated by other people's food.'

Some wicked imp persuades me to add, 'And whatever your decision, darling Humpty, I still love you!'

Oh, ho, ho.

And yet, and yet. Always the long drop after the high triumph. I am sad now because what he offered would have been everything I could desire, did I but desire *him*. Which I don't.

Still, I feel I have backed Humphrey into a corner and now he must commit himself fully. And then I can order my china and linen and cutlery and glass and go home again. The thought of Kelly Park possesses me. How could I have thought I would leave her? And what cliff-hanging tales I shall have to tell Tom when I get back. The thought of him leads me to plan supper for two. Mentally I check the game hanging in the larder. And from there, quite naturally fall to thinking of recipes.

Apart from a bunch of roses bought at a pavement stall, the basement flat, packed up and ready for clearance, has returned to anonymity. It is merely living space. Whereas down there in Cornwall, even in the ravages of neglect and decay, the spirit of Parc Celli lives on. She will be something special until they finally rase her to the ground. Will afterwards linger in the memory of those who have known her, to be seen in family albums, to be revived in anecdotes.

We are all mortal. The best we can expect is to be remembered kindly, lovingly, admiringly, as a person who was their own man, their own woman. Parc Celli has achieved that status. She exists in her own right.

And yet. Have I enough energy to deal with Humphrey's perpetual wriggles and evasions? Have I the stamina to take on the obligations of running a great house and making it profitable?

I am unsettled and dubious again. The noise of traffic keeps me awake. I think I can smell gas, and get up twice to check that all the taps are turned off.

On Saturday evening Humphrey concedes that we must talk about our business partnership and promises to book an appointment with his solicitor on Monday, but is then reluctant to agree to my personal proviso about planned and limited visits during Parc Celli's high season, and becomes querulous. We part in a state of mutual indecision.

On Sunday, uncertain of one option but unwilling to lose the other, I telephone Nick Rackham and ask for more time to consider.

On Monday, in a fine temper, I rearrange all my plans and ring Peggy Crowdy at the village shop to tell her I am staying on for another week. In that way I shall save at least half a dozen telephone calls, for she will broadcast the news. Also I am reluctant to talk to Tom, who has an uncanny knack of reading my mind.

On Tuesday morning, having heard no more from Humphrey, I ring him and say, 'Go to hell! You've lost your chance. I've finished with Parc Celli. I shall accept Nick Rackham's offer. And I'm not sure I love you after all!'

I dial Nick's number three times that day. Each time I put down the receiver before he can answer. Finally I sit on a tea chest and cry.

I have seen everyone who matters, and done everything I planned. I am weary of entertainment and grossly overfed. So I face an evening alone in London: an experience which so far I have lacked the courage to recall.

I don't draw my curtains at twilight because the world outside, though it cannot keep me company, does at least provide distraction. I make stories up about the legs which pass, or stop and meet other legs, or wait for legs to join them. I wonder what I might like to eat, and can neither decide nor care very much about food for myself. I fall into an old routine: post-Guy Pollard and pre-Jack Rice. I change into black velvet pants and a gold top, put on a Beatles record, pour myself a long stiff vodka and turn it into a Screwdriver with fresh orange juice and ice cubes, fill one Chinese bowl with peanuts and another with large green olives. I am back in the swinging Sixties: all dressed up and nowhere to go, trusting that someone will telephone or the doorbell will ring and fill the petrifying void.

Later, when every hope has dwindled, I shall soak for a long time in a fragrant bath, make a nightcap of milk and honey, take it to bed with a good thick paperback, and read myself into oblivion.

I remember that part very well.

And the Beatles singing 'Yesterday'.

A vehicle draws up outside. Since this is part of my solitary evening's entertainment I move over to the window and stand there, looking up. The van is newly sprayed a dazzling white, though travel has marred its purity. On the side is scrolled in a dashing green and gold script *Parc Celli Hotel and Restaurant.*

I repeat the words to myself in disbelief. I stare suspiciously into my empty glass. I look up again to make sure. The van is still there.

Presently, in leisurely fashion, a door slams shut and a pair of long legs stride across the pavement, dressed in navy-blue trousers. The trousers crease, in order to permit their owner to squat down and look into my window. They are followed by a naval jacket and an officer's hat, and beneath the hat is the bearded and sardonic face of Tom Faull.

I gape up at him, glass in hand. He salutes and grins. The legs stand up again and I hear them coming down the steps. Bemused, I stare through the window at the van. A brisk ring at my door forces me to take action. The action must have taken place in slow motion for the ring comes again, this time longer and more imperative.

I stumble across the room, calling crossly, 'All right! I'm coming!'

And open the door to find him leaning against the jamb with a derisive smile on his face.

He says comfortably, 'I knew you were up to no good here, Flavia. Thought I'd come to take you home. Do you like the sign on the side of the van? I had it done over the weekend. A favour somebody owed me . . . '

I am so delighted and relieved to see him that I castigate him as he makes himself at home.

'There are few things I dislike more than people marching into my flat, uninvited, helping themselves to my gin and tonic, and making black coffee for me in an ostentatious manner. I am not drunk, I am simply relaxing after a hectic day. And why you have taken it upon yourself to drive up to London in this high-handed manner I do not know! I have business to do here, and I have no intention of going anywhere until it's concluded. Nor am I returning in that van. I have a perfectly good ticket and should prefer to travel by train. You seem to think that you and Parc Celli own me. Well, you couldn't be more wrong. It may interest you to know that I might not be coming back at all. Except to collect my summer clothes. It may interest you to know—'

'Some tongue you've got,' says Tom pleasantly. 'I know more about this situation than you do, Flavia. And I'll tell you the news while we're eating. Have you got any bacon and eggs?'

'No, I have not. Not because I'm neglecting myself but because I don't eat bacon and egg for breakfast. I've been eating out mostly, you see. I've had an absolutely wonderful week here, and gone short of nothing, and I can't think why I ever went away. In any case I don't want to eat bacon and egg. It would make me feel sick. There's half a pint of milk in the fridge, and a small loaf in the bin. What are you doing in my kitchen, opening and shutting cupboard doors?' Following him, arms folded. 'I don't like it.'

'I'm checking up on your supplies, Flavia. Not exactly Parc Celli standard. More like a church mouse. Now you come and sit down,' he says kindly, steering me back into the bed-sitting room, 'and drink your coffee while I do some shopping. I saw a supermarket open on my way down the street.'

He finishes his gin and tonic and claps his hat smartly on his head.

I am weary, and weary of fighting, but have not yet thrown in the sponge. Nor will I be pushed around and taken for granted.

I say hardily, 'You may as well take yourself off to Cornwall, where you belong. I shall lock the door when you've gone out, and I shan't open it when you come back.'

He smiles down on me with genuine amusement.

'I shouldn't do that if I were you, my lass. I'd have to put a brick through the window.'

'You wouldn't do that!' I say positively.

He smiles again.

'Would you?' I ask uncertainly.

He smiles wider.

'Oh yes,' says Tom Faull, 'I would.'

CHAPTER NINETEEN

Tom had composed my simple supper with care. A slice of duck pâté lay in a scallop shell of fresh lettuce, from it spoked a wheel of thinly sliced tomato, dill pickle and cucumber, and round the rim of the dinner plate were arranged triangular snippets of toast. He had laid the tray with a cloth, and made me a pot of Earl Grey tea. He had peeled, cored and quartered an apple, and served it up with a triangle of Brie, a fringed stalk of celery and two Bath Oliver biscuits.

'All right, then?' he asked jauntily.

Despite the light-hearted attitude and tone, I detected a need for approval beneath this enquiry.

'Yes,' I said sincerely, 'it looks lovely. Very professional, I must say. And I'm sure it will taste delicious. Thank you, Tom.'

He adopted his storytelling stance.

'You say professional? Well, I suppose you might call it that. Did I ever tell you that I started off as a ship's steward? Wasn't my line of country, of course, and they chucked me out after a few months. The chief steward was a bastard. But I picked up a few ideas on the way.'

I was too tired to listen, and he knew it.

He said, 'Remind me to tell you sometime how I spilled a tray of soup over the petty officer. Now would the smell of bacon and egg make you feel sick?'

'No. I just couldn't eat it.'

'Then I'll fry up for myself and join you.'

He had the ability to make himself at home without being intrusive.

'Feet up!' Settling me comfortably on the sofa.

'Good concert on tonight!' Tuning in the radio.

'Cold this evening!' Turning up the gas fire.

'Now you tuck in, Flavia. Don't wait for me.'

But I did, and we ate together, trays on our knees, listening to the music in silent fellowship. Then when Tom judged me to be in a receptive mood he sat back in his chair, stretched out his legs to the gas fire, and began, 'Now I've had a talk with the squire . . . '

He had telephoned Humphrey as soon as Peggy Crowdy retailed my message, and found him totally disorientated. Leaving Vera to keep an eye on Parc Celli, Tom had then driven up to London, stayed with Humphrey overnight, put him together again, and taken him round to the solicitor that afternoon.

'I jotted down the main points,' he said, taking out a notebook, 'and made one suggestion which the squire accepted. There's a flaw in it, mind, which you might like to talk about – and there again, you might not, and it's your own business. Anyhow, the solicitor's setting up a contract along these lines, and he says he'll be communicating with you shortly. I think you'll find it to your liking. You can make your own amendments – and so can the squire, of course, though I don't think he will. I think you spiked his guns this time.'

I read the notes through.

'It seems fair enough, though there's no mention of any expenses I've incurred in the past months, nor my board wages,' I remarked drily. 'Still, you wouldn't know about that, and I'd more or less said goodbye to a refund. I also see that I must spend ten thousand pounds before Humphrey needs to put another penny into the business.

'But you've got a lot more than ten thousand to spend,' Tom pointed out, 'and I don't think the squire has. And you've got the edge on him. The business is to be run entirely under your jurisdiction.'

'Yes, I see that. What was the suggestion with a flaw in it?'

'I thought he should make a new will to protect your interests. So that, in the event of his death, Parc Celli was to continue to be run by you as a hotel and restaurant, and you were to pay the squire's percentage of profits to his family. But if for any reason the house had to be sold – such as the estate being bankrupt – you were to be given first option to buy it.'

He was far ahead of me in terms of progress. Wills were the next item on my long-delayed agenda.

'How did he take that?' I asked respectfully.

'He's thinking about it. There's another snag. If he snuffed it too early you might be in trouble.'

'Yes,' I said, seeing yet another bleak prospect. 'I'd need a few good years to amass enough capital.'

'That's what I thought,' said Tom. 'So I pointed that out to him, and suggested that he willed Parc Celli to you altogether.'

I lifted my head and looked at him in amazement.

'Did you, indeed? That *was* aspiring! What did he say to that?'

Tom looked directly back at me.

'He wasn't going to be pinned down on that one. He said you could have inherited everything he possessed but you'd turned him down.'

'Oh, he *did* have a heart to heart with you!' I said, avoiding his eyes.

'You made the right decision. It wouldn't have worked,' said Tom frankly. 'But he said he had to be fair to his family – meaning, I suppose, Flash Jack, Clarry Gibbon and the Bristol Mob. So he would only go part way.'

'I see.' I thought of my other partnership. 'When Jack Rice and I started Bon Appétit we made wills and left our shares to each other.'

Tom was brisk about this

'The circumstances were quite different. Neither of you had anybody else to leave it to, and the bistro wasn't your home.'

I was silent, feeling I don't know what: relief mixed with apprehension, a curious sense of being failed yet again by Humphrey. Still, that was not Tom's fault, and he had acted in my interests.

So I said, 'Thank you for all you've done, Tom.'

'I did my best, but you're not through the wood yet.'

'You've done very well. Marvellously, in fact.' I could not help adding, with a sense of failure, 'Better than I did or could.'

'I'm not as close to the problem as you are,' said Tom graciously.

'But you *are* closer to Humphrey.'

'He's never asked me to marry him!' said Tom, and made me laugh.

'It wasn't marriage,' I said at last. 'Not what I call marriage. Not that I know what marriage is.'

He sat looking at me thoughtfully, hands clasped between his knees, as he had on that wild whisky morning at Parc Celli. I had the feeling that he thought more of me than he was prepared to say. And then again, I could have been wrong. My judgement of men can hardly be called sound.

He said, 'Are you going to accept the contract, Flavia?'

'I'm not sure.'

He veered away from the point in order to tackle it from a fresh angle.

'I see you're all packed up. Is this furniture to go down to Cornwall? No? What about the tea-chests? We can take those in the back of the van.'

'They're going to be stored in London,' I said feebly, 'in case I stay here.'

He stared at me long and hard and said, 'The squire told me about that idea, too. It wouldn't work, Flavia.'

I flared up immediately.

'Why shouldn't it? What do you know about it? I loved Bon Appétit. It was mine.'

He remained steadily on course.

'Got a new name now, I hear. Isn't yours any more.'

He sat forward and spoke with authority.

'Flavia Pollard, you made yourself a reputation at Bon Appétit. You can't go back to a place you've once owned and work there as an employee. That'd be selling yourself short. Think about the implications – good word, that! – Flash Jack'd be round there in five minutes flat, putting in the needle and probably the knee. And the lad who owns it couldn't look after you from what I hear of him.'

'I don't need anyone to look after me!' I said defensively.

He smiled and said pacifically, 'We all need someone to look after us, for our different needs and in our different ways.'

It was true, and I was silent.

He spread out his arms to indicate the anonymous room. 'And when the bistro closes at night what have you got to come back to?'

'It looks very cosy when it's lived in,' I said defensively.

He shook his head.

'Flavia, I'm not talking about carpets and curtains. If it was a penthouse I'd say the same. There's nothing and no one in London for you now. But at Parc Celli there's both house and home and all of us, and a future you've marked out for yourself. Don't change gold for pinchbeck.'

'You don't understand,' I said captiously. 'I love being back in London again. I've enjoyed myself, doing exactly what I wanted, for a whole beautiful week. I like the convenience, the immediacy of city life. Whereabouts in Cornwall could you have found a shop open at this time of night? Where could I take my pick of theatres and concerts? Where could I drop in on an old acquaintance, or arrange to meet someone in half an hour, down there? I haven't even *got* an old acquaintance in Cornwall!'

He watched me shrewdly, spoke persuasively.

'Well, I can understand that. But there'll be slack periods at Parc Celli when you can take a week off and come up here and enjoy yourself. We'll keep the place going for you, while you're away. And once it's open you'll meet all sorts of people and make a heap of new friends.'

I wondered whether he was being eloquent on my behalf or his own. Uncertain of his motive, and of myself, I would not be cajoled.

'Samuel Johnson said that the man who was tired of London was tired of life.'

'That's because he'd got everything he wanted here,' said Tom reasonably. 'And if you had the equivalent of Parc Celli up here I'd be the first to advise you to hang on to it. But you haven't. What I'm saying to you, Flavia, is that there's nothing in London for you. And there's a whole world waiting for you back home. There's one more thing, too. You gave the squire a real fright.'

He smiled as he thought of it, and shook his head.

'I thought he was worried when I walked in and I made sure he stayed that way. Made out you'd been restless down in Cornwall. Said I'd been afraid you wouldn't come back. Shouldn't think you'd have any more trouble with him, Flavia.'

Then I laughed aloud, and conceded his point, asking him honestly, 'Tom, I've often wondered. What hold have you got over Humphrey?'

He pondered this and answered as honestly.

'He's always liked me, always taken my side, even as a boy. Oh, I know what folk say about my mother and the old squire – though they'd best not say it to me, unless they want to feel the weight of my fist. But I mean more to him than I am. I'm an idea that he cherishes. This sounds like boasting, but perhaps I'm what he'd have wanted to be and I've led the kind of life he dreamed about. I'm a dream, if you like. But the bond's there for both of us. I could turn up again after twenty years, and he was still glad to see me. And I think the world of him, make no mistake about that. Because he's an idea for me, too. For me he's the squire of Parc Celli. And because of what he represents I watch out for him and take care of him, and he knows it.'

I needed to understand where I stood in this tri-partite relationship, though I found it difficult to ask. I managed the question in a tone which endeavoured to be nonchalant.

'But you take care of me, too. What happens when the loyalties clash?'

He looked grave, and then impish.

'I could never resist a challenge!' he said cheerfully, dismissing the conundrum. 'Now what's your answer? This or Parc Celli?'

I said irritably, 'I don't know why I should choose to put myself in harness – and in jeopardy – for the sake of a house.'

He smiled then, in supreme understanding.

'I do,' said Tom. 'I reckon you'd call it love, Flavia. And love means responsibility without power – as someone said who seemed to know.'

He was taking me out of my depth, and my reply was vehement.

'Well, I don't like it,' I cried. 'I like to be in control.'

'You're always in control,' said Tom. 'You may not be able to help what you feel, but you can choose what you're going to do about it.'

That was also true.

'So what are you going to do?' he asked.

I thought of Jack Rice walking into Bon Appétit, smiling, knife at the ready. I thought of my way of life: providing a magical evening for other people, without having magic of my own. I thought of returning, tired out, to some flat like this, of the empty Sundays when no one called and no one cared. I thought of my sons, bored by having nothing to do and nowhere to go. I thought of the proximity of Lily, and the endless flow of futile chatter. I thought of Victoria in London: rusting in the street, an expense rather than a convenience, while I tried to pass my driving test. And yet how could I part with her? I even thought of the van, newly painted and inscribed with a legend I should never create. And lastly I thought of this big bearded Cornishman on whom, I now realised, I had begun to depend. A few months ago, the idea of life without Tom Faull would have been an immense relief. Now I was shocked at the thought of losing him.

I said abruptly, 'I suppose I can hardly let everybody down at this stage!' Which was not truth but expediency.

Tom met me more than half-way, and his tone was full of faith.

'I never thought you would, Flavia.'

Another silence.

I asked hesitantly, daring to put my trust in him, 'Will you keep up the pressure on Humphrey for me, Tom?'

'My word on it!' he said devoutly.

'Well then . . . oh, but I can't go home right away! Now I've made up my mind for the second time I've got shopping to do. For Parc Celli.'

He stood up, alight with pleasure and relief.

'I can wait,' said Tom. 'I'm only here to help. I can drive you round. Carry parcels for you.'

We glanced at each other at the same time, and smiled shyly.

'I expect you're tired,' he said, 'and I know I am. Time to doss down. Where did the boys sleep when they stayed with you?'

'On Z-beds, in here. But sometimes we all went down to Surrey and stayed with Lily.'

'That must have been a riot,' said Tom, and made me giggle.

'But I've sold the Z-beds!' I said, and giggled again.

'That's all right. I've brought my sleeping bag with me.'

'You can sleep on the sofa.'

'No, I can't,' said Tom. 'It's too short and too narrow. I'll sleep on the floor.'

I was feeling tenderly towards him for saving my hide and pride.

'Oh, but are you sure you'll be comfortable on the floor in a sleeping bag?'

'I can bunk down anywhere, Flavia,' said Tom. 'And I have done. I could tell you a few tales about that – remind me sometime. Now I'll cook breakfast tomorrow while you sleep in for a bit. And when you've done your telephoning we'll be off shopping. Might as well ring Peggy Crowdy and tell her when we're likely to be back. Then Vera will have your bed made up fresh, and a fire lit, and something in the oven for us to eat.'

He stopped and asked blandly, 'You going home by train, or coming with me, by the way? I've fixed the van up with new seats and head cushions. Proper job. We can stop whenever you like. Look around. But you just say the word and I'll drop you at Paddington station.'

I pictured us travelling home down the long green English coast, county after county, taking the journey easily. Lunch here. Tea there. And Parc Celli waiting for us at the end of the road.

'No-o,' I said slowly. 'I'd rather like to try the van out. And I think the respray and the logo looks splendid – though rather ambitious. We aren't a hotel or a restaurant yet, you know.'

'We shall be,' said Tom, with the utmost faith.

I slept fitfully and dreamed fearfully that night, waking from time to time as a taxi drew up, a voice shouted in the night, a bus rumbled away to its depot. We were only a partition apart, Tom and I: a situation which reflected real life. Close, but not together. So I lay awake and listened, and dozed and dreamed, and met him swimming in the bottom of a well of sleep, and rose again to the surface, alone. And wondered whether he, too, was plagued by our physical proximity and the emotional tension between us.

CHAPTER TWENTY

October

'Flavia!' said Tom. 'Stop cooking and come out for a spin.'

'Why?'

'Because it's a fine autumn day and there won't be many more. And it's a Sunday. That means a holiday for everybody. Don't you hold with holidays?'

'I just wanted to try out this recipe for apple soup.'

'Try it out on Monday. What were we having for lunch? Apple soup?'

'Well – yes.'

'I'm a guinea-pig, am I?' Grinning.

'I was going to eat it, too.'

'How long will it take to finish?'

'About ten minutes.'

'Proper job. I'll pack the rest of the food in one of those antediluvian picnic baskets. And I'll make a Thermos of coffee for you and a Thermos of tea for me, and fill the other Thermos with soup, and we'll take the afternoon off.'

One hand on hip, the other one stirring slowly, rhythmically, I protested.

'But I have to write my weekly letter to the boys this afternoon.'

'Ring them up this evening instead.'

'The school doesn't like parents to ring up unless it's important – besides, Guy might hear of it and be difficult.'

'Balls to the school. And sod Guy,' said Tom pleasantly. 'Write this evening. It won't make any difference. Jeff'll pick it up tomorrow morning.'

He hauled a picnic hamper from the recesses of a corner cupboard.

'Knew how to make them in those days,' he remarked. 'This'll be about seventy years old. Held some good provender in its time. Shooting parties—'

'Raised pies. Brawn. Cold meats. Hard-boiled eggs,' I said automatically. 'Rich fruit cake. Apple dumplings and cream. Wine cup.'

'And stew and ale for the beaters,' Tom finished prosaically. 'Which cake is for eating now?'

I shrugged, sighed, smiled in spite of myself. He had made up his mind I was to have a day off. The question was settled. The subject closed.

'The Dundee cake in that square Huntley and Palmer's tin.'

I do believe he knew every inch of my domain by now. Moving between the dresser and the refrigerator, deftly, softly, as big men can, he packed the basket, muttering,'bread, bread knife, butter, butter knife, plates, cups, saucers, spoons . . . '

'You sound like Rat in *Wind in the Willows*!'

Briefly he surfaced, grinning at me, 'Serviettes'. He corrected himself ostentatiously, mocking me. '*Napkins*, that is! – whether they be paper or fine linen. Napkins! Pepper, salt. We're having ham are we? Mustard . . . '

'And put a bottle of red wine in, as well as white. Then we can choose which we prefer. No, it doesn't matter which. None of them could be called great wines, but they're all reasonable and ready for drinking.'

'And four glasses – because you won't mix the wines, supposing we were to finish both of them, and you won't drink out of plastic cups. What it is to be fussy! Now you put on your bonnet and shawl, Flavia, and we'll be off.'

'Where are we going and in which vehicle?' I asked.

'It'll be new to you wherever we go,' said Tom. 'You've hardly put your nose outside the door since you first came here. And we'd best take Victoria. See how he's running since the rebore.'

'She. How much do I owe you for that?'

'Nothing.'

'Someone did you a favour, did they?' Cynically.

'Never you mind that. That's my business.'

I tied a silk scarf round my head, hung a plastic raincoat over my arm, and locked up.

'So long as I don't spend the afternoon sitting at the roadside while you have to mend something!' I remarked. 'Which has been known.'

Tom refused to take this bait.

'You want to drive?' he asked politely.

'No, thank you. I'd rather not have a row on my day off.'

We sat on the side of the hill and looked down into the bay. Lunch had been long and leisurely, and we had drunk a bottle of Cabernet Sauvignon between us.

'What do you think of that then?' Tom asked.

'Very peaceful. Very beautiful.'

'Two good reasons for living here. Fresh air and space make two more.'

He lay on his back, plucked a blade of grass and chewed it, staring up into the bowl of sky. We had come here for a purpose quite apart from the picnic. I knew by the way he screwed up his eyes and spoke placidly, casually. I sat and hugged my knees and felt a breeze tug the scarf knot beneath my chin, and suffered an old twinge of foreboding.

'I think you've been a mite hard on the squire,' Tom began. 'As I said, Flavia, he's a gentleman, and he was brought up to expect folk to fetch and carry for him, and to do what he wanted. You won't change his attitude, but it can be modified.'

'So?' Defensively.

'I thought you caught him up a bit sharpish last night, when he talked about coming down this month. You've got your contract now. I think you should ask him. Make him feel wanted. Make him part of the project.'

I could think of several objections to that idea, but for the moment I said nothing. My heart began its insistent beat of warning. My breath came shorter. He was trying to manipulate me.

Tom changed course.

'As you say, we can't open before the end of the year. Will wants to go over the whole roof before they leave, make sure all the slates are fixed. Not a big job, shouldn't cost more than a few hundred. And I'll clean all the jackdaws' nests from the chimneys – dozens of them. Clean the gutterings – miles of them. Must have the outside ship-shape, ready to face the winter. We don't know what the weather will bring. And we don't want any more catastrophes.' His tone changed. 'Those two lads of yours are coming down for half-term, aren't they?'

Anxiety and anger allowed me only to say, 'Yes!'

In London, half-terms had meant a day out for the three of us. I wished I was back there now. Wished I had never left. At least I knew how much was expected of me, and how little would be given. I was not at sea with a man who had Humphrey under control and was now seeking to control me.

'Pat's the squire's godson,' said Tom, ruminating, sucking his stalk of sweet grass, 'and it seems to me that he thinks a lot of them both. Pretty proud of them – as he is of you. Why don't you ask the three of them down together. Nobody else. Just a family party. For the week. Then they could travel together. There and back.'

I could think of no better reason than, 'Humphrey travels first-class.'

Tom answered, as I should have answered myself, 'I know you've got to watch expenditure, but you're not poor. You could pay the difference, just for once. Next October the house'll be full. There won't be room or time to enjoy them as much as you could now. Besides, it's your birthday round about the end of the month, isn't it? That's something for everybody to celebrate.'

'How did you know it was my birthday?' Instantly suspicious.

'I pick things up, here and there.'

Tom was pursuing his own course, unmindful of my turmoil.

'It's a way to show the squire that he is wanted, but only at certain times and for so long. Why not try it?'

I looked down at his dark secretive face and greying beard, at the strong heavy body which made his cheap clothes splendid. A ruminative smile moved over his mouth. He plucked another stalk of sweet grass, and chewed. I looked at mouth and stalk and looked away.

I jumped up and said, 'No!' vehemently. 'No! No! No!'

As he rolled over on to his side, astounded, I cried, 'No, I shall *not* try it. I'll do things *my* way. Meaning no interference from anyone. Anyone at all. Ever. And particularly you!'

He pushed himself up on to his feet, spoke softly, though his eyes were wary and his face colourless.

'Then *no* it is, Flavia.'

He wandered over to the picnic basket, whistling quietly to keep himself in countenance, and began to pack it.

I clenched my hands into fists and cried at his bent back. 'This isn't the first time you've tried to manipulate me, and I won't have it.'

He straightened up at that, kicked the basket over, stuck his hands in his pocket, and marched off.

'Where are you going?' I called. 'I haven't finished talking to you.'

He turned a pallid furious face in my direction.

'But *I've* finished talking to *you*,' he shouted. 'And this time you've seen and heard the last of me. I shall pack my traps and go.'

'Where to?' I shouted back with fierce pleasure. 'Where to? You've got nowhere to go, and nothing and no one to go to!'

I thought of the blackest truths I could, piled the sins of Guy Pollard, Jack Rice and Humphrey Jarvis on top of them, and yelled them after my scapegoat's retreating back.

'And you never will have. Because you don't know what love and trust and commitment means. You only know how to make yourself agreeable to people so that you can use them.'

He continued to stride away, shoulders hunched against the onslaught.

'*Use* them!' Louder. 'And *manipulate* them.' Louder still. 'And set them *against* one another.' Loudest of all. 'For your own *devious* reasons.'

Fears and frustrations had tormented me for so long that it was pure joy to translate them into words. And yet as they winged their venomous way towards Tom Faull they lost their power for me, and I knew them to be groundless. Certainly he liked to organise and influence the course of events, but with no ill intent.

There was mischief in him, but no malice. In this instance he had been trying to find the best solution for the problem of Humphrey.

The knowledge of his innocence mollified me. I recognised that an old personal nightmare had tricked me into panic. I felt washed clean, and sorry. I should have liked to wipe the last few minutes out and start again. But it was too late.

He had swung round and was striding back towards me, black brows drawn together, dark face flushed. I hesitated. To say I no longer believed what I had said would sound implausible. To run away would be spineless. So I stood my ground in mute agitation. I did not think he would hit a woman, but with Tom I could never be sure of anything.

He stopped a few inches away from me. He spoke in a low pent voice as if the rage in him had been bottled, and the cork was about to blow.

'Now that's done it!' growled Tom. 'You've been chipping away at me since we met, and I took it because you'd got no reason to trust me, though I tried hard to trust you. Then we sorted ourselves out. At least I *thought* we sorted ourselves out. But now it seems I'm in the wrong again, through no fault of my own. And I'm not taking any more. So you listen to *my* side of the story!

'All I wanted was to live in Parc Celli stables in peace and quiet, and help out the squire when and where I could. That was how he and I understood it, and nobody else was involved. Just him and me. And life was simple. Then while I was at sea you took over. And by the time I got back you were masterminding the squire and Parc Celli, and nobody else was welcome. Yes, Flavia, you were a very large pattern. That's a Cornish expression. Do you know what it means? It means you had a big opinion of yourself!'

'"Do your best for her," the squire said. "Life hasn't been easy for her, and she's going through a difficult time. You may find her over-sensitive at first."

'*Over-sensitive!* Let me tell you this, Flavia Pollard. The minute I saw that sour little face staring me up and down at the kitchen door, and heard that crisp little English voice advising me to go elsewhere, I thought, "By Christ, Tom, how're you going to live with this, boy?" But I hadn't any choice, and I'd given the squire my word, and I did try.

'I treated you with respect and made sure that everyone else did. And let me tell you this – you may have thought of *me* as an outsider who wasn't to be trusted, but in Elinglaze *you* were the outsider, and nobody trusted *you*. They thought you'd got your hooks in the squire! And some said you were rich and wanted to marry him for his position. And others said you were poor and wanted to marry him for his money. And all of them thought you were using him one way or the other.

'I put things as straight as I could, but some folk would sooner hear gossip than truth. I patched up misunderstandings between you and the squire, and thought of ways to make life easier for you, and I saved the day for you and Parc Celli more than once. But good, bad or indifferent, Flavia, I did my bloody best. I bloody tried. And yet according to you that's still not enough.'

He spread out his arms and asked the white and blue heaven above him to witness my ingratitude.

'What do I get by way of thanks?' A bitter pause. 'Bugger all I get!'

He shook a finger at me.

'So I don't know what love and trust and commitment means? Now that's the pot calling the kettle black! I'm pissed off with working for a woman who gives food instead of love, and service instead of trust, and only commits herself in black and white on a legal document. And if you're talking about manipulating people you must think of yourself! Pushing the old squire into a scheme that excludes him, cutting me down to size whenever I use my initiative, and using thanks and smiles like carrots to make a donkey trot. Just think of that, Flavia!'

He shook his head from side to side in sheer disbelief.

'May God forgive me!' he said. 'There are times when I've thought Guy Pollard and Jack Rice had a point of view!'

He shrugged, and thrust his hands back into his pockets. His colour and temper had subsided. His inner light grew dim, his aspect sallow.

'But that's all over and done with,' he said sombrely. 'I'll ring up the P & O tomorrow, and tell them there's a chief engineer looking for a berth.'

He had one shot left in his locker, and fired it.

'And now I'm walking home, and you can drive yourself back. There's a map in the car if you don't know your way. And you'll be able to make all your usual mistakes without me saying a word. You can bugger up the clutch and clash the gears as much as you like. It's all yours. And if you're caught driving without a licence that's your problem. And bloody good luck to you!'

His rage left him as abruptly as mine had left me. We stood, uncertain of the next step, glancing doubtfully at each other.

Around us the day was just beginning to wane. Sky, bay, turf, heather and gorse were being transmuted into gold by the light of an autumn afternoon. And up into the shimmering air rose two buzzards, riding the wind in ritual courtship. We watched them fly higher and higher, in smaller and smaller circles, to hang for a charmed moment upon the air, reach a decision, then fold their wings and plummet earthwards.

We glanced at each other again. The phantom of a smile hovered peaceably between us. He had been wrong in saying that I offered food instead of love. Food was an expression of love. About much else he had been right. It was my turn to make the first move.

Wordlessly, I set up our spurned picnic basket and extracted the bottle of Chardonnay. Held it out to him, and automatically polished the two clean glasses on a piece of Kleenex. Wordlessly also, Tom uncorked the bottle, poured out two measures of golden wine carefully, correctly. We raised our glasses in a silent toast of truce.

As we were finishing the bottle he said in an apologetic tone, 'I didn't mean to interfere, Flavia. About inviting the squire. I just thought that a gesture to him on your part would show good sense – and kindliness.'

I conceded the good sense, and pondered over the kindliness.

I asked him earnestly, '*Am* I unkind, Tom?'

He answered me seriously.

'Not by nature, no. And not nearly as prickly as you used to be. But you've had to fight to survive, and now you fight out of habit. Sometimes you come out fighting before the bell goes.'

The point was taken. Being too proud to admit it I hoped he might take my silence for agreement. He did.

'I suffer from the same trouble in a different way,' said Tom frankly, addressing his glass of Chardonnay. 'I've had to be cunning to survive. Sometimes I'll cover up the truth when I needn't do. Lay too many plans and seem like a rogue. Talk too much and sound like a liar.'

He turned his head to look fully at me. I made a grimace of understanding.

'Parc Celli is your house in all but your name,' he said factually. 'And the squire is your partner and nobody else's. So it's your decision. All the decisions are yours. And I'll say one more thing. Pat and Jem are your sons, whether the judge gave them to their father or not. And I'll bet you a hundred pounds – which I can afford to do because I know I'm right – that when they're old enough to leave home it's you and Parc Celli they'll be heading for. And now I've said my piece.'

Then he sat up and said, 'Are you going to bite my head off if I suggest driving us home? We've both had a skinful and we don't want to get caught.'

'No,' I said, smiling. 'I think that's a very good idea. Tom! Am I still such a bad driver?'

'I'd have said,' he replied judiciously, 'that you were about ready to take the test. Fact is, Victoria's not an easy car to learn on. You manage her very well, considering.' He paused, and added, 'Everything I said should have been said a long time since, or let be. It isn't true any more.'

'I know. *I* said a lot of things that aren't true any more.'

'But they needed to be said, so they could be put away for good.'

'Yes. We had to say what we felt then, in order to know what we feel now.'

Tom held out his hands, and I clasped them. For a charmed moment we hovered, like the buzzards. He gave my hands a little shake and said, 'All right now, Flavia?' in an enquiring tone.

He was uncertain about something. I reflected, with a pang,

that he might well feel about me as he felt about Vera: genuinely fond, but no more. Afraid of misreading him I plummeted to earth alone.

'The best of friends, Tom!'

He seemed to take his cue from that, and released me. The moment was over. We walked back to the car and drove home in a silence that was in no way less amicable, but heavy with unspoken feelings.

So I decided to invite Humphrey with the boys for half-term. And as Tom knew best how to deal with Humphrey I asked him to propose the visit, and listened in admiration as he shunted his squire tactfully into place.

'I think that the lady wants you to herself, if you know what I mean, sir,' he began delicately. 'She likes to concentrate on your food and comforts and your company – you know how she is, sir. And, to tell the truth, I'd like some time with you to discuss the house plans. We're looking two or three years ahead now, and I need your judgement on one or two ideas of mine.'

Enthusiastic murmurs from the telephone.

'That's not saying,' Tom added slyly, 'that you and I can't slip off and do a bit of off-shore fishing in the evenings. I've made a new bait. Called it the Parc Celli Magnet.'

Tremendous enthusiasm from the telephone. Followed by a cautious feeler.

To which Tom replied adroitly, 'Well, it's not my place, Mr Jarvis, to discuss any guest of yours, but if I might make so bold I'd say the gentleman wasn't on the Parc Celli wavelength. Yes. Quite. Very wise of you, sir. 'Nuff said. Then I'll be off, Mr Jarvis. Plenty to do here, morning, afternoon and evening. Yes, I'm helping out in any way I can. A general factotum, as you might say. And we want that new chimney ship-shape to welcome you, don't we? Yes, and to you, sir. All the best. Cheers. Yes, here she is.'

He put his hand over the receiver and said, 'Flash Jack's out of favour!'

'You conniving rat!' I said charitably, and took it from him saying, 'Hello, Humpty. How are you? Looking forward to the end of October? Yes, so are we! Humpty how do you feel about Cornish Riviera Fish Soup with Rouille? Well, it's the same as Mediterranean Fish Soup, but made entirely from local ingredients – and with one or two personal touches.'

Tom also spoke to the boys after I had done, in a tone which was both brisk and intimate.

'Now then, you lads. I want you to fetch your working clobber as well as your fishing gear. I need a couple of extra labourers. We're up to the eyes in repairs and decoration. All right? That's good, then. That'll be bonza. See you! Here's your mother again.'

He handed the receiver back to me, saying *sotto voce*, 'And you've no need to look like that. They're young men, not babies. They'll enjoy doing their bit and they understand me.'

I was not so sure. I spoke softly to my nurslings.

'Darlings, Tom was only joking. I don't expect you to work.'

'Oh, but we're looking forward to it, Mum,' said Patrick. 'And I can do heavy work. I've been weight-lifting this term.'

'Pat's been weight-lifting, this term, Tom,' I said, in an aside that was both proud and fearful.

'Good on him!' said Tom. 'I'll introduce him to Peggy Crowdy's uncle. He used to be a champion Cornish weight-lifter and wrestler. He taught me.'

I retailed this information to the boys.

'I'd like to wrestle,' said Pat promptly.

Divining my fears, he added, 'Truly we want to help you with Parc Celli, Mum – and we do like old Tom! We think old Tom's great!'

CHAPTER TWENTY-ONE

I stand in the lighted doorway. And up the broad front steps of Parc Celli, and out of the chilly autumn evening, come my three dear expected and invited guests: faces upturned and smiling, proffering cold cheeks and hands.

'Dearest Flavia, so good to be home again.'

'Hello, Mum. Where's Tom got his taxi from. Is it yours?'

'Mum, first time I've been driven by a chauffeur in a naval uniform!'

I have seen the combination of the uniform and this serviceable black London cab twice before, and my suspicions deepen as Humphrey also speaks warmly of them.

'Very good notion, that. Makes quite an impression. Eccentric but stylish. Just the sort of thing to meet guests at the station.'

From the embrace of my three menfolk I call a warning to Tom.

'You can tell Eddy Johns from me that I don't want it!'

'I only borrowed it for the occasion,' says Tom soothingly, bringing in Humphrey's suitcases. 'It'd be no use to us as it is. Sups petrol like Ben Quick sups ale. One swallow and it's all gone.'

Although I join in the laughter he provokes, I am not buying a taxi cab.

'Come in, come in, you poor, starved, travel-worn creatures!'

I am gratified by Humphrey's reaction.

'Good heavens, Flavia. This is even more splendid than last time!'

But my sons' comments fill me with rejoicing.

'Oh, great! What a log fire! And take a look at the fire-dogs, and the brass and copper whats-its. It's all too amazingly feudal for words.'

Jeremy smiles shyly at me and says, 'It's good to be back, Mum.'

Humphrey stands with his back to the flames and lifts his coat-tails, warming himself reflectively, smiling expansively. I go over to him and link arms.

'The squire in his domain?' I ask mischievously, affectionately.

'Well, well. Aha, ha. And you're looking very much the lady of the manor, if I may say so.'

For the first time one son pays me the compliment of teasing me.

'A vision in a gracious gown,' says Pat.

While the other pays me a compliment.

'You look very elfin in green silk, Mum,' says Jeremy.

'He's been reading *The Lord of the Rings*, Mum. Take no notice of him.'

'You look like the Lady of Lórien, Mum. How's that for a comparison?'

'Smarmy beggar!'

Tom's expression is benign, his tone slightly possessive.

'Whatever Flavia does, she looks the part,' he says proudly.

His praise gladdens me but makes me feel self-conscious.

'I'll put these in your room, sir,' Tom says to Humphrey. And to the boys, 'You two can carry your own bags up. Right?'

'Right!' they say, grinning.

He disappears.

'This is my London evening best,' I say lightly, of the green gown. 'I thought I should dress up for the occasion.'

'I'll tell you what I like about this elegance,' says Humphrey, holding my arm close, confiding in my sons. 'It means that Flavia intends to grace us with her presence instead of staying in the kitchen!'

'Quite right. Let me get you a drink, Humpty. Whisky for warmth? Sherry for refinement? Gin for jollity?'

'A small dry sherry,' says Humphrey. And adds, 'Doctor's orders.'

'Oh dear! And have you a little diet sheet for me? Yes, after dinner will do, Humphrey. Sherry, you two?'

They are flattered to be included.

Tom appears at this moment, minus his officer's hat. He is carrying the butler's silver tray on the outstretched palm of one hand. On it is a bottle of Tio Pepe and five of Grandmama's lead crystal sherry glasses.

'You'll drop that one of these days!' I say acidly.

'And then there'll be hell to pay,' Tom observes serenely. 'Sherry for you, madam? Sherry for you, sir?'

'Ha, ha, ha!' laughs Humphrey, enchanted with his protégé as always.

He loves Tom much more than me. But now I don't mind.

The boys wink at each other and exchange covert smiles with Tom.

More masculine conspiracy. I don't mind that either. I am intensely and completely happy. I love my boys' frank faces and obvious enjoyment. They are under no constraint on this visit. Though for seven years they were my loving and beloved sons, I had often doubted whether they still loved me. I had seen them too often try to please me because I was trying to please them, unable to conceal boredom with my flat and dislike of Jack Rice. It is sheer joy to know that they like this house and us.

Tom, as butler, serves everyone else with a flourish. Then sets down the salver and his persona, fills a glass for himself, and raises it to Humphrey.

'Good health, sir!' He reports progress. 'You'll be pleased with the stables this time. Roof on, and sound and true. New window-frames and glass in. New door hung.'

'You *have* been working hard!' says Humphrey, beaming.

'And wait until you see the new chimney-stack tomorrow,' Tom continues. 'They took the old one down as if it was made of eggshells. Will Soady said if he'd given it one good clout it'd have gone through the roof and taken him with it!'

'But now it's splendid, is it?' Humphrey asks, hanging on every word.

'Built back as good as it ever was.'

I love to see Humphrey laughing like the eternal open-hearted child he is. In sympathy I squeeze his arm, and feel amusement ripple gently under my fingers. I have been unkind to him. Bullied him. My conscience smites me hip and thigh. He turns a moist and friendly face to mine.

'Dearest Flavia, while I'm here, you and I must have a special little talk.'

Later we eat *en famille* in the dining room, lit by a chandelier of tapers, served by Marianne, whose demure enquiries and sidelong glances please all the men present. Marianne is a minx, but a very competent and attractive one. At sixteen she believes she knows everything, is superior with her equals, crushing with her inferiors, and respectful towards me only beause I represent something she would like to achieve. The toss of that butter-coloured rope of hair, as she retreats with a trayful of empty plates, is indicative of an independent spirit. Her ambition is to work in London: a heresy she has confided only to me.

Tom sits opposite Patrick and Jeremy. He has changed into his best black suit and finely ruffled shirt, and resembles an ageing Spanish grandee.

The boys wear identical grey suits, white shirts, and the Liberty silk ties I gave them last Christmas. They eat appreciatively, absorbedly, as they once did under my dominion.

The painted black eyes of Grandmama in her heyday stare down on us: arrogant, young and fiery. Humphrey is talking of the old days, of her days to be precise, since she reigned over Parc Celli for nearly sixty years.

'The women in our family have always been stronger characters than the men. It was great-grandmama who made the original quince preserve and thought of selling it. And they all outlived their husbands – except for my poor mama, of course. She was English, you know. And Saxon – I inherited her colouring. Quite a shock to the family at the time. Still, even though she died young, she made her presence felt. Apparently she was more than prepared to cross swords with Grandmama – to my father's everlasting terror. What a life he would have led between the pair of them. As it was, that fine lady,' gesturing towards the portrait, 'took the stage and held it unchallenged. She was only a little creature but she had a great fighting spirit.' He regards me thoughtfully. 'Rather like you, Flavia. I believe she would approve of you.'

'I hope so,' I say lightly. 'I like to think so. Otherwise her fighting spirit might have chased me off the premises before now.'

Humphrey laughs, well pleased, and wipes his mouth with his napkin, crying, 'True! True! The spirit lives on. Well, that's comforting to know.'

He has lost no weight, despite the diet sheet he will hand me with a sigh at bedtime. And I notice that he does not restrain himself, but asks for second helpings and likes his portions to be larger than those of anyone else.

'Just a *morsel* more, my dear!' Plaintively.

We have trodden this weary road many times, Humphrey and I. And the more ingenious I become at cutting his food or calories down the more adept he becomes at keeping the status quo. I have seen him at breakfast, confronted by a delicious dry-fried egg, glare at me and slap a lump of butter pettishly upon it.

'So, Tom, I hear that work on the stables has been set aside for the winter and you are now part of the general household,' he says, turning to his favourite.

Tom shows all his teeth and replies modestly, 'I've been allowed in, sir, but only on my best behaviour.'

And he glances slyly, first at me and then at his audience.

Meeting his eyes I look away again, and feel my colour rising.

'Oh, ho! Oh, ha ha. You behave, indeed. Why, Tom, you never behaved in all your life.'

'I'm a late learner, sir,' says Tom, easily but seriously, 'in everything. Let's say I'm learning.'

He raises his glass to me, and sips, looking meaningfully at me.

But Humphrey will not have this. He wants his sport, his jester.

'I could tell a tale or two on you, Tom,' he says, eyes shining.

He pours cream lavishly over his lemon pie. I signal Marianne to bring more from the kitchen.

'I hope you won't, sir,' Tom answers, with a grin that invites him to do so.

'Not even about fighting my cousin Jack Rice?'

Tom smiles in his beard and says nothing. Patrick and Jeremy perk up and take a quick look at me, to see how I take this.

'Only time in my life that I've seen Jack slink off – or be carried off! – with his tail between his legs,' says Humphrey.

He lifts the laden silver spoon and pops its offering into the cavern of his mouth. Chews, reflects, pleasurably. Turns to me.

'Delicious, Flavia. A new recipe?'

'A Shaker recipe, Humphrey.'

'I thought those sort of people were supposed to live simply.'

'Simply, but well.'

'Very well indeed, judging by their pie.'

Tom says with pride, 'That's Flavia's cooking.'

Humphrey and the boys look at him, and me, and each other.

'Quite right, Tom. Quite right,' says Humphrey, and the boys agree.

There is a short silence, then, which Patrick breaks, saying directly to Tom, 'Did you beat him up?'

Tom nods.

Jeremy says, 'How badly? Did you black his eyes?'

Another nod. Tom is not to be drawn, but Humphrey is.

'Blacked both eyes. Bloodied his nose. Loosened a couple of teeth. I was home on leave at the time. Your grandfather, boys – Flavia's father – was a major, and I was one of his young lieutenants. Yes, it was quite a fight. Martin Skeggs separated them. Said he thought Tom would have killed Jack otherwise, though I doubt that – they were only boys at the time. Such a to-do. I think Tom was three years younger than Jack, but big for his age. Whereas Jack Rice was never big.'

Patrick says quietly, 'No, not in any way.' And raises his glass to Tom and takes a sip of wine in acknowledgement of a favour rendered. Gravely, Jeremy follows suit.

'The funny thing was,' says Humphrey, heedless of deeper undercurrents, 'that everyone was on Tom's side, even though they said he was a bad boy and tutted and fussed over Jack. But nobody ever punished him for it, did they, Tom?'

'Only my father,' says Tom. 'He leathered me to a standstill. Left his mark on me, and not for the first time.'

The past, like a clenched fist, has also left its mark on him, and Humphrey is brought to himself.

'Ah yes, the father. He was always too hard on you, Tom.'

And seeing his favourite sit sallowly, his grandeur gone, his light dimmed by remembrance of past tyranny, Humphrey adds, 'That's long since behind you, my boy! Brighter days are here. Patrick, pass your mama's glass, if you please. Drink up, Tom. We must open another bottle and toast the chef.'

He is skilled in the art of social diversion, perceptive when you least expect him to be. The moment passes, as all moments do, but like Tom's father leaves its mark. It seems that men are always a challenge to each other. My sons now honour Tom all the more because he once fought Jack Rice.

This autumn visit is a reflective one: a pause between preparation and event. I am reaping the harvest of eight precious months' hard work and collaboration.

Our squire has breakfast in bed and comes down for lunch, takes a turn about the estate in the afternoons and chats with villagers, requires us to entertain him in the evenings. He is delighted with everything, and for the first time in his life climbs the servants' stairs to inspect the top floor, and is agreeably surprised to find it looking light and airy.

'We did pretty well for our people on the whole!' he says, satisfied.

He should have seen it before we started work.

I have taken over the right wing, formerly used as sleeping quarters for the female servants, who had their own staircase down to the kitchen below, and Tom wishes to transform it into a personal suite.

'Future plans, sir,' he says, 'strictly upon your approval, are as follows. I thought to separate Flavia's quarters from the rest of the floor by means of a private entrance door.' Humphrey nods agreement. 'This small room will convert fairly easily into a bathroom. And I'd like to knock this wall down – these aren't carrying beams – to make a good-sized sitting room. That leaves a small room apiece for the boys, or again I could turn it into one large guest-room.'

'Tom *is* looking after you!' Humphrey observes to me. And his tone is arch. 'Yes, Tom, by all means. Do what you think best. And whereabouts do you lay *your* head?'

In the left wing, where the male servants once slept, divided from the females by means of a separate staircase, he occupies the butler's bedroom and has made it comfortable and ship-shape.

'Very snug!' Humphrey remarks, and hums a tune under his breath.

Beyond here lie swept and empty cubicles which will be converted later in the year, and we talk of our plans for these.

Meanwhile the labours continue. Will Soady and sons are still busy refurbishing Parc Celli's various slate hats. Humphrey mounts to the roof to congratulate them all, and exchanges reminiscences with Will. On the way down he pauses once or twice to catch his breath, and holds my arm as we descend the main staircase.

'Always encourage your workers,' he confides to me, 'and look after your staff. That's the secret of a well-organised and happy household.'

He is making the most of his visit, even to the point of going to church. The boys are used to Sunday services at school but I am a fallen, perhaps an unconvinced Christian. Still, I am familiar with the service and hymns from my own boarding school days, I like old churches, and the Elinglaze peal of bells is a rare and lovely relic from its past. So we don our best and walk the half mile on a brisk late October morning.

To my surprise I find the cricket team there in force, with their wives and families, a few in new capacities: sidesman, warden, ringer. And everyone expresses the hope that when the house is fully restored Humphrey will return to take his rightful place in the community. He dodges this misguided hope gracefully, with a faint smile and a courteous murmur. He reminds them that Parc Celli is no longer a gentleman's residence but must earn its living. He raises one hand in mild protest when someone refers to him as the squire. He diverts them with small-talk and enquires after the health of aged relatives. His manner is as smooth as his thin fair hair. Irreverently but affectionately, I find myself thinking that he is indeed 'an altered Toad'.

Throughout the week there is a sense of expectation, as if he is withholding news of tremendous importance. Several times he has said, 'We must have our little talk, my dear.' And at that my stomach clenches, my throat thickens, because I fear being asked a favour which might be impossible to refuse. But opportunities of being alone are few: overridden by events, diverted by practical matters. So it is the afternoon of the last day, and I am packing for Humphrey when he says, 'And now we must have our little talk.'

There comes a pause. After which he adds, 'Speaking of Tom . . . '

My fears are laid at rest. I can pack the shoes Sean Angwin has polished.

Humphrey takes an armful of underwear from the drawer and sits on the bed, holding it. This is his way of helping me.

'About Tom, dear girl. I have been thinking. Of course, I know that we are using your money at the moment, so I feel a certain delicacy about . . . yet I feel I must. Not only for his sake, but for the honour of our partnership.'

I wrest the underwear from him, saying, 'You think he should be paid for the work he does?'

'We-ell,' padding back to the chest of drawers and returning with two cardigans, 'yes, I had thought so. I mean, I know we feed and house him, but his dignity, Flavia, is also important. Man does not live by bread alone. The labourer is worthy of his hire, you know.'

I find it difficult to talk about Tom in a natural manner, so I adopt a brisk and business-like tone.

'I'd thought of that, too. I told him that he was working like a third partner, and he should have a salary. He wouldn't take it.'

'Oh dear,' says Humphrey, clutching the cardigans to his chest. 'What about a title, with a salary attached? Steward, say. Or, as he seems to have adopted the role, your under-manager. Would that be acceptable?'

'I've thought of that, too. He doesn't want to be labelled or tied down. He wants to be his own man. He's prepared to render any amount of service, but he doesn't want to be regarded as a servant.'

Humphrey mumbles to the cardigans, 'I can't think how he's

managing for money, you see. I did help him out a little when I was last here – simply because he'd spent all his own, and needed more materials.'

I check the pile of laundered shirts and tick the list enclosed by Mrs Turner, his housekeeper, and speak casually so that I shall not throw him into confusion.

'I know. Tom offered the money to me a week later, to help me out. I wouldn't take it, of course.'

I pull the cardigans from him and he looks at his empty arms for a while and then pads over to the wardrobe. I interject a lighter note.

'And unless Jewson's swap building materials for scrap, he must have spent most or all of it by now!'

Humphrey creeps back with a tweed hacking-jacket and consults my face.

Reassured he asks, 'Then how can we help him?'

'I don't know. But he is making a living of sorts, somehow.'

This has puzzled me for a while, and I air the puzzlement.

'He never seems short of ready cash. And he disappears quite frequently on mysterious errands. He never explains where he's going, nor how long he'll be away. And though it's none of my business, really, I do *wonder*.'

I struggle for a few moments against a feeling of disloyalty against Tom, but Humphrey is sympathetic to him and I unburden myself.

'You see, Humpty, I'm afraid he's poaching.'

Humphrey chuckles. He enjoys roguery in others, provided it does not jeopardise his own interests. I launch into a catalogue of private torments.

'Oh, no one mentions the word *poaching*, but I'm not an idiot. He brings in game quite regularly. I've got a row of birds hanging in the larder this minute. They can't all be found at the side of the road, now can they? And then there are all the fish he catches. I know he goes sea-fishing, which would account for the bass, but Vera told me there was no trout-fishing here, and I'm always up to the ears in trout.'

Humphrey sniggers.

'Then he brings me presents – something for the kitchen or the house.' Afraid that this sounds too personal, I add, 'He's very appreciative of anything you and I do for him.' And launch into my confession again. 'But, Humpty, how does he pay for them? If I tackle him about it he says they were swopped for scrap or someone owed him a favour. *What* scrap? *What sort of* favour? It really worries me, Humphrey. Suppose the police come here asking questions and finding things? What shall I do if they put Tom in prison and arrest me for receiving stolen property? Parc Celli's reputation will be ruined before we've opened. It's very difficult when a person is so honest and so dishonest at the same time. I don't know where I am, you see.'

I realise that I am talking and packing at a tremendous rate, and stop. I breathe deeply, and smooth and re-smooth a sheet of tissue paper while I regain control of myself.

Humphrey bumbles up to me, portly and immaculate, and places a plump arm around my shoulders: amused and sorry.

'My dear girl. You really mustn't take on so. Tom knows how to take care of himself. Besides, he's a Cornishman born and bred, and the Cornish are a hardy and an independent race. They've been bartering for thousands of years. A great deal of trading goes on which doesn't involve money. And they're a law unto themselves. They'd far rather take a risk than pay a tax. They've produced active law-breakers for generations – pirates and wreckers and smugglers. And were supported by a group of passive law-breakers who kept them in business – brandy for the parson, baccy for the clerk, sort of thing. And "Watch the wall, my darling, while the Gentlemen go by!"'

I can think of nothing to say, and smooth the tissue, head bent.

'I'll have a word with him, if you like,' says Humphrey paternally. 'We're bashing off to Helston together this afternoon.'

I am relieved. Curiously, he also seems relieved. Glances at his watch and tuts over the passage of time.

'I really must be off, dearest.'

Surprisingly, for I thought we had just had our little talk, he says, 'So I'm afraid our own business must wait. Do you mind, Flavia, if I leave the rest of the packing to you? We seem to have done most of it. And then you can relax for a couple of hours before I take us all out to dinner.'

For it is my birthday today, and all the cards I have received, including a so-called humorous one from Jack Rice, assure me that now life begins. But I am still trying to assimilate the idea of being forty years on, growing older and older, and am not so sure.

So the two of them disappear in Tom's taxi, which is still with us, and return at six o'clock with a bouquet of cream and scarlet roses for me. They are both laughing as they walk up the steps and Humphrey has his arm around Tom's shoulders. The male conspiracy is still alive, and kicking splendidly it would seem.

CHAPTER TWENTY-TWO

November

I am forty years and one week. Our visitors have gone and we are by ourselves again.

Into my office Tom brings a long, thin scratchy parcel, painstakingly wrapped up in what I recognise as the florist's paper from my birthday bouquet, with the bow of ribbon sellotaped into position. His display of nonchalance is unconvincing.

'Happy birthday from me, Flavia,' he announces, holding the gift out at arm's length. 'And I didn't swop this for scrap – it's made out of scrap!'

Inside the roll of patterned paper is a long-stemmed wrought-iron rose on a three-legged base, very delicate and black and beautiful.

Tom whistles softly to himself to show that he is completely at his ease, and watches me uneasily.

'Didn't want to give it to you in front of the others,' he says. 'You know how folk make a lot out of nothing.'

My confused silence lasts too long for his comfort.

He says, 'If you don't like it I can change it for something else. Bought it from a retired blacksmith who makes them for pleasure. He does animals, too, if you'd rather have one of them.'

I say truthfully, 'I think it's perfectly lovely, and I shall keep it here in the window where I can look at it every day. Thank you very much, Tom.'

He is pleased, but not glad. Relieved, but disappointed. As I am, for I feel more, would like to say more, would like him to say more. A taut silence stretches to breaking point.

'Oh, well, must get back to work!' says Tom breezily. 'Terry

Soady's helping me patch up the old boiler and pipes. They'll do us for now, Flavia, but we shall have to put in a new heating system before next autumn.'

He has crossed over to the safe area of our business relationship, and I join him.

'I have that earmarked as a future expense.'

At the door he pauses, head bent, then turns resolutely round. We are about to have a confession. I brace myself. For what?

'Flavia, Mr Jarvis said you were worrying about me being short of money.'

'Oh!' Deflated. And then, 'Oh, yes?'

'I'm telling you there's no need. I've got myself a part-time job. All square and above board, as the squire would say. I may be a jack of all trades, but I'm master of one. Wasn't chief engineer for nothing. Know about engines.

'Being doing freelance work for a mate of mine. He owns the business but I'm in charge of the sideline. In fact I suggested it. Working mostly on boats. Fishing boats, private boats. People hear of me and pass the word on. I do a good job and charge a fair price, but I've got no overheads so I come cheaper than most.

'Doesn't mean I can't help you here, but it keeps me independent and puts a few pounds in my pocket. Way I'm doing at the moment I'll be back at work on the stables next autumn. Pay for it all myself this time. Not bother the squire. He's been good to me – and so have you, Flavia. Cheers.'

This admission is delivered at high speed. He pulls the door open and is moving out just as speedily when I speak.

'Tom! I'm so *delighted*!'

Relieved would have been a more accurate description, but I am delighted as well.

'Tom, come back a minute and tell me more!'

His return is unwilling.

'Who are you working for? Is he a boat-builder?'

'Not exactly,' says Tom, wringing the enamelled doorknob, face averted. 'He owns a general sort of business. Second-hand stuff. He' – the word is chosen carefully – 'renovates things.'

I take a leap into the dark, unexpectedly connecting everything. Car, van, taxi, swop, scrap and favours.

I say demurely, 'Tom, are you working for Eddy Johns?'

Then he fairly bursts out in protest, like a child wrongly accused.

'I'd have told you long since, but I was afraid you'd take it the wrong way. I've been buying and selling for him almost from the first, and bartering on my own account. We went to school together, Eddy Johns and me. Thick as thieves in the old days – at least, that's not what I – but I never took commission for Victoria or the van – at least, I did, but I knocked it off the price. I never made money out of you, Flavia. But if I'd said so at the beginning you wouldn't have believed me.'

I start to laugh. Tom strokes his beard sheepishly for a moment or two, then joins me. We revert to an amiable silence. Our equilibrium, so often threatened, is once again restored. I feel I can put the final question.

'Oh, Tom!' I say mischievously, as he is departing, 'What about the fish and game you give me? Is that another job on the side?'

His face is inscrutable. He grins into his beard, and delivers the answer in a Cornish speech so rapid that I can barely catch it.

'Them as asks no questions isn't told no lies!'

And grins again and goes out, leaving the grin dark and sly behind him.

I smile for quite a time after he has gone. And then sigh, and get back to work.

We are arranging two great events for the end of this eventful year. Humphrey, my sons, and my mother, will spend Christmas week with us. This is part pleasure and part placation, for I want Humphrey and Lily to feel they have been loved and wanted, and then to leave me alone so that I can open Parc Celli in peace. I have often had to cope with two things at the same time, but never enjoyed it, and always felt that I gave of less than my best to both. So I shall concentrate on my family at Christmas, and give Parc Celli my undivided attention from the beginning of 1979.

We are to open with a gourmet New Year's Eve Dinner at £6.00 a head, coupled to a bargain package for those who would also like to stay overnight. Afterwards they will be encouraged to linger with us in luxury at the reduced rates of £6.00 per person per day (bed and breakfast), or demi-pension (dinner, bed and breakfast) at £9.00, and weekly prices of £36 and £54 respectively, inclusive of VAT. Children charged according to age. For this is a lean time of year, and we must make guests doubly welcome.

Like the mother of the bride, I wallow in the bliss of preparing, dressing and providing for Kelly Park in her new role. Our stylish brochure is graced on one side by a drawing of the house by a local artist. On the other is a neat map, showing visitors how to find us. I have composed the local and national advertisements, designed and ordered the stationery, created the first dinner menus. We are working with a scheme of apple-green and snowdrop-white, fresh and pretty and wonderfully appetising as a background. Our white china is decorated in green and gold. Our white tablecloths have green slip-covers.

The Jarvises' original embroidered bedcovers, their linen sheets and lace-edged pillow-cases have been folded away for safe-keeping, to be brought out for Humphrey when he stays with us. Blankets and eiderdowns have given way to duvets. The new bed linen is all white cotton, and we provide everything from a face cloth to a bathrobe.

I have contacted the former London wine merchant who supplied Bon Appétit, chosen our house wines and set up a cellar. After much deliberation we have decided on a writing recess in the library as the best place in which to build a discreet cocktail bar, and we shall fold back the doors between library and saloon so that our guests can sit in either room after dinner. One of Will Soady's cousins is in charge of this transformation.

Meanwhile Tom has asked for a trial run as our future barman and maître d'hôtel. I insist on paying him a wage for this. But he says he will work for nothing while he is on approval, and we can talk about money later. I think he will be admirable, though this is purely intuitive on my part. His references for both posts are highly questionable, tied up with many tales about the iniquities of the chief steward on one ocean-going liner, and the way in which Tom outwitted him before being sacked. On the other hand his knowledge of cocktails is formidable and he is quick to watch and learn. So I accept his offer and do not enquire too closely. I have taught him how to flambé, an art to which he brings a tremendous sense of theatre. Since he feels that he should also be dressed to suit the occasion, he is looking out for a dinner suit in the Oxfam shops, though his best black and ruffles will do very well. He is also our odd-job man and chauffeur. And how he will ever combine all these duties with his Open University course and his part-time job with Eddy Johns I do not know, but that is his business. I have made only one stipulation. In all his dealings Parc Celli must come first.

We shall be transfigured when the house opens. Henry Blewett's widowed sister is coming in to do the rough cleaning and vegetables. Alice Quick will continue to pursue her own fell course. And Marianne is working here for a year, helping anyone who needs her, to make sure that the hotel business is her métier. If it is, she will then go on to Cornwall College to study catering while Julie helps out as a waitress. And rumour has it that I shall be set free to cook and supervise, with Vera as my second in command.

I have been taken on a long and garrulous tour of the newly repaired greenhouses by Martin Skeggs, who has consulted me as to my fruit and vegetable requirements for the coming year and made suggestions of his own. He speaks well of Sean Angwin: a shrewd and intelligent young man, possessed of considerable charm, who grows handsomer by the day, is a favourite among the village maidens, and shows so much initiative and manipulates the old gardener so skilfully, that I really do wonder if . . . but Tom's past is not my business.

I am spending my money lavishly, though sensibly, and enjoying every penny and every moment. I have bought an electric cooker to supplement the kitchen range, and an ice-cream freezer for my enjoyment as well as my convenience.

Let us say that an atmosphere of contentment reigns in Kelly Park. For once we can do no wrong. The family response to our Christmas holiday is ecstatic. The public response to our New Year's Eve Dinner is spontaneous, and our guest list overflows. All six bedrooms will be occupied by guests from upcountry and forty have booked for the meal itself.

Then the week before Christmas the telephone begins to ring.

'Mum? Patrick here. Look, Mum, I'm awfully sorry about this, but I'm afraid Dad's made some sort of a mix-up about Christmas. Apparently Anne didn't realise that Jem and I would be with you. She thought we were coming for New Year. She's booked us all into that place in Scotland.'

'I see,' I said.

For the arrangements had been made more than a month ago and were perfectly clear.

Patrick attempted to mend matters and worsened them.

'Apparently she thought we were having Christmas at home, and she didn't want the hassle of cooking for us all, and that's why she booked up this place. And now it's too late to cancel.'

In chagrin, I burst out, 'What's all the fuss about cooking a Christmas dinner for four people? You and Jem spend most of your lives at boarding school anyway. What cooking is she talking about?'

Tom was beside me, his face troubled by my trouble. He put one hand on my arm, which I shook off immediately. He put one finger to his lips.

I turned on him, inflicting the pain that had been inflicted on me.

'Don't interfere! This is my business! They're not coming for Christmas. It's always the same. He's done it a hundred times before.'

'Mum,' trickled Jeremy's voice through the receiver, 'we did say we wouldn't go with them, but there was so much flak we were afraid they might stop us from coming down to you altogether . . . '

'Flavia,' Tom persisted gently. 'Flavia, don't hurt the lads. It's not their fault. They're the ones caught in the crossfire.'

I was struggling against tears of rage and disappointment: the receiver hanging from my hand. Through it hollow sounds of apology and regret floated towards us.

Tom besought me, 'Will you let me talk to them if you're not up to it?'

'Do what you like,' I cried, thrusting the receiver in his hands. 'Nothing I plan ever goes right for me.'

Still, I stayed by the telephone to see if it would, while Tom smoothed the way for us all.

'Your mum's a bit upset at the moment,' he was saying. 'Suppose I put your suggestion to her and she calls you back? All right, Pat? Cheers, then!'

Rage had come uppermost.

I cried explosively, '*She* did it on purpose and *he*'s behind it all!'

'I shouldn't be surprised,' said Tom. 'They sound like a pair of bastards to me. But the lads do say they'd be allowed to come for New Year.'

'Yes. But only because I specifically told Guy that I couldn't *have* them for New Year because we were opening. That's why he's suggested it!'

'I know the score, and so do you,' said Tom diplomatically, 'but the lads are prepared to set out for Cornwall the day after they get back from Scotland, and if that doesn't show willing, I don't know what does. Now listen to me, Flavia, just listen. Here,' he said tenderly, putting a large warm arm round my shoulders, 'have my handkerchief, and wipe your eyes, my lass.'

I fought a hiccup and dried my tears. His arm was immensely comforting. I stayed within its circle and studied the border of the handkerchief, and wiped my eyes again.

'That's better,' said Tom. 'Now listen to me – and don't fly at me like a fighting bantam cock! – what's wrong with having them for New Year? They've got their own rooms here in your suite. They're taking up nobody else's beds. They're no trouble. They muck in like a pair of troopers. And you know that you want to see them. That's why you're piping your eye. And they want to see you. And how will they see you? Why, opening up Parc Celli with a big New Year dinner, and the place full of people – some of them their own age. Won't that be more fun than sitting round the fire with a few cranky grown-ups, trying not to listen to Lily and tripping over that perishing little dog?'

I began to laugh, and Tom joined me.

'Show that bastard Pollard he can't win every time,' said Tom. 'Ring him up and say what a marvellous idea. And if he starts prevaricating speak to Pat and Jem. They're young adults, not young children. They should be able to stand up for themselves and you.'

I nodded, and sniffed, and said inconsequently, 'I've made a mess of your handkerchief again.'

'Never mind, my lass,' he said, smiling down at me. 'It'll all come right in the wash – as they say.'

I was almost myself again. It was time to move away from him, and I did. He released me instantly, with an expression I could not define. The tension was there again between us. I avoided his eyes, and pretended it did not exist.

'Someday,' I declared, with a toss of the head, 'I'll organise something at Kelly Park that goes without a hitch!'

He took a great breath, shook his head, and managed a grin.

'Someday,' said Tom, 'the moon will be made of green cheese!'

I dried my eyes, blew my nose, and dialled the Pollards' number.

Humphrey's housekeeper rang next to say that he was indisposed.

'And he's afraid he can't come to the telephone at present, madam, but he says he'll ring you as soon as he can put foot to the ground.'

'What's wrong with him, Mrs Turner?'

'He's got the gout, madam.'

I wondered why such an agonising ailment should always strike me as being faintly amusing.

'Oh dear, poor thing. How very painful.'

'Yes indeed, madam. He winces even if I come too close. So he says he's very sorry but he can't come for Christmas, but he'll be better presently, and hopes to make other arrangements soon. And to give you his love.'

Among Tom's many accomplishments was an ability to draw up plans and diagrams. So he had made a house plan for the occasion, and he came into my office to find me playing Box and Cox with the guest rooms. I had adopted an easy, factual manner with him, in an effort to avoid difficult silences and the feeling that neither of us was saying what we meant. Tom responded in kind.

I said over my shoulder, 'Humphrey's laid up with the gout,

poor love, but will be better presently. Meaning New Year. I can hardly refuse if he does suggest it!'

But I had learned much from our previous discussions and arguments, and corrected myself in words as well as spirit.

'In fact, I shall suggest it myself. So I thought in for a penny, in for a pound. If I move the Baxters' two teenage sons Humphrey can have his own bedroom. Tom, I was thinking we could put the Baxter boys in the night nursery, next to the nursery bathroom. It's quite a large room. Do you think you could possibly decorate it in the next week? Nothing fantastic. Just a lick of paint and a slap of paper until Will Soady turns up again.'

'Give me the paint and paper and I'll start as soon as you like,' said Tom.

'The furniture is fairly basic but Mrs Thomas in the village will run up some more new curtains for us. And if I bring a few ornaments and pictures from the lumber room, and arrange a few flowers, it should look quite presentable.'

'You can rely on me,' said Tom courteously.

I smiled at him mock-sweetly, but heard myself answering honestly, 'You know very well that I couldn't even have *thought* about it without you.'

His black bright gaze softened as he considered me, and I wondered for the thousandth time how much he cared for me. For if he cared as much as I thought he did then why didn't he show it? But he looked away again.

'When they've all gone and there's a bit of a lull,' said Tom, 'I'll start decorating the rest of the rooms, ready for action.'

Returned to Parc Celli, I agreed, and sighed, and looked at the house plan.

Then, brightening up, 'Do you know, Tom, I'm pleasantly surprised how quickly we can fill up. Most of the guests who've booked in are staying on for a few days, and the Baxters are staying all week.' I thought of a snag. 'I'm afraid the family cancellations mean that you and I will have Lily with us, unadulterated, for Christmas.'

A Lily who would be most surprised, not to say displeased, by Tom's presence and importance in the house.

—

He followed my train of thought and said under his breath, 'Jesus Christ!'

Then he shrugged and smiled.

'Never mind, Flavia. You can't win them all!' he said philosophically.

We had an excellent relationship. We had a highly unsatisfactory one, too.

My mother rang two days later.

Beginning, 'Flivvy, bad news I'm afraid. Our precious Christmas . . . '

Mentally I assigned my bedroom to her, put myself up on the bed-settee in the sitting room, and added another guest to the New Year list. Lily continued to rattle on.

' . . . poor dear soul. Oh, I know I spoke harshly about her in the summer, but of course she *had* behaved in a very underhand manner, in fact tricked the poor man into marriage – I don't think the word *tricked* is too strong, though one shouldn't speak ill of the – and if at the time one tends to say things that one regrets later, still I never wished her any harm, and naturally I never expected this to happen . . . ' She paused for breath and said, 'Where was I?'

'I have no idea, Lily. You mentioned our precious Christmas.'

'Christmas, of course. I can't manage it, even for you, Flivvy, and I do hope you'll understand when I say that I cannot leave that poor man in his hour of sorrow . . . '

'Which poor man is this, Lily?'

' . . . because all he wants, as he says himself, is to come and sit with me in my peaceful little flat and think of the dear dead days beyond recall . . . '

'*Mother!*' I said pointedly. 'Would you mind telling me what you're talking about?'

The title stopped her abruptly.

She said, very dignified, 'Godfrey's wife died yesterday, and I can't come for Christmas because I won't leave him.'

She added, even more grandly, 'You don't listen, dear. You never did listen to what I said. Your father was exactly the same.'

So that was how he had survived?

'Well, I'm sorry about that, Lily. And about Godfrey's wife. I don't think I've ever met him, have I? Still, I am sorry. Do give him my sympathy or condolences or whatever you feel is appropriate.'

She was not listening.

' . . . and I said to him, "Godfrey, what you and I need is a little healing holiday in the sun. Life has exhausted us." *Les affaires du coeur*, you know, take their toll . . . '

I shifted the receiver from right to left, gripped it firmly between my shoulder and chin and pulled the house plan towards me. Now if only the stables had been habitable. As they were not, Pat and Jem could double up on camp beds in another place, leaving their rooms vacant for the unhappy happy couple.

Reckless with hospitality, I said, 'I can't manage the sun at this time of year, I'm afraid, but how would you like to come down for New Year's Eve, Lily, and bring Godfrey with you? Humphrey and the boys are coming then!'

' . . . so as soon as the funeral is over I shall pop into the travel agency, which has these wonderful cheap winter holidays. I'd thought of Jamaica, all that rum and rumba – are they the ones who do the rumba? – but that might be too far away . . . '

'Lily! Would you both like to come down here for New Year? *Mother!*'

Brought up short again she said in stately fashion, 'I'm afraid you'll have to manage without me for once, Flavia. Remember, dear, that I gave up the whole of my summer to you because I felt you needed me, and now poor Godfrey's in trouble you can't expect me to come running at your beck and call. Perhaps when the weather gets warmer. May, June . . . '

'Don't even think about it!' I said tartly. 'We shall be full.'

' . . . I can't help feeling that perhaps he strayed because I was selfish. I've never thought of myself as a selfish person, but being married to a wonderful man like your father rather spoils one, and I may well have taken Godfrey's devotion for granted, still one does learn to make sacrifices when . . . '

I considered the plan more closely. Tom had suggested we made a car park at the back of the stable-block. He had sketched them both in.

' . . . but of course I see it all quite clearly now, in fact it's quite obvious that when I turned down his last proposal he married Grace on the rebound . . . '

A knock at the door, followed by Tom in his work clothes, carrying my morning cup of coffee and his morning mug of strong brown tea.

I placed my hand over the mouthpiece and whispered, 'Lily. In full spate.'

'Give her my regards,' said Tom drily, spreading a newspaper on the chair and sitting down. 'I suppose she's coming for New Year, too? You can give her my bedroom and I'll doss down in the steward's room on a camp-bed.'

'She's not coming at all. Either Christmas or New Year.'

And as I spoke, it occurred to me with an exquisite leap of terror, that we should be all by ourselves.

'Good on her!' said Tom heartily.

Then his face changed, and he became very thoughtful, and stared down into his tea mug.

' . . . and yet, at my time of life, though I feel seventeen at heart, and people always say they can't believe my age, not that I tell them how old I am, I don't really want to leave my lovely home. Still, he and poor Grace did buy a *very* nice little house in Surbiton. Or perhaps he could be persuaded to sell? I never visited them when she was alive, though they did ask, but as soon as he told me she was No More I took a taxi and went right over. She had no taste, of course, but I see great possibilities. I'm not sure which would be best. Darling, would you like to pop up for a little holiday and look the property over – such a clever Flivvy, with all her bright ideas . . . '

'Lily!' I said loud and clear, to attract her attention, 'Terribly sorry! I've got to go now. Crisis in kitchen.'

'What? Oh yes. Don't work too hard, darling. And give my regards to dear Vera and Captain Faull. I'll ring you again when the funeral's over . . . '

I hung up, and forgot her immediately. Tom took a breath at the same time I did, and hit on the same safe topic.

'About the car park, Flavia . . . '

'Tom, I've been looking at your plan for the car park . . . '

He gestured that I should speak.

'I think it's an excellent idea. Out of the way, round the back of Parc Celli, and yet convenient for the guests. You can go ahead with that whenever you want to.'

I had not mentioned the stables, but he was on my wavelength.

'Flavia, I've had another idea as well. Looking ahead, that is, because it would cost a few thousand. We could turn the stables into a self-catering lodge, or an annex to Parc Celli.'

I counted to twenty, as being more considerate than ten.

'I couldn't consider it, Tom. I think of the stables as your home.'

So I protested: ashamed that I too had thought of converting them.

But he answered me directly.

'You house me here. I've got my own bedroom, and the steward's room downstairs where I can study and keep my things. What more do I need?' He pursued the point. 'That's all you've got, Flavia. A room to sleep in and a room to work in. And you don't ask for more.'

I summoned up an image which was no longer enough, but all I had.

'It's not quite the same for me. This house is my life,' I said.

But I spoke thoughtfully, careful not to shut him out.

He stared into the dregs of his mug, deliberating. When he spoke he did not look at me.

'It's become my life too,' said Tom.

I could think of nothing to say. The air was electric. Once more we were on the brink of self-discovery. Flurried, I began to chatter.

'Of course, the restaurant will be quite different from London. We were cosmopolitan at Bon Appétit. We brought food in from everywhere, because nothing is grown in a city, nothing is natural to it. We shall still have to import spices and luxuries, but so much of the food here is grown or reared or caught. I shall work out new menus which suggest themselves from the products available. Helford mussels. Germoe smoked salmon. Cadgwith crabs and lobsters. We could have a fish tank in the restaurant, and then customers can choose their own . . . '

His imagination was caught. He ceased to watch me quizzically.

'I'll clean out the conservatory and repair it,' said Tom, thinking. 'You could turn it into a restaurant annex. Put another cooking stove in it, along with the fish tank. Employ an assistant chef. Then they can see their fish cooked. And I know a man who's thinking of starting a venison farm—'

'—medallions of venison steak, marinated in wine and herbs—'

'Eddy Johns's brother is a farmer. Raises his own bullocks—'

'Fillets of beef, beaten out and fried in butter—'

'Plenty of mushrooms in the field at the back. I can collect them first thing in the morning. For breakfast – or whatever you like—'

'—with fresh field mushrooms and tomatoes, flamed in brandy—'

'Not forgetting the Home Farm – as we used to call it – with their poultry.'

'Free-range, of course!'

'Nothing but!' said Tom devoutly.

'Fresh eggs for breakfast: poached, boiled, scrambled, fried. Chickens every which way – too many recipes to mention. Pan-fried duck breast, deglazed with brandy and cassis—'

'And pigs. Handsome pigs! For a straightforward Sunday roast,' he reminded me. 'You'll pull the local families in for that.'

'Pork chops in foil with fennel and juniper berries or rosemary and garlic.'

'Saddle of Cornish lamb?' Tom suggested, getting into the swing.

'Racked, with mint and garlic, served with baby carrots, new peas, new potatoes—'

'And sweets,' said Tom, eyes shining. '*Desserts*, as you would say! Lots of them, eh?'

I spread out my hands to indicate the impossibility of saying how many.

'Pies, puddings, tarts, gateaux, poached and fresh fruit, home-made ice-cream and sorbets—'

'You need a proper cold room. I've got a mate who's a refrigeration engineer. He could do it in his spare time. Probably find us a good second-hand one.'

We paused, smiling at and through each other on this vision of the future Kelly Park.

'I reckon,' said Tom reverently, 'that it'll be the best restaurant in the country, never mind the West Country.'

'Oh, Tom!' I cried, genuinely shocked, genuinely moved by his faith in me. 'Never in a thousand years will we come up to that standard. If only you knew how many marvellous – oh, but it'll be a good restaurant all the same. They'll hear about us!'

He sat with his big brown hands clasped between his knees and shook his head in wonderment.

'Never thought I'd see the day.'

'I sometimes wondered whether I would.'

'Oh no,' he said soberly. 'You always would, Flavia, because you have it in you. It was always possible for this to happen to you. But I've had nothing and been nobody, and this is a miracle to me.'

'Tom!' Terry Soady was shouting hopefully, to anywhere Tom might be.

'That'll be about the boiler,' said Tom, rousing himself. 'Got to get it right for the winter. I'd best be off, my lovely.'

The endearment, which had slipped off his tongue, immobilised me.

Deliberately, he repeated, 'My lovely.'

Shocked, entranced, I kept my face averted and said nothing.

He stood up smiling, lifted my right hand very gently from the desk and put it to his lips. He laid it down again as if it were very fragile and valuable, nodded at me twice, and went out.

I sat looking at the hand for quite a while after he had gone.

I was about to realise the dream of a lifetime, and it seemed to count for nothing beside this.

CHAPTER TWENTY-THREE

23 December

Saturday afternoon. For once I have time on my hands. I stretch them out before me on the kitchen table, which Vera has left scrubbed and clean, and contemplate them. They are good little hands, even though they do work hard and I am forty. Competent and neat and smooth. I don't wear a ring and they don't need one. Like me they are sufficient unto themselves. Almost.

Every member of Kelly Park staff has gone home for the Christmas holiday and will not be reporting for duty until the end of next week. They have taken their wages, and a Christmas bonus of five or ten pounds, according to status. And Tom went to Helston some hours ago to collect the shopping. Lord knows what else he is doing and where else, but he will turn for home in the end. I sit in my shining orderly kitchen, and reflect.

This first Christmas in Cornwall will not be lonely. The vicar has invited Tom and me to attend a candlelit service tomorrow evening. Vera has asked us to share their Christmas lunch on Monday. And on Boxing Day we are having tea with Mrs Will Soady and family. The dresser is bright with cards: none of your sophisticated works of art, ceremonial greetings or seasonal quips, but the proper old-fashioned sort: robins and holly berries, stagecoaches dashing up to venerable inns, candlelit lanterns, wassail cups, merry gentlemen, Victorian ladies, rosy children, and plenty of snow. And round the tree is an assortment of parcels for both of us, Christmas gift wrapped in more holly berries, robins and snow.

The tree began all this.

A week before Christmas, without a word of warning, Martin

and Sean hauled a splendid specimen of the fir family up to the house, and Tom helped them to plant it in a vast tub. Because, I was informed at least twice, they did always have a tree in the old squire's time.

The symbol towers majestically towards the plasterwork ceiling, appearing to be only a foot or so shorter than the one in Trafalgar Square. Its size and presence demands more than my humble string of Woolworth's fairy lights, two dozen coloured glass baubles, and an angel with tarnished wings and a crooked halo. Since the tree will be with us until Twelfth Night, and the staff have hinted about an estate tea-party, and I should not like to disgrace Parc Celli on either count, I have asked Tom to use his initiative.

Sean also brought up sacks of cheerful holly, luscious mistletoe and trails of ivy, which seemed a lot at the time and dwindled to nothing much when spread about the hall. For the honour of the house I enquired about paper chains, though personally I dislike them, but apparently this was not done.

'But we do have a candle in the lodge window,' said Alice Quick, 'which do burn through Christmas night. And old Mrs Jarvis did have a candle in every window at the front of the house.'

I have compromised with one slow-burning candle in the kitchen, shaped like a church tower and having an imitation stained-glass window in each of its sides.

'And a yule log,' said Martin Skeggs. 'They did have a yule log, and we did carry him in on Christmas Eve. But seeing as Mr Jarvis won't be here Christmas Day I'll find one for New Year.'

The sound of the van brings me to my feet, alive and faintly apprehensive. I set the kettle on the range and peep out of the window. The roof rack is laden. The back doors of the van are partly open and laced together with rope. Covertly I watch Tom taking off his seat belt. His long legs slide forth. He ducks his head as he gets out, turns back to retrieve something from the passenger seat, straightens up and strides towards the house. He cannot see me, but I can see him. His face is serious to the point of sadness. He cradles a long cardboard box in his arms. He marches like a soldier to battle: fearful but resolute. What on earth has he done now?

I sit down again and commune with my hands. Once again we are in this strange place, he and I, where there is no time and all the space in the world and some great event is about to happen.

I should open the door for him. Instead, I sit and listen to him going through the process of setting down the box, lifting the latch, and picking the box up again.

I should act as if I had just heard him, and call, 'Is that you, Tom?' But I sit and contemplate my hands, head bent.

He is standing before me, black eyes glowing.

He says, 'These are for you, Flavia. First of the season.'

And lays the box reverently before me.

I cannot speak so I smile instead. The smile is a travesty and we both know it. My hands are more sensible than I am. They move forward, lift the lid and discover layer upon layer of cold gold scented trumpets.

My voice says breathlessly, 'Oh Tom! Oh, Tom!'

My hands move over the daffodils, touching them gently, lifting some up to my face to sniff them, almost in disbelief that they can be so beautiful and so many.

'Oh, Tom. They're lovely. Oh, how extravagant! Oh, how lovely.'

His voice says bravely, rapidly, 'They're a measure, a very small measure, of what I think of you.'

He must think a great deal. There are over a hundred flowers here.

'Not only what I think,' Tom continues, braver yet, 'but what I feel.'

My voice replies at random, 'I must put them in water.'

'Flavia,' he says in desperation, 'will you leave the bloody flowers alone for a minute? I'm trying to tell you something. Flavia, you mean all the world to me, my love.'

My hands are intuitive. They lay down the daffodils, who will manage without water for a while longer, and place themselves one on either side of his face. His beard feels delicious, springing beneath my fingers. His mouth is full and warm. His arms come round me in a bear hug. And we kiss for a very long time, because we have waited a very long time to do just that.

We part and look and smile for a moment. I am shaking, and so is he, and he wraps his arms round me again and holds me to him, to quieten and comfort us both.

He mumbles into my hair, 'I've been wanting to tell you that for months.'

I say vehemently into his shirt front, 'Then why didn't you?'

'You take some tracking, my lovely. Every time I got within a yard of you – you moved off.'

'No, *you* moved off. *I've* been waiting.'

I feel his chuckle rumbling beneath me.

'You're the ringmaster in all else,' he says, stroking my hair. 'Why didn't *you* speak out?'

'I wasn't sure – of you – or myself. I've made two bad mistakes already.'

We kiss again, longer and deeper, and come up for breath.

'By God,' says Tom, as though he had walked the desert for days and at last was able to drink, 'that was good.'

I begin to laugh, breathless and tremulous, since this is my feeling exactly.

He shakes his head from side to side, wondering. He tries to explain the inexplicable, to rationalise the irrational.

'I'm no bargain, you see,' he says. 'I've come forward and stepped back a hundred times, and thought – Why should she want *me*? What have *I* got to offer her? Nothing but goodwill and good intentions – and myself, of course.'

I cannot resist answering, 'I'll settle for the last offer. I expect I'll come to terms with the rest.'

He grins then and says, 'Sharp!'

He holds me away from him and looks at me steadily.

'All right, then?' he asks.

A great many questions are contained in that one. I know them all, and the single answer that is required.

'All right, Tom!'

He looks round the kitchen and asks unnecessarily, 'Everyone gone home now, have they?'

'Yes, there's only you and me and Parc Celli until next Saturday.'

'Well, then?' hopefully.

He reads the answer in my eyes and asks, jokingly, 'Your place or mine?'

I come of age in the house.

'Neither. Let's have Grandmama's room while it's vacant. Humphrey always thought I should use it, and I rather like the idea of occupying a four-poster.'

He does not answer, looks irresolute, and I laugh.

'You're not turning all feudal on me, are you, Tom?'

'No. I just want to be certain, before we start, that you're sure about me and sure of me.'

'I've been sure for a long time.'

He smiles then, a slow wide smile which lights his dark face.

'Well, you had a funny way of showing it!' he says, without blame.

We are wordless, walking together up the broad staircase, arms round waists. Words are superfluous. Outside the wind has come up and it begins to rain, but the roof is sound, the walls strong, and we are safe within. We have come upon an island in time, been given a space for ourselves, and all harassments fall away. Though it is not yet dark Tom draws the heavy curtains and shuts out the rest of the world. We shall make free of each other, in quite the grandest setting either of us has ever experienced. And I think how much knowledge and joy and bitterness in both our lives it has taken to bring us together, and to make us what we are to each other now.

Then I stop thinking and start being.

A long time later, Tom reaches across me and turns on the bedside lamp.

Half asleep, I move further into the circle of his arm. The tip of my nose tests the chilly air of a world outside our bed and I relish the warmth within it. I have often, when too tired to check the thought, remembered the way he hugged Vera on the first day he arrived at the house. I envied her that embrace, despite myself. Now I revel in it. Turning my face I can see a bush of greying beard, a fine Spanish profile, and the dark glitter of an eye beneath its lid. This is my man.

'Sometimes,' says Tom drowsily, contemplating the ceiling while I contemplate him, 'just sometimes, life seems to say "Yes!"'

My tongue is awake even if I am not.

'I expect it gets tired of saying "No!" so often!'

Tom turns a quizzical look upon me.

'You're only a little thing,' he says, 'a pretty little thing, but you pack a big punch.'

Unfairly, I enjoy saying, 'I thought you said I was sour-faced?'

'I'm not answering that one,' Tom remarks to the ceiling. 'It means trouble.'

'I wonder what time is it?' I ask, too lazy to lift my head and consult the clock on the mantelpiece.

'Going on eight o'clock.'

Having become one flesh we appear also to have become one mind. We wonder whether we are hungry, but drift away from making an immediate decision.

'A whole week to ourselves,' I say, marvelling. Then, becoming aware of my cold nose, 'Tom, are you sure these radiators are working?'

'I'll take a look at them when we get up. They need nursing along. Must have them right for the guests.'

I stroke the soft fur of his chest, thinking.

'It is strange, when you think of it. Life, I mean. Quite suddenly, a weekful of visitors gone at a blow. And all for us.'

I prop myself up on his chest and look into his dark quiet face.

'You've very black and hairy, aren't you?'

'That's me, my lovely.'

'I like it.'

'That's good, then.'

I settle back again: retelling the miracle of our time together.

'Not just one visitor cancelling for Christmas, Tom – which might be expected – but all of them. Lily and Humphrey and the boys. So that we could be by ourselves. Oh, Tom,' remembering, 'did you find any ornaments for the tree?'

This room faces south-west. The rain upon its windows, becoming louder and more insistent, sounds like a tattoo.

'Yes, by God!' he says. 'And I haven't unloaded the van. The boxes on top and at the back'll be wet through!'

He eases his arm carefully from under me, jumps out of bed and strides about the room, picking up his clothes, unconcerned about his nakedness or the cold, talking. I luxuriate in watching him, in knowing that we are now together in all things, that we are the stewards of Kelly Park, that this bed is our centre, that our single separate selves have become an us.

Tom's mind is elsewhere.

'Wait till you see what I bought in Helston market. We'll be all night dressing that tree, Flavie, I'm telling you.'

I slide out of bed also and begin to dress, but in a leisurely fashion, pausing and yawning and stretching with sheer pleasure. It is a splendid thing to feel a desirable woman again instead of an overworked and undesired body. Already I am thinking, What I shall cook for us? For us. Us. Us.

But Tom does not linger in Eden. He steps into his trousers, hauls a fisherman's jersey over his head, laces up his sneakers, says, 'See you downstairs, Flavie!' And is off to rescue the contents of the van.

In the kitchen I stand, hands on hips, considering menus. My delicious lethargy, the lateness of the hour, and an assortment of left-overs, make up my mind for me. We shall have Spanish omelettes and salad, and Tom can finish off the weekly fruit cake as a dessert, with three sorts of ice-cream on top if he wishes, as he probably will.

Then I catch sight of the long cardboard box, remember my daffodils, and put them up to their necks in a wash-tub of cool water before cracking a single egg.

Meanwhile Tom is striding to and fro in his glistening yellow mackintosh and hat, piling up the results of his Saturday shopping expedition. Boxes of Christmas tree ornaments seem to dominate the rest.

'How much scrap did you swop for that?' I ask impudently.

'He let me have the lot half-price because it was almost closing time. I waited until then and made him an offer.'

'Clever old you. What do I owe you?'

'My treat! I mended someone's engine on the way to Helston this morning and he gave me a Christmas tip on top of the pay.'

'Things *are* looking up.'

At ten o'clock we begin to decorate the tree, which is no mean task. Even Tom, standing on a pair of long stepladders, can only just reach the top. And when we have hung a hundred and fifty baubles all over it, and looped dozens of tinsel ropes along the boughs, and used up six boxes of fairy lights, the giant is still asking for more.

'Parcels!' I say. 'Imitation gifts. We'll use that Christmas paper,' for Tom's bargain buy included a dozen assorted rolls, 'and cover cardboard boxes with it – not the ones that held the ornaments, we shall need them when we come to undress the tree.'

So we hunt up empty boxes of all sorts and shapes and sizes and transform them into kingly tributes.

At half-past one on Christmas morning Tom plunges the hall into darkness, and we stand together by the door while he switches on the fairy lights. The tree looks quite something.

Then he holds a piece of mistletoe over my head, gives me a devout and caring kiss, and says, 'Happy first Christmas, my dear love!'

CHAPTER TWENTY-FOUR

The quiet delight of Christmas was replaced by feverish excitement as we prepared for our grand opening. My plans had been so often altered and delayed, my hopes so frequently lifted and dashed, that I could not believe Kelly Park was about to be launched. Humphrey had contributed a case of champagne, which stood by to welcome in a new year and a new era in our lives. Between us, Tom and I had stopped every loophole, reckoned every possibility, forearmed ourselves against every potential crisis, and made ready. The guest list was backed by a reserve list. All our staff had cousins prepared to step temporarily into their shoes if necessary. Tom had mended the generator and patched up the heating system. And I, who had lived so long with disappointment and disaster, now nourished a small but steady flame of faith in the future.

The previous weeks had been wet and dismal and a forecast of snow came as a welcome change. I had heard that Cornish winters were mild, and snow a rare visitor: quick to come and quick to go, resting lightly, decoratively. But Saturday dawned as grey and gloomy as its predecessors, and was raining heavily by the time Humphrey, Patrick and Jeremy arrived in the afternoon.

This time my sons did not hang back shyly or politely while Humphrey paid his addresses, but were ahead of him with their hugs and greetings, laying claim to me as it were. And I noticed that they were delighted to see Tom, whom they treated as part-mentor, part-entertainer.

The outer climate might be gloomy but the inner climate

glowed. A mutual glance between Tom and me established that we were both pleased with this new state of affairs.

Humphrey threw up his hands at the sight of our decorated giant, crying, 'Ah! The tree!'

And then as Martin and Sean ceremoniously carried in their gnarled green offering, guaranteed to burn well and long, 'Ah! The yule log!'

He kissed my hands humbly, and his eyes were moist.

On the final evening of Parc Celli's life as a private house we ate simply but well, *en famille* in the dining room. It was not easy for Tom and me to be so much to each other, and to seem less. But we concentrated on our guests and monitored our responses: a nod, a lifted eyebrow or a quick smile, conveyed a silent message. And afterwards Tom and the boys cleared away and stacked the dishwasher, and I ushered Humphrey into his armchair before the drawing-room fire with his reading-glasses, a balloon of brandy and *The Times* crossword. Drawing the curtains I noticed that the rain had changed to sleet and snow, which drove fiercely against the windows.

Humphrey, peering at me placidly from over the top of his newspaper, said, 'There are few situations in life more pleasurable than being safe and warm within the house, and hearing the wind and rain beat in vain against these granite walls. Though – as my dear grandmama rightly used to say – God save all poor souls at sea on such a night.'

Later we sat round the hearth and talked of the year which was almost gone and the one which was to come, and Tom, encouraged by Humphrey and brandy, began a series of naval yarns about drunken skippers, autocratic chief stewards, bad cooks, fights in foreign bars, parties below deck and storms at sea. He sat forward, hands on knees, and communed with the flames, and I was able to watch him with the others.

His voice rose and fell, his black eyes glinted, his eyebrows signalled astonishment or incredulity. Sometimes he slapped his thigh for emphasis, sometimes threw back his head and shouted with laughter. We sweated through the Suez canal with him. We wandered the night streets of great ports. We became acquainted with ships' engines and their idiosyncrasies. We rubbed shoulders with the likes of Squib Bristowe and his mates. How much was plain truth, and how skilfully that truth was embroidered, no one knew. But it was all good stuff and we loved it.

Long past midnight, on his way upstairs to bed, Humphrey paused many times, apparently to speak of many things, but in fact to regain his breath. Outside the Green Room he kissed my hand most courteously, and spoke pensively.

'Dearest Flavia, it still seems unfitting to me that you should be housed in the servants' quarters, however comfortable Tom has made them.'

I felt sad myself, for Grandmama's room was forbidden until the visitors had gone, and Tom and I must be celibate as well as circumspect.

Misinterpreting my silence, Humphrey said, 'Well, well. *Tempora mutantur, et nos mutamur in illis!* The times are changed, and we with them. I say no more, my dear. I know you have the best interests of Parc Celli at heart.'

Then he patted Tom on the shoulder, and spoke wistfully.

'A thousand thanks, my dear fellow, for those sea yarns. Listening to you – d'you know – I feel as if I had never lived. Well, well. Goodnight to you both. God bless you. I appreciate all you have done for me.'

My sleeping quarters, which had once been all I desired, seemed to have shrunk: a nun's cell, complete with pallet, and none too warm. And how I should miss the lovemaking, and the comfort of Tom's body in our opulent four-poster.

'Yes, you're a fine and private place,' I said to the little bedroom, 'and that's about all!'

As I drew the chintz curtains at one o'clock in the morning, I noticed that the snow was falling thickly and had begun to settle.

I sat up in bed with a start, thinking I had forgotten to set the alarm and would be late, for I woke to a muffled world and an unearthly light. My window was iced up on the inside, and breathing a hole through the stiff lace I saw outside a strange immaculate snowscape. Oddly enough, I felt that this was a good omen, a sign that the weather was on our side, and a childlike joy possessed me. I imagined myself as one of our first visitors, rounding the drive and seeing Kelly Park in her bridal splendour, crisply veiled under a pale blue sky. I dressed quickly, looked in on the boys, who still slept, and went downstairs to the kitchen, where Tom had already dug a path to the shed, brought in the coal, and coaxed the fire to burn.

'You're early. I was going to bring you a cup of tea. What about this, then?' he cried, flushed with exercise and cold.

'Oh Tom, doesn't it look wonderful? And no one else will be up for ages. We can have breakfast together by ourselves.'

We kissed as if we had been parted for twelve months instead of a night.

'I've made up the boiler,' said Tom. 'Ben won't be here for quite a while.'

We smiled at each other and stood together for a minute or two, hugging, and staring into the red-gold heart of fire. Then, as if proximity had fuelled us, we began to make breakfast while pursuing our own train of thought. Consequently the conversation, though intimate, was dislocated.

'Tom, if you'll make the toast I'll cook the eggs. Tom, I feel badly about concealing us from Humphrey and the boys but I don't know how to tell them. I was wondering whether to mention it when we let the New Year in. Or would it be better to write to them when they've gone?'

He said, filling the kettle, 'Alice Quick won't get up here unless Ben and me dig towards each other, and that'll take us all morning. As for Vera and the girls, I don't know that we'll see them at all. Wouldn't be surprised if the road to the village wasn't one big drift.'

'I just worry about how they'll take it. Men are so possessive. Though Humphrey and the boys think you're wonderful.'

Tom dropped one large warm brown hand to my shoulder and squeezed it.

'Never mind your men, my lovely. You can sort them out later. First things first. I'm going to find out what's happening.'

He lifted the receiver of the kitchen telephone, which had at last been installed, and dialled a number. He reverted to the Cornish mode.

'That you, Peggy? Tom Faull here. All right? Snowed up, are

you? So are we! Well, I'm glad to hear that. Yes, you do that. Set them all to it, Peggy. We need a road between here and Elinglaze. You tell Arthur I'll stand him a pint when we meet. Yes, Parc Celli's supposed to be opening tonight but I can't see it. Five inches in Falmouth, they say? Ah well, they would brag about nothing, wouldn't they? We've got more than that here! And more to come, looking at the sky. Said anything about a snow plough, have they? No, they wouldn't. They'll be clearing the main roads. Won't bother with us down here. We have to look out for ourselves, don't we? Cheers, Peggy.'

He stood for a while, head bent, hands on hips, pondering. Then he looked up and smiled reassuringly. I had not fully grasped the situation and was busy with practicalities.

'Alice Quick's no use on her own, Tom. I really do need Vera and Marianne and Julie. You *must* get through to the village. Pat and Jem can help you. Otherwise I don't see how we're going to manage. The overnight guests will be arriving this afternoon.'

He consulted the barometer, tapped it, shook his head.

'Power lines aren't down yet. That's one thing. And we've got plenty of batteries for the radio. You listen in to it while I'm away. We need to hear all the weather reports. We might be snowed up to Plymouth or Exeter – or even beyond.'

Still one step behind him, I was saying, 'The bedrooms were all made up yesterday, and between us – you and me and the boys, with Humphrey playing host – we could cope with people wanting things like a tray of tea and their luggage carrying up, but a four-course New Year's Eve dinner is something else altogether. For that, Tom, I must have a full staff!'

Tom kissed me to stop me from talking, and said when I was silent, 'Listen to me, my lovely. Peggy Crowdy's been ringing round since seven o'clock this morning. She says we're snowed up worse here than anywhere else. The main road from Helston to the Lizard is blocked, and every village cut off. Some of the telephone lines seem to be down, and there's drifts no one knows how deep. That means no transport – no planes, no trains, no buses, no cars, no nothing. Means that nobody can get through to Parc Celli. The only vehicle to clear the way would be a snow plough, and we shan't see that down here until it's all over.'

I opened my mouth to protest, and he held my shoulders and kissed me again and said, 'But we'll do what we can for ourselves. We'll have our breakfast first, Flavia, and then you wake those lads of yours – and feed them well because they won't be back for a while. Tell them to find a spade apiece in the shed and join me. I'll be out there digging.'

Amicably, he toasted his face and the bread in front of the kitchen grate: buttering each slice generously and popping it between two plates to keep warm, while I scrambled eggs, made tea and brooded.

I found my voice and raised it in dissent.

'I don't *believe* it! I *won't* believe it! Peggy Crowdy's probably exaggerating. Even if she isn't it'll probably start to thaw in a couple of hours. Even if it doesn't the snow ploughs will clear the main roads in no time. Tom, Tom are you listening? We are opening tonight with a New Year's Eve dinner, and I need Vera and Marianne and Julie up here just as soon as you can fetch them.'

He laughed, and shook me gently, and called on heaven to witness the astonishing obstinacy of Flavia Pollard.

Then he said, 'All right, my love. Have it your own way. I'll be off as soon as I've eaten, and I'll get all the help I can. And make some good hot soup and keep it going. I may be sending folk back for a warm up.'

So we returned to our personal probem, and ate and drank and wondered how to tell Humphrey and the boys that we two were as one, and came to no conclusion. Until Tom set down his cup, pushed away his plate, pulled on his boots, pulled down his Balaclava helmet, donned his reefer jacket, shouldered his Cornish shovel, and creaked off in the snow.

I roused my troops and fed them.

'I say, Mum, isn't the snow super? Hard luck on you, though. What about opening night? Will anyone be able to get through?'

'Of course they will. Lots of Cornish people booked in. Some only live a few miles away. You and Tom and the villagers are digging us all out. So hurry!'

I fed them and sent them forth. I took up Humphrey's breakfast on a tray, and did not stint him. He was in reminiscent mood.

'Ah, my dear, the white world of childhood! But, Flavia, what of our New Year guests? No one will be able to reach us.'

I was brisk with him, and forthright.

'Certainly they will. The Cornish contingent will, at any rate. Tom and the boys are digging us out and we're opening tonight. I'm making a gallon of soup for the workers, and I haven't got any help until the staff arrives, and the fires aren't lit, so please don't ring because I can't answer the bell. Come to the kitchen if there's anything you want. In fact, on second thoughts, I should stay in bed if I were you, Humphrey.'

At ten o'clock the telephone rang with the first cancellation from a family of Londoners, trapped in Exeter. I took comfort from the fact that they said Parc Celli sounded so lovely that I could book them in for the Easter weekend.

In clear black script on a sheet of thick cream paper, I had written out my menu for the New Year's Eve Dinner: balanced, harmonious, satisfying. Now I pinned it up defiantly on the cork-board on the kitchen wall. Above it, two permanent notices reminded me and all who worked with me YOU EAT WITH YOUR EYES! and FAIT SIMPLE!

At lunch-time Henry Blewett plodded up the drive with a borrowed horse and cart, and delivered Alice Quick, a large churn of milk and a small churn of cream. They were received into the haven of the kitchen and accepted soup. Henry brought a message from Tom, saying that he and the boys and Ben Quick were on their way to Elinglaze. Would I send food and tea? Henry also told me that everyone was out digging, and he was delivering where he could, but mostly leaving a crate of milk at the nearest collecting point and hoping folk could get to it. And what would happen tomorrow he didn't know. If the weather was like this the farmers would be pouring milk away because the tanker lorries couldn't get through. I packed a basket for Tom and the boys and he departed.

At intervals the telephone rang, and each time I crossed two or more names off my guest list. Still I was hopeful, for these were all people outside the county, and I was relying on the Cornish to be faithful.

Alice Quick, inclined to be querulous, was lighting fires,

flourishing her dusters, and prophesying disaster. Metaphorically speaking I went on cutting bread and butter: in fact turning out sheet after sheet of meringue shells.

When Humphrey appeared, apologetic but petulant at the kitchen door, I sat him down at the kitchen table and gave him a bowl of soup and a hunk of bread. Stupefied, he ate it without a murmur and disappeared.

At two o'clock Jeff Kennack arrived to say that there was neither post nor newspapers. But he brought back the basket and a message from Tom to say that they had cleared the way almost to Elinglaze, and were keeping the road open with a farmyard muck-scraper. They would then press on to see if they could connect the village to the B3293, the secondary Lizard road.

Just before three o'clock a tractor trundled up the drive, bearing Vera, Marianne and Julie in a state of high excitement. I gave them their work lists, and the tractor trundled back again with Alice Quick.

'But what if nobody comes, Mrs Flavia?' asked Vera.

I repeated obstinately, 'This is our opening night and we shall open.'

'How many covers shall I lay, Mrs Flavia?' Marianne asked, her eyes on the decimated guest list. I conceded that my forty covers were a dream.

Grudgingly I said, 'Thirty.'

'Do you want me to do all these vegetables, Mrs Flavia?' Julie asked, surveying the assorted mountains.

'Yes, please.'

The three Angwin women exchanged meaningful glances, decided not to argue with me, and set to work.

The presence of our menu on the cork notice-board was a talisman. From time to time each of us consulted it and returned to our labours refreshed.

The light faded. The mercury in the thermometer slid inexorably down. The snow froze. Hills had become toboggan slopes. Fields were skating rinks. At four o'clock it was growing dark, and the diggers came back exhausted, bringing Sean Angwin with them. They had failed to reach even the secondary road. I gave them the rest of the soup, put out a loaf, a hunk of Cheddar and a jar of chutney and brewed a large pot of strong brown tea. A forgotten Humphrey joined them, bringing a bottle of Johnnie Walker, and they laced their mugs with whisky. Huddled at the end of the long kitchen table the men talked, heads together, in low voices while we women worked on in silence.

And in silence the snow began to fall again.

Five o'clock, and dark. The telephone had not rung for two hours and there were still twenty Cornish names on my guest list. Now the group of men rose, and Tom came forward as if they had designated him to act as spokesman.

'Flavia, you'd best put this party food in the freezer for next time. There's nobody coming here tonight, my lass. Make up your mind to that.'

The men all nodded: gravely, sagely. We four women stood spellbound, for the menu had carried us along with it, and if the food existed then logically there must be diners to consume it.

I said uncertainly, 'But no one else has cancelled, and there are still twenty guests who could come.'

'Their telephone lines may be down,' said Tom gently, 'or they may well think that you don't expect them in this weather.'

Humphrey had been standing with his back to us, reading the paper banquet on my notice-board. Now he came back to the kitchen table, took off his reading glasses and cleared his throat. Everyone fell silent as he spoke in his cultured, fly-away voice, looking over my head in order to avoid my eyes.

'Flavia, my dear, I have spent the last few hours listening to national and local weather forecasts on the radio and they are absolutely horrendous. It would seem that Cornwall has suffered the worst snowfalls for twenty years. Public transport is at a halt. Cars have been abandoned. My dear, it is total chaos. No one will find their way here tonight.'

'But our people have been digging all day,' I cried, 'and other people will have been doing the same. Someone must connect somewhere.'

The men looked at each other, then studied their empty tea mugs.

Sean Angwin said thoughtfully to the boys, 'Visibility warn't no more than thirty yards. You and us was on top of one another almost, when we met.'

Vera, Marianne and Julie now joined in, for they had been listening to the radio while they worked, whereas I had listened only to myself.

'. . . been giving out bulletins all day, and they've set up a help-line.'

'. . . 'undreds of villages cut off, and some with no power and no water.'

'. . . leastways we've still got they. Power and water, I mean.'

Humphrey completed the Greek chorus.

'Flavia dear, they are actually advising people to stay at home for their own safety.'

The men kept their faces averted from my disaster, but the women looked to me to rectify matters.

Within myself I was raging, thinking how extraordinary it was that when I didn't want people they turned up in droves, and when I invited them they couldn't come.

Outwardly I maintained a rigid calm, and I was not yet beaten.

I said, 'Humphrey, the kitchen staff have come to a natural break in the preparations. And all the men have been working hard. Suppose we have a beer or a glass of wine apiece while I mull the situation over?'

His face brightened. He counted the heads.

'Tom,' he said grandly, 'bring up a couple of bottles of champagne.'

Faces shone as the corks popped. It had been a cruel day.

Humphrey raised his glass and said, 'Success to Parc Celli!' And added, chin raised, tone earnest, 'The Lord's delays are not denials!'

His retainers applauded him, and sipped appreciatively. There was a reverent silence which threatened to become an awkward pause.

Then Tom adopted his storytelling stance, and began as if he were talking aloud to himself, though actually intent on the company at large.

'Worst cook I ever remember was on the Federal line, travelling to the Antipodes. Scabby little chap called Spud Murphy, who looked like a garden gnome—'

'Now Tom, Tom,' Humphrey cried, delighted, pointing his forefinger at the teller of tales, 'remember there are ladies present. None of your gaudy language, if you please!'

'Certainly not, sir,' said Tom urbanely. 'Just the occasional mild adjective.'

As they gathered round him, laughing, I sat down with my prickling, glittering glass of champagne, and began to rewrite the guest list.

PARC CELLI

New Year's Eve, 1978

Humphrey Jarvis
Flavia Pollard
Patrick Pollard
Jeremy Pollard
Tom Faull

'The only food he couldn't ruin was cornflakes. And he had a way of frying eggs so hard that a knife couldn't stab them. So you peeled the top off the yolk like a watch-glass and ate the powder underneath . . .'

Staff
Alice and Ben Quick
Vera Angwin & husband (Brian)
Sean, Marianne & Julie Angwin
Martin Skeggs

' . . . the only thing you could do with the white was to nail it to the sole of your shoe.'

Builders
Mr & Mrs Will Soady and Four Sons

'Now the ship's baker was an ex-Regimental Sergeant-Major chef, and he *could* cook, though he hadn't signed on for that. But he was a good bloke. So I used to slip him a bottle of whisky and he supplied us with food, and the lekkies bodged up an electric grill for us. Lekkies? Electricians. They work hand in glove with the engineers . . . '

Other Helpers

Mr & Mrs Henry Blewett (milk deliveries)

' . . . could smell this food through the engine-room vents . . . '

Mr & Mrs Jeffrey Kennack (postal deliveries)

' . . . realised what was up when the third engineer reeled out, singing "Danny Boy", with a whacking great bacon sandwich in his hand . . . '

Peggy and Arthur Crowdy (village centre and communications)

' . . . finally made up our minds we were going to get shot of Murphy. So we put these barrels outside the door of his cabin . . . '

Vicar and wife? Doctor and wife?

' . . . left him in hospital in Auckland with a broken leg, and fed like kings for the rest of the voyage.'

Total: 29

When Humphrey had finally subsided, laughing and wiping his eyes, I pushed my jotting pad over to him, saying, 'What do you think?'

He sat next to me and read it at arm's length, head well back. Set it down and tapped his mouth with his spectacles, thinking. Turned to me, smiling.

He said for my ears alone, 'If we agree to go ahead with your idea, does this mean that we shall all eat together? And will you wear your green silk gown and take your place at the foot of the table as my hostess?'

At this tender moment the power failed, plunging the house into darkness, and we all gasped or cried out.

'No need to fret!' cried Tom, out of the gloom. 'I can start the generator!'

A hiss, a pop, and a harsh glow. He had lit his hurricane lamp and was holding it aloft. We all smiled at each other, in a state of relief.

'Best have a light or two while you're gone,' said Vera, finding the matches.

'Just so long as you've got plenty of candles and paraffin,' Tom warned us, on his way out.

'Cartloads of them,' I replied.

Humphrey pressed my hand under the table and said, 'Now we shall all dine together by candlelight. So much nicer!'

Myself again, I turned to Humphrey and said, 'Yes, Humpty, if you would like that. I think we should make it more of a party than a formal occasion. A sort of thank you to all the people who have been concerned in restoring Parc Celli. I don't see why they shouldn't accept an invitation. They've got nowhere else to go. And we could transport them to and fro in batches. Vera and Marianne and Julie and I will have to keep popping in and out of our seats to see to things, but that won't matter. We can let in the New Year with a bang, and declare Parc Celli well and truly open.'

Humphrey reread the list and put his forefinger on two names.

'The Crowdys have an aged mother living with them, who can't be left. And two of the Soady sons are married, with – I believe – toddlers or babies.'

'That's no problem. I was expecting forty guests. Let them all come!'

Someone said, 'Tom's a long time!' and took a torch and went out to help.

'Is there anyone else you can think of?' I asked Humphrey.

'Not without opening the doors of the whole of Elinglaze. Each of these people has a particular claim upon us. Let us leave it there.'

'Then perhaps, dearest Humphrey, you'll set the scheme in motion?'

But before he could do so both men returned to a candlelit kitchen saying, 'Can't start him. Diesel oil's frozen!'

'What shall we do about the freezer and the refrigerator?' I cried.

'Don't you worry!' said Tom reassuringly. 'I can cover them with duvets for twenty-four hours. If the power doesn't come back tomorrow I'll move them outside. It's cold enough there.'

'Best light the lamps then!' said Vera prosaically.

Her attitude towards Tom and towards me had changed. She was factual with him now, instead of worshipful. Upon me she occasionally turned a quizzical look.

Humphrey kissed my hand and held it in both of his.

'My dear, you are a wonderful woman,' he said. 'And when this is over you and I must have a very important little talk about the future. I am speaking personally now, not as your business partner.'

Don't fail, heart! Beat on! You have a dinner to serve and a party to give.

'In fact, with the future in mind,' Humphrey continued, 'I have taken the liberty of bringing you a New Year present which will best express my feelings and intentions. In fact, I have spent today thinking of a good hiding place, and you must guess where it is! We'll have a little treasure hunt, you and I, tomorrow morning.'

Oh will he never give up? Oh, not an engagement ring, pray God! Never mind, I'll face that symbol of bondage when it confronts me.

'Humpty, I shall wait with baited breath for tomorrow!' I said speciously. 'And now, perhaps, I think you should tell everyone what you have in mind.'

Satisfied, he wheeled slowly round, raising his arms to garner their attention, lifting his voice to deliver an invitation no one present had ever expected.

My sons appeared to take me in charge, turn by turn about, as if I were an invalid with a fascinating ailment and they my physicians. This time it was Jeremy who offered to help me turn thirty napkins into thirty water lilies while Marianne instructed her sister in the art of table-laying.

'When and why did you learn to do that?' I asked, surprised.

'I had nothing else to do, mooning round one wet afternoon at Dad's place, and Anne was having four people to dinner – big deal!' He glanced at me, making sure that I was receiving the right messages. 'She's got a book called *The Perfect Hostess*, and I looked through it while she was fussing over the table. So I read the instructions and tried them out. I can do bishops' mitres, too, and a conical tower.'

'You clever old thing!'

He sat, fair head bent over his task, a little smile on his mouth. We worked peaceably together, somewhat apart from the rest.

He said, 'I suppose you'll be teaching Marianne how to do these, Mum?'

'Yes. Among many other accomplishments.'

'And Tom tells us that you've taught him how to flambé – let's hope he doesn't set fire to Kelly Park!'

I felt uncomfortable, talking about Tom, and kept my eyes on the linen petals of the water lily, and laughed to show that I appreciated the joke.

I was aware of Jeremy looking up and smiling.

He said, 'Old Tom's made himself pretty well indispensable, hasn't he?'

'Yes. Yes, he has. I don't know how we'd manage without him now.'

Then catching sight of Marianne coming into the kitchen, empty-handed and looking for further orders, I escaped from the conversation, and left my son to create water lilies.

Ignoring the weather, life in Elinglaze was continuing its natural course, and neither the doctor nor the vicar could oblige us with their company. For the one was bringing a baby into the world and the other ushering an elderly soul out of it. But everyone else arrived in every possible kind of vehicle, dressed in their very best. Had the jewels been real they would have outshone Cartier's window. And, though our guests may have felt shy at first, they behaved with a natural dignity and shook hands as if they were used to dining with the local squire. Though I noticed that the older members tended to group together for safety: smiling and silent with the honour and terror of the occasion.

From Parc Celli's domestic recesses came a cornucopia of paraffin lamps and candles, and even an iron candle chandelier, which Tom hoisted to a hook in the hall ceiling and lit with a taper fixed to a long wand. It was a pity about the Christmas tree's fairy lights but its glass baubles reflected dozens of burning yule logs. And there was a living quality about the flames, a softness of light, which excelled mere brightness.

Humphrey was superb: pale hair plastered to his skull with brilliantine, clad in white tie and tails, with a starched front that kept his second chin well up. His smile of welcome, his gentle hand pressure was just right.

'So good of you to come at such short notice!' he cried to the men, murmured to the ladies.

Shining, gracious, he waved his guests towards the drawing room where Tom stood in his Spanish best, holding a tray of drinks.

At Humphrey's side, my smile on the company, my mind on the food, I shook hands, played hostess, and prayed that the range was behaving itself and not either shooting up in high fever or dropping below zero. But by good luck or ingenuity Vera and her family were the earliest arrivals. Giving me an understanding nod, she disappeared towards the kitchen at once; while Marianne and Julie, unable to resist an excursion into the high life, giggled over a glass apiece of Bristol Cream until Tom hissed, 'Be off with you! Your mam needs you back there!' Whereupon they fled, still giggling.

The air was supercharged with purpose, and with more than purpose, with a kind of magic as the occasion took over. Vera, Marianne, Julie and I discarded our Cinderella image by casting off our overalls and emerging in full evening dress. Tom became a chameleon, taking on the colour of whatever place he happened to be. And Humphrey, at his finest, kept the company occupied in small talk.

As I moved between kitchen and drawing room, I had a bird's-eye view of the event.

Martin Skeggs, wearing the suit in which he proposed to Lily, staring raptly at one of Grandmama's portraits, with never-thought-to-see-the-day written all over his face.

Grandma Crowdy's personal closet being carried into my office because, as Peggy explained, 'She won't use nobody else's toilet and she do have to go sudden these days!'

A small troupe of children, clad in their night-clothes and clutching favourite soft animals, being bedded down in the Lilac

Room. Tom rigging up an intercom system so that they could be heard in the event of trouble.

Will Soady, Jeff Kennack and Brian Angwin at one end of the room, rocking in lordly fashion on their heels, sherry glass in hand, discussing cricket.

Sean Angwin and my two boys laughing about heaven knows what.

All the wives in a huddle at the other end, discussing every detail of the soft furnishings, occasionally making forays upstairs to see the children, or taking Grandma Crowdy on one of her frequent visits to the office.

And that steady busy hum of conversation which means that everyone is enjoying themselves and looking forward to the meal.

Tom was changing roles so fast that I could hardly keep up with him.

'Another sherry, sir?'

'I'll just put some more logs on the fire.'

'Should I take that trolley in now?'

And being himself with me for a few moments in passing: a compliment, an endearment, a reminder of what we are to each other.

Finally, standing at the door in saturnine grandeur, as the butler.

'Mr Jarvis. Ladies and gentlemen. Dinner is served.'

And there was I, as if the word catering had never been known to pass my lips, translated to the foot of the table in my green silk gown, while Vera and Marianne and Julie, their duties done for the moment, slipped into their places, a little breathless and flushed, but now members of the party.

Humphrey said, 'Shall we say grace?' and there was a scraping back of chairs and a fumbling and rumbling of people standing up, bending their heads in deference, and listening to a sixteenth-century prayer which aptly matched the present time.

> God bless our meat,
> God guide our ways,
> God give us grace our Lord to please.

Lord long preserve in peace and health
Our gracious Queen Elizabeth.

Then we all sat down with a great sigh of pleasure, and began to butter hot rolls, and to sample the game soup.

CHAPTER TWENTY-FIVE

The yule log fell with a crash and showered sparks and occasioned cries of amusement and mock terror. The candles flickered in their sconces. The banquet was at the nutshell and tangerine peel stage. Now, made easy with wine and soothed by food, conversation did not languish. Outside, the wind might gust down the chimney and shiver every pane in the great hall window, snow fall and icicles hang three feet long beneath the eaves. Who cared? Though God save all poor souls at sea.

They were talking of other storms, of wrecks and rocks and smuggling.

'Of course, smuggling was regarded as a general occupation until the 1840s or thereabouts,' said Humphrey, wiping his mouth on his napkin. 'Many a Cornishman brought up his family on the proceeds. Then the customs men made it too hazardous for any but the most daring adventurers.'

'Now my mother was a Williams from Mullion . . . ' Martin Skeggs began.

A little hush fell on the company, to think that a member of the Elinglaze Skeggses should marry such a foreigner. Someone muttered, 'Mullion Gulls!' but fortunately Martin was deaf, and wandered away on the wind of his tale.

' . . . and her grandfather was cousin to Dionysius Williams. I daresay you've heard tell of *him.*' With tremendous emphasis. 'Regular old rogue he was, smuggled all his life, never got caught, retired happy and lived long! I seen a photograph of him when he was ninety-three, and as hale and hearty as – as . . . ' Then he eddied to the ground again, mumbling to himself, 'Ninety-three. 'Es, we'm a long-lived family on my mother's side . . . '

Ben Quick moved in, saying, 'There's many an old house has a secret chamber from them days, to hide a man or hide his goods. They built 'un behind a cupboard and put a false back in it. Customs men might look where they would, they wouldn't find nothing.'

Humphrey said, 'My grandmama told me there was a secret room in Parc Celli. I was always trying to find it, as a boy. But even if it existed I don't believe it would be used for contraband.' Then he looked round the table and said, 'Would it, do you think? Surely not?'

They glanced at each other and at him, and smiled slyly.

Arthur Crowdy, encouraged by wine and proximity, said with rough good humour, 'Why not, Mr Jarvis, sir? You was always one of us, warn't you?'

Whereupon everyone laughed and raised their glasses, and Humphrey neighed with delight.

Martin Skeggs, off on another eddy, said, 'My grandma told me she heard the smugglers go by many a night, when she was a maid. They would fetch the brandy barrels by packhorse, and muffle their feet . . . '

Now Will Soady joined in.

'There was an old house in Elinglaze by the church, a long time since. And I've heard my grandad tell that the folk who lived there was friendly with the local smugglers. Said they had a tunnel running from the garden right under the churchyard. But nobody found nothing and the family died out, and time went on. Then a year or two before the war the house was pulled down to make way for a proper road through the village. And when they brought the digger through the garden the ground caved in – and there was that tunnel, right enough.'

The women listened to their men, fingers tracing the gold rim of a plate or the ivory handle of a knife: keeping their silence, possibly as their female ancestors had done all those years ago, knowing much, saying nothing.

'Tomorrow, Flavia,' said Humphrey archly, 'you and I must go a-hunting, and see what we can find!'

The clock struck eleven. At a signal from me my helpers rose for the final effort.

I said, 'Ladies and gentlemen, coffee will be served in the drawing room.'

But Humphrey lifted a lordly hand.

'One moment, if you please!' he cried.

We all subsided.

'Tom, my boy!' said Humphrey. 'I believe it is time to open the champagne. Make sure everyone's glass is charged!'

While this was being done, he took a slip of paper from his waistcoat pocket and spread it on the cloth in front of him, put on his half-moon spectacles, smoothed his hair, cleared his throat, and stood at his ease.

With admirable presence of mind Patrick cried, 'Speech!'

And immediately, to the accompaniment of laughter, the clapping of hands and the banging of knife handles on the table, came a universal cry of, 'Speech! Speech! Speech!'

Gratified, Humphrey inclined his head, smoothed the swelling arc of his waistcoat, and waited for the applause to fade. Again I was reminded of Toad in his hour of glory, and with such an intense affection that my eyes filled.

Silence now.

The voice began on a low note, was mellifluous, and brought us all together in two charmed words.

'My friends . . . '

He paused for the murmur of appreciation and respect, smiled benignly, and began again on a stronger note.

'My friends – for so it is my pleasure and privilege to call you! I shall not detain you long. And lest you fear I am not telling the truth these few notes shall bear me witness!'

He held up the scrap of paper, and we all laughed and clapped again.

He became serious, and we copied him.

He addressed his people.

'I must first thank my old friends from Elinglaze, for accepting an invitation at such discourteously short notice, and for turning a sad failure into a delightful celebration. I raise my glass to you. God bless you all.'

One wit cried, 'Any time, Mr Jarvis!' which amused everyone but his wife, who reddened and hushed him.

'Tonight,' Humphrey continued imperturbably, 'should have been the official opening of Parc Celli in its new role as a country-house hotel. But fate and the inclement weather deemed otherwise. And yet I cannot find it in my heart to regret this present occasion. On the contrary it has given us a breathing space in which to enjoy each other's company, to look back on almost a year of dedicated effort, and to look forward to a future in which we shall all participate.'

They had settled down, prepared to hear him out.

'Houses, as well as people, must change with the times. I cannot deny that I should have liked Parc Celli to remain my beloved home, to have been forever enshrined in a past which I – at least – found perfect.'

A nostalgic murmur rippled round the table. Alice Quick nodded her head, lifted worn hands as if to see them for the first time, and clasped them again.

'Once upon a time this house sheltered some of you or your families, provided work and security for the others. And then, for more years than I care to remember, the house declined and so did the people of Elinglaze. We were caught between a past which was no longer viable and a present which placed a higher regard on money than on personal relations. For we meant a great deal to each other in the old days. Relied upon each other. Made each other's happiness complete – as we have done tonight, my friends – as we have done tonight . . . '

Martin Skeggs wiped his eyes and looked down upon his handkerchief as if scrutinising the answer to an imponderable question.

Humphrey's tone changed, became purposeful.

'But none of us can escape the pressures of the outside world, nor can we change it to suit ourselves. We must change with it or be left behind, to soldier on as best we may. And in this remote county – whose needs, I fear, are often misunderstood by the powers that be, and sometimes clean forgotten – we shall founder if we do not fight. So Parc Celli must go forward with the rest of us. Must earn her living if she is to survive. And so she will. And in earning that living she will once more give work and care and shelter to the people of Elinglaze.'

His voice lifted, lit, turned many faces towards him.

'For in this momentous year a solution was found which affects all of us, as well as this dear house. Found, I may say, by two people: one of them a man who was born and bred here – I believe you all know Tom Faull!'

And here he winked and drew down the corners of his mouth and laughed. And they all laughed with him. And Tom laughed at himself like the giant he was: throwing back his head, and the laugh coming loud and long and deep from the bottom of his lungs, so that they laughed again in sympathy.

'Yes,' said Humphrey humorously, 'we all know Tom, and we love him. No doubt about that. We even love his faults – and he has one or two, I believe. I've heard mention of trout and pheasants . . . '

More laughter. Humphrey became bland.

'I can't remember in what connection,' he said.

Uproar. Cries of, 'He's got you there, Tom!'

And Will Soady called, 'Where did you get they tarpaulins, Tom?'

Humphrey raised his hand, and they were quiet at once, like children waiting for further treats.

'But underneath the fun and devilry he's sound and true, is Tom. I hold out my hand to you, Tom, in honour and friendship. My hand, Tom.'

Then Tom came forward and shook it, and returned to his seat wiping his own eyes.

I sat enthralled. And was to be further exalted.

'Finally, I must come to the lady who was a stranger among us, and whom – I am proud to declare it! – I honour above all women.'

They were hushed now, glancing uncertainly from him to me to Tom, and back again. For though nothing was known all had been surmised.

'Without the inspiration and dedication of Flavia Pollard,' Humphrey continued, looking straight at me, 'this house would eventually have come to dust. She is a lady whose purpose is equal to her great talents – and one does need both in this world. I don't mind telling you that she has put me right, many a time, and kept me straight.' He lightened the moment. 'I daresay she's done the same for Tom!'

Tom raised his hand in rueful acknowledgement, and they laughed, but softly this time and with understanding rather than merriment.

Humphrey said, 'Tonight's banquet – and we have dined sumptuously – ' another murmur of agreement, 'was due entirely to this lady's determination not to give in to circumstances. She had cooked a dinner and therefore she intended it to be eaten. And at that moment of determination came also inspiration. At that moment she thought of all of you. Her exact words were, I believe, "A sort of thank you for all the people who have been concerned in restoring Parc Celli." '

Everyone turned to look at me, and clapped. Tom saluted me gravely. And the boys said joyfully, 'Well done, Mum!'

Humphrey said, 'I shall be keeping an eye on things, of course, and coming down here from time to time. But for the greater part of the year I shall be absent while the house earns its living. I commend the lady to you. I ask you to take care of her and to do your best for her – and she will do the same by you. Ladies and gentlemen,' in a louder voice, as they were all pledging themselves audibly to my service, 'just one more moment, if you please?'

In the instant silence he raised his glass and said, 'I ask you to drink to your hostess, Flavia Pollard. To you, Flavia. Thank you, and God bless you!'

They rose in acclamation, and I sat pressing the palms of my hands together to steady myself, pressing my lips together so that they should not tremble. Then I lifted my head, saw the double row of cordial faces, of glasses held aloft, heard my name on their lips, looked around at my boys, at Tom, and finally in joy and tears at Humphrey.

He had set down his wine and begun to clap. He stood very upright, holding his hands high, striking them purposefully, as though he were at the opera, applauding a prima donna.

* * *

His face changes. He clutches his chest, shouting ah-ah-ah at the onslaught of pain, and falls back in his chair.

Tom is the first to reach him, saying, 'Hold up, sir. You'll be right!'

He loosens Humphrey's white tie, unbuttons the starched front.

'Somebody phone the doctor!' he says urgently.

Humphrey is being crushed to death. He fights and gapes for breath, and every gape is a groan. His eyes roll in panic towards Tom, and then towards me, who has somehow arrived from the foot of the table and knelt on his other side. I slip my hand into his coat pocket and find the little enamelled snuff-box in which he keeps his tablets. With difficulty Tom slips one on his tongue. I put my arm round Humphrey's shoulders and try to comfort him. But he is convulsed with terror and torment and no longer heeds us.

All round us our guests are jumping up, pushing back their chairs, crowding us, despite Tom's appeals to give Humphrey air, asking each other questions to which no one knows the answer.

Patrick sprints back from the telephone, very white and tense, to say that the line is dead. But in any case the world outside is buried under a weight of snow and no one could get through in time, because Humphrey is being pressed too hard, and is losing the struggle.

He makes a final snoring effort, falls back, and is tranquil.

All sound and motion ceases. We are imprisoned in the moment.

Will Soady standing helplessly beside us, asks, 'Has he . . . is he . . . ?'

'Yes,' says Tom. 'He's gone.'

All over the house the clocks begin to chime the New Year in.

Looking back, I find gaps in my recollection of events.

I will say to Tom, 'How did everyone get home that night?' or 'Did everyone go home?' or 'When did they leave?'

I know that the doctor and the vicar arrived eventually, the one to pronounce Humphrey dead and the other to pray over him. Their previous duties had been accomplished and the population of Elinglaze balanced. For on New Year's Eve we lost old Kezzie Thomas and Humphrey, but Loveday Pengelly had twins.

Memories are few but vivid. They leap back and forth.

Humphrey is lying in state upstairs on his bed covered with a clean white sheet. Hands folded on his chest, he looks remarkably like a Roman emperor, face portentous with a knowledge he cannot share.

'I don't know when we can bury him,' said the vicar. 'The nearest funeral directors are in Helston, and we can't get through. But I can send Mrs Collings up to lay him out. She used to be the local midwife until she retired.'

'There'll be an inquest, of course,' said the doctor. 'A formality, in fact, but necessary. And that will have to wait until things get back to normal.'

'Are you – concerned – about having the body in the house, Mrs Pollard?' the vicar asked. 'There's no way, you see, of removing him to a Chapel of Rest. Of course, he could lie in the church, if you wished.'

I said, 'Parc Celli was, and is, Mr Jarvis's home for as long as he needs it. There's no problem.'

So Humphrey presided over the household in marble dignity behind the closed door and drawn curtains of the Green Room.

The pipes froze and our water supply failed. Tom was all for unsealing the well in the courtyard, but I vetoed this idea. We had enough trouble without enraging the South West Water Authority. So he drove the van to and from a natural spring, and filled containers for us.

On the third day, a slight thaw overnight and rumours of a snow-plough, gave us hope of connection to the outside world. But the thaw merely made the ground more treacherous underfoot. On the fourth day the road to Helston was closed again. Farmers who could not reach it by tractor were pouring their milk away. Only the children remained liberated, exhilarated. They skated on fields, tobogganed down hill slopes. For them it was all shouts and glee, woollen gloves and cold red noses.

The drifts were deep, and strong winds blew snow from the fields into the narrow ways we had dug. There was no electricity. Everything had to be done and carried by hand. Life slowed down to a fraction of its usual pace. We lit paraffin lamps against the night and watched our fuel supplies getting lower. And we waited. For five long days.

Tom said ironically to me, 'Did I ever wish you a Happy New Year, my lovely?'

A bleakness overlay the pair of us.

From the moment we could contact the outside world it descended upon us. Jack Rice, as official administrator of the estate, and self-appointed spokesman for the family, took over on the first day.

Both Tom and I had guessed that this catastrophe would delay our plans for Parc Celli while the will was proved. We were further bedevilled by the fact that though Humphrey's body and property were here in Cornwall his daily life had been led, and his business affairs conducted, in London.

Jack Rice was in his element. I communicated with him first of all by telephone, and he became both ferret and mediator: contacting his family, organising the funeral from a distance. I coped with an influx of Humphrey's relatives, some of whom I had never met before, others with whom I was not best pleased to be reacquainted, and none of whom I particularly liked. Some brought dogs with them, and the dogs fought, and all of them expected something from Humphrey's will and took it for granted that I would feed and house them until the ceremony was over.

The staff whispered among themselves, wondering what would become of them, knowing they were powerless without their squire's patronage.

'A word with you, Flick,' said Jack breezily, sticking his head round the kitchen door.

I was not about to jump at the crack of his whip. I replied briefly.

'I'm busy at the moment. Tell me where you'll be, and I'll come as soon as I can.'

Even more briefly he replied, 'Library. OK?'

I washed and dried my hands, took off my overall, thinking.

Vera asked apprehensively of the universe, 'Now where's he to?'

I would have liked to reassure her, but could not think what to say. I knew Jack. His confidence filled me with foreboding. Yet the library was tranquil in the cold January sun. And from the window I could see the narrow green leaves and bright yellow blossom of a hardy winter jasmine, growing at the foot of a garden wall; viburnum, still covered in a pinched flush of flowers; gold and silver variegated holly; heathers in every shade of colour: symbols of beauty and endurance.

'Yes, Jack?' I said incisively, and sat down facing him.

Of course he was acting as usual, pretending to be terribly concerned for me, prepared to be tremendously considerate with everyone. But not meeting my eyes, I noticed.

'I felt I had to have a private word with you before the contents of the will were made known. Look here, Flick, this is an awful mess, and nobody could be sorrier than I am. But I did warn you about poor old Humps.'

I steeled myself to repeat non-committally, 'Yes, Jack?'

'Since I was the most business-like person in the family, Humphrey asked me some years ago to deal with matters in the event of his death. So I've been checking things out, and his will does seem to have left you in the lurch. Thought it best to warn you. I didn't want you to have a nasty surprise.'

That brought my heart into my mouth.

'How can that be?' I cried, unable to hide my concern. 'He told me in September that he was making a new will which would stipulate that Parc Celli was to be run as a hotel, that the profits from his share were to be divided among members of his family, and that if it had to be sold for any good reason then I should be given first option to buy.'

Jack shrugged his shoulders, spread his hands and smiled.

He said, 'I'm sure he meant to do it – but he didn't. You know Humps.'

'Is there any mention of Parc Celli being run by me?'

'None whatsoever. His will was drawn up about seven years ago. He leaves two thousand to you, whom he describes as "my dear friend Flavia Pollard". Five hundred to his housekeeper, Mrs Turner. Two hundred to each of his godchildren – there are about a dozen altogether, I believe. He's left some jewellery and furniture to be given out here and there – you've got some little item, I forget what. Then small legacies. He was living in the past, as usual. For instance, he would like Alice and Ben Quick to have a couple of hundred if they are still alive. Martin Skeggs to have a hundred pounds if he's ditto. And so on down to the last retainer. The residue of the estate is to be divided amongst the living members of his family.'

He timed his next piece of information accurately.

'Oh, yes. He did add one codicil. Last March, apparently. Five hundred pounds to Tom Faull.'

He must have read my face, and its momentary chagrin that Humphrey had remembered Tom but forgotten me.

'It's always the way, Flick. The prodigal son gets the fatted calf, and the worker who stayed at home is taken for granted.'

I had no answer to that either.

'Otherwise,' said Jack, 'apart from my share of the pickings, he leaves me Parc Celli, which sounds generous now but at the time was a white man's burden. He tried to leave it to the National Trust at one stage, you know, but they weren't having any, and no one else could be bothered with it. He expresses the pious hope that I will find a way to restore it and put it to family use once more. And d'you know, looking at the date, it struck me that he thought you and I might marry and produce. The two of us had just opened Bon Appétit.'

The irony of this struck both of us. He gave a contemptuous snort. I laughed, and not in amusement.

He said, 'Although it works out so well for me I must say that old Humps really was an ass. Imagine not updating his will! He never knew who his best friend was, did he? Even when she gave him back a slice of his youth.'

I was silent, but the set of my mouth must have alerted him.

He said warningly, 'I should advise you not to contest the will, Flick, because you haven't a legal leg to stand on. It'll take some time to retrieve your investment in the property but there won't be any trouble about it. I believe you did persuade Humphrey to sign a contract eventually – and aren't you glad you did? And the estate will settle all its debts, large and small. You'll have no cause for complaint, business-wise. But personal sentiment is another matter, and you'd be a fool to think you could reverse the will in your favour. You're not even a relative – though apparently you could have been if you'd played your cards right!'

He waited for comment. I made none.

'Naturally you can stay on here for two or three months while you make other arrangements. In fact I'll be glad to have someone looking after the place through the winter. Do I remember your saying something about board wages last summer? Well, I'm quite prepared to cough up whatever old Humphrey paid you. But you'll have to cut back on staff. Perhaps Vera, one day a week, to put a duster round the place – I'm not paying to have the silver polished and fresh flowers arranged in vases. And you can get rid of old biddy Quick and that doddering husband of hers as from now. Our roving mariner can stoke the boiler and keep an eye on the property in return for temporary accommodation. I have no great regard for Tom Faull, but I mean to be fair all the way round.'

Still I said nothing.

Jack said, 'I like to be fair.'

I would not answer.

He said, 'Actually, Humphrey hasn't left a fortune. Although he had a comfortable lifestyle and was surrounded by what people call "lovely things" he wasn't a rich man. Even that plush flat didn't belong to him. It was rented. In fact it may interest you to know that in the past year he's squandered all his spare capital on this place – a country-house hotel which hasn't yet opened, and a partly restored stable block which is no use to anyone.'

He was aiming to hurt.

He said, 'Unlike you, I have no sentimental feelings for Parc Celli. I'm going to use the money from Bon Appétit, and my share of the estate, to convert this house into exclusive self-catering holiday flats. The stables will be demolished, and the space used for a car park. Incidentally, my offer to you as general manager still stands. I'll make it worth your while, Flick.'

I lifted my head at his and said with cold savagery, 'Sod off, Jack!'

He gave an abrupt laugh.

'That's my girl!' he said, and took a turn about the room. 'Biting the hand that offers to feed her.'

He stopped short at the window, looking out on to the winter garden.

'Still, I can't say I blame you for being scratchy. Old Humps has let you down properly. But remember this, you've nowhere else to go and not enough capital to launch yourself in business, unless you're thinking of running a tea shop or a snack bar. I'd advise you to think very seriously about stringing along with me for a few years while you make your pile.'

Then he turned round and smiled, and spoke with quiet deliberation.

'You needn't worry that I'm going to bore you with my attentions. That's all over as far as I'm concerned. Nor do I give a damn whether you hate me or not. You're good at your job, and I'm talking business. It's your skill I want, not your devotion. And before you answer me, remember that if you'd tackled Humphrey and this Parc Celli lark in a sensible fashion you'd have been sitting pretty this minute, and I'd have been the one who was biting his nails. So don't let your heart speak for your head and muck you up yet again. Think things over.'

Grief and fury were throttling me.

Slightly breathless, I stood up and said, 'You can forget the offer and the advice, Jack. There's just one good thing coming out of this mess. I need never have anything to do with you ever again, and my God I'll make sure of that. And one more thing. Keep well out of my way while you're here, or you're likely to find yourself left without a caterer for the funeral, and that could be very embarrassing.'

Then I walked out and into Vera, who had been listening at the door.

Flushed and sorry, she said, 'That be telling him!'

But I was too full of tears to answer her.

Death of Local Landowner

The funeral took place at Elinglaze Church of Humphrey John Curtys Jarvis of Parc Celli. The Reverend George Millmore officiated. Aged 62, Mr Jarvis was the last surviving member of a well-known and highly respected local family who had headed the community for over a century. Though he lived much of the time in London during his latter years he still retained close ties with the village, and was proud to call himself a Cornishman. He was educated at Rugby and Oxford, where he proved to be a keen sportsman, and later served his country as an army officer during World War Two. The family home, Parc Celli, had recently been restored and renovated and was to be opened as a country-house hotel. It was there that Mr Jarvis died suddenly on New Year's Eve. He will be sadly missed.

Local mourners included villagers and members of the Elinglaze cricket club which was founded by Mr Jarvis's father. The church was full to overflowing. A member of the household had fixed up speakers, and many stood outside and listened to the service being relayed. Family mourners were headed by Mr Jack Rice (cousin) and Mrs Flavia Pollard (business partner). Also present were relatives Mr and Mrs James Starky, Mr and Mrs Richard Gibbon and their two daughters, Mr Charles and Miss Georgina Jarvis, Mr and Mrs Harcourt Rice, Mrs Pollard's two sons, Mr Patrick and Mr Jeremy Pollard, and her mother Mrs Lily Clough. Among the floral tributes were several from Mr Jarvis's friends in London . . .

CHAPTER TWENTY-SIX

January, 1979

When the last car had moved away, and the last member of staff gone home, Tom and I locked up and regained possession of our house. The three of us were alone again, as we had been just over a fortnight ago, but this time the atmosphere was one of impending departure whereas the other had been a long-awaited arrival. Vera and Alice had already stripped the beds and remade them, and bagged up the laundry. Tonight, Tom and I would resume our honeymoon in the four-poster. The weekend was ahead of us, and we were determined to forget the future for a couple of days, because Monday would fetch us all back to the present again.

On that day I should have the disagreeable duty of telling Vera that her proud post as my full-time assistant had been diminished to six hours a week as a cleaner, and there was no guarantee that she would be employed after Easter. Her three youngsters, Martin Skeggs, and Alice and Ben Quick would be given a week's wages and declared redundant. The services of Henry Blewett's widowed sister would not be required. Will Soady and sons were to cancel present plans and wait for future orders, which might or might not be forthcoming. And the hopes of all those villagers who had thought to help us, or profit by our business, would be wiped out.

I should have one small pleasure: that of making up an official hotel bill for the family mourners and sending it to Jack, but it was precious little solace compared to the general distress I would be forced to inflict. Meanwhile Tom and I were reduced to being caretakers of Parc Celli while we made up our minds where to go and, in his case, what to do. And when I had dismissed or demoted my staff there were Humphrey's clothes to pack up and send to London. Not a happy prospect.

And yet, when I had undergone the difficult interviews, the numbed silences or disbelieving protests, the pained looks and sorry faces on that awful Monday, I would be grateful for this final task.

His room was tranquil. Alice Quick had made it orderly and bright. Sean Angwin had brought down Humphrey's heavy leather suitcases from the luggage room and laid them on newspapers on his bed.

'I give them a bit of a polish as well as a dusting,' he had said, 'and I cleaned all the squire's shoes. Thought it was only right.'

I thanked him, and thought how like Tom he looked, and wondered what he thought of Tom, and Tom of him, and whether there was anything to think about anyway.

As I opened the top drawer of the chest I felt incredulous rather than sad to think that Humphrey was here no longer. For sixty-two years he had lived on this earth, and now there was a space where he used to be. It struck me, as I transferred little heaps of immaculate underwear and beautifully laundered shirts from drawers to suitcase, that we all occupied a portion of space in our lifetimes: a Tom-shaped space, a Flavia-shaped space, on loan as it were. And when we were gone the space would be given back, leaving our empty clothes behind for someone else to deal with.

I thought of this quite composedly as I was walking to and fro, and the work was soothing and easy. So it was a shock to find myself suddenly in tears over the remembered scent of gentleman's toilet water when I opened his wardrobe. Floris No. 89 emanated from a handkerchief in the breast pocket of a hacking jacket which he had worn on that last day. I held the rough tweed to my face and cried into it until I felt better. After a while I wiped my eyes on his handkerchief, mopped up the lapels of the jacket, laid it on the bed and emptied the pockets.

There was a letter in one of them, sealed in a creamy parchment envelope, and the inscription was written in Humphrey's hand. *For Flavia – Happy New Year!*

I stood looking at it for a full minute. The envelope had been stuck down so lightly that I was able to pull it open without tearing.

New Year's Eve, 1978

Dearest Flavia,

Originally, I intended to hand over my little gift when our first guests had gone to bed on New Year's Day, so that you could open it in peace and privacy. However, this wretched blizzard has changed all our plans. I am sitting in the library as you prepare a dinner which I fear will be served only to the freezers. The Elinglaze peal of bells (if it be rung at all tonight!) will sound a sad toll to your hopes of opening Parc Celli. So I thought of a diversion to amuse you. I have had enormous pleasure in thinking this out, and I must confess that I take a sly delight in the prospect of seeing your face when you finally unwrap my offering.

The gift is cunningly concealed. I have been cudgelling my brains and pottering about all day here, trying to find a suitable and *subtle* hiding place, and I think you will find it taxes your wits to the utmost. I am giving you a trail of riddles, augmented with clues. I always loved riddles when I was a boy! As you unravel each one it will lead to another. Parc Celli being rather too large a place to hunt from top to bottom each time, I have indicated which floor you should search. There will be no guessing or skipping. I have made sure of that! However, I do want you to find my present, so if the game proves too difficult you can throw yourself on my mercy, and I promise to give you a hint.

At this stage, of course, you are on your own. Good luck, my dear!

Y^r^ LOVING HUMPHREY.

From the envelope I shook out a little cocked hat of paper. Unfolded, it read:

I am Spanish by origin. Look at my face, I am somebody. Look at my back, I am nobody – but there I am. First floor.

For the first time since Humphrey's death I smiled. For the hundredth time my eyes filled with tears.

In sorrow and exasperation I asked the void, 'Oh Humpty! Do

we have to go on playing games? Well, this one will have to wait until I've finished packing. Because I'm not in the mood for it!'

So I laid the envelope aside while I brushed and folded his suits, and spread sheets of rustling tissue between each layer.

His presence was almost tangible. I could see the particular expression of pique upon his face, like that of a favourite child baulked of a treat. Almost, I felt that if I turned round he would be standing there, silently demanding my attention.

'I don't want your engagement ring!' I said snappishly over my shoulder. 'I never did!'

But certain phrases continued to pluck at me.

I have been cudgelling my brains and pottering about all day here, trying to find a suitable and subtle *hiding place.*

Still I continued to pack until all the drawers and cupboards were empty.

I have had enormous pleasure in thinking this out.

I collected his toilet things from the dressing-table and wash-basin and zipped up his toilet bag. I snapped the locks of the final suitcase.

I thought of a diversion to please you.

'All right, Humpty,' I said, 'I'll find the bloody ring if it kills me. But only for you, Humpty, only for you.'

Half-past ten. Time for morning coffee and a chat with Tom. I stuffed the envelope into my trouser pocket and ran downstairs.

The kitchen was warm but empty and quiet. Looking out of the window I saw that the van had gone. On the table was a note saying:

Flavie love, Eddy Johns rang. Engine job on fishing boat. Sounds ominous. Don't do lunch for me. Will ring you later. Love, Tom.

I drank my coffee and wrote out my daily list. I decided we should have roast pheasant for dinner tonight, and brought it from the larder in a ripe state. But before I began plucking it I took out the envelope and read the clue again. And as the movement mesmerised me and feathers drifted on to the newspaper I pondered it.

Look at my face, I am somebody.

I could feel Humphrey's enigmatic smile at my back.

'A picture!' I cried. 'Of Spanish origin. A Spanish picture on the first floor.'

I bundled up the pheasant and left it on the draining board.

He had warned me there were no short cuts, but nor were there any pictures of Spain nor any by a Spanish artist. Finally, I examined every painting of any kind on the first floor, and they were very many. I found nothing, and Alice Quick had evidently not dusted the backs for a long time. I cursed Humphrey aloud, for his presence was full of glee, as it would have been in his lifetime.

'Keep your bloody ring!' I shouted, in a fine old temper.

The clock chimed one. 'Look at the time!' I accused him.

I passed the mirror on the stairs and glimpsed myself, hot, cross and tired with a grey dustmark across one cheek.

'Just look at my face!' I cried, and stopped.

Look at my face, I am somebody.

My breath came quickly.

'Oh, I wonder?' I asked myself, and ran back up again.

Of Spanish origin. Spanish. Spanish. Black and gold and inlaid. I consulted my reflection in it each morning. The oblong Spanish mirror on the wall opposite the bed.

It was too heavy for me to take off the wall, but I lifted the bottom corners and moved it sufficiently to allow a little cocked hat of paper to flutter down.

A mouth that can't eat, eyes that can't see, ears that don't hear, a coat you can't wear. I am bare and boneless. Pause for thought! Second floor.

I took that one down with me, and considered it over a late cheese sandwich. While I finished plucking the pheasant I reviewed all the rooms on the second floor. I couldn't imagine Humphrey, in his gentlemanly way, invading our sleeping quarters, so that left the bedrooms along the front. One had suffered a hasty conversion for the Baxters' teenage sons. The others had been cleaned and their furniture stacked. They were devoid of carpets and curtains. So what had prompted him to pad all the way upstairs, no doubt grievously out of breath, to hide a clue in that deserted sector?

Then it occurred to me that I was seeing the rooms through my eyes instead of Humphrey's. To me they might be future guest rooms. To him they were his old nursery quarters.

A sepia photograph flashed on the inner screen of my mind: a chubby little boy of four, sitting smiling on the summer lawn, holding his teddy bear.

The mind is a clever thing. Obligingly it threw up a play on words. Bear. Bare. Pause. Paws.

A mouth that can't eat, eyes that can't see, ears that don't hear, a coat you can't wear.

I bolted the rest of my sandwich and dashed up two flights of stairs. Halted at the door of what had once been the day nursery. Headed for the cupboard in the wall. I remembered Vera and I spending a morning sorting out toys. We had put Humphrey's teddy bear in a bag with a Mothak to protect him, but his owner had found him and lifted him out: with what fond memories and poignant feelings I could well imagine. There he was, paws outstretched in welcome, and underneath one rubbed arm was tucked another cocked paper hat.

Two bodies have we, though both joined in one, the stiller we stand, the faster we run. A cook could use one of us. A country parson did use the other. A country gentleman collected us. Ground floor.

I was beginning to enjoy this, and made myself an extra cup of coffee.

It took me quite a while to work out the meaning and to find the two Georgian hour-glasses in the library. One was egg-timer size, the other sermon-length. Presumably Humphrey's father or grandfather had bought them. Beneath the larger hour-glass the paper cocked hat, unfolded, read:

Formed long ago, yet made today, employed while others sleep;

what few would like to give away, nor any wish to keep. I wanted you to have one of the best of these but you chose a humbler version. First floor.

Looking round the library I had a leap of inspiration. The sight of all those books, and the fact that he had composed the clues here, made me suspicious of his cleverness. I could not believe that Humphrey had carried all this knowledge in his head from childhood or any other time. I stuffed the paper in my overall pocket and began to hunt through the shelves. One book, slightly advanced from the others, as if someone had borrowed it and returned it carelessly, was entitled *The Oxford Nursery Rhyme Book* assembled by Iona and Peter Opie. On reading the list of contents I discovered a section devoted to Riddles, Tricks and Trippers.

As I turned over the pages it was my turn to be gleeful, and Humphrey's to shout in anger. But his protesting cry of, 'Not fair! Not fair, dear girl!' left me unmoved.

'Don't you believe it!' I answered him. 'All's fair in love and war, and this seems to be a mixture of both!'

My inspiration and discovery speeded the game up considerably. The answer to riddle number three was a four-poster bed, and I found the fourth clue tucked under a pillow in the Lilac Room.

Despite help from the Opies, he really had gone to extraordinary trouble and some considerable ingenuity to lay the trail. And though I might know what I was looking for there could be many versions of it, and many places in which to find it. But I was in hot pursuit now, and by the time Tom blew into the kitchen at five o'clock with an armful of daffodils and a boxful of fresh fish in ice, the game was almost played out.

I made tea for both of us and he fried a bacon sandwich for himself while I recounted the day's efforts, and read out the final clue. Buoyed up by his previous doings, Humphrey had gone so far as to compose a riddle, for I could not find it anywhere and it was more cryptic than the previous ones.

When others are finely dressed I am nothing. When I am clad in my glory they are nothing. Last clue. Ground floor.

Tom reflected long and deep. He skimmed through the riddle pages.

'The nearest is a tree,' he said, pointing it out, 'but you don't have trees indoors.'

Then we looked at each other and cried simultaneously, 'It's the Christmas Tree!'

We both made for the hall and stopped halfway. For the tree had been dismantled on Twelfth Night, the evening of our release from snowdom, and Martin and Sean had carried it away goodness knows where.

Tom said, 'The bloody tree's gone!'

'Oh no!' I wailed. 'I can't believe it! He must have stuck one of those little paper hats in the branches and it's been lost.'

'No,' said Tom, 'not if it was the final clue, as he says. And it's a gift. Probably a parcel.'

'A *parcel*!' we both shouted, and looked at each other.

'A parcel like the boxes we wrapped in Christmas paper—'

'—and he found an empty box and put the present in it, and wrapped it up again. Cunning old Humpty!'

'But where is it?'

'In the lumber room. We put everything in the lumber room in plastic bags and cardboard boxes. Even the imitation Christmas presents.'

Tom bolted the rest of his sandwich, as I had bolted mine, and we headed for the lumber room.

Two hours later, in the midst of innumerable cardboard boxes and discarded wrappings, we found a jeweller's leather case and a letter.

'*Not* an engagement ring!' I said to myself, as I opened the box.

It was a small enamelled fob watch, very fine and old and pretty, which must have belonged to his grandmother.

I sat back on my heels and smiled, and spoke to the presence which was now fast fading, but had been with me all day enjoying the game.

'Sorry, Humpty! Humpty – thank you!'

'Misjudged him once again, did you?' said Tom, knowing me. 'I told you the squire was all right. Are you going to read your letter, then? No, no. Not out loud. Not just yet. You can read it to me later if you like. He wrote it to you.'

New Year's Eve, 1978

Dearest Flavia,

Bear with me a little longer, my dear.

We have had our little treasure hunt, you and I, and it was only right that you should find some jewel at the end of it. The fob watch belonged to my grandmother, and calls forth one of my oldest memories – that of sitting in her lap as a very small boy, and being allowed to hold it to my ear and listen to the tick. She was a lady who filled every moment of time, as you do yourself, and I feel the gift is appropriate. I hope you will think of her, and of me, when you wear it. And now to speak of the greater treasure.

Faint heart never won fair lady. My heart was ever faithful to you, Flavia, and ever fearful. I am an incorrigible romantic, and when you turned down my proposal for the third time your words stayed in my mind. I believe you said that you would never marry again because you didn't wish to know another person so well. I realise, far too late in life, that these are my own feelings precisely. To possess is to lose the dream. 'Forever shalt thou love and she be fair!' Flavia dearest, quite without knowing it, I must have pursued you for twenty years hoping never to catch you! And now I never shall. Regret mingles with relief, but my dominant feeling is one of fatalism. This simply was not meant to be.

I am not such a duffer as I must often appear, and you two dear people are not so skilful at hiding your emotions as you think. So I shall save you and Tom from further indecision and embarrassment by telling you that we are all fully aware of your changed relations. Furthermore we accept and bless them. Your two sons and I had our suspicions in October, which we confided on the journey down and confirmed on the journey back. What a set of gossips we are! I think they will be as relieved as myself if you will both come out with the truth and allow us all to stop pretending!

How you manage this new relationship is of course entirely up to you. I foresee its difficulties, as no doubt you do yourselves. But speaking as an onlooker who has spent his life on the sidelines, I can see no way out but onwards. So on you both go, and good luck to the pair of you. I will say, Flavia, that if you had a fault (apart from being a bit of a pepperpot!) it was your inability to choose a man who loved you for yourself instead of for his own convenience. This time I think you have found him. As well as the mutual affection and respect you have for each other, I think I can prophesy that neither of you will ever be dull, nor able to take each other for granted – rather a good recipe for any partnership, come to think!

But now to the crux of the matter. When Tom dashed up to London on his rescue mission in September – which was the first time I suspected *him* of having fallen in at the deep-end! – he suggested that I willed Parc Celli to you, in order to protect your interests. I forget my reply, but I know it was an evasive one. Too much had happened far too suddenly throughout this strange and wonderful year, and I needed to think the matter through. But when I came down with the boys at half-term, I found that you too had become deeply involved. (I suggest that you accept the 'poaching' side of him, my dear! He needs to take risks!) I realised then that the pair of you had committed yourselves one hundred per cent to each other and to Parc Celli. My cogitations were long and searching, and it was only when struck down by the gout that I made my final decision.

Parc Celli could not have better stewards nor I better friends. So, as far as I am able, I have tried to take care of you and the house in the event of my death, and I should like you to know where you stand, so that you may feel as secure as anyone can in this unstable world. I have not yet had time to deposit the will with my solicitor, though it is all in good legal order (the two witnesses are neighbours of mine from the flat above), but this shall be done the moment I return. I shall also inform my family of the new state of affairs.

I am afraid that Jack will feel somewhat miffed, as he was the inheritor of Parc Celli in my previous will. But at the time I made it the house was more of a curse than a blessing, and Jack has since shown himself so lacking in sympathy towards our present plans that he cannot blame me for changing my mind about him. He will still have his fair share of my estate, and so has no cause – legally or personally – to make trouble. In fact, apart from the bequest of Parc Celli – which nobody wanted until you got hold of it! – the will remains largely unaltered, so no one should be upset. Nevertheless I think it wise, under the circumstances, to choose a neutral and professional executor. I have appointed my solicitor to take care of everything.

I also decided to make the knowledge of this bequest part of my New Year Gift to you, and to deliver it in person. So I have spent this snowy day, while you conjure up one of your magic banquets, in thinking how best to present the news. I wished to avoid the somewhat lachrymose atmosphere in which such matters are usually conducted, and so thought of a treasure-hunt. I hope you have been entertained!

If all goes according to plan and we are by ourselves tomorrow – for I do not think, my dear, that anyone will plough through this blizzard, even to sample *your* succulent feast! – Patrick and Jeremy and I shall be waiting for you and Tom in the library, with two bottles of champagne to celebrate.

My love to you, undimmed and undiminished, as always.

God bless and keep you both.

Humphrey

P.S. On reading this through I realise that I have talked at length without explaining myself fully. You, my dear Flavia, become the legal owner of Parc Celli and its contents, but *my* shares (50 per cent) in it are to go to Tom.

An extract from The Good Food Guide, 1981

ELINGLAZE Cornwall

map

Parc Celli
Helston (032 623) 993
off B3293

This impressive E-shaped Elizabethan manor, set in a grove of trees on the Lizard peninsula, is in fact a pastiche which was built in the late nineteenth century by a wealthy Bristol merchant. Now converted into a country-house hotel, and one of last year's promising newcomers, Parc Celli scores in all departments – décor, setting, service, ingredients, cuisine. On entering the great hall there is a strong feeling of *déja vu*, and sensitive efforts have been made to keep the house as it must have been whilst constantly improving the amenities. Some lovely antiques mingle with engaging Victoriana, and the four-posters are equipped with comfortable modern mattresses.

Kelly Park, as it is called by the *cognoscenti*, is the inspiration and creation of Flavia Pollard – formerly *chef-patronne* of the quirky and highly popular Bon Appétit in South London – who has changed her French Provincial cooking pot for a Cornish oven, and is the presiding spirit of this establishment. Her partner and husband, Cornishman Tom Faull, plays a variety of supporting roles from genial host and late-night raconteur to mender of fuses and provider of maps and mackintoshes on a wet day. He will also meet train travellers in the Parc Celli taxi, wearing a naval uniform. For the evening performance, order any flambéed dish, sit back and watch!

This two person team works like a well-oiled machine. The atmosphere is unstuffy and a feeling of goodwill pervades the house and the cooking. Resident guests are treated like special friends but left to their own devices during the day (lunch boxes provided on request) and come together again in the library for drinks before dinner.

The set-price menu changes once a fortnight and has a choice of four dishes for each course. Real foods and high quality ingredients, from fresh-caught sea-bass down to clotted cream, provide the basis. Local fish figure in many of the main courses. Vegetables from the kitchen garden are plentiful, plain and excellent.

We tried a delectable smoked trout pâté, and the crab soup with croûtons was mouth-watering. Rack of Cornish lamb with tarragon sauce intrigued one of us, and fillet of Cornish beef *en croûte* with *duxelles* and red wine sauce delighted the other. Cheese comes before the sweet, French-style, and the cheeseboard, besides local Cornish Yarg and goat's cheese with a crust, has some superb French examples, and a good selection of walnut bread. Sweets please! Try any of the imaginative ice-creams and sorbets. House favourites are profiteroles, the cream boozy with brandy, topped with a wicked dark chocolate sauce; and in summer a feathery Pavlova piled with fresh raspberries in Kirsch. Good strong coffee comes with petits fours.

Breakfasts constantly improve. Try Parc Celli muesli one morning and porridge with Cornish cream the next. Pork sausages with herbs are home-made, tomatoes home-grown, eggs from the Home Farm served in half a dozen ways, mushrooms often newly picked by our host Tom Faull, orange juice freshly squeezed, honey supplied by a local bee-keeper, and the jams are delicious (particularly the Kea plum and Kelly Park strawberry and elderflower).

The wine-list is thoughtfully composed and provides plenty of choice for under £10, with some stars hidden away – Ch. Pape-Clément '61 at £28.40 or Ch. Beychevelle '71 at £14.40. A few more half-bottles would help. House French £3.25.

CHEF: Flavia Pollard   PROPRIETORS: Flavia Pollard and Tom Faull

CLOSED: Jan to March

MEALS: D only. 7.30 to 9 (7 to 9.30 summer). Must book.

PRICES: Tdh £10. VAT inclusive. Seats 40. No smoking in dining room. Wheelchair access. Car park. Pets by arrangement.

CARDS: Access, Diners, Euro, Visa

ACCOMMODATION: 10 rooms, 3 bath/4 shower. Stables Annex to be opened next year. Garden. Tennis. Fishing. TV. Phone. Scenic. Autumn breaks.

RECOMMENDED: Flair and flamboyance in the country house you always wanted to own!